Don't Do It

The voice in her head was silenced by her first step toward him. How close would he let her come? After all, his back was against the tree, so he couldn't easily retreat.

She took another step, and another, and her full skirts brushed his legs. One more, and the fabric was crushed between them. There was no more room for steps, so she leaned forward, opened her cloak, and wrapped it around them both as she slid her arms around his neck.

He swallowed convulsively. "This really isn't a good idea."

"What?"

"*This.*"

"Sharing our warmth on a cold night?"

"Letting me kiss you."

"You haven't kissed me."

"But I'm going to if you don't…"

She gazed up at him. There was a look in his eyes she knew well—desire. Hunger. And a look she didn't know at all. Panic? Fear? Was he afraid of kissing her? Afraid of wanting her? Afraid she wouldn't want him?

Or afraid she would?

Also by Marilyn Pappano

SOME ENCHANTED SEASON
FATHER TO BE
FIRST KISS
GETTING LUCKY
HEAVEN ON EARTH
CABIN FEVER

SMALL WONDERS

Marilyn Pappano

A DELL BOOK

SMALL WONDERS
A Dell Book / September 2003

Published by
Bantam Dell
A Division of Random House, Inc.
New York, New York

ISBN 0-440-24119-7

Manufactured in the United States of America
Published simultaneously in Canada

OPM 10 9 8 7 6 5 4 3 2 1

A List of Characters

Leanne Wilson,
*owner of children's shop Small Wonders and
four-time loser at love*
Danny, *son*

Cole Jackson,
liar, con man, and charmer
Ryan, *son*

Nathan and Emilie Dalton Bishop,
*New York City detective turned small-town cop
and assistant manager at the local inn*
Michael, *son*
Alanna, Josie, and Brendan Dalton,
Emilie's nieces and nephew

Berry Dalton,
the Dalton children's drug-addicted mother

Corinna Winchester Humphries and Agatha Winchester
Grayson, *Bethlehem's grand dames and matchmakers
extraordinaire*

Ross and Maggie McKinney,
CEO of McKinney Industries and wife/mother
Rachel, *daughter*

J.D. and Kelsey Grayson,
psychiatrist and social worker
Trey, *J.D.'s son*
Faith, *J.D. and Kelsey's daughter*
Caleb, Jacob, Noah, and Gracie Brown-Grayson,
adopted children

Bud, *J.D.'s father and newly wed to Agatha Winchester*
Grayson

Gabe and Noelle Rawlins,
engineer at McKinney Industries and angel-turned human
Sophy, Gloria, and Norma,
guardian angels; Noelle's replacements

Tom and Holly McBride Flynn,
second in charge at McKinney Industries and owner
of McBride Inn

Ben and Lynda Barone Foster,
carpenter and top executive at McKinney Industries
Alanna Dalton,
Ben's daughter

Sebastian and Melina Dimitris-Knight,
carpenter and private investigator
Chrissy and Alyssa, *daughters*

Julie Bujold,
Alanna's homeless friend and caretaker

Bree Aiken,
Holly McBride Flynn's half sister

Alex and Melissa Thomas,
lawyer and plant nursery owner

Mitch and Shelley Walker,
chief of police and wife/mother

Harry Winslow and Maeve Carter,
owner and waitress at Harry's Diner

Chase and Nolie Wilson,
lawyer and feed store owner
Micahlyn, *daughter*

Chapter One

WHEN HE REACHED THE RESTAURANT, JACK Coleman's first stop was the men's room, where he checked his reflection in the mirror. The elderly attendant who watched him seemed to think it was vanity, or so his barely suppressed grin indicated, but it wasn't. In Jack's business, appearances were important. The people he was meeting for lunch put a lot of stock on the cut of a man's suit and the names on the labels. They would take him far more seriously in his Hugo Boss suit, with his diamond tie clasp and cuff links, than they would if they saw him in his usual scruffy jeans and T-shirt.

He wanted them to take him seriously.

He adjusted the knot in his silk tie and combed his fingers through his hair, then gave his reflection a critical once-over. Satisfied that he looked the part he was playing today, he drew a deep breath, then left the men's room. In the broad entrance to the dining room, he skimmed his gaze over the crowd until he located his marks—uh, prospective clients.

Sissy and Marvin Ravenel were among Savannah's historically and socially prominent residents. Marvin's however-many-times-great-grandfather had owned the biggest and most profitable plantation in pre-Civil War Georgia, along with the biggest and most lavish plantation house. Over the generations, the family had produced senators, governors, doctors, lawyers, professors, and a whole regiment of military leaders. Then there was Marvin. Not the brightest bulb in the box.

He was a lawyer by education, a gentleman of leisure by occupation. One thing every generation of Ravenels had excelled at was making money, which left Marvin in the enviable position of never wanting for anything. Why spend time in a stuffy office, taxing his brain, when he could play golf, sail, or travel with Sissy instead?

"Jack." Sissy presented her cheek for a kiss, which he pretended to give. *She* was part of Savannah's socially prominent, only through Marvin. Until their marriage, she'd been just another pretty girl who didn't want to live the rest of her life on the wrong side of the tracks. Having come from the wrong side of the tracks himself, Jack understood her ambition.

He shook hands with Marvin, ordered a martini from the waiter who hovered nearby, then traded small talk until the drink arrived. Truth was, he hated martinis and would be happier with a bottle of beer or, better yet, a Coke, but the Ravenels liked to drink, and liked company while they did it.

The waiter asked if they were ready to order and Sissy waved him away. "Tell us again about this investment opportunity," she said in her husky Georgia drawl. Her gaze seemed sharper than usual, her smile more satisfied.

Movement near the entrance distracted Jack for a moment. Two men in suits were talking to the maitre d', and all three were glancing in the general direction of the table Jack shared with the Ravenels. Granted, men in suits weren't out of place in this restaurant—every male diner wore them—but the two men were. They didn't look as if they made a habit of dropping seventy-five bucks for a meal and a drink or two.

Sissy reached across the table and laid her pampered, manicured hand on his. "Come now, Cole. We're about to hand over a very large check to you. Don't you think that entitles us to your attention?" she gently chided as she gave his fingers a squeeze.

The two men moved away from the door—and toward them. Every muscle tensed as he debated whether to stay where he was or make a hasty excuse and get the hell out. There were only two ways out of the dining room— through the main entrance, pretty much cut off by the men, and out the kitchen door. A glance that way showed a third man leaning against the wall, waiting.

He decided to stay put. If the bad feeling making his skin crawl was right and these men were looking for him, they'd caught him. If he was just being paranoid, taking flight would cost him the Ravenels' investment, which was apparently a sure thing. What had Sissy said? *Come now, Cole. We're about to hand over . . .*

Come now, Cole. Not Jack.

Oh, hell.

The two men reached their table and stood one on either side of him. One pulled a credentials case from an inside pocket, giving Jack a glimpse of the weapon hidden by his jacket. He showed the badge inside the case, then said, "Cole Jackson?"

Jack forced his most charming smile. "Close, but no cigar. Jack Coleman." He rose from his chair, offered his hand, and the silent cop snapped one-half of a set of handcuffs around his wrist.

"Mr. Jackson, you're under arrest."

Jack's smile slipped. "Gentlemen, there appears to be

some confusion. Obviously, my name is similar to this man you're looking for, but I assure you, I'm not him. I'd be happy to show you some identification if you'll just—"

The cop pulled his arms behind his back and secured the dangling bracelet around his left wrist. "We'll clear up the confusion at the station," he said in a seen-everything-heard-everything-didn't-believe-any-of-it voice.

Everyone in the dining room was staring. Most faces showed surprise, a few disinterest. Only one person was smiling. She eased to her feet, came a few steps closer, and raised onto her toes, to murmur, "I've worked way too hard to get Marvin's money to let some two-bit hustler walk away with even a dime of it."

He took offense at the *two-bit hustler* crack. He was a con artist, not a hustler, and he was damn good at it . . . most of the time. This time it appeared he'd made a fatal error. He'd underestimated the competition.

But they'd made a mistake, too. They'd arrested him *before* he took the Ravenels' money. The DA wouldn't have an easy time convicting him of theft, fraud, or anything else, when every Ravenel penny was safe in the Ravenel bank.

He grinned at Sissy as the detectives started him toward the door. "Oh, well . . . better luck next time, huh?"

She smiled smugly, picked up his martini, and polished it off.

Jack—or Cole; he was comfortable answering to any number of names—was still grinning when they walked out of the restaurant into the muggy Savannah afternoon. So he was being arrested. It had happened before and would probably happen again. He would bond out, then disappear and never set foot in the city again. That had happened before, too.

Then he saw the vehicles parked at the curb in front of

the restaurant. The first two, sedans marked as police cars only by the Kojak light on the dash, belonged to the Savannah cops. The third was a black-and-white SUV with a seven-pointed star on the door, and leaning against the front bumper was a uniformed cop.

Sergeant Nathan Bishop. Of the Bethlehem, New York, Police Department.

Cole's grin disappeared and icy dread spread through him, making him shiver in spite of the heat. For one crazy moment he considered making a break for it. At best, he would get away. His hands would be cuffed, but finding someone to remove that little problem wouldn't be difficult. At worst, the cops would shoot him for fleeing.

No, at worst, they would turn him over to Bishop and send him back to Bethlehem.

He was gauging the distance between them and the cars, judging the route most likely to lead to freedom, when the cops beside him took hold of his arms. They both outweighed him by thirty pounds or more, and they both had a grip that could stop a stronger man than he in his tracks.

They stuffed him in the backseat of their car. Just before the door closed, he heard one of them tell Bishop to follow them to the station. They would turn him over there.

As the car pulled away from the curb, he tilted his head back and closed his eyes. He'd made a fatal error, all right. Now, if he could just die before he had to face the consequences of it. . . .

TIME HEALED ALL WOUNDS, OR SO PEOPLE LIKED TO say—particularly people who weren't suffering—and Leanne Wilson considered herself living proof of it. Just once, though, she would like to prove true some other adage. Second time lucky, maybe, or third time's the charm. Even three strikes and you're out. If her third broken heart had taken her out of the game, she wouldn't have been around to go through number four.

But she was better now. Really. So what if she still didn't have a social life? If she spent every minute of her free time with the kids or her brother and sister-in-law? If she had zero desire to ever go on a date, share a kiss, or have sex again? She'd just turned thirty-three. She was older and wiser. She knew better than to get involved with a man again.

The bell over the door rang, signaling a customer's arrival. Dredging up a smile that she doubted would fool anyone, she rose from the wicker sofa, stepped into her shoes, and walked to the centrally located checkout counter. The smile faded a bit when she saw Mitch Walker. There wasn't much chance he was there to buy—Small Wonders was a kids' store, and Mitch's wife, Shelley, did all the shopping for their kids. Maybe it was just a friendly visit, but she'd discouraged friendly visits from everyone but family over the past few months.

The only option left was a professional visit. Considering that Mitch was the chief of police in Bethlehem, she would really prefer a friendly hello instead.

"Leanne."

"Mitch."

He removed his hat and glanced around the shop. Big, broad-shouldered, gun on his hip, he should have looked out of place in the pastel surroundings, with all the tiny clothes, toys, and child-sized furniture. Being every inch the family man, he didn't.

"How's the family?" she asked.

He smiled briefly. "They're fine. The kids are doing well

in school and are already looking forward to Halloween at the end of the month. How're your boys?"

"They're fine, too." For more than four years, her own little family had consisted only of her son, Danny, and herself. They'd added Ryan Jackson at the end of May. Twelve years old, abandoned—again—and angry as hell, he'd needed a home, and she'd needed to give it. There had been other choices, probably better choices, but she'd been the only one in town who really knew him, and since they'd both been abandoned by the same man, it had seemed fitting they should deal with it together. "Ryan's wondering why he has to go to school again this year when he just went last year, and Danny's whining because he *can't* go yet."

"Yeah. Give him a couple days in kindergarten, and he'll get over that." Mitch glanced around again, then, clearly uncomfortable, met her gaze. "I just got a call from Nathan. He's on his way back."

And that was significant because? . . . "I didn't know he'd gone anywhere."

"To Georgia. To pick up a prisoner. Cole Jackson."

Leanne stiffened. She'd thought they would never see Cole again. He was a con artist, a liar, and a thief. He'd run an investment scam in Bethlehem, then disappeared with more than $250,000 of their money, while leaving his son behind. The fact that he'd returned all of the money a few weeks later didn't even begin to undo the damage he'd done. He'd befriended them, gained their trust, even their affection, and he'd betrayed every one of them. That wasn't easily forgiven.

She didn't intend to ever forgive him, and neither did Ryan.

"So . . ." Her voice was breathy. "He'll go to trial."

"Yes."

"And to prison."

"Probably."

Cole in prison. He'd been so good-natured, so charming and outgoing. It was hard to imagine him behind bars. . . . Not that it would be a new experience for him. After he'd taken off with their money, Mitch had uncovered an extensive arrest record under various names. He'd spent his entire life ripping off people who trusted him. If he'd worked half as diligently at a legitimate job, he could have succeeded at anything.

"When will they be back?"

"Tomorrow night, maybe the next morning."

"I'll have to tell Ryan."

Looking as if he didn't envy her the task, Mitch nodded.

"Will this affect my having custody of him?"

"Nah. In fact, Family Services will probably look into terminating Jackson's parental rights. If he goes to prison, he can't take care of the kid, and if he doesn't go . . . well, he's proven he's not fit to be a father by abandoning the boy."

To say nothing of lying, cheating, and stealing his way through life, Leanne added silently. But he was still Ryan's father, and Ryan loved him. If he didn't, he wouldn't be so angry and bitter right now. He wouldn't feel so betrayed. She knew from her own experience.

"Anyway . . ." Mitch ran his fingers through his hair, then put his hat on. "I wanted to tell you before you heard it on the street. I figured you and the boy need the time to get ready."

"Yeah. Thanks, Mitch."

As he left, she sat down on the counter where she bagged purchases, rattled a hanger, then shifted away from it. So Cole had gotten caught. Ryan had been convinced it would never happen. Cole was too good, too smart, according to the boy. He was a con artist, not a hustler . . . not that Leanne understood the distinction. To her they were just different ways of saying the same thing—criminal. Crook. Bad guy. Besides, he'd had all those previous arrests. Not in a long time, granted, but still . . .

Oh, man, she really didn't want to tell Ryan his father was coming back to stand trial. Life was already tough enough for the kid, and having the entire town know what scum his father was, would only make it worse.

The bell rang again, this time announcing the arrival of her part-time help. Sophy Jones came to the counter, heaved her backpack underneath it, then flashed a grin. "Afternoon."

"Hm."

"Is something wrong?"

"Hm? Oh, no. I was just . . ." Leanne glanced at the clock. "You're early."

"I knew you were planning to decorate for Halloween today, and since I didn't have anything else to do, I came on in." Sophy grinned again. "I can leave again, and spend the next fifteen minutes sitting in the park across the street, if you'd like."

"No. Oh, no. In fact, I need to run upstairs for a few minutes." Without waiting for a response, Leanne got her keys from her purse, left the store, let herself in the door at the west end of the building, and climbed the long stairs to her apartment.

Today was the first holiday of the new school year, a warm Friday off for a teachers' meeting, so the television was tuned to a children's show, which she knew from experience only Danny would be watching. Ryan would be stretched out on the couch, reading one of the dozen books a week he checked out of the library. Books were his refuge, the places he went to forget that neither of his parents wanted him.

Sure enough, Danny was giggling at the antics of a cartoon dog, and Ryan had his nose in a book. She stood unnoticed in the doorway and watched them, feeling the protectiveness only a parent could know—though, apparently, not all parents.

There was enough similarity between the two boys that a stranger could mistake them for brothers. While Cole was a blond-haired, blue-eyed surfer type, Ryan was dark-haired, dark-eyed, dark-skinned. So was Danny, and so was she.

Ryan noticed her first, closed the book, and sat up. The kid must have read something in her face, because suddenly he looked years older. "Hey, Danny, why don't you go in the bedroom and get the video game set up? I'll be in in a minute, to play you."

If Leanne had made the same suggestion, Danny probably would have balked before obeying. Because it came from his big brother/idol, he said okay and jumped right up. He gave her a hug on the way past, then disappeared down the hall.

She crossed the room and sat at the opposite end of the sofa. The antique wicker gave a soft, comforting creak.

"You heard something about Cole." Ryan said it as fact, without emotion, as if he couldn't possibly care.

"Yeah. He . . . was arrested in Georgia. They're bringing him back here to stand trial."

Ryan's expression remained impassive. "Is he going to jail?"

"Most likely."

"Good." He opened the book again.

"He'll be back in town in a day or two. If you'd like, we can make arrangements for you to see him."

"I don't want to. I don't care if I never see him again as long as I live."

"Ryan . . ." What could she say? *He's your father?* What kind of father sneaked off in the middle of the night and left his son behind? *He didn't mean to hurt you?* Yeah, sure, like waking up in the morning to find he'd been tossed away like yesterday's garbage, wasn't guaranteed to hurt. *He loves you?* She wasn't sure Cole Jackson gave a damn about anyone but himself. He used people. He preyed on the trusting, then destroyed their trust.

And she had loved him, had thought he was the man she'd been looking for all her life. God, what a fool she was!

"You don't have to see him," she said at last. "I assume the trial will be fairly short, since he can't possibly defend what he did, and then he'll be transferred to prison. Chief Walker thinks it's likely his parental rights will be terminated this time, so you'll never have to see him again."

Ryan flinched, then his gaze shifted her way, filled with uncertainty and bravado. "Good. I hope he rots there."

Leanne knew she should respond to that, to gently chastise him or say something wise and insightful, but she remained silent because there was only one thing she wanted to say.

So do I.

COLE SAT, STIFF AND SILENT, IN THE BACKSEAT OF the SUV. His hands were cuffed in front of him, then attached to a chain around his waist, restricting any movement of more than a few inches. He wore leg irons, too, attached to a chain that passed through a steel loop bolted to the truck's floorboard, then to the waist chain.

His muscles ached from holding the same position all day, but he had no one to blame but himself. He'd been more comfortable the day before—handcuffed, but otherwise free to move. He'd been so comfortable, in fact, that when they'd stopped that evening to gas up and hit the bathrooms, he'd tried to move right on out of Bishop's custody. The chains and leg irons were the thanks he got for his effort.

He stared out the side window, barely noticing the woods and the occasional house. They'd passed through Howland sometime back. Soon they would start the descent into the valley where Bethlehem was located. Soon they would be there, and there wasn't a damn thing he could do about it.

From the moment the Savannah cops had turned him over to Bishop, Cole had wanted to ask about Ryan— Where was he? Was he all right? Who was taking care of him?—but had stubbornly refused to do so. The kid was better off without him. He needed a mother, a stable home, someone to teach him right from wrong. It hadn't escaped his notice or Cole's how hypocritical it was for Cole to try to do the teaching when he hadn't done an honest day's work in his life.

But he wanted Ryan to be a better man than him. That was why he'd left him behind. It didn't matter that it had been a lousy thing to do, or that Ryan would hate him for it. It had been best, and that was all that mattered.

Realizing that the road was curving steeply downward, he spoke for the first time all day. "How much longer?"

"Five, ten minutes."

Cole's gut knotted. It was a short walk from the parking lot outside the Bethlehem courthouse to the police department on the first floor and the jail in the basement. Was it too much to hope that he could make it without running into anyone he knew? Probably. But as long as he didn't see Ryan—or Leanne, a sly voice inside him whispered—he would be all right.

He'd had a whole lifetime of learning to be all right.

The church steeples came into view first, followed by rooftops. Long before he was ready, they were passing Hiram's Feed Store, owned by Nolie Harper. One Saturday night last spring he'd gone there with Leanne to take Nolie, suffering from a bad case of food poisoning, to the hospital. She'd been seeing Leanne's brother—probably still was—and had welcomed Cole into her home and trusted him with thirty grand and change, that was earmarked for her daughter's education.

The next business, just barely within the town limits, was a gas station and garage. Leon, the owner, had contributed five grand to Cole's scheme. Melvin Fitzgerald at the hardware store on the right had chipped in another five grand. Elena who owned the bookstore, Betty who worked there, Harry and Maeve at the diner, the Knights, the Graysons, the Winchester sisters, the pastors of most of the churches belonging to those steeples . . . He'd been an equal opportunity cheat.

Bishop turned on the far side of the square, drove to the end of the block, and parked outside the courthouse. Cole did his best not to look in the direction of Small Wonders, Leanne's shop across the street, or the Miller mansion, the house he'd shared with Ryan for his short residence in town. As usual when it came to good intentions, his best wasn't good enough.

The shop was closed and dark except for a few lights shining on the window displays and another over the cash register. There were also lights showing through the apartment windows upstairs, though neither Leanne nor Danny came near the windows for the few moments he could see.

Bishop opened the rear door and unlocked the chains,

then the leg irons, but he left the handcuffs in place. Cole slid to the ground, his joints creaking, a rush of pain shooting through his muscles at the sudden movement. He did his best to stretch, then with a nudge from Bishop, he started toward the courthouse. Jillian Freeman—in to him for seventy-five hundred—was standing outside the house across the street that was home to both her and her law office, her expression less than friendly. An officer leaving the courthouse—in for two grand—held the door for them and called Cole a thieving bastard when he passed.

He'd ripped off two of the three judges in town, both lawyers, and a fair number of cops. This was *not* a good place to stand trial.

After Cole was booked, Bishop escorted him downstairs and past the first and second cells, both empty, before locking him in the last cell. It was the only one with a window, set high in the wall and too small for even Ryan to wiggle through, and when Cole lay on his back on the cot and gazed out, all he could see was Leanne's apartment.

His punishment had already begun.

W HAT'S ON YOUR SCHEDULE TODAY?"
Alex Thomas slid his arm around his wife's waist as she topped off his coffee, then drew her into his lap, grunting for effect when he held her fully. "The usual stuff. Appointments, wills, dealing with companies who don't want to be dealt with, and"—he lowered his voice and mumbled the rest—"an arraignment."

Of course, Melissa heard him. "Really? For whom?"

"Cole Jackson."

"You sure know how to make a Monday even worse than usual." She wrinkled her nose in delicate disapproval. "I can't believe he had the gall to ask you to represent him when we're one"—she laid her hand protectively over her stomach—"two and a half of his victims. Isn't that a conflict of interest?"

"He didn't ask me. Judge Monroe left the choice to Jillian and me, and since Jillian's feeling less forgiving than me, I volunteered. Besides, we got our money back."

"That doesn't make him any less a thief."

No, Alex agreed, but it did show remorse on Jackson's part. About two weeks after he'd disappeared, Alex had received a check at the office for the full amount, down to the penny, along with a list of the people it belonged to. No one had understood why Jackson had returned the cash—regret, guilt, conscience?—and the only person who truly knew him, his son, hadn't been able to shed any light on the matter. Truthfully, though, few besides Alex cared about the why.

"You're not going to try to get him off, are you?" Melissa asked.

"I'm going to provide him with the best defense I can. It's the jury or the judge who will let him off, or not. Not me."

"But—" With an accepting sigh, she got to her feet again. "I know you don't have any choice. You're a lawyer. It's what you do. But you'll have to forgive me if I hope you lose."

"You've hoped I would lose every criminal case I've ever taken. It's a good thing that's a very small part of my practice, or we'd be in trouble."

"Wrong. I didn't hope you would lose Emilie's case. In fact, I prayed very hard you would win."

Winning Emilie Dalton Bishop's case had been more a matter of good fortune than legal skill. When she came to Bethlehem, she'd been running from kidnapping charges for taking her two nieces and nephew on the road, to prevent the state of Massachusetts from separating them in the foster-care system. Of course, the charges had caught up with her, but by then she'd found the support she needed to care for the kids herself.

Besides, it had been Christmas. Prime time for miracles in Bethlehem.

Whereas now it was October, and rather than trying to save his son, Cole Jackson had abandoned him, so he wasn't likely to find much support. Even the good citizens of Bethlehem had their limits, and helping a career criminal avoid prison most likely exceeded them.

Truth was, it exceeded some limit of Alex's, too, but that wouldn't stop him from ensuring that Jackson received a fair trial.

Across the kitchen, Melissa was rinsing their breakfast dishes. She still wore her nightgown, a thin clingy thing that molded to her seven-months-pregnant belly. Every time he looked at her these days, he wanted to get on his knees and thank God again for this baby. They'd married twelve years ago with the intention of starting a family right away, but they hadn't been so blessed. She'd had trouble getting pregnant, and every time they'd managed, she'd miscarried before five months. They'd both been through endless exams and tests, had consulted fertility experts, and after the fourth miscarriage, they'd accepted that having a child of their own wasn't going to happen.

Then, when they'd given up trying, she'd gotten pregnant. It hadn't been the happy celebration all the other pregnancies had been. Alex had been afraid to hope, afraid of those hopes being crushed again. But once she'd passed the four-month mark, then the fifth and the sixth, and both she and the baby had remained healthy and strong, the hope and dreams had overwhelmed him.

Now that she'd made it to seven months, he felt almost

like any normal father-to-be. He caught himself at odd times, thinking about swing sets for the backyard, about tricycles and baseball gloves, video games and soccer and driving lessons and dating rules. He wanted a son, but would love a daughter just as much, and wondered if whatever miracle had allowed this pregnancy to be normal could work a second time and maybe a third.

He'd become a greedy man.

Melissa turned, caught him staring at her, and smiled sweetly. "You'd better get going."

"Huh?" He looked at the clock, gulped the last of his coffee, and took the cup to the sink. Sliding his arms around her, he kissed her soundly. "I love you."

"I love you, too."

He bent and kissed her stomach. "Love you, too. Take it easy today."

His office was a five-minute drive from their house, located on the second floor of a circa-1840 building on Main Street. Next to him was an accountant, and next to her was a part-time tax preparer. On the other side of the hall was Earl Wilson's insurance office, and a title and abstract company. The space directly across from Alex was empty now, but had been home to Jackson Investments last spring.

Alex checked in with his secretary, returned a few phone calls, then walked the short distance to the courthouse. While he waited in an interrogation room, the jailer escorted Cole Jackson up from the basement.

Surprised, Jackson stopped just inside the door. "I didn't ask for a lawyer."

"The judge asked for you. Sit down."

After a distrusting look at the jailer, Jackson reluctantly pulled out the wooden chair across from Alex, sat down, and rested his cuffed hands on the tabletop. "I don't need a lawyer."

"You're charged with fraud, embezzling a quarter of a million dollars, and abandoning your son. You sure look like you need a lawyer to me . . . unless you're planning to plead guilty. Are you?"

"I haven't given it much thought," Jackson said, but from the evasive way he dropped his gaze and jerkily shrugged, Alex suspected he was lying. He'd been locked alone in his basement cell since Saturday evening, with nothing to do but think. Pleading guilty would be the honorable thing, if there really was any honor among thieves, and avoiding a trial was the kindest thing he could do for his son.

"You're scheduled to appear in front of Judge Monroe after lunch. You'd better think about it." Alex opened his briefcase and removed a legal pad and ink pen. "I need your full name, date and place of birth, and social security number."

"Why?"

"So I can start preparing your defense."

"And what would that be?"

Alex leaned back and studied him. Getting a hostile witness on the stand, who wasn't interested in helping convict or clear a defendant, wasn't unusual. Getting a hostile client, who wasn't interested in helping to clear himself, was. "I don't know yet. Our best bet would probably be to gain the jury's sympathy. Show them you had a lousy childhood, that you were neglected, misguided." He paused. "How was your childhood?"

"Perfect. Two parents, five brothers, and a dog. We lived in a great house, sat down to dinner together every night, and went to church every Sunday. Couldn't have been better."

Once again Alex was pretty sure he was lying, though there was nothing concrete he could point his finger at. Jackson's expression was cool, his gaze level, his eyes empty. Wait, that was it—they were *too* empty. As if he'd slipped behind a mask that showed nothing and protected everything.

Alex returned the pad and pen to his briefcase and closed it. He could get the necessary biographical data from the arrest report—assuming Cole Jackson was his real name, and the social security number he was using this time actually was his. He stood up, slid the chair close to the table, then faced Jackson again. "Why did you do it? Why did you steal from people who offered you trust and friendship?"

Jackson shrugged callously. If his hands were free, he probably would have raised them in a who-gives-a-damn gesture. "Because that's what I do. It's what I am."

Judging by his previous arrests, that was true. He'd been living off other people's hard work all his life. Once more Alex started to leave. Once more he stopped. "What about Ryan? Why did you abandon your own son?"

That question pierced the mask. For one very brief moment, Alex saw a range of emotions in his eyes—regret, shame, hurt, defeat. Then the cool blankness returned, and Jackson said nothing. It was as good an answer as any and better than most, because *nothing* could excuse what he'd done.

For that reason alone, like Melissa, Alex also hoped he would lose this case.

Chapter Two

THE FIRST FLOOR OF THE BETHLEHEM COURT-
house was taken up with the police department
and the sheriff's office. On the second floor were
administrative offices and the courtrooms, and on
the third were more offices. There were only two courtrooms, and the one Cole was escorted into shortly before
one P.M. was small. Three tall windows let in light, but the
dimpled frosted glass blocked the view outside. The paneling, woodwork, and plaster were probably original to the
room—such quality work would cost a fortune these days.
A mural depicting blind justice covered most of one wall,
and wooden benches, worn to a sheen by years of use,
filled the back half of the room.

He kept his head up, his shoulders back, and his gaze on the
floor. He caught vague images of people sitting in the gallery,
but didn't look to see if he knew them. He would rather not
see any more familiar faces. They made him feel guilty, which,
of course, he was. He just wasn't used to *feeling* it.

The jailer, accompanied by a deputy, nudged him into a
seat at the defense table. This time the older man hadn't
handcuffed Cole, and he'd been allowed to wear his own
clothes. It was an improvement over the times in the past

when he'd been forced to appear handcuffed and shackled and wearing a butt-ugly orange jumpsuit.

Alex Thomas already sat at the long oak table, looking none too friendly or hopeful. That was okay. The only thing Cole hoped for was to get out of Bethlehem as quickly as possible, and he didn't care where he had to go to do it—prison, hell . . .

At precisely one o'clock, the judge came out of her chambers and took a seat on the bench. Cole tuned out the proceedings, fixing his gaze on the glossy wood floor where it met the wall, willing his mind to go blank. It was a state he usually achieved without much effort, but this afternoon it wouldn't happen. Words from the prosecutor's speech kept slithering in—*defrauded, stole, abandoned*. Unfamiliar emotions kept seeping to the surface—regret, guilt, shame.

Every profession had its downside. Lawyers lost cases. Doctors lost patients. Teachers couldn't teach everyone. This—arrest, a trial, jail—was the downside of his business. Avoiding it was the challenge that made his work fun. Accepting when it couldn't be avoided, was the cost of doing business. It was a common setback, and it shouldn't make him feel so damn lousy. It never had before.

For the fact that this time it did, he blamed Bethlehem. Ryan. Leanne.

Thomas's chair scraped as he stood up, then he touched Cole's arm, gesturing for him to rise. Cole refocused his attention on the proceedings and his gaze on the judge, who was looking annoyed at obviously having to repeat herself.

"How do you plead, Mr. Jackson?"

You'd better think about your plea, Thomas had told him that morning, but when Cole had returned to his cell, he'd lain on the cot, stared at the windows of Leanne's apartment, and considered how completely he'd wasted his life. He was thirty years old, and he'd contributed *nothing* to society. He'd never made anyone happy, never helped anyone in need, had never done a damn thing that justified his continued existence. The world would be a better place without him in it.

That was one sorry epitaph.

The judge watched him, her mouth pursed in a thin line. If he tried to speak, he wasn't sure he could find his voice. The words he wanted to say, needed to say, didn't come easily to a man like him. From the time he was five years old, his father had taught him to always proclaim his innocence. To never admit guilt, even if he was caught red-handed.

Owen Jackson would box his ears for even thinking what he was thinking.

"Mr. Jackson," the judge prodded impatiently. "How do you plead?"

Thomas was looking at him. So was the prosecutor, the court reporter, the bailiff, and everyone in the gallery. He drew a breath, but his chest was tight and refused to accommodate more than a gasp. His voice was strong in spite of it, though his jaw was clenched so tightly that his mouth barely moved. A lifetime of learning could be difficult to overcome . . . but it *could* be overcome.

"Guilty."

The relief rushing through him was almost equal to the panic. No son of Owen Jackson's *ever* pled guilty. A jury might judge them so, but they always put up a fight. What the hell was he doing, rolling over without even trying?

He was accepting responsibility for what he'd done. No son of Owen Jackson's ever did that, either, and it felt damned scary, but good. Now he would go to prison. He would leave Bethlehem for the last time, and this time it really would be the last time.

He would never see Ryan again, or Leanne.

That was also one of the downsides of his line of work.

The judge set a sentencing date for the following Thursday, which brought more relief. He knew from experience that sentencing dates four weeks or more after a conviction or entering a plea weren't uncommon. If he was incredibly lucky, he could be out of town by Friday. He could stand four more days. As long as he didn't have to see anyone but the jailer or the officers who delivered his meals, he could stand anything.

The judge dismissed the court, and the deputy signaled Cole to leave the courtroom. He circled the table and walked behind the jailer and in front of the deputy, and was halfway to the door before some indefinable something jerked his gaze to the left. Standing just inside the door was Leanne, and she was giving him a look of pure loathing.

The deputy gave him a push, and Cole realized he'd stopped in his tracks. He started walking again, came abreast of her, gave her a cocky grin and a wink, and said, "Hey, sugar."

As if he hadn't stolen her money, or broken her heart, or done some damage to his own heart in the process.

Her expression didn't change—not a flicker of surprise, not a hint of temper. She just watched him as if he were scum scraped from the bottom of somebody's shoe.

In that moment, that was exactly how he felt.

As if he didn't have a care in the world, he walked through the doorway, then followed the jailer to the stairwell. A few minutes and three flights of stairs later, he was back in his cell with no place to go, no one to talk to, and nothing to do. He stretched out on the cot, with his head at the end where he couldn't see out the window, used his clasped hands for a pillow, and tried to concentrate on his future. Not the years he would spend in prison, but after that. Where he would go. What he would do. How he would live.

But it was hard to think about all that when other images kept intruding. Dark hair and dark eyes, filled with condemnation, contempt, confusion. Hell, he couldn't even say exactly whose image he was seeing. Ryan, Leanne, and even her son Danny, whom Cole had fallen so easily into the habit of calling *son,* all had identical dark hair, eyes, and skin.

And they all had good reason to hate him.

He closed his eyes, hoping that would chase away the vision. For a moment it worked, and the tension slowly started seeping from his muscles. Then he heard a sound—the soft scuff of a shoe on the concrete floor—and it came rushing back.

He opened his eyes, turned his head, and saw Leanne standing on the other side of the cell bars. He wished he could ignore her, pretend she wasn't there, make himself disappear. Of course, he couldn't, so he sat up, grinned, and leaned back against the stone wall. "I'd invite you in, but I seem to have misplaced the key."

For a long stiff moment she stared at him, looking as if any expression at all would cause her face to crack. Then she stepped forward, slid a plastic bag through the bars, and let it drop. It landed with a particularly loud *thump.*

He looked from her to the bag, then back. "What's that?"

"Books. Ryan thought you might be bored."

"Then why didn't Ryan bring them?"

"Because he's hoping he'll never have to see you again."

Pain slashed through Cole, tightening his chest, forcing him to swallow hard. It had been too much to hope that Ryan would understand why Cole had left him behind. He was a kid, after all—just twelve years old. When he got a little older, though, he would see that Cole had owed him better, and had done his best to see that he got it. A kid couldn't ask for a better place to grow up than Bethlehem, or better people to grow up with.

Cole shrugged callously, as if he didn't give a damn about Ryan's hopes. "If that's all you wanted, you can leave now."

She didn't. Instead, she came closer to the bars, resting one hand on the crossbar. "I talked to the jailer, and to Alex, and to Nathan. You haven't even asked about Ryan."

He shrugged again. "He's not my problem anymore."

Her mouth worked, but no sound came out, and her fingers tightened around the steel bar until they turned white. After a moment, she found her voice. "You worthless, lying, coldhearted *bastard,* I hope you burn in hell!"

Spinning away, she stormed off toward the opposite end of the corridor, and he watched her go. Once the heavy steel door closed after her, his shoulders slumped and he bowed his head. Burning in hell sounded preferable to the mess his life had become. All he'd wanted was to do the right thing for Ryan, for Leanne, even for Danny—to get out of their lives and make room for someone who deserved them—but as usual, he'd screwed up. It was proof that he wasn't cut out for being decent, and he damn sure didn't deserve to care about anyone.

THE STARLITE LOUNGE DIDN'T OFFICIALLY OPEN until five, but Leanne knew the owner was there most afternoons. This one was no exception, she found, when she tugged the heavy door and it swung open. The bar was more brightly lit than usual, no music blared from the jukebox or the corner where live bands performed on weekends, and the air, though smelling of smoke and beer, was clear enough to actually see through.

Christian Rourke, owner and chief bartender, was sitting at a table, papers spread in front of him. For obvious reasons, he went by his last name only—what tough-guy bartender wanted to answer to a sissy name like Christian? She would bet half the people who considered him a friend had forgotten or never known his first name.

He looked up as she approached. "Is business so good at the store you can take off in the middle of the afternoon, or so bad?"

"It's good enough that I can afford a part-time clerk, but not so good that we both need to be there every minute." She slid into the chair opposite him and glanced at the papers spread out. Timecards and work schedules. Her business would never be so good that she would have to bother with those things, and she wouldn't want it to be. She harbored no dreams of great success. She simply wanted to provide a comfortable living for herself and the kids, while still having time for a life.

"Want a drink?" Rourke was already on his feet, moving toward the bar.

"Or two or three," she muttered. She wasn't the sort to drink herself into oblivion. In fact, she couldn't remember the last time she'd been even a bit tipsy. Certainly not since Danny was born. But her brief visit to the jail had left a bitter taste in her mouth and a fire in her gut that anything less strong wouldn't touch.

He returned with a bottle of scotch and one glass, sat down, poured, and served her. She took a sip, felt it burn all the way down to her stomach, took another, then set the glass down and watched Rourke watch her. Leanne drinking in the middle of the afternoon was a rare enough occurrence that anyone else she knew in town would be on their fifth question by now, trying to ferret out the problem, but not him. If she wanted to talk, he would listen, but he wouldn't ask questions. She wasn't sure whether he respected her right to privacy, or just didn't care, or what. Whatever the reason, she was grateful.

She gestured toward the schedule. "Go on with what you were doing. I don't mind."

He took her at her word—another thing she liked about him—and turned his attention back to his work. She sat quietly, sipping her drink, gauging her tension level, sipping again. The bad taste was gone from her mouth, but all the scotch in the world wouldn't diminish the fury inside her. She wanted to hurt Cole. She wanted to make him sorry he'd ever set foot in Bethlehem.

Just as she was damned sorry she'd ever met him. If she could go back to the spring and undo meeting him, dancing with him, kissing him, loving him, she would. Even with a string of broken hearts behind her, wanting to totally erase one bad affair from her life and her memory was a first. But she would do it if she could.

By the time she neared the bottom of the glass, Rourke was stacking his paperwork and setting it aside, then fixing his gaze on her again. His hair was brown with a hint of auburn that gleamed in the sun, and his eyes were hazel. At the moment, he was wearing contact lenses, but when he tended bar at night, he switched to glasses because the smoke irritated his eyes. At a few inches under six feet, he was shorter than Leanne generally liked, but physically he could hold his own against any man in town. He jogged, lifted weights, and had, at some point in his past, been a pretty good amateur boxer, which explained why his nose sat just a hair off-center in his face.

He was handsome, intelligent, and nicer than a lot of guys, and they'd both been single in the same town for years, but they had never considered being single together. She wondered why, thought of Cole, and answered her own curiosity. She attracted losers the way bug lights attracted insects. Rourke was way too respectable for her.

"How's the kid?"

"Danny's fine."

"And the other kid?"

She shrugged. Ryan had pretty much brooded all weekend, then had tried to get out of going to school that morning. She'd been tempted to pack him and Danny into her SUV and steal away for a day or three or five, so they could pretend nothing was happening back home. But since she wasn't *that* good at pretending, and Ryan was having a tough enough time in school without missing an entire week, she'd resisted the temptation.

She wished she had resisted the temptation to go to Cole's arraignment or to take the books to him. She'd certainly had no intention of setting foot in the courthouse, but that morning, while staring out the window at the jail, Ryan had commented how boring it would be to have nothing to read for days at a time. He'd been clutching one of his own books at the time, as if losing them would be a fate worse than death, and like an idiot, she'd asked if he would like to take some books to his father.

No, he'd answered immediately, sharply, then hesitantly added, *But you could.* So she had. And to repay his son's concern, Cole had carelessly shrugged and said, *He's not my problem anymore.*

Bastard. Low-down, unfeeling snake. Forget the money he'd stolen, the trust he'd betrayed, the people he'd used. Forget that he'd broken her heart. He deserved a lifetime in prison for nothing more than what he'd done to his son.

"I went by your store last night. It's all decorated for Halloween."

She steered her attention back to Rourke and the cynical note in his voice. "Hey, Halloween is a profitable holiday for a place that sells costumes along with everything else. I've got the most adorable bunny-rabbit baby outfits this year and some princess costumes to die for." She grinned when he responded with a very un-holiday-friendly grunt. "You know, you could have a hell of a party here. Put up some spiderwebs and crepe paper and glow-in-the-dark stuff, have everyone dress up in costumes, have plenty of beer on hand, and *voilà!* Lots of customers, lots of profit."

"Have a costume party," he said skeptically. "Here, at the Starlite."

"Your customers would love it."

"Halloween is already a busy night for us. Everyone who wants to get away from all those little buggers ringing the doorbell nonstop comes here."

"Coming here to have a burger or a drink or a dance is fine. Coming for a party would be even finer."

He grunted again, as if he might consider it, then nodded toward her glass. "Want a refill?"

She studied the empty glass for a moment. She didn't feel great, but she wasn't quite as sick as when she'd walked in the door, or quite as angry. "No, thanks," she said at last. "I'm okay."

"Are you really?" It sounded as meaningless as the *How are you?* everyone greeted everyone else with, but the look in Rourke's eyes made it quite possibly the most personal question he'd ever asked her.

"I am," she replied softly. "At least, I will be." In time. A few months, a few years—who knew how long it would take her to get over Cole? But she would. Life and love had made her a survivor. Maybe she was slow to learn, but she did learn. She wouldn't make the same mistake again.

She pulled a few bills from her purse to pay for the drink, but Rourke waved them away. "We're not open for business yet, so you're a guest, not a customer."

"Thank you, sir. Drop by the shop sometime and I'll return the favor—at least, if you have a taste for raspberry tea."

"Me—drinking prissy tea in a store where kids go?"

"Oh, yeah, I forgot. You went into the saloon business because it was the only one you could legally keep kids out of."

"It was either that, a liquor store, or an adult bookstore. Bethlehem already has a liquor store, and I don't think they'd stand for an adult bookstore."

"I don't think they would." She stood up and slid her purse strap over one shoulder. "I appreciate the drink and the conversation."

"We didn't talk about anything."

"I know. And that's exactly what I needed."

WHEN THE JAILER CAME WITH BREAKFAST AT SIX-thirty Thursday morning, Cole sat up, looked at the food, knew the knot in his gut wouldn't let him eat, and lay back down to snooze again. The next time he awoke, several hours had passed and a man was sitting outside his cell, his wooden chair rocked back on two legs and a newspaper open in front of him. Instead of a cop's or deputy's uniform, he wore jeans and a button-down shirt, but looked way too young to be a detective. He looked way too young to be much of anything.

When Cole sat up, the cot squeaked and the kid put down the paper, let the front chair legs hit the floor, and stood up. "Good morning."

Cole offered no response. In an hour or so he was going upstairs to face Judge Monroe while she sentenced him probably to the maximum prison term possible. It wasn't a good morning for him.

"I'm Eli." He gestured to the breakfast tray sitting on the

floor. "You should have eaten. The food comes from Harry's, and it's just about the best you can get in Bethlehem . . . unless you get an invitation from the Winchester sisters. You remember them—Miss Corinna and Miss Agatha? They delivered homemade cinnamon rolls when you first moved in, and they invited you and your son to Sunday dinner, and you stole about six thousand dollars from them."

A scowl settled over Cole's face. Of course he remembered the two old ladies. They always had a crowd for Sunday dinner, and both sisters and every guest had made him and Ryan feel as if they belonged right smack dab in their middle. *That* had made him feel as low as a snake in a ditch.

But he'd taken their money anyway.

"What do you want?" Cole asked harshly.

"What makes you think I want anything? Because that's the way *you* operate?"

Cole decided to ignore the kid, but that was easier said than done. He was a captive audience, and Eli knew it.

"You always have an ulterior motive for everything you do, don't you?" Eli asked. "You haven't made a selfless or sincere gesture in longer than you can remember."

"I took in Ryan three and a half years ago." *And left him four months ago.*

"What choice did you have? He's your son . . . isn't he?"

His scowl sharpening, Cole looked at the kid. Eli looked back, his gaze level and unwavering. Unable to maintain his bravado, Cole dropped his gaze away first and stared at the floor instead.

"Besides, taking him in wasn't selfless. You were just recruiting another sucker for the family business, weren't you?"

That brought him to his feet. "That's not true! I've kept him out of it completely!"

"So it was just coincidence that he got caught stealing back in Cleveland."

Cole paced the length of the cell, then tilted his head back to gaze out the window. At such a sharp angle, all he could see was the top edge of Leanne's building, a few tree branches, and clear blue sky. He hadn't realized how much Ryan loved books until the kid had gotten nabbed by store security in Cleveland and a search of his room had turned up a full box of them in his closet and another under the bed, not a single one obtained honestly.

Books. As a kid, Cole had stolen a lot of things—food when he and his brothers were hungry, medicine when one was sick, money to pay the rent or keep the utilities from being shut off. But he'd never risked getting caught over something as trivial as a book.

He'd paid for all the books Ryan had taken, then made the kid work to pay him back, and he'd wondered how they had lived together for nearly three years without his learning something so basic about the boy. It was just one more example of his failures as a father . . . which he *didn't* need pointed out to him by some stranger barely two-thirds his age.

"Who the hell are you, and what the hell do you want?"

"I told you—my name is Eli." He conveniently ignored the second half of the question. "You're going to be seeing a lot of me."

"I doubt it," Cole said dryly. "If you were going where I am, you'd be on this side of those bars." His gaze narrowed suspiciously. "Are you from social services?"

Eli considered it a moment, then shrugged. "In a manner of speaking."

The response made Cole feel about as cold as Leanne had accused him of being. There was only one thing social services could want from him—Ryan. To ensure that he never got within a million miles of the kid again. Hell, he had no problem with that. Wasn't that why he'd left the kid in the first place?

But judging himself an unfit father was one thing. Having the state do the same, was worse.

The opening of the steel door at the end of the corridor made Eli look that way. So did Cole. This time the jailer was accompanied by two deputies, as if the officials feared Cole would run at the first opportunity. They were probably right.

"See you," Eli said, then walked away, nodding politely to the three men as he passed them.

"You ready, Jackson?" the jailer asked as he unlocked the door.

"Aw, you mean it's check-out time already?" Cole stood in the center of the cell, arms at his sides, wondering if they were counting on the deputies' sizes and presumably quick reaction times to intimidate him, or if he'd wind up in handcuffs and leg irons. If he were them, he would truss himself up. After all, what did he have to lose by making a break for freedom?

The question lingered in his mind as they took the stairs to the first floor. The sun shone through the glass double doors of the main courthouse entrance, drawing his gaze that way. What *did* he have to lose? His pride? Dignity? Self-respect? All long gone. Ryan's respect, or Leanne's? Gone, too. His life? In prison or out, it really wasn't worth much.

But when his escort started up the next flight of stairs, he turned away from the doors and followed.

They walked into the second-floor courtroom, then stopped abruptly due to a tie-up in the aisle up ahead. He risked a quick look around and saw Eli, grinning from his seat in the last row and, a few rows up, Leanne. He would recognize her dark hair and slender shoulders anywhere.

The redhead beside her was Nolie Harper, and next to her was Leanne's brother, Chase.

Maybe he *should* have tried for an escape downstairs. Whatever the results, it would have been better than knowing Leanne had come to see him sentenced to prison.

At least Ryan wasn't there. Thank God for small miracles.

Finally they reached the defense table at the front, where Alex Thomas was waiting. Cole sprawled in his chair, shooting for a casual effect. The jailer left, and the two deputies took up position a few yards away, leaning against the nearest wall.

Conversation in the gallery was muted but ongoing. Thomas made a few polite attempts at small talk, then gave up. Cole watched the second hand on the clock high above the judge's bench sweep around and around and tried not to fidget, but by nine-ten, he was antsy. "Let's get this show on the road," he muttered.

Thomas looked at him. "Are you so eager to spend the next few years in prison?"

"There are all kinds of prisons," Cole replied. Restlessly, he drummed his fingers on the table, then gave in to the impulse to look around. There were more people in the courtroom than he'd drawn Monday, but still not many. Jillian Freeman scowled at him from the opposite side of the peanut gallery. The Winchester sisters sat beside her, both prim and pursed-mouthed. Kelsey Grayson, another social worker, sat next to Thomas's pregnant wife. The chief of police and the sheriff shared a bench with Judge McKechnie.

Except for Eli and a handful of old men who looked like regular benchwarmers, that was all . . . well, except for the Wilson-Harper contingent. Knowing it was a bad idea, Cole turned the few degrees necessary to see them. Chase was scowling. Nolie's sweet gaze was full of sympathy—

surely for Leanne and Ryan, not him. And Leanne . . . she still wore that look of loathing.

Just as he'd done Monday, he grinned and winked at her, making her jaw tighten, but she didn't look away.

The bailiff announced the judge's arrival with the command to rise, and Cole slowly turned and eased to his feet. The woman taking the bench wore a judge's black robes, but that was where the resemblance between her and Judge Monroe ended. Monroe was maybe forty, tall and slim, with carefully styled hair and carefully schooled expressions, and she took herself very seriously. This new judge was probably ten years older, give or take, none too tall, and chunky. The robe reached to her ankles, where a pair of sturdy old-lady shoes peeked out. Her hair was about equal amounts brown and gray, and though it was cut in a simple enough style—short, parted down the middle—it looked as if she'd combed it with an eggbeater.

The biggest difference, though, was her smile. It stretched from ear to ear as she settled onto the bench and surveyed the courtroom. Judge Monroe was stern and straitlaced, while this woman looked as if she didn't know the meaning of the words. "Good morning," she greeted after the bailiff commanded them to sit. "I'm sorry for the delay, but I didn't find out until this morning that I'd be filling in for Judge Monroe. Let's see . . ."

She perched a pair of glasses on the tip of her nose, opened a file, and looked through it. "Hmm . . . oh, dear . . . really . . ." Peering over the top of the glasses, she focused on Cole. "It appears you've been a busy boy, Mr. Johnson."

"Jackson," he corrected her.

"All right—Jackson. You can call me Gloria." She beamed a motherly smile in his direction.

Judge Gloria? Sounded like some crappy TV courtroom show. He glanced at Thomas, who didn't seem to find anything the least bit odd about the woman. No one did, apparently, except him.

"Let's see . . . you've pleaded guilty. Oh, good. It's always best to tell the truth, you know. And you gave the money back, every penny of it. That's good, too. Shows you have at least a passing acquaintance with the notion of honesty. So we're here today to . . . hmm, to sentence you for your crimes." Her forehead wrinkled in a frown, and she rested her elbows on the desk, then her chin in her hands. "You know, some people believe the consequences of a crime should be punishment, nothing more, nothing less. Personally, Jack, I think you should learn a few lessons in the process and emerge from the experience a better man for it. Therefore, I sentence you—" At a gesture from the bailiff, she rolled her eyes. "Oh, I forgot. Please stand up. You, too, Alec."

Bewildered, Cole got to his feet, as did Alex Thomas.

"Now, where was I? Oh, yes, Jack Johnson, I sentence you to five thousand hours of community service, to be served right here in Bethlehem under the supervision of Eli. Hi, Eli." She waved, and from the back of the courthouse came a familiar voice.

"Hi, Gloria."

"Any questions?" she asked, but didn't wait for an answer before she banged the gavel. "Court is adjourned." Then she grinned at the gavel. "I always wanted to do that."

"But—Wait—You can't—I don't want—" Cole's protests were cut off as the deputies began moving him toward the door. In front of Thomas, he stood his ground. "What the hell is this? I don't want to do community service!"

Thomas shrugged as he picked up his briefcase. "It's only for a couple of years, two and a half at the most."

"I'd rather be in prison!"

"It's an unconventional sentence, I admit—"

"It's crazy as hell! I don't want to stay here! I *won't* stay here!"

Thomas went on as if he hadn't spoken. "—but Bethlehem's an unconventional town. The judge is giving you another chance, Jackson. You don't get that often, so don't blow it."

"But—"

Apparently tired of waiting, the deputies herded him away. As they approached the last row, Eli grinned. "Told you so."

"Go to hell," Cole muttered.

"No can do," Eli said cheerfully.

That was what Cole was facing if he stuck around to serve out his sentence—two years or more of pure hell. The key word there, of course, was *if.* Now he had the best reason in the world to make an escape attempt. If he succeeded, he could leave town. If he didn't . . . well, surely that would convince loopy Judge Gloria that he couldn't be trusted, and force her to send him off to the nearest penitentiary with high walls and armed guards.

"Don't try to run," Eli advised. "You won't get away, and it won't change Gloria's mind. Nothing will. Besides, I'd find you. No matter where you go, no matter where you hide."

As the deputies nudged him out the door, Cole looked over his shoulder at the kid. He couldn't be much more than twenty-two, and he didn't look even that old. His expression was open and friendly and innocent.

So how did he manage to make his last words sound so damn threatening?

Chapter Three

I T WAS A SOMBER GROUP GATHERED AT NOLIE AND Chase's house Friday evening for their weekly hot-dog night. Only the two younger kids—Danny and Nolie's five-year-old daughter, Micahlyn—were their usual cheerful selves. Huddled in a sweater against the chilly night air, Leanne stood near the grill on the small patio, her back to the fire, and watched her brother watch the hot dogs. "It's a stupid sentence."

She'd said that a dozen times before, though repeating it only annoyed her . . . which didn't change her utter belief in the truth of the statement.

"Sometimes sentences are."

"He should be in prison." She'd said that a dozen times, too, and she believed it almost wholeheartedly, though there was still a silly part of her that flinched away from the idea of Cole in prison.

"A lot of people should be who aren't, and some who shouldn't be are," Chase said without emotion, but his gaze had taken on a distant tinge. He was a prime example. After being convicted of a crime he didn't commit, he'd spent twenty-two months in a Massachusetts prison. She shuddered at the thought of her brother, bewildered, frustrated, and estranged from his family, *knowing* he was innocent, but helpless to prove it.

She didn't need any proof beyond knowing him, and neither did Nolie. He'd been wise to marry her as quickly as they could throw a wedding together. A woman like Nolie was a rare find.

Besides, Leanne added with a rueful grin for her own selfishness, it had been the only bright spot in her recent life, and she'd really needed that brightness.

"Maybe he won't stick around," she said with a shiver as a brisk wind gusted through the trees. "How closely will he be supervised?"

"I don't know. I never represented anyone who got that kind of sentence. Besides, this is Bethlehem. They have their own way of doing things." Picking up the tongs, he transferred the plump hot dogs from the grill to a pan, handed it to her, then shut off the gas. She warmed her fingers on the bottom of the pan as she hustled inside, then deposited them on the counter next to the stove, where chili and sauerkraut heated in saucepans.

Her sister-in-law glanced up as she finished shredding a chunk of cheddar. "Your cheeks are red. Standing too close to the grill?"

"Freezing my butt off," Leanne retorted. "It's a little nippy out there."

"Hmm. Weenie-roast weather. Maybe we'll do that next Friday night."

Leanne shivered at her words, but it was only for effect. She loved weenie roasts on cold fall nights—the velvety dark sky, the popping and crackling of the fire, the fragrance of wood smoke mingling with fresh, crisp autumn scents . . . oh, and the ooey-gooey sweetness of a perfectly roasted marshmallow dripping off a stick and into her mouth. Mmm.

And someone to share it with. Not just kids or family or friends, but someone special. Someone to snuggle close to and keep her warm, to steal smoky kisses from, to stargaze with.

Even as the image formed in her mind, she sharply rebuked herself. *No, not someone like Cole.* If she got near him with a blazing fire and a sharp pointed stick, marshmallows weren't likely to be the only thing she would roast.

"You want to call the kids?" Nolie asked as she lined up the various bowls and pans of their dinner on the counter, along with all the usual condiments.

"Aw, do we have to?" Leanne went through the living room to the bottom of the stairs. "Danny, Micahlyn, dinner's ready!" Upon hearing the resulting thunder of small feet, she headed for the recliner, where Ryan was pretending to read a book. Instead, he was staring out the window, a lost, wounded look on his face. When he realized he wasn't alone, he quickly jerked his gaze to the book. She didn't mention his distraction as she sat on the arm of the chair. "Good story?"

"Uh-huh."

"You hungry?"

"A little."

"Give your eyes a break and come fix your hot dogs— but save some room for dessert. Nolie made banana-split cake—your favorite."

With a grudging smile, he slid a bookmark into place, laid the book aside, and followed the younger kids into the kitchen. Leanne remained where she was. He'd been listless and blue for a week, and she didn't have a clue how to shake him out of it. She'd tried to talk to him about his father several times, but each time he'd bluntly changed the subject. So she'd tried *not* talking about his father, but that didn't seem to help, either.

That afternoon she'd decided to get professional advice. After school Monday, the two of them had an appointment with J.D. Grayson, a psychiatrist at the local hospital whose specialty was the treatment of children. His years of practice were complemented by real-life experience, with six kids of his own at home. Faith in his abilities gave her a sense of hopefulness for the future, but damned if she was looking forward to getting there.

Squaring her shoulders, she returned to the kitchen where Nolie and Chase were fixing plates for Danny and Micahlyn, and Ryan was leaning against the opposite counter, waiting his turn. She leaned next to him, folded her arms over her chest, and loudly said, "Man, some people are *slow*. I bet I could have already fixed and eaten one whole hot dog in the time I've been standing here, waiting."

"That's because you've got a big mouth," Chase retorted.

"A big mouth? *Moi?*" She feigned offense. "I resemble that remark."

Micahlyn peered up at her through her thick glasses. "I don't think your mouth is big, Aunt Leanne."

"That's 'cause she never yells at *you*," Danny said with a giggle.

"Oh, and we can tell she yells at you all the time." Holding a plate in one hand, Nolie placed her other hand on Danny's head and shepherded him toward the living room. "She looks like such a mean mama, and you look so scaaared."

"I'm not scared of nothin'," Danny boasted. "Except vampires. And mummies. And monsters."

Chase gave Leanne a dry look. "Letting him watch old horror movies with you, huh?"

"Just getting him in the Halloween spirit." As he delivered Micahlyn and her dinner into the living room, she gently elbowed Ryan. "Want me to fix your plate for you?"

He didn't answer, but took a plate. On good days, he ate like the growing boy he was. On moody days, he just picked, even at his favorite foods. She could have guessed how down he was by nothing more than his dinner—one wiener, one bun, a squirt of mustard. As she loaded the extras on her two hot dogs until they overflowed onto the plate, she cursed the man responsible for the hundredth time.

It didn't make her feel better, but at the moment, she didn't have a clue what would. She could blame Cole for that, too.

But things were bound to improve. Look at Chase. When he'd gone to prison over two years ago, he'd thought everything was over—his legal career, his marriage, life as he knew it. He had probably never guessed that, soon after his release, he would meet the love of his life and get a daughter and an even more wonderful life in the process. And Nolie . . . after losing her parents when she was seventeen and her husband when she was twenty-two, she hadn't expected to be this much in love again three short years later. And Alex and Melissa Thomas, about to have the baby they'd worked so hard to get . . .

Bethlehem was filled with miracles. Surely two of them—*please, God*—had her and Ryan's names on them.

SATURDAY MORNING FOUND COLE LYING ON HIS COT, eyes closed, his mind wandering to Pennsylvania, where his father lived, and to Tennessee, where his mother stayed sometimes. He hadn't bothered to notify them or his brothers that he was out of commission for a while. Owen wouldn't offer much sympathy, not after a guilty plea, and Eloise . . . hell, sympathy wasn't one of her strong suits. Neither was concern or consideration or any of the gentler emotions a mother was supposed to feel.

As for his brothers . . . they all looked alike, they were all in the same business, and they all had their own lives to worry about. They wouldn't even notice that he and Ryan had dropped out of sight until one of them needed Cole's help executing a con. That would be soon enough for them to find out.

The heavy steel door opened, then footsteps echoed along the corridor. When they stopped in front of his cell, he forced himself to keep his breaths slow and steady, and he didn't move a muscle until the person spoke.

"Are you ready to go?" It was Eli, the baby-faced kid who was supposed to tell him what to do and when and how to do it for the next two and a half years.

Cole didn't open his eyes or sit up. Instead he folded his hands under his head and settled more comfortably. "I'm not going."

"Sure, you are."

"I'd rather go to prison."

"That's not gonna happen, if I have anything to say about it."

Finally Cole turned his head and looked at him. "You don't."

Eli smiled. "My word counts for a lot more with Gloria than yours does."

"You take me out of here, I'm skippin' town."

"No, you're not."

Cole sat up, drew his feet onto the edge of the cot, and let his arms rest on his knees. "What are you gonna do?

Keep me in handcuffs and leg irons twenty-four and seven?"

"No. I'm going to finish the job your being in Bethlehem has already started."

"And what job is that?"

"Reforming you." Eli said the words with a smile.

Cole greeted them with a snort. "Don't waste your time trying. I've been a crook all my life and I like it. I choose my own jobs, set my own hours, and never have to struggle with issues like honesty, morals, ethics, or a conscience."

"You have a conscience."

Cole shook his head. He came from a long line of lawbreakers with a different view of right and wrong, good and bad. He knew what he did was wrong. He just didn't let that stop him.

"Then why did you give the money back?"

A shudder of something uncomfortable swept through Cole, and he disguised it with a careless shrug. "I figured it would keep the police from looking for me."

Eli didn't look convinced. "Everytime you leave a place, the police are looking for you, but this was the first time you returned what you'd stolen."

Another shrug. "I didn't need the money."

"You haven't *needed* the money since the time you were eighteen and your brother David was about to get his right hand cut off for borrowing from the wrong guys."

Cole let his arms drop to his sides, his feet slide to the floor, and stood up. He crossed the cell in three strides. "How do you know about that?"

"You're my responsibility for the next five thousand hours. It's my job to know. So . . ." Eli opened the cell door, then stood back. "You ready to go?"

Hell, no. But Cole picked up his only belongings—the books Leanne had delivered from Ryan—and walked out the door. He was going along for one reason only—because escape from outside might be tough, but from inside it was damn near impossible.

Ten minutes later he stepped outside for the first time in a week, officially released into Eli's custody. The sun was shining brightly, though the air was cool. It was a busy morning downtown, with all the weekday workers taking advantage of the day off to run errands and shop. The grocery store parking lot was crowded, and more parking spaces around the square were occupied than not.

He wondered how business was at Small Wonders this morning, and was glad the massive stone courthouse blocked his view.

Eli gestured toward the parking lot, and Cole turned in that direction. The kid didn't head for any vehicles parked there, though, but cut across to the sidewalk on the opposite side, then turned left. They were headed straight for the intersection where Leanne's store sat.

He didn't want to look, but couldn't help it. The display windows across the front and one side of the building were decorated for Halloween, with scarecrows and witches and ghosts. A crescent moon swayed from side to side, and so did the eyes and tail of the black cat perched on it. A cauldron sat on a fire of red cellophane illuminated by a light inside, while gray crepe-paper smoke streamed to the ceiling.

When he was a kid, Halloween was an occasion for mischief. What better time to snatch a purse or wallet than when every kid around was wearing a costume and mask? He'd been able to stand face-to-face with his victims, and the best description they could give was, "He was a goblin."

He followed Eli across the street, then they immediately crossed again. There on the corner was the Miller mansion, the house he had "bought" for his stay in Bethlehem. The family had wanted to unload the old place, so they'd readily agreed to let him live there while waiting for the loan to go through. Of course, by the time they'd found it would never go through, he was already a half-dozen states to the west.

When Eli turned in at the gate of the old house, Cole stopped short, still on the sidewalk. "You've got to be kidding."

Eli stopped, looking from the house to him. "About what?"

"Why are we here?"

"Rather than have it stand empty, the Miller family has offered it as a home for our program, at least until it sells. This is where we'll be staying."

Cole shook his head. "No freakin' way."

"You say that as if you have a choice in the matter."

"I'm not staying—" In the house he'd stolen the use of. The house he'd shared with Ryan. The house directly across the street from Leanne's. The house where he'd had great sex with her for the better part of a few incredible nights.

Eli came back to the gate. "Maybe I didn't make myself clear. You don't have a choice."

"I can go back to jail."

"They don't want you."

That wasn't news. He'd spent his entire life not being wanted by someone or other. His mother had regularly gone seeking greener pastures, leaving all six kids behind, and his father had raised them as accomplices rather than sons. Most towns where he'd run his scams had been happy to see the last of him, particularly if there was a little jail time involved, and God knew, most of his victims hadn't wanted him around after they'd discovered the truth about him. Unfortunately for them, they'd always discovered it too late to protect themselves.

Except for Sissy Ravenel. Even if she was directly responsible for his being back in Bethlehem, he had to admire her ability to look out for herself and her husband's fortune.

Eli was waiting without the least bit of impatience. The kid had no doubt Cole was going to do exactly what he wanted, and it pissed off Cole that in this, at least, he was right. Reluctantly, he walked through the gate, forcing one foot in front of the other. When he reached the steps, he hesitated again, clenched his jaw, and climbed to the porch.

Eli unlocked the door, then stepped back for Cole to enter first. He did, stopping a few feet inside the foyer. On the left was the living room where Ryan had watched too much TV and read too many books. Straight ahead was the kitchen where Cole had cooked their meals, usually just for Ryan and him, but a couple of times for Leanne and Danny, too. The stairs on the right led to the second floor and four bedrooms. Ryan's had been at the back of the house, near the back stairs, and Cole had chosen the room at the front—the one that faced Leanne's bedroom.

This time he'd just as soon sleep in the basement.

Eli tossed his keys on the hall table. "I had the hotel where you were staying in Savannah pack up your belongings and ship them here. They're in your room upstairs. I took the liberty of returning a few things to their rightful owners—a Mont Blanc pen, a Rolex, an antique money clip, and the diamond cuff links."

Cole didn't ask how he'd found out who their rightful owners were. He wouldn't get a straight answer, and it didn't matter anyway.

"Go on up, unpack, then meet me in the kitchen. We'll discuss the rules of the program."

Grudgingly, Cole started up the stairs, resisting the urge to point out that he'd never been big on obeying other people's rules. Every rule was meant to be broken, his father used to say, and Cole had spent his entire life doing just that. It was too late to change.

He was halfway to the top when Eli spoke again. "It's never too late to change, not until the last breath has left your body."

His fingers curled tightly around the bannister, Cole slowly turned to look at the kid, but all he saw was Eli's back as he disappeared down the hall. Coincidence, he told himself, starting his climb again one slow step at a time. Just as it was coincidence that Eli's do-gooder program was housed in the same place Cole had called home during his short time in town.

Just as it was coincidence that the idiot had given him that same front bedroom where he'd slept before.

Cole discovered that after futilely checking the other three bedrooms for his stuff. Two were unoccupied; the third had a stack of books—social work mumbo jumbo—on the nightstand and a jacket tossed across the foot of the bed.

Two large boxes stood at the foot of the bed in the front room. Both bore the return address of the hotel in Savannah, and both had been opened. He didn't bother unpacking them, but walked past and to the window. His gaze went straight to Leanne's window, its blinds closed, then dropped to the shop window below before shifting to a group of boys on the sidewalk. It slid past the four strangers and zeroed in on Ryan.

He was leaning against the stone wall of Leanne's building, and the other kids were apparently trying to talk him into something. He shook his head several times, and finally the other boys left, heading toward Main Street. Ryan stayed where he was, staring off into the distance, until Leanne came around the corner. They talked a moment, then she slid her arm around him and together they disappeared back around the corner.

Long after they had gone, Cole expelled the breath that had caught in his lungs. Some people believed the consequences of a crime should be punishment, the judge had said—nothing more, nothing less. *This* went beyond punishment. This was torment, plain and simple.

And damned if he was going to stick around for it.

WITH THE EXCEPTION OF THE EARLY MONTHS OF her marriage, Melissa Thomas couldn't recall a time when life had been more perfect. It was her favorite season—autumn, with the leaves turned rich shades of crimson, bronze, and gold, and the air smelling clean and sharp with a hint of the winter to come. Physically, she'd never felt better, even though she was carrying an extra twenty-six pounds around and her back ached with the burden. Spiritually, she was more satisfied and hopeful than ever. And in December, the month of miracles, their baby would join them, just in time for Christmas.

Life couldn't get any better.

She'd gone downtown to pick up a few things for dinner, but found herself parked in front of Small Wonders instead of the grocery store. Fearing yet another miscarriage, she'd stayed away from the shop through the first five months of her pregnancy. Even after that, she hadn't allowed herself to buy much for the baby. Alex had painted one of the guest rooms green, and she'd picked out a crib and dressing table, sheets and curtains, and a few whimsical pictures for the wall. But she hadn't bought any *real* baby things—no sleepers or tiny shoes or outfits, no diapers or pacifiers, receiving blankets or bibs.

She'd waited long enough.

Easing out of the car, she shivered as a chilly wind rustled around her, then hurried across the sidewalk and inside. The bell announcing her arrival was soft, its melodic chimes designed not to disturb sleeping babies. It was *so* soft and melodic that it didn't penetrate the mental fog Leanne was drifting in.

Melissa walked to the window Leanne was staring out, glanced at the courthouse and the square, saw nothing worthy of such concentration, and gently nudged her friend. Eyes widening, breath catching, Leanne jerked her gaze to Melissa's. "Oh. Hi. I'm sorry. I didn't hear . . ."

"You were a million miles away."

"Actually, less than a mile. Ryan should have been home from school fifteen minutes ago."

"I'm sure he's all right."

"No, he's not." Leanne looked at her again, then smiled weakly. "Of course nothing's happened. It's just . . . he's been having some problems since his father was brought back."

Melissa nodded sympathetically. She couldn't understand how a person could possibly abandon his own child. She and Alex had tried for so long, had grieved for every baby they'd lost, had prayed and pleaded and hoped, and Cole Jackson, who'd been blessed with such a gift, had simply turned and walked away. If the police hadn't caught him, he probably never would have looked back. She wasn't a vindictive woman, but she wanted him to suffer for that.

"How are *you* dealing with his father being back?" she asked gently.

Abruptly, Leanne began straightening shelves that didn't

need it. "There's nothing to deal with. I'm so far over him that he doesn't matter anymore, except for how it affects Ryan. I couldn't care less. I think he belongs in prison and the judge's ruling showed astonishingly poor judgment, but it doesn't affect me in the least."

Melissa wanted to hug her close and remind her that they'd been friends ever since Melissa had married Alex and moved to Bethlehem. She knew Leanne threw herself into love wholeheartedly, and that every broken heart hurt as bad as the one before, and mere months weren't enough to render Cole Jackson insignificant in her life. But they *had* been friends forever, and if Leanne wanted to pretend Cole meant nothing, who was she to argue?

"What can I help you with today?"

Looking around the shop, Melissa smiled. "I don't suppose you could pack up all your baby stuff and deliver it to my house."

"It might take a while, but, yeah, I could do that. Then I could take the boys off to some distant beach for a vacation."

"A beach is exactly where I feel like I belong, along with the other whales."

Leanne looked her up and down. "Oh, honey, you're doing just fine. When I was pregnant with Danny, I gained nearly sixty pounds. Of course, I spent about five months of that time trying to eat away my misery."

Melissa remembered. Danny's father had been handsome, charming, and totally unwilling to face fatherhood. The day he'd found out they had a baby on the way, he'd bowed out of Leanne's life so fast her head had spun. Just in case she hadn't hated him enough for it, Melissa had despised him, too.

After another look at her watch, Leanne forced a smile. "So . . . are you looking for anything in particular today?"

"Just some hopes and dreams."

"You're in luck. We just got in a new order of hopes and double that of dreams. Why don't you look around and see what you can find? I'm going to try to track down Ryan."

As she headed for the counter near the back, Melissa turned to the Halloween costumes. Some were mass-produced, but the ones she liked best were made by Hailey Montgomery, a local seamstress and cousin of Leanne's. It was too easy to imagine her own little boy in the faux-fur rabbit suit with floppy pink ears and a matching pompom tail, or a sweet little girl in the green-and-brown turtle costume—so easy, in fact, she considered buying one of each for next year, just to be prepared. She resisted the temptation, though she did pick out two of Hailey's crib quilts, one an appliqued sampler, the other a three-dimensional landscape that bore a resemblance to Bethlehem and the valley that sheltered it.

Next she debated the merits of one-piece footed sleepers versus gowns with drawstrings at the bottom, then opted for three of each . . . for starters. She'd waited so long for this child that he would no doubt be the best-provided-for child in town.

She was browsing through hooded bath towels on her way to tiny shoes of satin, cotton, and the softest leathers when the doorbell rang and Ryan Jackson came in. His book bag was slung over one shoulder, his head was down, and his lower lip stuck out. He looked the very picture of a sullen teenager as he slouched his way to the counter.

Melissa couldn't resist smiling. She couldn't wait for the terrible twos and the terrible teens and everything in-between. She was looking forward to separation anxiety, temper tantrums, first-day-of-school jitters, and first-date jitters. She couldn't wait to get up-to-date on the latest in video games or computer technology, to learn the name of every significant cartoon character, to add new slang to her vocabulary and new concerns to her worry list.

She couldn't wait to be a mother in fact, as she already was in her heart.

Y OU'RE LATE," LEANNE ANNOUNCED.
Ryan ducked his head and mumbled something unintelligible.

"We have an appointment with Dr. Grayson in ten minutes."

That made him look up. "I don't need no shrink."

"Don't call him that. He's a psychiatrist and, sweetie, I think we *all* could benefit from some time with him." Especially Ryan's father, though of course she didn't say so out loud.

"There's nothin' wrong with me." His tone was defensive, as if he wanted very much to believe that, but harbored a few doubts. Being abandoned by one parent was easy enough to blame on the parent, but when *both* parents chose to walk away, a kid couldn't help but wonder if he was to blame.

"You're right," she said with a cheerfulness she didn't feel. "There's nothing wrong with you—or with me, either, for that matter. But there's something about our . . . situation, that Dr. Grayson might be able to help us with."

His gaze narrowed. "You mean, you havin' to take me in 'cause Cole ran off."

"I didn't *have* to take you in. There were plenty of families who wanted you." She ignored his snort at that. "I just happened to want you more. Come on."

He folded his arms over his chest and scowled at her. "I don't wanna go."

She reached under the counter for her purse, then went

to the storeroom door, opening it a few inches. "Sophy, I'm leaving now. If you need anything, call my cell. Melissa, when you're ready to check out, give a holler for Sophy in the back room."

When she came even with the counter again, she looped her arm through Ryan's as if he wasn't being difficult and turned him unwillingly toward the door. "It won't hurt at all," she teased in the same cheery voice she used to reassure Danny, "and if you're really good, I'll treat you to ice cream when we're done."

Ryan shot her a chiding look, but quit dragging his feet as they reached the door.

It was such a pretty day that they could have walked to J.D.'s office at the hospital if Ryan had come straight home. Since he hadn't, she pulled him around the corner, to where her SUV was parked. She settled into the driver's seat, glanced at Ryan, slumped against the passenger door, then backed out and headed for Bethlehem Memorial.

Truthfully, she wasn't looking forward to this meeting with J.D. any more than Ryan was. She didn't want to talk about Cole, didn't want to even think about him. The first was pretty easy to avoid, except for the occasional well-intentioned questions like the one from Melissa earlier. But not thinking about him was one of the toughest things she'd ever tried. Anytime she relaxed her guard, he weaseled his way into her thoughts like the slippery crook he was. She didn't have to see him—she hadn't done that since Thursday—or even hear his name. If she just closed her eyes and let her mind wander, it wandered straight to him.

J.D.'s office was on the first floor of the hospital, a compact space with battered furniture, two narrow windows, and a small library's worth of books. The family photographs on the walls overshadowed the Harvard medical degree, and the man waiting there overshadowed it all. He was tall, broad-shouldered, and looked as if he would be more at home on a construction site than behind a desk. He was the only doctor she knew who liked filling his spare time with hard labor, and he had the muscles to show for it.

"Leanne. Ryan." He brushed a kiss to her forehead, then extended his hand to Ryan.

The boy grudgingly shook hands, then dropped into one of the two chairs that fronted J.D.'s desk. Leanne chose the other, and J.D. shoved a stack of papers back to sit on the edge of the desk. "How's school this year, Ryan?"

He shrugged. "Okay, I guess."

"My son, Caleb, is in your grade. He says you're quite a runner." When Ryan's eyes widened, J.D. hastened to reassure him. "Nothing we talk about leaves this office. I don't discuss work with my kids, my wife, or anyone else. No one will know you've come to see me unless you choose to tell."

A bit of the tension that held Ryan stiff seeped away, but not enough, Leanne thought regretfully.

"Have you seen your father since he came back to Bethlehem?"

Ryan gave another of those derisive snorts she was beginning to hate. "No, and I don't want to. They should'a put him in jail."

He spoke as if seeing his father behind bars wasn't an unusual thing. She tried to imagine her own father locked up, but it was too unlikely an image to form. It would be a horrible thing . . . but then, her father wasn't a career criminal. Cole was.

A career criminal with a *son*. The day he'd helped give

life to Ryan, Cole should have given up his crooked ways and taken the first honest job to come along. He'd had an obligation to his child, to not get himself thrown in jail, to not do anything to threaten that child's safety and well-being, to never hurt or shame him.

But she knew better than most how many fathers failed to live up to their obligations. Danny's father was a perfect example. The man had never paid a penny to take care of his son. He'd never even laid eyes on him.

And Danny was wonderfully happy and well-adjusted anyway. Someday Ryan would be, too.

J.D. moved to sit behind his desk. "Tell me about your mother, Ryan."

The change of subject caught Ryan off-guard. His gaze narrowed and he sank lower in the seat. "What about her?"

"Whatever you want to tell me."

The question piqued Leanne's curiosity. She knew nothing about Ryan's mother except that she had abandoned him three years ago and he still had nightmares about his time with her. She didn't know if Cole had married the woman, or if he'd loved her, or if she'd been just one more victim in one more of his scams. She didn't know if the woman hated Cole as much as *she* did, but she was pretty sure the answer was yes.

Ryan seemed at a loss for anything to say. He hunched his shoulders and let his chin sink to his chest. The posture made him look small and vulnerable, an impression emphasized by the shadows in his eyes.

"When did you last see her?" J.D. asked, his tone soothing, nonconfrontational.

"A while ago."

"How long?"

Ryan shrugged, as if he didn't have a clue. Leanne would bet he knew, right down to the day.

"Where is she now?"

Another shrug.

"Are she and your father divorced?"

Ryan let a put-upon sigh escape. "They weren't ever married. Cole's not real big on doing things the way other people do."

Like working for a living, Leanne thought. Setting a good example for his son. Obeying the law.

J.D. gave him a chance to go on. When he didn't, the doctor leaned back in his chair. "Okay. Let's talk about your father."

"You mean Cole."

"Isn't he your father?"

Scowling, Ryan got up and walked to the window. There wasn't much out there—yellowed grass, a few of the hospital's outbuildings, a wooded area—but he concentrated on it even as he shrugged yet again. "I guess."

"How do you feel about him leaving the way he did?"

The question brought the boy's head jerking around. "How do you think it feels? It sucks."

"Why do you think he left?"

"Because that's what he does. He uses people, and then he leaves 'em." His voice quavered there at the end, and as if to make up for it, he adopted a belligerent stance and a cold stare. More than anything Leanne wanted to wrap her arms around him and promise with all her heart that he would never be left again. Only her faith in J.D. kept her in her seat.

Ryan turned his back on them again, and his voice took on a low, careless tone. "It's no big deal. I knew it was gonna happen sooner or later. I don't need him anyway."

After another brief silence, J.D. asked his next question. "What was your first reaction when you heard he'd been arrested and was coming back to town?"

Her first reaction had been shock, joined quickly by dismay, anger, grim satisfaction, regret. She would like to think she'd hidden it from Mitch Walker, but there was no way she'd hidden it as well as Ryan had. When she'd told him, his expression had been utterly unemotional, as if she'd said nothing more important than *Your shoelace is untied.*

Ryan leaned against the windowsill and folded his arms over his chest. "I was surprised. I didn't think he'd get caught. He's a con artist, not a hustler."

"What does that mean?" J.D. asked.

"A con artist plans his cons and chooses his marks. A hustler just hustles anyone who's ripe for the pickin'. A con artist leaves town when he's ready, but a hustler leaves when someone else, like the cops, decides it's time." He flashed a mockery of a smile. "Owen taught me that. He's a con artist, too."

"Who's Owen?"

"Cole's dad."

"Your grandfather," J.D. clarified.

For an instant, Ryan went still, as if he'd never considered the relationship before, and for the thousandth time, Leanne wanted to hurt Cole. Mitch had been right that day in her store. Cole wasn't fit to be a father, and apparently, his own father wasn't fit to be a grandfather.

Which suggested he probably hadn't been much of a father to Cole, some sly little demon whispered. After all, he was a crook who'd raised his son to follow in his own footsteps.

"Sounds like you spend a lot of time with your grandfather," J.D. remarked.

"I stay with him sometimes when Cole's workin', and we always go there—" Ryan caught himself and his expression tightened. "We always went there for Christmas and in the summer sometimes."

"How do you get along with your grandfather?"

Dragging the toe of his sneaker back and forth, Ryan watched the scuff marks appear in the carpet, then disappear, before finally lifting one shoulder. "He's okay. He doesn't treat me like a kid and get all bossy. He doesn't have a bunch of rules, or get upset about things like other people do."

Oh, Owen Jackson had rules, Leanne thought scornfully. Just not the sort any self-respecting parent would pass on to his child or grandchild.

"Do you like staying with him?"

"It's okay." Ryan made another careless gesture, but all the shrugs and casual responses in the world couldn't hide his hurt and vulnerability. "It doesn't matter much to me where I stay, and I like Owen. He's cool."

J.D. made a note in the file open in front of him, then changed the subject. "What do you think of the sentence the judge gave your father?"

It wasn't *fair,* Leanne silently insisted, and expected Ryan to echo her thought. He didn't.

"It's kinda cool. He'll hate it, 'cause he never sticks around after he takes people's money. He'd rather be locked up." Then the pleasure that had appeared briefly in his expression disappeared. "But he won't stick around. Unless they watch him real close, he'll be outta here first chance he gets."

But maybe he would think twice before he tried to con an entire little town like Bethlehem again.

"Maybe he won't stick around, or maybe they are watching him closely," J.D. said. "But as long as he's here, you're liable to run into him sometime. What will you say to him?"

"It ain't gonna happen."

"Bethlehem's a small town, and he's living right across the street from you. It will—"

"He's what?" Leanne's face flushed hot, and too late she realized she shouldn't have interrupted, but J.D. couldn't drop a bombshell like that and expect her to take it in quietly.

The doctor shifted his gaze to her. "He's living across the street. I figured you'd heard. The Millers have donated temporary use of the mansion to the program he's in."

"Why didn't I know that? There should have been gossip, talk—"

"Complaint?" J.D. paused. "You're familiar with the not-in-my-backyard syndrome, aren't you? Prisons, garbage dumps, nuclear facilities, and halfway houses are all well and good, as long as they're not in our own backyards. I imagine the news has been kept relatively quiet in case folks decided they didn't like the idea of a convict serving his sentence in their neighborhood." He smiled dryly. "Not that you would be so narrow-minded."

She forced her own smile. "I have nothing against convicts." But she held one hell of a grudge against Cole.

Ryan reclaimed the conversation, repeating, "It ain't gonna happen. I don't wanna see him, and no one can make me."

And if he did see Cole, he could ignore him. That was certainly a skill *she* was going to cultivate.

"Just play along with me, will you?" J.D. asked reasonably. "If, by some really rotten luck, you should run into him, how will you handle it?"

Tight-lipped, Ryan shook his head.

They waited, the silence growing heavier with each moment. When it became too much for Ryan to bear, he shoved himself away from the window ledge and headed for the door. "This is stupid. Talking never fixes anything. I'm outta here."

The slamming door punctuated his words.

Leanne slowly got to her feet. "Well . . . I'm sorry. . . ."

J.D. grinned. "You didn't think this would all get straightened out in one visit, did you?"

"A woman can hope, can't she?"

"He's a kid without a whole lot of stability in his life. His mother abandoned him, then his father. Now Jackson's back, but not because he wanted to come back, not because he regretted leaving Ryan. The kid's got a lot of anger, resentment, hurt, and fear inside him, and he doesn't know what to do with it. That's our job—to help him cope. I'll do what I do best, and you'll do what you do best, and we hope."

She nodded in agreement, then blankly asked, "What is it I do best?"

"Love him. Make him feel safe. Be there for him."

"Sounds like I've got the easier job."

"It bodes well for the kid that you think so." Coming around his desk, he walked into the corridor with her. Where the hallway ended in the hospital lobby, Ryan stood, staring out the window. He looked so alone that her heart ached.

"Thanks, J.D."

"My secretary will call to set up a schedule with you."

She said good-bye, then walked a half-dozen yards before he spoke again. "Leanne? You need to be thinking about your own answer to that last question I asked Ryan. When you run into Jackson—and you *will*—how will you handle it?"

She held his gaze for a long time before walking away. She had only one answer to give, and she didn't think it would satisfy him any more than it did her.

Damned if I know.

Chapter Four

COLE AWOKE BEFORE DAWN TUESDAY MORN-
ing, eased from the bed, and went to the window that looked out on the courthouse, the
square, and Leanne's shop and apartment. He
wasn't looking to see if she was up. Really, it was the
courthouse that drew him—his daily reminder that, lack of
bars and guards notwithstanding, he was in prison.

Though he guessed Eli was a guard of sorts. Not that he
couldn't take the kid in a fight. Eli was a few inches shorter
and twenty pounds lighter, and his old man probably
hadn't taught him to fight dirty practically from the cradle,
like Owen had.

What Eli mostly was, was annoying. The only peace
Cole had found in the house since he'd moved in was in
this room or the bathroom. Outside those two places, he
was apparently fair game for Eli's company, nosy questions,
psychological mumbo jumbo, and constant scrutiny.

Prison—the uniform, the eight-by-ten cell, the bad
company, the restrictions—couldn't possibly be worse.

He was about to turn away, take a shower, and grab
some breakfast when lights came on across the street. He
stopped and watched, even though the blinds were closed,

even though Leanne was one of the last people he wanted
to see, and he waited, hardly breathing, moment after long
moment. Finally, disgusted, he forced himself to walk away.
He hadn't engaged in such juvenile behavior even when
he was a juvenile. He was too damn old to start now.

By the time he'd finished his shower and dressed, Eli
was in the kitchen, flipping pancakes and frying sausage.
Not so long ago, Cole had fixed that same breakfast, and
had eaten his at the sink while Leanne's little boy made a
mess at the table. Afterward, he'd cleaned up Danny, then
delivered him to his mother across the street, fully intending to start backing off from their affair. Then she'd come
to the door, so pretty and sweet, and had given him one of
those smiles that drove all rational thought from his mind,
and backing off had zoomed to the top of his list of things
he wanted least.

Well, he wouldn't have to worry about getting any
more of those smiles. She was more likely to snarl.

Eli set two loaded plates on the table, added two glasses
of milk—Cole couldn't comprehend how anyone could
prefer milk over coffee first thing in the morning—then
sat down. "What kind of work have you done? Besides the
scams, I mean."

Cole slid into his chair and spread butter and syrup over
his pancakes before he shrugged. "Nothing."

"Nothing? You've never held a legitimate job?"

"Nope." Though he'd been tempted a time or two—
had wondered what it would be like to make an honest
living, to not feel that vague little anxiety every time he
saw a cop, wondering if the guy was looking for *him*.

I once considered going straight, his father used to say. *But I
laid down and soon the temptation went away.*

"So what can you do? Besides scamming people."

"You put unreasonable limits on your questions, you don't leave me many answers."

Eli grinned, knocking about ten years off his appearance—probably not the effect he was going for, since he had such a baby face anyway. "Okay, forget the limits. What can you do?"

"I can lie, cheat, and steal with the best of 'em. I can pick a pocket so smooth the mark never knows what's happened. I can pick locks, hustle the best pool players in town, palm cards, sell things that don't exist, and charm a woman out of her money while making her think it was her idea to give it to me. Give me a laptop computer"—one thing that hadn't been returned to him with his clothes—"and I can steal a name, a social security number, a credit card number, or the contents of some sucker's bank accounts. I don't do that often, though. It lacks the challenge of the face-to-face con."

"And you can cook."

Cole blinked. He'd expected more of a reaction to his boasting, but Eli acted as if he'd recited a perfectly normal resume instead. "Yeah, I've done some cooking." It had been his responsibility all those times his mother had gone off looking for greener pastures, and most of the times when she came back. Eloise had lacked all maternal instincts, as well as those of a housewifely nature. No cooking or cleaning or laundry for her, but maternal or not, she'd still managed to turn out six sons. *Someone* had to take up the slack, and Owen had been too busy providing for them, to do all that homemaking stuff.

"And you've taken care of Ryan."

He snorted, to hide the ache the mere mention of the boy stirred. "Ryan never needed taking care of. He probably changed his own diapers and fixed his own bottles."

"You weren't around to know?"

Cole's jaw tightened. "No. He was nine when he came to live with me."

"But you saw him before that."

"Nope."

"Oh. I see."

See what? he wanted to demand. That he was as sorry an excuse for a father as ever lived? There was a reason he hadn't known Ryan when he was young, and a good one—he didn't know the kid existed. But telling Eli that would only lead to other questions, other assumptions . . . unless he told the truth.

He could probably count on one hand the number of times he'd done that in his thirty years, so why start now?

Eli carried their dishes to the sink and rinsed them. "We're going to be working in City Park today. Ever want to be Paul Bunyan when you were a kid?"

"Those weren't the kind of bedtime stories my old man told." No, he'd gotten primers on hiding the larcenous soul of a devil behind the smile of an angel, on when to talk and when to shut up, on the arts of distraction, flattery, and subterfuge.

"Grab a jacket and meet me out front," Eli said as he headed down the hall.

Cole climbed the back stairs to his room, took a leather bomber jacket from its hanger, then put it back and reached for a sweatshirt instead. He wasn't up on kiddie lore, but as far as he could recall, Paul Bunyan had been some kind of outdoors guy. No need to risk a four-hundred-dollar jacket on whatever dirty work Eli had dreamed up.

It was a good decision. Their work in City Park involved cutting down dead trees. More than a dozen of them had been flagged with yellow strips tied around their trunks. Eli pulled his beat-up old truck onto the grass, got out, and lowered the tailgate. In the truck bed were chain saws, a couple cans of gasoline, work gloves, plastic safety glasses, and an axe.

"Aren't you concerned about putting a potential weapon in my hands?" Cole asked dryly.

Eli didn't look the least bit concerned. "Just about anything has the potential to be a weapon. Besides, you've never resorted to violence, except for the time you broke that guy's nose, arm, and jaw, when he'd tried to kill Frank."

God, that had been a lifetime ago. He'd been nineteen, and Frank, the youngest and wildest of the Jackson boys, had just turned fourteen. No one had believed he was going to make it to fifteen, but he'd surprised them. Hell, he'd really surprised them when he'd turned twenty-five, especially having suffered nothing more serious than a few broken bones.

Eli gave him a how-to on the chain saw and the finer points of cutting down trees, and they set to work. It was dirty, hot, and frustrating. The saw blade kept getting hung up, no matter how precisely he followed the kid's instructions. When the first tree fell—and in the direction he'd wanted it to, no less—he was surprised. By the time the sixth one went down, he was dirtier, hotter, not so frustrated, and tired of the effort. About the only good thing he could find about the whole job was that the chain saws were so loud, conversation was kept to a minimum. He hadn't known Eli could say so little for so long.

After what surely must have been hours, Eli signaled him to stop. When he cut off the saw, the kid said, "Let's get some lunch."

Cole automatically glanced at his left wrist, but the Rolex he'd worn for the past five years was gone. "Why don't you go ahead and bring it back?"

Eli's look was as dry as the desert. "Like you'd be here waiting? Come on."

Still Cole didn't move. "Where?"

"Where everyone goes for lunch. Harry's."

"Nope." Cole started the saw again, revved the engine, and prepared to remove a limb from the tree he'd just downed. Before the blade touched the wood, though, the saw died. He started it, it sputtered for a moment, then went dead again.

"Come on," Eli repeated, pulling the saw from his hands. "Let's go."

Against his will, Cole climbed into the truck. In his weeks in Bethlehem, he'd become a regular at Harry's. He'd known all the other regulars, had his own usual table. He'd made so many contacts in there, that he'd joked with Harry about splitting the commissions with him. Of course, there'd been no commissions because there'd been no investments.

And Eli wanted him to walk in there and face everyone now that they knew the truth.

He wasn't sure he could do it.

He had only a few minutes to find the courage to pull it off. Then Eli was pulling into a parking space, shutting off the engine, and waiting pointedly for him to get out.

According to the sign outside the bank down the street, it was twelve-thirty-five. That alone was enough to tell him that Harry's would be busy. Looking at the sidewalk, he walked beside Eli to the diner entrance, took a deep breath, lifted his gaze, and walked in the door.

The reaction inside wasn't anything so dramatic as a sudden silence. No one yelled obscenities at him, pointed their fingers in censure, or snickered at his predicament, and neither Harry nor Maeve, the longtime waitress who seemed to think the joint was as much hers as Harry's, threw him out. But there were looks—some quick and furtive, others long and judgmental, some disdainful, some expressionless.

There was Fred Miller, who'd invested five grand in addition to letting Cole live rent-free in his mother's house while waiting for a nonexistent loan to go through. And Dean Elliott, an artist who lived outside town, where he created strange but valuable pieces, some of the profits of which he'd sunk into Cole's scheme. And Mrs. Larrabee, widow of the former mayor and as grandmotherly as anyone he'd ever known—as trusting, too, as her buy-in had shown. And Leanne—

He stiffened. She was sitting in a booth next to the plate-glass window, looking outside while the woman across from her chattered. Her dark hair was pulled back and tied at her neck with a fat red bow that matched her sweater, and she looked beautiful. Untouchable.

"Afternoon, boys," Maeve greeted. Her smile dimmed as she looked from Eli to Cole, then brightened once more when she spoke to the kid. "If you can find a place to sit, I can serve you."

"You're having a busy day," Eli remarked.

"Every day's a busy day. Thank the Lord for that."

Cole scanned the room, careful not to make eye contact with anyone, and saw no empty seats. He was about to suggest they eat at the house when Eli gestured. "There . . . she'll share her table with us."

Never bring attention to yourself, Owen had taught, *but once you have it, don't cower from it.* Keeping that in mind, Cole kept his head up and shoulders back as he followed Eli between tables. He was so busy wishing he was elsewhere, that when the kid stopped, he almost plowed into him.

"Imagine meeting you here," Eli said, his tone too friendly, too phonily surprised. "Mind if we join you?"

Cole shifted to the side so he could see this *friend,* and recognized the pretty blonde with Leanne. "No," he said flatly. "Huh-uh."

He turned to walk out, but Eli caught his arm, his grasp unexpectedly strong. Cole could break it, and maybe even a few of his fingers in the process, but that would draw even more attention his way, when he was smothering with what he already had.

"Ladies?" Eli prompted.

"You can have my place," Leanne said, grabbing her purse and sliding toward the end of the bench. "I've lost my appetite."

Eli blocked her way. "You've hardly touched your food. No one walks away from Harry's lunch special. It's the best food in town. Slide over, Sophy. Let Cole sit beside you."

With a narrow-eyed scowl for Eli, the blonde obeyed, leaving more than half the bench for Cole. Unwillingly, Leanne did the same, so Eli could sit next to her.

"This is *not* a good idea," Sophy announced, still scowling at Eli.

Her annoyance had no effect on him. "It's lunchtime. You're hungry. We're hungry. The place is packed. It's an efficient use of time and space. What could possibly not be good about it?"

"Spoken like a man," she muttered.

Maeve appeared with an order pad and pen, and a smile for Eli. "What can I get you?"

While he ordered, Cole stared at the tabletop, acutely aware of Leanne doing the same. A moment later he felt the weight of Maeve's disapproving stare. "What about you?"

"I'll have the same," he murmured, not knowing what he'd just asked for, and not caring. As soon as the waitress left, he stood up, but managed only one step before Eli was on his feet, too.

"Where are you going?"

"To the bathroom, to wash up."

Eli studied him, as if debating whether to trust him. Leanne helped him along with a sarcastically sweet smile. "It's safe. That hall goes to the bathrooms and nowhere else. There are no windows, no way to escape."

Relaxing, Eli sat down again. "Go ahead. We'll be right here when you get back."

Not if she could help it, Leanne thought belligerently. It was bad enough she had to live with Cole in town—had to lie in bed at night, unable to sleep, knowing he was only a few yards away in his own bed. She damn well wouldn't have lunch with him.

As soon as he disappeared through the door marked REST ROOMS, she offered Sophy a tight smile. "I'm going to head back to the shop. I've been gone too long."

"Fifteen minutes," Sophy scoffed.

"I don't close during the day."

"It doesn't hurt once in a while. Anyone who wants to shop and finds it closed, will come back later. After all"— she smiled wheedlingly—"where else can they buy all the wonderful stuff you carry?"

Feeling her temper rising, Leanne took a calming breath. It didn't ease the tension in her voice. "Okay, no subterfuge. I couldn't care less about the shop being closed in the middle of the day. But you were right when you said this is a bad idea. I'm not sitting here with him."

"Why? What did I do?"

Leanne glared at the young man beside her. She'd seen him in court last week, had heard the judge call him Eli, but that was all she knew about him. He was new to Bethlehem, new to her, and at the rate he was going, they *weren't* going to become friendly enough to learn more.

She didn't bother to answer his questions, but turned her attention back to Sophy. "Tell your friend to get out of my way."

"He's no friend of mine," the girl replied with a toss of her blonde curls. "He wouldn't listen to me anyway. He never does."

"I'd listen if you had something important to contribute," Eli said, his voice smug and condescending.

As Leanne had ignored him, so did Sophy. "You have to eat, Leanne. Besides, Cole's going to be around a long time. You can't run away every time you see him. You can't let him make you afraid to go out. What kind of lesson would that teach Ryan?"

The same lesson Cole had already taught him the hard way—when things got tough, the tough got going. But she wasn't ready to be in the same building with him, much less at the same table. Besides, he had run out on her. Wasn't it only fair that she should be allowed to run out on him?

But who guaranteed that life would be fair? God knows, *hers* certainly hadn't been. Or Ryan's. Or Cole's—

No. No sympathy. He didn't deserve it.

The question became moot when the REST ROOMS door swung open and Cole returned to the table. He'd washed his face, arms, and hands, combed his fingers through his hair, and dusted away the layer of sawdust that had coated his clothes. He looked amazingly handsome.

He sat down beside Sophy—two blonds, both blue-eyed and tanned, looking more like brother and sister than virtual strangers—and fixed his gaze on the table. Where were the cocky grin and wink and the *Hey, sugar* that she'd wanted to smack him for last week in the courthouse?

Where was all that arrogance, that don't-give-a-damn-about-anything attitude? Surely a lousy one and a half day's work hadn't beaten it out of him.

Almost as if he sensed her thoughts, he took a breath, raised his head, grinned, and transformed into the Cole who'd first come to town last April. The difference was as obvious as night and day, and it made her stare, wondering which was real and which was an act. Or was it all an act? Was there anything at all about him that was real?

"Did you miss me while I was gone?" he asked, a drawl more apparent in his voice than when he'd first come to town. Of course, he'd been masquerading as an L.A. native then, and they all knew now he'd been born and raised in the heart of Texas.

"Yeah, I did," she replied carelessly. "But my aim's getting better every day."

"How's Danny?"

"He's fine. He's forgotten all about you." She didn't look at him as she spoke—didn't want to see if her jibe had any effect. Instead she focused on cutting a piece of tender pork chop, dipping it in gravy, and lifting it to her mouth.

"Nolie still seeing your brother?"

"They're married now. You know, that thing two people do when they're in love and want to be together and have a family." Then she faked a big regretful frown. "Oh, that's right. You wouldn't know anything about that, because you don't care about anyone but yourself."

His voice was hard and stiff. "Well, you finally got one thing right."

She forced another bite of pork chop, a forkful of mashed potatoes, three baby carrots, then laid her fork down and stared at him. "Ask about Ryan."

Maeve gave him a moment of reprieve as she served two specials and two glasses of chocolate milk, but then she left again. He sprinkled salt over his potatoes, buttered his roll, and started to cut into the pork chop.

"Ask . . . about . . . Ryan." It was her sternest voice, one guaranteed to make small children snap to attention—and grown men, too, for that matter. It made his fingers tighten around the fork until his knuckles turned white, and formed thin lines at the corners of his mouth.

He exhaled, put the utensils down, sat back, and looked at her head-on for the first time. "What about Ryan?"

"He's living with Danny and me, since we're the only people he knew in town when you dumped him here without so much as a 'So long.' He's making C's and D's in school, and he had a nightmare last night, even with the light on. He's lost weight; he's sullen and uncooperative; and he's headed for big trouble because of you. And you can't even be bothered to *ask* about him?"

For a moment, she thought she saw a flicker of something on his face—bleak regret? Sorrow? But it disappeared so quickly behind that impassive mask, that she feared she was kidding herself. His next words confirmed the fear.

"He's an adaptable kid. He'll get over it."

Leanne was stunned. How could he keep surprising her? He'd seduced her, made her fall in love with him, then ripped off the entire town. He'd played such a good father, then walked away and left his son behind. He was as dishonest as the day was long, self-absorbed, and superficial. He wasn't even worth the cost of the air that kept him alive . . . and yet he'd shocked her again.

This time when she moved to get up, she didn't let Eli stop her. If he hadn't scrambled out of the booth as quickly as he did, she would have knocked him to the floor and stepped in his middle on her way out. Clutching her purse so tightly she might just grind the leather to powder, she rushed out of the diner, darted across the street, and covered the block to her shop in record time. There she would have taken the stairs two at a time to her apartment, where she would have ranted, raved, and broken things, but a slender figure was waiting impatiently outside the shop door, arms folded, toe tapping.

A visit from her mother usually ranked somewhere between a root canal and a near-lethal case of food poisoning on Leanne's list of favorite things, but today she actually welcomed the distraction. Anger with an absent Cole would take a backseat to dealing with Phyllis in the flesh.

"Mom," she greeted her more warmly than she had in years, as she slid the key in the lock. "I'm glad you stopped by. Come in, please."

L OOKING AS IF HE'D SWALLOWED SOME DEVILISH little horror movie creature that was now killing him from the inside out, Cole left his lunch uneaten, muttered that he would be outside, then left the diner as quickly— and with as much attention—as Leanne had. Sophy watched as he stopped in front of Eli's old green truck, leaned against it, then bent his head as if he just couldn't hold it up anymore. Then she glared at Eli. "I told you it was a bad idea."

"We had to do something to get them together."

"Not like this. Not with half the town for an audience. But, no, you couldn't listen. You think you're so hot. Well, let me tell you—"

"Do *you* think I'm hot?"

She stared, mouth open, before remembering to shut it. He was the most arrogant guardian she'd ever known . . . and the handsomest, too, with black hair and dark eyes and a smile that could light up the heavens. Not that she was susceptible to a pretty face. She had a job to do here, and thanks to him, it had just gotten harder.

"You—you—" Frantically, she tried to recover the thread of the conversation before he'd interrupted and seized it with relief. "You can't just come in here and do things your own way. Gloria and I *know* these people. We know how to handle them."

He was absolutely unrepentant. "And I know how to handle Cole."

"You don't know squat about Leanne."

"She's a woman. What's to know?" He shrugged dismissively, then pointed to the pork chop on her plate. "Are you gonna finish that?"

Too numb to think of anything at all to say, she slid the plate toward him, and he speared the meat on his fork. He was obnoxious, arrogant, rude, chauvinistic, brash, egotistical, arrogant—

"You already said *arrogant*. Don't start repeating yourself." He ate a bite, then grinned. "Besides, those are awfully uncharitable thoughts for a guardian to be having. Face it, Soph. We have different styles. Yours is gentle, gradual, and subdued, and mine gets results. You'll see that soon."

Styles? Results? Soph?!

She couldn't speak for fear of sputtering. It was just as well, because he gulped the last few bites, then grabbed the ticket and got to his feet. "Gotta go. See you around."

Not if she could help it, she thought with a sniff. She would rather transfer to the North Pole than work with a guardian like him. He was too obnoxious, too smug, too arrogant—and, yes, she knew she was repeating herself, but something so dead-on accurate deserved repeating. She'd worked with many guardians over the years, some whom she'd liked better than others, but this one . . .

For heaven's sake, he'd called her *Soph!*

• • •

THE STREETLIGHTS WERE BUZZING SOFTLY WHEN Leanne locked up the store Wednesday evening. For a time she stood on the sidewalk, breathing deeply of the nippy air, letting it seep into her bones and chase away every last bit of heat from her body. She was tired—sleepless nights tended to have that effect on her—but the chill gave her a new burst of energy, enough to face the one-block walk to the grocery store without groaning inwardly.

She'd called upstairs on the intercom, to let Ryan know where she was going and to ask for meal suggestions. He hadn't offered any. She'd nagged him to finish his homework, and he said he already had. She really hoped he hadn't lied to her.

As the wind whipped down the street, she zipped the jacket to her chin, shoved her hands in the pockets, and started toward the store. Ryan had another appointment with J.D. on Thursday, and she had Halloween costumes to acquire, and she was on the decorations committee for the haunted house at the town's celebration, and there were pumpkins to carve and treats to bake, and she was suffering from the worst case of lack of concentration she'd ever experienced.

And she knew exactly who to blame.

She was scowling as she crossed the grocery store parking lot—had been scowling every time she thought of her run-in with Cole at Harry's the day before. She wasn't sure what bothered her more—that he was walking around free, that she still found him so damned handsome, that he'd pulled off his chameleon act so completely, or . . . no, no doubt about it. His uncaring attitude about Ryan won hands-down.

A close second was the act. She'd had to face that she knew virtually nothing about the man she'd fallen in—and out of—love with. He'd been playing a role with her, and he'd succeeded magnificently. She'd seen only what he wanted her to see, and none of it had been the real Cole Jackson. She doubted even he knew the real Cole anymore.

It was too bad for Ryan's sake. For herself, she didn't care anymore. Whatever tender feelings she'd had for him were gone. She might not be the quickest learner in the world—four broken hearts proved that—but eventually she *did* learn. But Ryan . . . it broke her heart all over again, to see him grieving for the father he'd believed loved him.

Inside the brightly lit store, she got a shopping cart and headed for the produce section. Cooking wasn't her strong suit. Before Danny's birth, all her meals had come from Bethlehem's limited choice of restaurants or the freezer case. Now she relied too much on sandwiches, hot dogs, and dishes such as spaghetti, chili, and stew. Maybe she should surprise the kids and cook a real dinner—roast beef with all the veggies or baked ham with wild rice and broccoli casserole. Maybe meat loaf and mashed potatoes or fried chicken, potato salad, and baked beans.

Or maybe one of her old fallbacks, such as chicken stew, she decided as she bagged carrots, potatoes, celery, and onions. It was a good thing her boys were easy to please. She added catsup and canned corn to the cart, then a box of cornstarch just in case she needed it for thickening the gravy, along with apples and caramel dip for dessert. She was browsing through the meat section, looking to be tempted on her way to the packages of boneless, skinless chicken breasts, when she bumped carts with another shopper and glanced up, an apology at the ready.

It died unspoken.

Cole didn't look any happier than she felt. His gaze narrowed, pulling the skin across his cheekbones taut, then slid into a wince. She noticed the nasty scratch across his left cheek and wondered whether one of his former *clients* had demanded a little interest on a failed investment. Not that she could imagine anyone in Bethlehem resorting to physical retribution, but he'd taught her plenty of things that had been unimaginable before.

She didn't want to speak, didn't want to even make eye contact, but he and his cart were blocking the chicken she needed. She tried easing her cart forward so he would have to retreat, but he just planted his feet and held his ground.

She unclenched her fingers from the cart's handle and made a show of looking around. "Where's your watchdog? Surely he's not foolish enough to let you out, unguarded."

A muscle in his jaw twitched. "Eli's getting dessert."

"And you haven't crept away like a thief in the night?" Then she smiled sarcastically. "Bad choice of words, huh? Since you really *are* a thief."

That muscle twitched again. "You all got your money back."

"And that somehow makes up for the fact that you stole it in the first place?"

"No one forced you to buy in."

"No. We did that because we trusted you. No one forced *you* to betray that trust and steal from us."

He shrugged, but without the cockiness she was coming to expect. Instead, he merely looked . . . weary. "It's what I do."

"And you don't regret it at all, do you? You're sorry you got caught, sorry they brought you back here, but you're not at all sorry for committing the crime in the first place, are you?"

He stared at her a long time, his expression unreadable, then abruptly took a few steps back so he could maneuver his cart around her.

Perversely, she swung her cart around, to block him. "What? No answer?"

"You wouldn't believe it if I gave it." He succeeded at the same technique she'd tried, pushing his cart forward until she had to either move or get run over. He walked a few yards, then turned back. "Hey . . . Ryan's birthday is next month—the thirteenth."

She should have known that, Leanne thought—should have asked him or found out from his social worker or the school or *someone*. What if it had passed unnoticed? How insignificant would that have made him feel? How badly would they all have felt?

All she could do in response was nod, and even that seemed more than he expected. With a curt nod of his own, he walked away.

Numbly she took a package of chicken breasts from the refrigerated case, then turned her cart toward the registers at the front of the store. That wasn't so bad, was it? Sure, she felt as if she'd been turned inside out and upside down, and there was a knot in her stomach that was taking its own sweet time at relaxing. But she'd seen him, talked to him, and hadn't cried, punched him, screamed at him, or anything else. That was a good sign.

Even if she'd *wanted* to do all those things and more.

She'd paid her bill and was on her way out the door, purse over her shoulder and a shopping bag in each hand, when someone called her name. She turned to see Eli, who'd spoken, and Cole, leaving the next register down. Eli was grinning as if seeing her had just made his day.

After lunch at Harry's yesterday, she could have happily gone a few years before seeing him again.

"How about a hand with that?" he offered, nodding toward her bags.

"I can manage."

"I didn't mean to imply that you couldn't. But it's not proper for a man to stand by with empty hands while a woman carries heavy bags."

"They're not so heavy, and I don't have far to go."

"And we're going in the same direction." With the grin brightening a hundred watts or so, he took the bags Cole was carrying, then gestured again with a nod. "Why don't you help her with those?"

Though Cole made no move toward her, she tightened her grip anyway. "It's not necessary."

"No, it isn't. That's what's nice about it."

Cole could refuse to take the bags. She could refuse to give them up. She could tell Eli to mind his own business and leave her alone. She could do a lot of things, and every one of them would be noticed, dissected, and passed on by the curious shoppers watching from nearby checkouts.

Grinding her teeth, she managed a semblance of a smile, let Cole have the bags, then spun around and walked out. He matched his pace to hers. Eli fell farther and farther behind—deliberately, she guessed. When they reached the sidewalk at the far edge of the parking lot, she glanced over her shoulder, to see the young man chatting pleasantly with Mrs. Franks—not an easy task, given the woman's sour disposition. "What's his problem?"

"He's very young."

"He can't be that much younger than you."

"I was never that young."

If that was true, it was very sad, but he seemed neither sad nor bitter. He was simply stating an opinion.

"He sets Sophy's teeth on edge," she remarked as they passed the courthouse. "I think she likes him."

"I don't know about that. *I* set your teeth on edge, and it doesn't have anything to do with liking, does it?"

In spite of the chill, her face flushed hotly. "No," she agreed, tight-lipped. "Nothing at all."

When they crossed the street that ran in front of her shop, she stopped, faced him, and held out her hands. When he didn't immediately give the bags to her, she took hold of the handles, but he didn't let go. "Ryan's smart enough to make straight A's with a little effort. He just doesn't see much reason to bother. He's not convinced that book-learning has much value in the real world."

Unwilling to acknowledge that he was actually demonstrating some concern for—to say nothing of understanding of—his son, she fell back on sarcasm. "Gee, where would he get that idea? From his father, the con artist? Or maybe his grandfather, who's also a con artist?"

Cole's forehead wrinkled in a frown. "His grand—oh. You mean Owen."

In J.D.'s office, it seemed as if Ryan hadn't made the connection that Owen was his grandfather, and even Cole had needed a moment to realize it. What kind of father had Owen Jackson been? He hadn't brought up a son, but a chip off the old cellblock, and the grandfather/grandson relationship had apparently been so tenuous that it had gone unrecognized by both Cole and Ryan. How much responsibility did the elder Jackson bear for Cole's choices in life?

She gave herself a sharp mental shake. She wasn't making excuses for him, remember? No matter how inadequate his father had been, the choices Cole had made were his. Certainly his father had influenced the boy, the teenager, and probably even the young man, but he was thirty years old. Old enough to make decisions for himself, and to suffer the consequences for them.

Too bad she and Ryan had to suffer with him.

She tugged until he released the bags, then took a few steps back. "Tell me something . . . is there anyone in your family who *isn't* a criminal?"

He pretended to think about it a moment, then gave a callous shrug. "No one I can think of at the moment. Besides Ryan."

"Why is that? Because you didn't have enough time with him, to teach him the tools of the family trade?"

His expression turned as hard and cold as the concrete beneath their feet. "Because that was the deal we made from the beginning. I'd take care of him, and he would stay out of the business."

"So even a little kid knew better than to make the choices you did." Thoroughly disgusted with him—and with herself for getting into the situation where they could even have this conversation—she shook her head disdainfully, turned her back on him, and headed toward her apartment. Just before she went inside, she surreptitiously glanced to the right. Cole was still standing there, shoulders slumped, hands at his sides. He looked about as defeated as a man could get while still standing.

But that wasn't her concern. Nothing about him was, except how to relegate him to the darkest corner of her mind.

And how to stop feeling that little shock every time she saw him.

And how to quit finding him so amazingly attractive.

And how—

"Oh, hell," she muttered as she reached the top of the stairs. Two small words that summed up her life quite well at the moment.

Oh, hell.

Chapter Five

ON THURSDAY THEY GOT A NEW RESIDENT at the house—an older man by the name of Murray, who would be with them only for a week or so, according to Eli. His age was difficult to guess—somewhere between fifty and seventy, Cole assumed. He carried an extra thirty pounds in his belly, his thinning hair was white, and he was either living someplace else in his mind or doing a damn good act of it. He would probably be completely harmless if not for his habit of driving after spending a few hours with his best friend, Jack Daniel.

He joined them before breakfast and went along afterward when they drove to City Park. He was no more familiar with a chain saw than Cole had been a few days earlier, but he followed directions well.

By Cole's count, they had cut down twenty-one trees, cleaned them up, and piled the discarded branches nearby. Today they were cutting the trunks into firewood, which they would deliver to elderly people who used it to keep their winter heating bills down. Later, the branches would be fed through a chipper, to make mulch. Then they would have the pleasure of mulching every tree planted along the sidewalks in the business district and every flower bed in the square. One more job he was going to hate.

Though, he had to admit, if not for the people, it hadn't been bad so far. He liked being outside, and he'd spent so much time behind a desk in his last couple of cons, that he could use the physical activity. Even getting scraped across the face by a falling branch yesterday hadn't amounted to anything more than a nuisance.

But he could live easier if he didn't see Leanne again. If she wasn't always looking at him as if she could barely contain her hatred. If he wasn't tempted to explain himself to her. It didn't matter if she knew the real reason he'd left Ryan behind, or if he told her details about his upbringing that he'd never shared with anyone else. It wouldn't change a thing if he tried to make her understand, other than costing him whatever pride he had left.

It would just all-around be easier not to see her.

Seeing Eli approach, Cole let the chain saw idle, then die. Even after he set it down, he still felt the vibrations in his hands and all the way up to his shoulders. He took the paper cup the kid offered and drank half of it in one swallow, then grimaced. The drinks offered under Eli's supervision were better suited to preschoolers than grown men—usually water and milk. This was the hard stuff— lemonade, made from a mix and tart enough to turn Little Mary Sunshine sour.

"Let's load up some of this wood and get it delivered," Eli said, bending to gather an armful of logs.

"I thought wood had to dry out before it could be used for firewood." Cole drained the last of his lemonade, tossed the cup in a nearby trash can, then picked up an armload himself.

"It does. Most of these trees have been dead so long they

could have been burned standing upright. The city just hadn't budgeted for removing them, until we came along."

Whoever would have thought that a baby-faced do-gooder and a convicted felon could be the solution to their problem?

While Cole had been cutting, Eli and Murray had unloaded the tools from the back of the truck. When they finished loading the wood, there was no room left for them. "What about that stuff?" Cole asked.

"We'll leave it here. No one will take it."

Of course not, since the only bona-fide criminal in Bethlehem would be otherwise occupied. "It's a park, Eli," he pointed out impatiently. "Kids come here to play. You can't leave chain saws, gasoline, and an axe lying around."

"Oh." Eli glanced toward the playground equipment in one direction, the baseball fields in another, then shrugged. "Why don't you stay here and keep working, while Murray and I make this delivery?"

Stay here. Truly alone for the first time since Eli had gotten him out of jail. Free to disappear into the thick growth of woods that formed the back boundary of the park and never come back. The thought made Cole's chest tight, made his breaths shallow and unsteady. "You sure you trust me to be here when you get back?"

"No." Eli tossed the last logs into the truck bed, then slammed the tailgate shut. "But I guarantee, if you're not, I'll find you before sundown."

Not in those woods, Cole thought cynically.

"Even in those woods," Eli retorted.

After giving him a sharp look, Cole put on the ear protection and safety glasses, gave the chain saw a jerk, then revved the engine and went back to work. Though he was careful not to be obvious, he watched as Eli and Murray climbed into the truck, then drove across the dead grass.

The old pickup dipped and bounced over the curb into the nearest parking lot, then turned onto the street. Within moments it was out of sight.

And Cole was free to go.

But he didn't shut down the saw and make a run for it. He was almost finished cleaning up this trunk. It wouldn't take him ten minutes to get the job done, and another five to drag the branches to the side. Besides, as Owen always said, *A man needs a plan.* He'd already decided that the first chance he got, he was outta there, but that wasn't a plan.

Where would he go, and how would he get there? He needed money and transportation. Like an irresponsible kid, he wasn't allowed to have money in this program; what he'd had on him when he was arrested was in Eli's safekeeping. So he would have to find out where the kid had hidden it, or he would have to steal a stash.

As for transportation, he couldn't buy a bus ticket there in town, and he damn sure couldn't hitch a ride. That left his own two feet, stealing a car, or getting help. Crossing these mountains on foot when the nighttime lows were in the forties struck him as promising a low probability of success, and hot-wiring a car was one skill he'd never picked up in his checkered past.

But he could get help. All he had to do was get a message to the family, and someone would show up.

He was working on automatic pilot, caught up in his thoughts, when some sixth sense made him cut off the saw. An instant later, a small boy flung himself against his legs and climbed into his arms.

"Cole!" Danny Wilson squealed with delight, then threw his arms around his neck and gave him a sloppy kiss. "I didn't know you was home! Ryan's been stayin' with us and we're sorta brothers now, only we're gonna be real brothers someday and—hey! Know what I'm gonna be for Halloween?"

Cole couldn't think of an answer—couldn't think of anything but how good it was to see Danny, and how it felt even better to just once see someone who didn't hate him. He hugged the kid tightly, then became aware of an unholy screeching rapidly approaching. It was Phyllis Wilson, Leanne's banshee of a mother, and she was so furious she was shaking.

"Put him down! Danny, get away from that—that man right this instant! How dare you touch my grandson?" She snatched Danny away, careful not to touch Cole any more than necessary. He felt a sense of loss at the only friendly contact he'd had in a long time being pulled away.

She settled the boy on her hip, then shifted so he was away from Cole. "Don't you ever go near my grandson again. Do you understand? This is outrageous! What could they be thinking, letting a convicted criminal run around, armed and free, to terrorize the citizens of this town? I'm going home to complain to Chief Walker and Judge Monroe right this minute."

"I'm not armed—"

Spinning on her heel, she marched away, her back ramrod straight. Danny gave him a frantic look over her shoulder and wiggled to get down. "Grandma, I wanna talk to Cole. I wanna tell him what me and Ryan have been doin'! Grandma— Grandma—!"

As they disappeared into a brick house across the street, Cole leaned back shakily against the nearest tree. This was just what he needed—less than three days into his five-thousand-hour sentence, and already one of Bethlehem's law-abiding citizens was making a formal complaint against him. The best he could hope for was that the police chief and the judge knew Phyllis and would automatically discount her gripe. In her dealings with Leanne, at least, she was neither kind nor reasonable.

On the other hand, maybe her complaint would result in the cancellation of Eli's program and a quick transfer to the state pen. In the meantime, though, he was getting a letter out to his brothers immediately.

One way or another, he was getting out of this town. Before it killed him.

Alex Thomas was sitting at his desk, thinking about holidays and kids, Halloween costumes and Easter eggs and fireworks on a hot July night, when his secretary buzzed him. "Mitch just called—wanted to know if you could get over to the courthouse ASAP."

"Did he say what it was about?"

"No. There was a lot of loud talking in the background. Sounded like he had his hands full."

"Thanks, Eleanor." He loaded his briefcase, shrugged into his suit coat, tightened his tie, then left the inner office. "I'll head on home from there, so you can take off as soon as you're finished."

"Will do, boss," the older woman said with a salute. He knew better, though. Quitting time was five P.M., and while she might stay later, she never left earlier. She was worth every penny he paid her and then some, and he'd sworn he would do what he could to keep her happy, because no one else could possibly compete.

Passing his car, he half-wished he could ignore Mitch's call and go on home for a long, quiet evening with Melissa, but Mitch wouldn't have called unless it was important. Maybe Murray Walker—no relation to the chief—had gotten behind the wheel again, or the Smith boys had gotten caught, egging houses again. They were the only repeat offenders in his small criminal practice.

There was a lot of loud talking in the background, Eleanor had said, and Alex heard it for himself when he walked through the police department door. The desk sergeant, wearing a grimace, nodded toward a conference room halfway back, and Alex headed that way.

Judging by the sheer volume, he'd expected to find a roomful of people, but there weren't many—Mitch, Judge Monroe, the assistant DA, Eli, Danny, and Phyllis Wilson . . . which explained the noise. Smiling even though the mere sight of her made him grind his back teeth together, Alex closed the door. He stood next to the chair where Danny was sitting on the wooden arm and quietly asked, "What's up, Danny?"

The boy raised a teary gaze to him, with his lower lip stuck out. "Grandma's being mean."

She wasn't *being* mean, Alex thought uncharitably. She *was* mean. He wasn't sure what terrible wrongs life had done to justify her behavior, but she had more than most people—a family who tolerated her when they should have cut her off years ago, a grandson who loved her, a nice home, and no money worries.

"You watch your mouth, young man," Phyllis said sharply. "I am *not* being mean. I'm simply looking out for your welfare the way any reasonable person would."

"And what's threatening his welfare?" Alex asked, sliding his arm around Danny's middle and feeling the boy lean back comfortably against him.

"Your client," Phyllis declared.

"At one time or another I've done work for probably half the people in town, including you and your husband, your daughter, and your daughter-in-law. You have to be more specific."

"Cole Jackson."

Alex looked to Mitch, whose expression suggested he'd rather waste his time elsewhere. "When Mrs. Wilson took

Danny to the park to play this afternoon, Cole was over there working."

"Alone!" Phyllis added. "And he was armed!"

"He wasn't armed," Eli said.

"He had a chain saw and an axe."

Eli made an impatient gesture. "He was cutting down trees. Do you expect him to do it with his teeth?"

Phyllis flung her hand in his direction. "This person left that criminal alone with a weapon in City Park, where our children play. Not expecting such irresponsible behavior, I took my grandson there, and that man *grabbed* him!"

Before Alex had a chance to react to the accusation, Danny's small hands tightened on his. "He did not! I hugged him 'cause I missed him and he missed me, too. We was talkin', and *she* was mean and made me leave."

"Have you talked to Jackson?" Alex asked, and Mitch nodded.

"He tells the same story as Danny."

"Well, of course he does!" Phyllis's cheeks burned hotly. "He's a liar! Of course he's going to back up Danny's story!"

"Mrs. Wilson, he doesn't *know* what Danny said," the ADA said patiently. "He only saw the boy for those few minutes at the park, and they had no time to get their stories straight."

The facts had no effect on his grandmother. "That man should be in prison. He's a thief and a liar and a criminal. He has no right to be walking the streets of our town and making it unsafe for us to leave our houses in the middle of the day!"

"And what do you want us to do about it?" Mitch asked.

"Lock him up! Make him serve his sentence."

"He's serving his sentence," Eli retorted. "Five thousand hours of community service."

"That's a stupid sentence. Change it." She directed that to Judge Monroe, who shook her head.

"It's not my sentence to change. I'm not convinced it's the sentence *I* would have given, but I'm curious to see how this program of Eli's works out. It appears to have great potential."

"Potential for disaster, you mean." Phyllis sniffed haughtily. "I cannot believe you people see nothing wrong with what's happened. That man is a dangerous criminal who has caused nothing but trouble. You mark my words— you'll be sorry, every one of you. Come along, Danny."

Though he clearly didn't want to go, she gave him no choice, sweeping him up and stalking from the room.

The silence following her passage seemed to vibrate. Mitch broke it when he closed the door, then glanced around the room. "Any of you think Jackson is dangerous?"

Everyone shook their heads.

"Any of you besides Eli think it's a good idea to leave him out working on his own?"

The assistant DA shook his head, along with the judge. Alex chose not to answer.

"You've got to trust these people sometime," Eli said in his own defense. "Sure, he could have taken off . . . but he didn't. He could slit my throat and disappear in the middle of the night, but he hasn't. Cole's not violent. Even if he did escape, he wouldn't hurt anyone in the process."

"You sure of that?" the ADA asked.

"You wanna know if he is capable of violence? Yes, he is. So are you. So is everyone. But Cole's been a criminal practically from the cradle. He's not going to make that kind of abrupt change in his methods. Besides, if he takes off, I'll find him."

This time it was Judge Monroe who asked, "Are you sure of that?"

Eli flashed a cocky grin. "I haven't lost one yet."

"Yeah, like you've been doing it so long," the ADA muttered. "How old are you? Twenty?"

"Older than I look." Eli sprawled back in his chair. "So . . . you gonna let Mrs. Wilson scare you off the program?"

"Her? No." Then Mitch smiled grimly. "But be prepared. She recognizes Jackson as a troublemaker, because she's one herself. Don't take any chances for a while. Don't give her any ammunition to use against you. And *don't* leave Jackson alone in her part of town."

When Mitch signaled the end of the meeting by opening the door, Alex stepped aside and waited for Eli to approach. "Can we talk?"

"Sure." Once they were alone, Eli sat on the table, his feet propped on a chair seat, and asked, "What's up?"

"You said Cole has been a criminal practically from the cradle. What did you mean?"

"Just that. I imagine his father was using him in some sort of scam when he was still in diapers. The first time he got picked up by the police, he was six. Got caught shoplifting."

"A childish prank," Alex said tentatively, unable to imagine a six-year-old thief.

Eli shook his head. "Hungry brothers. He was stealing food because their parents weren't around. He was raised by the best con artists the great state of Texas ever produced, who occasionally went to jail and left the boys to fend for themselves. He and his brothers turned out just like them. I'm not sure they ever stood a chance at anything else."

How was your childhood? Alex had asked Cole last

week before his arraignment, and he'd given a careless answer. *Perfect. Two parents, five brothers, and a dog. We lived in a great house, sat down to dinner together every night, and went to church every Sunday.*

At the time, Alex had thought there was more—or less—to the answer than it appeared, but he hadn't really given it any thought since Cole entered his guilty plea. "He told you all this? He didn't even want to give me his date and place of birth."

"Nah. I don't think he would give a straight answer, even if it was to his benefit. I've got friends all over the place. Anything they don't know, isn't worth knowing."

Interesting. Apparently, there was a whole lot more to Cole Jackson than anyone, with the possible exception of Eli, was giving him credit for.

THE CLOSED SIGN HUNG ON SMALL WONDERS' unlocked door; Sophy was gone for the evening, and Leanne was standing at the register, trying without much success to balance the drawer. Ryan had had another unproductive session with J.D., or so it seemed to her; her mother had insisted on picking up Danny at day care that afternoon, which meant Leanne would have to see her twice in three days; she couldn't make the cash and checks in the drawer add up to the total on the register tape; and her head was pounding a rhythm that made her want to crawl into a dark corner and stay.

And she still had dinner and a haunted-house-committee meeting to face.

The door flew open, catching her off-guard, and Danny stalked his way up the center aisle to the counter, his little face like a storm cloud looking for a place to unleash its fury. A few yards behind him was Phyllis, wearing pretty much the same expression. Her stomach suddenly going queasy, Leanne managed a sickly smile. "Hi, guys. What's going on?"

Danny didn't slow his dogged steps until the counter was between him and his grandmother. He climbed onto the stool there, stood up, and folded his arms over his chest. "Grandma is mean and I don't like her no more."

"Whoa, honey—"

"This is all *your* fault," Phyllis said spitefully. "If you'd ever shown any taste whatsoever in choosing the men you sleep with—"

"Hey!" Leanne glared at her mother. "That topic isn't open for discussion, especially in present company."

Nostrils flaring and jaw muscles tensing, Phyllis averted her gaze to the ceiling, as if praying for patience, then looked at Leanne again. "You're right. We'll take that up later. Suffice it to say, though, that once again your abominable taste in men has come back to cause trouble."

Her abominable taste in men had *been* back nearly two weeks, and there was no doubt Phyllis had known before today. She wasn't much of a mother or a wife, but she was an exceptional gossip. Little things like the return of her daughter's ex-lover who stole a quarter of a million dollars registered big-time on her rumor radar.

Already fed up with Phyllis's interference, even though it had hardly begun, Leanne figured her best bet at getting a semi-accurate picture of events was Danny. Sliding her arm around his waist, she gave him a kiss. "I missed you today."

"I missed you, too, and I ain't ever goin' to Grandma's again."

"Why not, sweetie?"

" 'Cause she's mean and I don't like her."

Phyllis shook her finger warningly. "I warned you at the police station—"

The police— "What was my son doing at the police station?"

Too late, her mother realized what she'd said. She lifted her chin, straightened her shoulders, and pursed her mouth, while two spots burned in her cheeks. "I went to make a complaint with Mitch Walker and Judge Monroe. Naturally, I couldn't leave Danny waiting in the car, so I took him inside with me."

A chill of dread spreading through her, Leanne lifted Danny to the floor. "Why don't you run upstairs and see what Ryan's up to? You guys can figure out what you want for dinner, okay?"

"Okay." He chose a route that avoided his grandmother by a dozen feet on his way to the door. Of course, she couldn't take a hint.

"Come give Grandma a kiss."

"No!" he blurted, then dashed out the door, ran the few feet to the apartment door, and disappeared inside.

"That child is spoiled rotten," Phyllis declared when she turned back to Leanne. "One of these days you'll regret that you've let him get away with so much."

There was a part of Leanne that wanted to protest mightily. *She* didn't spoil Danny—she *loved* him. And if a four-year-old didn't deserve to be cut a little slack, who did? Besides, it was her mother who had bought him more toys than any three kids could play with, who took him out of day care on a whim, who let him get away with misbehaving.

But they'd had this argument before, and it wasn't worth the energy to repeat tonight. Phyllis believed what she wanted, and all the reality in the world wasn't going to sway her.

Instead, Leanne took a calming breath, wished for an

elephant-strength headache pill, and asked, "What were you complaining about to Mitch?"

With self-righteous indignation, Phyllis told her story. By the time she finished, Leanne was ready to skip the headache pill and go straight to a drug-induced coma. She pressed her fingertips hard against her temples, massaging for a moment, then dropped them. "Okay. So Cole was working in the park and Danny saw him."

"That criminal *grabbed* him. I had to take him away."

She didn't doubt the second part . . . any more than she believed the first. Cole wouldn't just grab a child, especially one whose shrew of a grandmother was yards away. Besides, Danny wouldn't have given him a chance—he would have leaped into his arms as soon as he saw him. He'd liked Cole from the beginning and had treated him to the same hero worship he lavished on Ryan. Like a lot of little boys, Danny wanted a father figure, and for a while, Cole had been it.

"Danny greeted this man whom he was very fond of, and you didn't like it, so you went to the police and filed a complaint?" In spite of her best efforts, Leanne's voice rose significantly by the end of her question.

"Of course I did. I told them I wanted him put in prison, and you know what they said? That he's serving his sentence, and that this program has great potential. Potential for disaster, I told them. I cannot believe the idiots we have working for us."

Leanne was appalled, but not for the reasons her mother expected. Phyllis didn't want Danny having any contact with Cole, so she'd tried to screw with his community service program? When she knew any problems with the program could result in his being sent to prison, after all? How mean-spirited could she be?

Of course, Leanne wanted him in prison, too, but that

was different. She had very good reasons for it. Her mother didn't even *know* the man.

And neither did she, whispered that sly voice she hated.

"All you had to do, Mother, was let them talk for a few minutes, then Danny would have gone off to play. There was no need to make such a huge incident of it."

"No need? *No need?*" Phyllis was close to sputtering. "So you're blaming *me*? You're saying it was *my* fault?"

Leanne's natural inclination was to say, *Of course not; no, you misunderstood*—anything to keep whatever little bit of peace they could manage. But she was flat-out of peace in every other part of her life. Why should her relationship with her mother be any different?

"Yes," she said calmly. "You overreacted. If you'd just stayed out of it, the whole thing would have been over in five minutes. Danny would have been happy, you could have spent the rest of the afternoon playing with him rather than at the police station, and you would have saved yourself some embarrassment."

Phyllis took a few steps back as if the impact of Leanne's words had been physical. Instead of a hot flush, her face was drained of color. Even the blue of her eyes was washed out and icy cold. "Embarrassment?" she echoed in a stiff voice. "I show concern for the safety of my grandchild and you think I embarrassed myself?"

"You didn't complain out of concern for Danny's safety. You wanted to cause trouble for Cole."

"You are so wrong." Tears welled in Phyllis's eyes, and she made a show of dashing them away before pressing her hand to her heart. "I don't understand how you can be this way, Leanne. Your father has never appreciated me, and your brother . . ." She made a dismissive gesture. "But *you*—you should see I've done the best I could for this family. I've sacrificed and struggled . . . and this is the thanks I get. You accuse me of being a troublemaker just because I'm trying to be the best grandmother my only grandchild could want."

Her mother should know better than to try to use her father and brother against her in an argument, Leanne thought dispassionately. Phyllis's life hadn't been any less happy than Earl's, and as for Chase . . . Leanne still hadn't forgiven her parents for the rift that had kept her brother away and out of contact for years.

Grimly she gathered the money spread on the counter into a bank bag, zipped it, and dropped it in her purse. She began flipping off lights, leaving her mother no choice but to move to the door or be left standing in the dark. There she opened the door and pointedly waited for Phyllis to walk through it. As soon as she did, Leanne locked up, then faced her. "You know, Mother, your poor-pitiful-me speech would go over a little better—with me, at least—if you would remember that Danny's *not* the only grandchild. You have a stepgranddaughter in Micahlyn and a foster grandson in Ryan."

Without a good-bye, she covered the distance to the apartment door in long strides, darted inside, and locked the door behind her, then gave a big sigh of relief.

The phone was ringing by the time she got to the top of the stairs. She heard Danny's voice—much closer to normal now, with no hint of the anger or the pout from earlier—then he bellowed. "Mom? Miss Maggie's on the phone!"

She mussed his hair as she took the phone from him, then dropped her purse on the kitchen counter. "Hey, Maggie May, I'm not already late for the meeting, am I?"

Maggie McKinney laughed. "No, you've still got an hour or so. But there's been a change in plans. Instead of my house, we're meeting at the Miller mansion. I hope that's okay."

Leanne inhaled deeply. "Oh, that's perfect." The perfect ending to the crappiest day she'd spent in a long time.

"I know it might be awkward, but Eli and his . . ."

"Convicts? Felons?"

"*Clients* are going to provide the labor for the haunted house, so it seems a good idea to get them involved right away. If you aren't up to this, I'm sure Miss Corinna can find something else for you to do, and we'll manage to get along without you."

It was an easy out, and Leanne wanted to grab it more than she could say. For reasons she couldn't even begin to put into words, she didn't. "Hey, my life has become a house of horrors lately. Let me share some of it with the rest of you."

"Are you sure?" Maggie's voice was rich with sympathy. She'd been through some tough times with her husband, Ross, a few years earlier. They'd grown so far apart that they'd forgotten why they had ever fallen in love, and had even reached the agreement that after the holidays, they would divorce and go their separate ways. But it had been Christmas, the season for miracles, and they had rediscovered their love and themselves instead.

Leanne didn't harbor such hope for herself. The first three men she'd fallen in love with had been happy to go their separate ways, and the fourth didn't even exist. It would take one heck of a miracle to turn Cole into the man he'd pretended to be.

"I'll be fine, Maggie. Don't worry. I'll see you in an hour."

After hanging up, she turned to greet the boys . . . and stared in surprise. They sat at the wicker table, set for three with paper plates, napkins, and soft drinks in cans. In the middle was a platter of sandwiches, along with two bowls of potato chips. To the left of each plate was a candy bar, sneaked from the Halloween stash she'd been collecting.

"You guys made dinner," she said, as pleased as she was surprised.

"And dessert," Danny said, holding up his candy bar.

"You said you had a meeting tonight." Ryan shrugged as if it was no big deal.

"Bless you both." She caught both of them in a hug, kissing first Danny, then Ryan. Whatever her feelings toward Greg, the rat who said so long when she told him she was pregnant, and Cole, the rat who'd sneaked out of her bed without so much as a so long, she was grateful to them both . . . for giving her a family.

Chapter Six

"WE'RE HAVING COMPANY THIS EVENING."
Cole glanced at Eli as he rinsed the last sink-
ful of dinner dishes and stacked each piece in
the drainer. Since Eli didn't seem about to
volunteer more and Murray was wiping down countertops
in another dimension, Cole played the sucker. "Who?"

"I'm not sure. Maggie McKinney, for one. Holly Flynn,
I think. It's the ladies in charge of the haunted house for
the city's Halloween celebration. I told them we'd supply
the labor, if they'd give us directions."

Was a haunted house the sort of thing Leanne would
get involved with? Probably, he thought grimly, remembering the elaborate decorations in her shop windows. But
surely having to deal with more than one Wilson woman a
day qualified as cruel and unusual punishment. He would
just spend the evening in his room.

"Maggie's bringing dessert," Eli went on. "I told her we
would provide coffee and tea."

"Coffee? In this house? Hallelujah." Cole hung the
dishtowel over the towel bar, then started toward the stairs.

"Where are you going?"

"To my room."

"But I just told you—"

"You didn't say I had to hang around."

"Yes, you do. And don't worry. It'll count toward your accumulated hours."

Cole scowled. If he had a reasonable sentence, like Murray, he might be eager to burn off another hour or three. But when he had approximately 4,968 hours left, it was tough to get excited about a few hours.

"Why don't you get the coffee started?" Eli suggested as the doorbell rang.

"With what?"

Eli pointed to a cabinet on his way out. When Cole opened the door, he found a coffeemaker, still in the box, and a one-pound can of coffee, along with a package of filters. As he washed the pot, he listened to the two new voices down the hall, both women, neither of them familiar.

He'd met a lot of people during his weeks in town, but he'd kept his distance from a specific few, including the two women Eli had mentioned. Their husbands, Ross McKinney and Tom Flynn, along with Lynda Foster, were the top dogs at McKinney Industries, were all richer than sin, and were, financially speaking, tougher than nails. Driven people like them didn't give up control of their money easily, and never would have let it walk away in his pocket.

"Smells good," Murray remarked as the aroma of brewing coffee filled the air. "I thought we would have to wait for Eli to reach legal age before we could have coffee again."

Cole glanced at him. That was only the second time he'd spoken since his morning arrival. If asked, Cole would have bet that he was totally unaware of everything going on around him, and he would have been wrong. That had happened before.

Murray breathed deeply again. "But don't you think it'd

taste better with a drop or two of Baileys Irish Cream? Or a dram of Irish whiskey, or maybe just a bit of Galliano." He closed his eyes and smiled dreamily as if he could taste it.

"Except for the occasional beer, I'm not much of a drinker."

The old man smiled at him. "That's okay. Except for the occasional DUI, I'm not much of a criminal."

He'd been called a criminal and much worse, but somehow the word had more of a bite to it when it came from a drunk. Everybody needed somebody to look down on, he guessed, and he was it for Murray. Didn't that feel great?

In the foyer, more voices joined the first two. He thought he recognized Kelsey Grayson's, and that was definitely Nolie Harper's, damn it, which just about guaranteed Leanne would be joining them. She and Nolie had been well on their way to becoming best friends even before Nolie had married her brother.

Despite Eli's decree, he considered disappearing upstairs. There wasn't a lock on his bedroom door, but there was plenty of heavy furniture that could be used to block it. What could the kid do?

Besides boot him out of the program and into the nearest penitentiary?

Wasn't that what he wanted? Wouldn't it beat the hell out of living in Bethlehem and seeing these people all the time? Besides, he'd been in prison before, once for ten months and another for sixteen. It wasn't so bad. Three meals a day, a place to sleep, and no expectations of a man beyond keeping his nose clean. He could handle that.

He couldn't handle *this*.

"Murray, Cole, come on in the dining room," Eli called.

Like a good obedient convict, Murray shuffled off. A knot growing in his gut, Cole stared at the coffeepot as the last drops splattered in with a gurgle. Sure, prison hadn't been so bad . . . not when he was nineteen or again when he was twenty-one. Not when he'd had the energy and optimism to carry him through.

He didn't have either anymore. He was tired of playing the games, of constantly moving, of always looking for the next mark. Most men his age were settled—had regular jobs, families or girlfriends or both. Their only thought when a cop pulled them over was, *Did I run that stop sign?* Or, *Was I speeding?* Winding up in jail wasn't even a possibility for most of them.

Neither was having to abandon their kids because the kids were better off without them.

"Cole?" Eli called.

Nah, he wasn't going to jeopardize his place in the program. Someday soon, one of his brothers was going to show up to rescue him. Escaping from this house would be a piece of cake. Escaping from the pen, he'd be lucky to survive, and tired or not, he was a survivor. All of the Jackson boys were.

He went down the hall and turned into the formal dining room as the doorbell rang. Eli glanced up. "Get that, will you?"

Thinking about that letter to his brothers he had yet to write, he pivoted, continued down the hall, and opened the door. He was wondering which brother would show up—Frank, maybe, since Cole's first stint in prison had been for saving his butt. Or Adam, who was the oldest and thought that put him in charge. Or maybe—

"Can I come in?"

Blinking, he cleared the thoughts from his head and stared at Leanne. She wore black pants, a rust-colored sweater that fell past her hips, black leather gloves, and the cold had turned her cheeks pink. Her lips were pink, too, a dark rosy shade, and her hair fell in straight lines to her shoulders. She looked incredible.

When he didn't move or speak, but just stood there like an idiot, she slipped through the half-open door, started down the hall, then turned back. For a moment she looked as if she thought better of her hesitation, then her mouth thinned. "I heard about your run-in with my mother today. I'm sorry."

A blast of cold rocketed through him, bringing him to his senses. He closed the door, then slid his hands in his hip pockets. "You can't apologize for her."

She made a gesture that might have been a rueful smile if it had fully formed. "Why not? This isn't the first time, and it won't be the last."

"She was concerned."

"No, she wasn't. She was . . . Phyllis being Phyllis." She gave a palms-up shrug that conveyed her frustration and helplessness fairly well. "Did she succeed in causing trouble?"

He shook his head, though it had certainly felt like trouble when a police officer had shown up at City Park, to invite him and Eli to a little sit-down with the chief. They'd put him in an empty room two doors down from the conference room and closed the door, but he'd still been able to hear Phyllis's side of the conversation. "I got the impression that her story didn't jibe with Danny's, while mine did. They did agree, though, that I'm too dangerous to let run loose among the decent folk in town."

He flooded the words with sarcasm, to hide the effort it took to say them. It was a sorry thing when average people found a man's mere presence offensive . . . and even sorrier when a man's character was so questionable that a hug from a little boy resulted in both of them being hauled in to the police station.

And he had no one to blame but himself.

He might as well have spoken that last thought aloud. She shrugged callously as she peeled off her gloves. "Hey, you steal people's life savings, you can't expect them to invite you into their homes."

He smiled. "I don't expect anything, sweetheart." It was better to expect nothing and be surprised, Owen said, than to hope and face certain disappointment.

Put off by his smile and/or answer, she turned on one booted heel and walked away.

Just as he'd expected.

He stood there a long time before following.

The dining room was second only to the living room in terms of size, and was the only one he and Ryan had never used during their residence. Seven-foot-tall china cabinets stood at each end, their shelves holding a small fortune in antique dishes, and the table stretched across the space between them. A large marble fireplace filled the third wall, with tall windows on the fourth. Two crystal chandeliers, small but worth a couple more small fortunes, illuminated the room. It was a great room for entertaining, Fred Miller had proudly pointed out.

The only entertaining Cole had done, was upstairs in his bedroom.

Leanne sat at the far end of the table, which left the near end for him. Eli sat on his left, Holly Flynn on the right. She gave him a look that was half-appreciative, half-disdainful—as if she despised him for ripping off her friends, but couldn't quite negate her feminine appreciation for his good looks. He gave her a cocky grin in return.

It wasn't conceit to say most women were attracted to him. Looks could be an important part of a con. If you've got 'em, use 'em, Owen had always advised. A man could empty a lonely widow's bank account with nothing more than a pretty face and a bit of charm. Cole was living proof of that.

He sat back, one ankle resting on the other knee, elbows braced on the carved wooden chair arms, hands folded across his belly, and listened to the discussion with half a mind. Name aside, the haunted house wasn't supposed to be scary to anyone over the age of two. It would serve Eli and his ladies' committee right if he covered himself with fake blood, attached a phony butcher knife to his chest, and staggered out of the dark corner to scare the bejeebers out of the kids. If he did, they'd think twice before making him work on their next Halloween project.

That thought stopped him cold. Serving his five thousand hours was likely to take two to two and a half years, Alex Thomas had said. He could be around for two more Halloweens. Jeez, he'd never stayed that long in one place in his life.

It was a scary thought . . . but he was leaving, remember? As soon as he wrote that damn letter, then it eventually caught up with one of the boys and they found time to come after him. Sooner or later—though a hell of a lot sooner than two and a half years—he was gonna blow this town.

And everyone in this room would go on with their lives as usual. Oh, they might pull the plug on Eli's program, but he was an ambitious kid, and Bethlehem took care of its own. He would find some other way to do good. No one would really notice Cole's leaving, except Leanne, and she would be happy to see the last of him.

And maybe her mother, who would also be overjoyed to see him disappear.

Ditto Ryan.

The women and Eli had been at the discussion for some time when Kelsey Grayson changed the subject. "Okay, you guys must be *way* stronger than me, but I can't sit here smelling that incredible aroma any longer. I need sugar, and I need it now."

Maggie McKinney lifted the lid of a pastry box and fanned the air toward Kelsey. "Are you hungry?" she asked innocently. "I'll warn you—it's a new recipe. A chocolate-cookie crust, cream-cheese filling, nuts, and whipped cream and cherries. The other is an Italian meringue with strawberries—from the freezer, I'm afraid, but still good."

Amid a chorus of groans, Eli spoke. "Cole—"

He stood up. "I'll get the plates." In less than a week, the kid had gotten damn good at ordering him around, and Cole had gotten pretty damn good at obeying.

He took plates and silverware into the dining room, then returned to the kitchen, to pour himself a cup of coffee. Standing at the sink, he gazed out the window into the dark yard while he drank it. When he heard footsteps, his fingers tightened around the mug, but he didn't turn to look—didn't even shift his gaze the few inches necessary to see the newcomer's reflection in the window.

The voice that broke the silence was soft, the accent not too different from the one he'd grown up with. "Wouldn't you like some dessert?" Nolie asked.

His glance was so brief that he caught just an impression of red hair, pale skin, and a green shirt. "Eli's got the sweet tooth around here."

"I noticed." She came closer and lifted one hand toward the cabinets. "Cups?"

He opened the door next to the sink, and she took one out, then poured herself some coffee. Instead of returning to the dining room, though, she leaned against the cabinet, partly facing him. "It hasn't been easy coming back, has it?"

The window reflected his mocking smile back at him. "It's punishment. It isn't supposed to be easy."

"At least now I have a better understanding of why you tried to talk me out of investing Micahlyn's money with you . . . sort of. I don't suppose you'd like to explain the finer details for me."

"What's left to know?"

"Why you warned me. You didn't do that with the others."

By the time she'd offered her thirty grand, he'd been feeling the first stirrings of a conscience—something Owen and Eloise had done their best to excise from their offspring. He hadn't known whether it was the town getting to him, or Leanne, or just life in general, but he hadn't wanted to rip off a twenty-something widow raising a kid by herself.

The attack of conscience hadn't lasted long. When he'd left town, her money had gone with him.

A few weeks later, he'd sent it back.

Since he didn't have an answer to offer, he shook his head instead and changed the subject. "I hear you and Chase got married."

Her smile was sweet and brightened her entire face. "Yeah. Hard to believe, isn't it?"

"Why do you say that?" As soon as the question was out, he remembered her insecurities last spring. Chase's ex-wife was beautiful and tiny and Nolie considered herself overweight and plain. Maybe she'd finally learned that smart men everywhere knew that curves were a lovely thing on a woman. "He's lucky to have you."

She blushed. "I'll tell him you said so."

Finally he faced her head-on. "No," he said quietly. "You probably shouldn't. He'll wonder why you were talking with the enemy."

"He doesn't—" She didn't complete the lie. Pushing

away from the counter, she started toward the hall, then returned. "Thank you."

"For what?"

"Returning the money."

Cole felt lower than scum. How could she thank him for giving back what he'd stolen? She should be damning him to hell . . . though she probably realized he was already there.

When he managed to respond, it was by breaking another Jackson rule. *Never apologize . . . unless it'll save your sorry ass.* "Nolie? I, uh . . . I'm ~~sorry~~."

She nodded gravely, then walked away.

Quickly, quietly, Leanne ducked back into the dining room as if she hadn't been on her way to the kitchen for a drink. Leaning against the paneled wall, she let Cole's last words repeat in her mind. *I'm sorry, I'm sorry, I'm sorry.*

Cole Jackson had apologized to one of his victims, and had even sounded as if he meant it. Would wonders never cease?

Of course, the key phrase there was *sounded as if.* Anyone could fake sincerity, and he was much better at it than most. His entire life was nothing but lies and manipulation, telling people what they wanted to hear, pretending to be what they wanted him to be. If he was truly sorry, if he had even one regret about everything he'd done, he would be making that apology to Ryan. He would be on his knees, begging his son's forgiveness. Instead, he hadn't even tried to see him.

A fact for which he didn't *deserve* forgiveness.

• • •

THE SMACK OF WOOD AGAINST WOOD ECHOED sharply through the cold night. Sophy directed a dry look toward Gloria, who was caressing the polished gavel she'd been toting around since last week's court session. Heavens, she'd been a judge for ten minutes. Just how long would they have to endure her judicial behavior?

"This meeting is now in session," Gloria announced. Her formal declaration was diminished, however, by her tinkling laugh. "The court recognizes Sophy."

She was about to bang the gavel again when Sophy caught hold of it. "Don't do that." As an afterthought, she added, "Please."

"But it has such a nice authoritarian sound to it." Even as she protested, Gloria released the gavel and Sophy laid it beside her on the railing.

They were gathered at the bandstand in the middle of the square. Sophy sat on one section of railing, Eli on another, and Gloria stood midway between them. A million stars twinkled overhead, and Sophy took her time gazing at each one. They were lovely and reassuring—a constant in a life that often didn't seem to have many.

Gloria's great sigh broke the stillness. "Louanne and Jack have a lot to overcome, you know. This is gonna be a tough one."

"You always say that," Sophy answered automatically.

"And I'm always right."

"Don't worry, Gloria." Eli smugly patted her shoulder. "You've got me to help."

Sophy didn't even try to restrain her delicate little snort. "Some help you've been—forcing Leanne and Cole together at Harry's."

"They've got to actually spend time together in order to resolve their problems."

His condescension grated on her nerves. "Of course they do . . . *when they're ready.* They weren't ready Tuesday."

There was nothing delicate or little about his snort. "By the time *you* pronounce them ready, they'll be too old to care."

Her fingers gripping the railing tightly enough to vaporize it, Sophy counted to ten, then added another ten. By the time she reached forty-seven, she acknowledged it wasn't working and gave up. Faking a sugary sweet tone, she asked, "If you're such an expert in these matters, why did they send you to Gloria and me for training?"

Eli jumped to the floor and spun around to face her. The outrage in his expression made her smile that much bigger. *"Training?"* His voice cracked, and he tried again, stronger this time. *"Training?!* They sent me here to *help,* because they didn't think you and Gloria could handle it this time!"

"In your dreams," she retorted. "We've been getting along just fine without your *help* for . . . well, forever."

"Yeah, right. When I showed up, you didn't even have a plan. *I* had to come up with the whole community service thing *and* give Mr. Miller the idea to let us use his mother's house."

Sophy couldn't argue with that. Of course, she and Gloria would have handled things just fine without his interference. Neither of them was really so big on plans. They liked to let things unfold more or less naturally, with a gentle nudge here, maybe the tiniest of pushes there. It had always worked before, and there was no reason to think this situation was any different.

"Anyone can come up with a good idea every millennium or so," she said airily. "The bottom line is . . . we don't need you."

He changed tacks then, the arrogance disappearing, the

smugness easing away, and smiled a most charming smile. If she didn't know better, she would think that even he, the most conceited guardian that ever existed, had a few redeeming qualities.

"You do that almost as well as Cole does," she remarked, and wondered if that was why they'd been cursed—er, graced with his presence. All guardians had the ability to transform themselves in one way or another. Noelle, who'd watched over Bethlehem before Sophy and Gloria, had once disguised herself as a geeky male clerk, complete with oiled hair, spectacles, and a bow tie, and no one had ever suspected a thing. That was before she'd fallen in love with Gabe Rawlins, one of her charges, and had traded her angel wings for womanhood.

But Eli seemed more skilled at it than most. Why, he could almost make himself appear likable.

Almost.

"Aw, you'd hurt my feelings . . . if I cared." He chucked her under the chin as if she were five years old. "Pay close attention on this one, Soph, and I'll show you how to do it *right.*"

Her temper surged, but before she could say anything, he disappeared. One instant he was there, the next he wasn't.

"Such a nice boy," Gloria said with a satisfied smile.

Because she suspected that *nice boy* was still around even though they couldn't see him, Sophy limited her response to another snort. "We'd best be going."

Gloria vanished, too, but Sophy took her time, fading out a little at a time. Just before she disappeared into nothingness, she saw the gavel rise from the railing, then smack down with a hard *cra-ack*.

"Court is adjourned," Gloria's disembodied voice intoned,

then her sweet laugh sounded like distant chimes. "Oh, I like doing that!"

SINCE SATURDAY WAS HER DAY OFF, LEANNE SLEPT IN late that morning, making it all the way to nine-fifteen before the creak of the bedroom door opening woke her. She kept her eyes closed and breathing steady, hoping whoever had wandered in would wander right back out. The ploy didn't work.

A shadow fell across her face just before a small finger-tip touched her eyelid. "I can see your eyes moving inside," Danny remarked, then he climbed onto the bed.

She lifted the sheet for him to scoot under, then cuddled him close. "Mornin', sweetie pie."

"Mornin', sleepyhead."

"What are you doing?"

"I'm bored."

She stifled a yawn. "What would make you un-bored?"

"I dunno. But I'm hungry, too. Can we go to Harry's for breakfast?"

"Sure. Why not?"

"But Ryan can't go. He'll have to have cold cereal, but without milk, 'cause I just drunk the last of it."

Ouch. That was a sure sign of trouble, since Danny would stick to Ryan like cockleburs to socks if he could, *and* since Ryan liked milk a lot and Danny drank it only under threat. Hey, hero worship only went so far.

She rolled onto her back, shoved her hair from her face, then stuffed an extra pillow under her head. "Leaving Ryan behind while we went out wouldn't be nice. How would you feel if we did that to you?"

"You go see Dr. J.D. without me."

Rather than try to explain, she tickled him. "Oh, so you want to go to the *doctor*? I thought you hated doctors."

"I do, but not Dr. J.D. I like playing with Gracie and Noah. They got cats, and their neighbor gots horses, and sometimes we go to the creek and wade."

"But the kids don't go to the office with him, and neither do the cats or the horses. It's just Dr. J.D. in a room with a desk and chairs."

"Oh." He rubbed his nose while considering that, then shrugged. "You know why Ryan can't go to breakfast with us? 'Cause I told him, let's go see your dad, and he said no, he ain't his dad and he don't want to see 'im. And I said *I* seen him the other day and he is, too, his dad, and I was gonna ask you if he could come spend the night like he used to, and Ryan said a bad word."

A curious sensation passed through Leanne at the mention of Cole spending the night. She ignored it and focused tightly on the conversation. "So he can't go because you're mad at him?"

"No, 'cause he's not here. He ran off and banged the door real hard after he said the bad word, and I thought he prob'ly waked you, so I come to see."

Throwing back the covers, Leanne disentangled herself from Danny and jumped to her feet. She grabbed jeans and a sweatshirt from the closet, scooped underwear and socks from the bureau, and hustled across the hall to the bathroom. "Did you look out the window to see which way he went?" she called through the barely-opened door.

"Nope."

Dressing in record time, she returned to the bedroom and sat down, to put on her shoes. "Get dressed, sweetie. We've got to look for him."

"After we go to Harry's?"

"Now." She lifted him to the floor, then swatted his

bottom when he dawdled. She brushed her teeth and combed her hair, then helped him with his shoes. He'd chosen black sweat pants and a pumpkin-orange Halloween sweatshirt with a glow-in-the-dark jack-o'-lantern.

As they clomped down the stairs, she said a silent prayer that they would step outside and the first thing they would see was Ryan walking down the sidewalk, sitting on a bench in the square, or holding up traffic in the middle of the street. But he wasn't among the people on the sidewalk, the benches in the square were empty, and traffic was moving along as it always did.

So where was he? Where would an angry kid go when he was mad at the world?

He wasn't throwing rocks at the Miller mansion. That was a good sign. And he hadn't hot-wired her SUV and gone for a joyride. Also a good sign.

They walked the block to Main Street, but saw no sign of him in either direction. He wasn't in Harry's, and no one there had seen him. He wasn't at the library, either, though the librarian promised to call Leanne's cell phone if he showed up. They returned to get her truck and set out to cover the entire town.

And if they didn't find him?

She would call the police. In the meantime, she was trying not to panic . . . yet. Bethlehem was a safe place. Bad things just didn't happen there.

But kids occasionally ran away. J.D.'s son, Caleb, had done it twice. Heaven knew, if anyone had a reason to run away and never stop, it was Ryan.

They had covered more than two-thirds of the town and were sitting at a STOP sign when Danny casually said, "There's Ryan," as if they hadn't spent the past hour searching for him.

"Where?" she demanded, and he pointed toward the

veterinary clinic across the street. Sure enough, in the yard at the back stood Ryan, holding a leash attached to a Great Dane doing his business.

She pulled into the vet's parking lot and ordered Danny to stay put. Just to be safe, she activated the child safety locks, then marched around to the back of the building. "Ryan Matthew Jackson, what are you doing running off like that?"

He startled when he heard her voice, but quickly hid it behind a resentful look. "Does it matter?"

"Oh, no. I *like* starting off my Saturdays by searching all over town for one of my kids." The Great Dane, practically big enough for her to ride, came over to sniff, starting at her feet and working his way up. When he'd gone far enough, she pushed his head away and scratched under his chin. "Be a nice brute," she admonished, then turned a stern look on Ryan again. "Whose dog is this?"

He shrugged.

"Where did you get him?"

This time the shrug was accompanied by a jerk of his head toward the clinic.

"I'm a little thickheaded before I've had my coffee. Clear things up for me. You got mad at Danny and you went out without permission and . . . ended up over here, taking a giant dog to the bathroom?"

Rolling his eyes as if she was too dense to believe, he hunched his skinny shoulders. "She was takin' the dogs out one at a time—"

"She who?"

"I don't know. Some lady. And I was lookin' at 'em, and we got to talkin' and she said I could help with 'em if I wanted."

Leanne studied him while she thought. Presumably, *she* was Dr. Collins, the vet, or one of her staff. Also presumably,

Dr. Collins had no clue that Ryan had sneaked out without permission or she would have made him phone home before turning any of her patients over to him. And—no presuming about it—Ryan liked animals.

"If you're done yelling, I need to take him in and get the next one."

"Oh, child, I haven't begun to yell," she warned him in a mild tone. "Go on. I'll wait." While he was gone, she stepped to the corner of the building, to check on Danny. On his knees in her seat, he was pretending to drive. He took his hand off the steering wheel long enough to wave at her, then immediately jerked the wheel as if he'd drifted into oncoming traffic.

Shaking her head, she returned to find Ryan coming down the steps with a smaller dog—though if his feet were anything to judge by, he wouldn't be that way long. The animal was so happy to be outside that he seemed to have forgotten what he'd come out for, sniffing everything and everywhere.

"Cute dog," she murmured.

"His name is Jerome. He's a 'found' dog. That means he's a stray. She's keeping 'im until she can find a home for 'im."

Leanne crouched to pet the dog. "Did you get lost, puppy, or did someone—" Abruptly she broke off, then stole a glance at Ryan. If he realized what she'd been about to say—*or did someone throw you away?*—he gave no sign of it.

Rising again, she leaned against the stoop. "I didn't know you liked dogs."

He shrugged as if it were inconsequential.

"Have you ever had one?"

"Nah. We never had the money or the space."

She looked from him to the puppy again, trying to stave off the idea forming in her mind, but failing miserably. They didn't really have the space, either, especially for this creature who looked like he might rival the Great Dane in size once he reached his full potential. And she didn't want to imagine what his feet would do to the wood floors she loved.

But, sheesh, every kid needed a dog. She'd had one when she was growing up—a dachshund named Barney who'd hated to see her leave, greeted her ecstatically every time she'd walked into the room, and slept with her at night. And she'd always planned to get Danny a dog. She'd just thought she would wait until he was old enough to be responsible for a pet . . . and she'd planned on something small and cuddly like Barney. Something that didn't already weigh as much as Danny.

After the dog finally remembered the purpose for his trip outside, Ryan sat down on the steps and the animal crawled into his lap, licking his face. Ryan scratched behind his ears and made the dog's entire body quiver so much he slid off his feet, which made Ryan laugh.

When was the last time she'd heard Ryan laugh?

Better question—*had* she ever heard Ryan laugh?

"Are there any more animals inside, waiting for you to give them a potty break?"

"A couple."

"Why don't you go ahead and do that? I want to talk to Dr. Collins for a moment."

He gave her a wary look, then stood up and carried the dog inside. She followed him, bypassing the kennels in search of the vet. A few minutes later, she and Dr. Collins joined him out back, with Jerome on a leash again.

"I already brought him out," Ryan said.

"I know." Dr. Collins bent to cup the dog's face in her hands. "You're a good boy, Jerome, and you be good for your new people, okay?" After pressing a kiss to the top of the dog's head, she straightened, then offered to trade leashes with Ryan.

He was confused. "You want me to take him back in?"

"I want you to take him home. Jerome is now officially a Wilson. Take good care of him."

As the doctor returned inside with the other dog, Ryan clutched Jerome's leash and stared at Leanne. "Really? You got Danny a dog?"

She slid her arm around his shoulders. "I got *us* a dog. He belongs to all of us—or, more likely, we now belong to him. Is that okay?"

"Yeah," he murmured. "That's okay."

Despite his subdued response, she knew it was better than okay when they reached the truck and he lifted the dog into the backseat. For a moment, he held the puppy close, and a single tear seeped from the corner of his eye.

Yep, it was way better than okay. In fact, Danny said it best in his most awed voice. "Wow, Mom, a dog! Woohoo!"

Chapter Seven

COLE WAS LYING ON HIS BACK, HANDS FOLDED under his head, when Eli rapped at the door. "You awake?"

"Yeah."

Opening the door, the kid stuck his head inside. "We're leaving for church in an hour. That'll give you time for a shower and breakfast."

"Uh, gee, you guys go without me."

"Uh, gee, that's not your call. Come on. Get moving."

Cole sent an unamused look his way, but Eli was already down the hall, knocking at Murray's door. Frowning, he rolled onto his side and stared out the window. It was dreary, gray, and threatening rain—a perfect day for doing nothing. Unfortunately, if Eli was insisting on church this morning, he probably had some kind of work lined up for the afternoon.

He wondered if this counted toward his time served.

He wasn't grousing because he really minded church. He had a fine appreciation for old gospel tunes—"How Great Thou Art," "In the Garden," "Will the Circle Be Unbroken"—and there was something appealing about the acceptance a person could find in a good church. He and Ryan had attended services in Bethlehem several times last spring, but that had been part of the job.

Now it was part of his punishment.

He showered and dressed in some of his investment-scam clothes—just about the only thing he'd been allowed to keep after his arrest. The things he'd stolen had been returned to their rightful owners, the laptop was probably tagged as evidence and in police custody, and his cash was locked up somewhere. After all, he needed clothes, but not the rest.

After eating breakfast, he climbed into the truck with Eli and Murray. The older man was humming a tune as Eli backed out of the driveway, and before they'd gone a block, the kid was singing it with him. He had a good voice: strong, clear, and rich.

Cole's brother, Bret, had a voice like that, but he wouldn't be caught dead singing "Amazing Grace," unless it was part of a con. Frank had pulled one of those a few years back, involving a tent revival and a handful of small towns in east Texas, and had made a pretty good haul. When he'd gotten caught, he had repented and asked for forgiveness . . . and gotten it. The folks he'd scammed, refused to prosecute.

Frank had always had an incredible streak of luck.

They arrived at the church a few minutes after the service had begun. Eli led the way into the last pew on the left, then decided for some reason to change places with Cole, then again with Murray. As he started to sit down, Cole saw the reason—the kid had wanted to be out of striking distance when Cole realized he would be sitting a mere two feet from Leanne.

He glowered at Eli as he slowly sat down, but the kid refused to look his way.

"I thought I felt the walls trembling," she whispered as the pastor instructed everyone to rise for a prayer.

As soon as that was over and they were seated again, he murmured, "I go to church."

"Casing the joint doesn't count. Remind me to tell the deacon to keep an eye on the offering plate."

"I've never stolen from a church," he retorted. That was another piece of advice from Owen. *Never steal from a church. That's what television evangelists are for.*

His gaze moved around the large room, scanning familiar faces, looking for the most familiar of all. He saw Leanne's mother—wasn't it wrong to give a man the evil eye in church?—and her father, with more distance between them than separated Cole from Leanne. He spotted Danny, sitting near the front with Miss Agatha and her husband, Bud Grayson. He saw a lot of people who had considered him a friend . . . but not Ryan.

Leanne leaned a few inches closer. "Ryan's helping out in the nursery this morning. All the older kids take turns."

"I wasn't looking for him." Inwardly he grimaced. If giving the evil eye in church was wrong, then lying certainly was. He'd be lucky if the walls didn't tremble, then fall on him.

The pastor's sermon was on forgiveness. Since that was something he neither wanted nor expected, he listened to little and thought about Leanne a lot. She wore a navy-blue dress that fitted as if it had been sewn onto her body. Her heels were black, and so was the jacket hanging over the back of the pew. Her hair was pulled back and tied with a black bow that didn't stop wispy strands from falling loose on her neck, tempting him to stroke them back into place. Of course, if he tried, if the Lord didn't strike him down, she would.

She looked lovely. Elegant. Like a doting mother and a

successful businesswoman. She looked strong and capable and soft and amazingly feminine. She looked . . .

Like the best time he'd ever had.

He hadn't meant to get involved with her when he'd come to Bethlehem. When he'd discovered that was easier said than done, he'd backed off on his restrictions enough to allow himself an affair with her, as long as an affair was all. That had been easier said than done, too. While he'd liked her from the beginning, at some point she'd become too important. No matter how he tried, he hadn't been able to walk away from her . . . until that last day.

At least he didn't have to worry about getting too involved this time. She wouldn't allow it, and even if she would, Eli was a pretty good guard dog. He didn't do nightly bed checks—yet—but he also didn't let Cole leave the house alone. Cole was pretty certain if he asked permission to go across the street and have wild, hot sex with Leanne, the kid would say no.

Thinking about sex in church was probably even worse than lying. He glanced over his shoulder to ensure that the stone walls were still straight and solid.

The minutes crawled past until, after one final prayer, the service was over. Cole's first impulse was to jump and run. Eli and Murray showed no inclination to do either.

"Gee, you survived," Leanne said, sliding forward on the bench and slipping into her jacket. "No bolts of lightning, no columns of fire and brimstone."

"Disappointed?"

She shrugged, an easy, fluid movement that made his breath catch. When the moment passed, he shrugged, too. "I told you—I'm not a total stranger to church."

"Too bad you never learned anything there."

He watched her pick up her Bible and a larger, brightly

colored kids' Bible, then find her keys in her bag. "Why are you talking to me?"

She seemed vaguely surprised by the question. "I've never refused to talk to you."

That was true, except for the times he'd seen her in the courtroom. Both times his actions had been designed to anger her into speechlessness, and both times there'd been little opportunity to see how well he'd succeeded.

She glanced at her watch, settled comfortably on the bench, and crossed her legs. Waiting for Ryan, he guessed, assuming that parents had to pick up their kids before the nursery workers could leave.

"Did you grow up in church?" Her tone was polite, a few shades too cool for friendly. Like someone just making conversation, but not really caring what was said.

"Oh, yeah, sure." The closest he'd gotten to church as a kid was when times were rough and the family was on the receiving end of a donation. He'd hated having people feeling sorry for them, hated being given food, clothes, and Christmas presents because Owen was in jail or Eloise had disappeared again. Given a choice between stealing and the pity and smug self-righteousness that accompanied most charity, he would choose stealing anytime.

"Oh, yeah, sure," Leanne repeated. "That's a lie, isn't it?"

He turned on his best used-car-salesman smile. "You wound me, sweetheart."

Her gaze darkened and the line of her jaw turned taut. "Knock it off. If you can't quit playing some part long enough to answer a simple question, then forget it." Chin raised, she got to her feet, stepped into the outside aisle, then headed for the door.

Cole stared hard at the wall. It was a sad day when a man couldn't smile at a woman without making her mad.

Hell, what did she expect? For him to sit there and agree face-to-face that he was a liar?

It probably would have been the first bit of honesty he'd given her.

The exchange hadn't gone unnoticed. Beside him, Murray leaned closer and said confidentially, "Women don't like phonies."

Cole grinned sardonically. "You're wrong, Murray. Women like me, and I am, first and foremost, a phony."

The old man studied him before slowly smiling. "They say you're the best at conning people. But you know who you've conned the best? Yourself. You don't have a clue who or what you are. Is it any wonder Leanne doesn't know, either?"

He was wrong, Cole thought, as Eli finally ended his conversation with a tall, white-haired woman and herded them toward the double doors at the back. He had no illusions about himself. He was a thief. A liar. A con artist. He was untrustworthy, undependable, and dishonest. He'd known wealth and extreme poverty, and he preferred wealth, any way he could get it. He'd done the best he could with Ryan, but it hadn't been good enough. Leaving him behind had been the hardest thing he'd ever done, and he was going to pay for it for the rest of his rotten life.

And that was okay, as long as Ryan didn't have to pay, too.

Getting out the church doors was only half the battle. They were stopped a half-dozen times on the way to Eli's truck to talk. Everyone greeted Eli and Murray, but few acknowledged Cole. Alex Thomas did, and Nathan Bishop and Maggie McKinney. Kelsey Grayson gave him a speculative look as she passed, and he wondered if the reason was personal or professional. She and her husband had invested money in his scheme, and, being the only social worker in town besides Eli, she was overseeing Ryan's foster care. Maybe she wanted to place the kid in a permanent home. Maybe she wanted to fix it so Cole could never see him again. It was no less than Ryan deserved.

And no more than Cole deserved.

Finally they reached the pickup, parked near the back of the church. He was waiting for Murray to climb in, then slide to the middle of the bench seat, when he became aware of a hard, unyielding gaze. He glanced up, then saw Ryan leaning against the building. He wore black pants and a white shirt, the sleeves rolled up to his elbows. He'd jammed his hands in his pockets, and was looking at Cole with pure disgust.

"Ryan."

He thought he'd spoken the name aloud, but it lacked sound. Numbly he took a few steps away from the truck and toward the church, then faltered to a stop when Ryan spun around and disappeared behind it.

The ache as he returned to the pickup was sharp and raw and, for a moment, it robbed him of breath. He climbed in beside Murray and slammed the door, then stared at the place where Ryan had stood, as if he could somehow bring him back. Of course, he couldn't.

And that, too, was no more than he deserved.

AFTER WORK TUESDAY, LEANNE CHANGED INTO JEANS and a sweatshirt, then found Ryan in his usual spot—stretched out on the sofa with a book. Jerome lay curled on his stomach as if he were normal puppy size, grunting softly as Ryan scratched behind his ears. "You two look comfortable."

Ryan glanced up. "He's just trying to escape all the noise from the video games in Danny's room."

She thought of the responses she should make—*It's your room, too* and *Jerome's lying with you because he likes you* and *You're part of this family whether you like it or not*—but instead took the easy way out as she sat on the coffee table. "Listen, I've got a committee meeting this evening. We're going to start decorating the haunted house over at the hospital. My dad's picking up Danny for dinner and a movie. You're welcome to go with me or with them, but I'll warn you—your father is working on this project, too."

Something flickered in his eyes at the mention of Cole, but was gone again too quickly for her to identify. "Can't I just stay here?"

"No."

"I'm *twelve* years old."

"I know. But them's your choices, partner—Dad and Danny or your father and me." Inside she winced. That sounded so . . . normal, as if she and Cole were a pair, which they'd never been, not for real. She'd been a fool, falling for his act, offering herself to be used. Who could blame him for taking her up on the offer?

"But what about Jerome? He's never been home alone at night."

"He'll go in his kennel and be just fine." On Dr. Collins's advice, one of her first purchases had been a jumbo-sized traveling kennel that occupied a quiet corner of the living room. When they were gone, that was where Jerome stayed—and her furniture stayed unsoiled and unchewed.

At least, he'd stayed there the few hours they were at church on Sunday. And for an hour or so Monday morning before she'd decided to see how he liked the shop. And for an hour or so Tuesday morning before she'd decided she liked the shop better with him in it. Hey, she'd taken

Danny to work with her when he was a baby. Why not Jerome?

"The movie at the theater is for kids," Ryan announced in a superior tone.

"How convenient since"—she faked a huge surprised look—"*you're a kid.*"

For a long time he stared at the puppy, then asked in a low voice, "Doesn't it bother you—being around him?"

Oh, jeez. This was a discussion she didn't want to have, with him or herself. It demanded too close a look—too honest a look—at what she was feeling. Was she getting used to having Cole around? Getting over him? Getting to know him, albeit in some very small, minuscule, insignificant way? Was she still attracted to him? Letting lust overcome disgust? Still thinking, in that incredibly moronic part of herself, that *just maybe* he could be Mr. Right, after all?

She preferred to believe she was getting over him. When she'd first opened the shop more than eight years ago, Melissa Thomas had sent her flowers with an inspirational message—*If you can dream it, you can do it.* It had taken a lot of dreaming to get Small Wonders into the black and keep it there, but she'd succeeded. That first year or two had been on the lean side, but the shop had supported her, and later Danny, then Ryan, comfortably ever since.

So now she was dreaming of getting over Cole. She intended to be outrageously successful at it, too.

"You know, Ryan, we can't control the world around us. There are always going to be people we don't like or can't get along with, so it's up to us to learn how to manage in spite of them. Would I be happier if your father didn't live across the street? You bet. Am I going to let it make me crazy that he does live across the street? No way."

"But you have to see him. He's hangin' around town, workin' on the spook house, even showing up at church."

"How do you know he was at church?" The parents had been slow picking up their kids at the nursery Sunday. By the time Ryan had met her and Danny in the parking lot, Cole had been long gone—or so she'd thought. "Did you see him?"

He dropped his chin and mumbled something she took as a yes.

"Did he say anything?"

Ryan's shoulders lifted, then dropped. "He just looked at me like . . . like . . . I don't know. When he acted like he was gonna come over, I took off." Finally he met her gaze, his expression both defiant and vulnerable.

Leanne clasped his hand in hers. "It's all right to talk to him, Ryan."

His jaw jutted forward and he jerked his hand back, on the pretext of needing to scratch the dog. "I don't wanna."

"That's all right, too. But you know, sweetie, this is part of living in a small town. We're going to run into people all the time, and we just have to deal with it."

The doorbell rang—one long and two shorts—and she glanced toward the hall. "Danny, let your grandfather in!"

A moment later he zoomed past, then thundered down the stairs.

"So what's it gonna be? Dinner and a movie or work?"

"Dinner and a movie," Ryan said with a sigh, closing his book.

She ruffled his hair affectionately. "Good choice. Now make sure you don't enjoy that kids' movie *too* much. Run Jerome outside and let him pee, will you, then put him in the kennel."

As they both got up, her father followed Danny through the kitchen and into the living room. He greeted Ryan with the same affection he showed Danny and Micahlyn, then hugged Leanne. "Call your mother, princess."

"Call her what?"

He tweaked her nose with cold fingers. "She's been hell on wheels ever since your run-in with her last week."

"Ah, yes, her run-in with me, which was also part of her bigger run-in with Cole, Mitch Walker, Judge Monroe . . . Besides, Daddy, she's always hell on wheels."

Earl Wilson's only response was a shrug. His relationship with her mother was the great Wilson family mystery. She, Chase, and Nolie—in addition to a fair portion of the town—had spent hours speculating on why he stayed with Phyllis. There was certainly no affection between them, the kids were long grown, and it didn't seem possible they could ever have loved each other. He deserved better than he was getting, but he didn't seem to mind.

"How's Ryan?" he asked, dropping his voice even though both boys were outside with the dog.

She made a so-so gesture in the air. "He's seeing J.D. Grayson."

"Good. Has he seen his old man?"

"Just once. They didn't talk."

"Want me to have a talk with him?"

"Ryan?"

It was Earl's turn to shake his head. "Jackson. Explain to him that any man worthy of the name shouldn't lose touch with his own son."

Leanne's throat clogged. He was speaking from experience. The sixteen-year silence between him and Chase had finally ended a few months earlier. They still weren't best buddies, and there was a lot of wariness on both sides, but they were trying. If Cole would try . . .

"I'll keep that in mind," she said as the boys and Jerome raced up the stairs and into the room. "Right now you've got two hungry little goblins to feed. Thanks a bunch for helping me out." Rising onto her toes, she kissed his cheek.

"What's a grandpa for? Have fun, princess."

Once they were gone, she stood at the kitchen counter and ate a sandwich, washed it down with a Pepsi, then grabbed her coat and gloves and headed for the hospital grounds.

The building they were using for the haunted house was at the back edge of hospital property. More properly, she guessed, it was an equipment barn, though there was rarely any equipment inside. This was where they turned out every year to work on the hospital's float for the Christmas parade, a project she donated time to, since Small Wonders didn't have a float of its own. Besides, the float-decorating always turned into one great party.

She parked on the shoulder of the dirt road that circled behind the hospital to the barn. Nolie's station wagon was on one side, Kelsey's van on the other, along with a half-dozen other vehicles.

Including Eli's old green pickup.

She walked quickly to the barn, then stopped just outside the light spilling out the open doors. Rubbing her arms briskly, she took a few deep breaths and, for one wild moment, considered returning home and claiming illness. The sudden onset of an allergic reaction to convicted felons.

More likely, the sudden onset of a severe case of yellow-belly.

She forced herself through the broad double doors and into the brightly lit garage. "Why in the world are the doors open?" she asked as if every cell in her body wasn't aware of Cole on a ladder near the back of the room. "Haven't you realized it's *cold* outside?"

"Honey, it's cold in here, too," Holly Flynn replied. She was standing next to a second ladder with streams of orange and black crepe paper draped around her neck.

Cole looked Leanne's way—she could feel the impact of his gaze—but she refused to acknowledge him. Instead, she zipped her jacket, then shoved her hands in her pockets and looked around. Bales of hay, donated by Nolie's feed store, were stacked outside the doors, and a variety of lights, ranging from small spots to strings of tiny orange bulbs, was spread around. There was crepe paper, colored cellophane, yards of black fabric, fake cobwebs, and stuffed witches, goblins, and cats, along with one very realistic-looking skeleton. She sidled close to the skeleton, wearing a black top hat and bow tie, and asked, "Hey, big boy, you come here often?"

"I think I used to date that guy," Holly said.

That brought a laugh from Maggie. "You used to date every guy in town."

Holly had been Bethlehem's original party girl . . . until Tom Flynn had decided to take a wife. Their courtship had been more public than any other Leanne had ever seen, a fact which Holly had publicly bemoaned but secretly liked, Leanne thought. What woman wouldn't like having a man make it clear that he was crazy about her?

Unlike Cole, who'd rarely been seen in public with *her*.

Of course, he hadn't been crazy about her, either.

And she'd been just plain crazy.

Following Maggie's rough sketches, they blocked off a winding trail through the barn with the hay bales, then began setting up the scenes. Stuffed bats and a vampire would fly through the air from one side of the barn to the other, along with a witch on a broom, swirling in circles while a tape of creaking doors, screams, and witchly cackles played. The skeleton would be rigged to rise from its half-buried coffin and dance a merry jig and, her favorite, three grotesque witches—Holly, Maggie, and Emilie Bishop—would stoop around a giant cauldron while another skeleton "boiled" inside, courtesy of water and dry ice.

It was gonna be great, Leanne thought as she started her first job—using a chisel to turn a slab of old barn wood into an ancient tombstone. She'd completed about two-thirds of the inscription when a quiet voice spoke behind her.

"You people are weird."

She concentrated on keeping her hand steady and not looking at Cole. She knew he would be standing too close, and her traitorous mind would immediately leap to other times he'd been too close—so close she hadn't known where either of them stopped and the other began. So close she'd thought they would be that way forever. So close she'd fallen right into the dream trap.

If you can dream it, you can do it.

Wrong, Melissa, she thought flippantly. Some dreams were fulfilled. Others were shattered.

Just like some hearts.

"Why do you say that?" She was proud of the fact that her voice didn't quaver one bit.

"A town named Bethlehem, as in the Christmas song, getting all excited about witches and goblins and ghouls? That doesn't strike you as odd?"

She bent over, putting a bit of distance between them—necessary so she could get the R.I.P. just right. Not because the hairs on the back of her neck were standing on end and her skin was tingling. "It's all in fun."

"Some towns don't even allow Halloween celebrations."

"Some towns don't allow convicts to take up residence right in their midst."

Silence radiated from him for a moment. When he did speak, his voice was stiff, tinged with bitterness. "Yeah. I'll have to include that in my research before my next scam."

Finally she looked at him, and he *was* too close. She compensated by moving to the opposite side of the work-table that held her headstone. "I think part of the purpose of Eli's program is to ensure that there's not a next time."

"But there's always another fool waiting to part with his money. How am I supposed to resist such easy pickin's?"

"I don't know. By developing a conscience?"

"A conscience is a bad thing to have in my line of work. It'll just get you into trouble."

Gripping the chisel too tightly, she studied him. His blond hair was mussed, his faded jeans fitted snugly to his narrow hips and long legs, and his sweatshirt was too big. If she didn't know better, she would think he looked adorable. Handsome. Sexy. Dangerous to a woman's heart and virtue, but otherwise harmless.

But she did know better. If she needed proof that he was a coldhearted, self-serving crook, all she had to do was look around her. Virtually everyone in town had offered him friendship, and he'd thanked them by stealing their money. She had offered him both money and love, and he'd taken one but not the other, breaking her heart in the process. He had abandoned his own son with near-strangers. He would stoop to anything that suited his purposes, and she would do well to remember that.

The muscles in her jaw tightening, she returned to her work, making her words suitably scornful. "You talk about it as if it were a real job—your line of work, research."

"You think breaking the law without getting caught doesn't take effort? It's work, darlin'. Sometimes a lot of hours with very little payoff."

"Then why not get a real job?"

"Most real jobs are also a lot of hours with very little payoff."

"And very little chance of going to prison."

Abruptly he grinned, not that big phony grin that made her want to smack him, but just a regular everyday, amused grin. "Where's the challenge in that?"

"For most people, earning a living, taking care of their families, being happy, and being able to face themselves in the morning is challenge enough."

His gaze narrowed on her before he shifted and picked up one of the other headstones against the wall. It looked like stone, heavy and unwieldy, but in fact it weighed only a few pounds. The writing where the name and dates were carved was distorted by the inhuman figure emerging from the stone, hair streaming, mouth open in a silent wail. It was one of a set of four, with the figures in various stages of emergence. On her favorite, only the outline of the face and a pair of hands were visible, while on another only the legs and feet remained out of sight.

"Dean Elliott did those," she remarked. "You remember him. He was also one of your victims."

Grinding his back teeth, Cole carefully replaced the piece on the floor, then crouched there and studied the others. Elliott's work sold for a fortune—seventy-five grand wasn't unusual—yet he'd donated this stuff to the haunted house. Alone with a telephone and the pieces, Cole could probably unload them for twenty-five grand with minimal effort. A fraction of their worth, but not bad wages for an hour of his time.

He ran his finger across the face of the ghost that was just taking form. The texture was smooth, cool to the touch. "This one looks like you." Like when she first awoke in the morning, mind still hazy and lazy before she opened her eyes and faced the new day.

"Thank you. Most people don't notice the resemblance."

When he stood, she was smiling smugly. Suspiciously, he looked from her to the gravestone, then back again. "You modeled for Elliott?"

"Not exactly." She laid the chisel down, stepped back to study her work, then picked up a cloth and a pot of what looked like black shoe polish. "He did it from memory, I suppose."

Damn. And Cole didn't feel like laughing.

He hadn't known she'd been involved with Elliott, though it shouldn't come as a surprise. After all, when they'd met, she was thirty-two, had never been married, was mother to a four-year-old boy, and certainly wasn't a virgin. And, really, he wasn't surprised. He was . . .

Jealous? He wasn't sure. He'd never been jealous over any woman in his life.

"So you slept with him."

Her gaze narrowed at his accusing tone, reminding him once again of how unpredictable she'd been lately. She was like a hand grenade that may or may not be a dud, that might seem perfectly safe, then blow a man to bits without warning.

"I fail to see how that's any of your business," she replied, her voice as frosty as the night.

It wasn't. Logically, he knew that. But what did logic matter when the subject was a woman?

"Were you in love with him?" Before she could speak, he went on. "I know—that's none of my business, either. I was just wondering how often you fall in love. Is it something you do with every man you sleep with? Or did it actually mean something when you said it to me?"

A hot flush spread across her face and extended down her throat as she stared at him. Her mouth worked a time or two before she managed to form words. "You—you bastard."

He'd been called that all his life—by his mother when she was tired of messing with him, by most of the women he'd known. He wouldn't argue it with her, and damn sure wouldn't let on that, somehow, it hurt more coming from her. He just wanted to know . . .

He rested his hands on the tabletop next to the marker and kept his tone as casual and careless as he could. "They're simple questions. All they need is a yes or no. In fact, you can answer any one of them— Were you in love with Elliott? Do you fall in love with everyone you sleep with? Or did it mean anything with me?"

She was still staring at him as if he were a sight so horrible she couldn't look away. Finally, her breath catching with an audible gasp, she leaned toward him. "Go to hell."

When she would have spun around and stalked off, he caught her hand and leaned closer. "Honey, I'm already there."

Her gaze didn't waver, and neither did his. He just wanted to know—*needed* to know . . . but why? So he could feel worse than he already did? Whether she'd really loved him or not, she'd felt *something* for him and he'd hurt her. Running out on a woman who'd cared for him was bad enough. Running out on a woman who'd loved him was . . .

Well, hell. He didn't know what it was, because no woman had ever loved him. Oh, a couple of them had told him so, but they'd also loved everything else—chocolate, expensive wine, a new outfit, red sports cars, *Friends.*

Except Leanne. She'd said the words as if she'd meant them.

Judging by the anger in her eyes, she would certainly never say them again—at least, not to him. Maybe to someone like Elliott. He was more her type anyway. At least he had a real job and could face himself every morning.

She pulled steadily until her hand slipped free, then turned and walked away. He wanted to say something to stop her, to make her come back, but he was pretty sure she thought he'd said enough already.

When she joined a couple of her friends, drinking hot chocolate from a thermal carafe, Cole realized that she wasn't the only object of someone's scrutiny. Eli, going over the sketches with Maggie, was watching *him,* a grave look on his face. Great. Now he would probably get a lecture for being too chatty with one of the decent folk in town, for obviously making her uncomfortable, for daring to touch her. It didn't help any that she was Phyllis Wilson's daughter. That family very well might get him thrown in jail in spite of his best efforts.

He turned away, picked up a string of lights, then climbed the ladder to plug them into the last string he'd hung. They were like Christmas-tree lights, except the bulbs burned bright orange—too bizarre for his tastes, though they had nothing on the set of black-and-white lights in the shape of a giant spider. That one, Maggie had told him, couldn't go up until Halloween night, when it would hang in the corner of the doorway, right in the middle of an elaborate fake web.

He kept to himself the rest of the evening, taking instructions from Maggie and Eli, trying really hard not to even glance in Leanne's direction. By the time they called it quits, he was tired and about as stressed as he ever got. But good ol' Eli managed to ratchet it up another few notches as they approached the pickup.

Between them, Eli and Murray were carrying the skeleton, arms draped over their shoulders as if it were a drunk unable to stand. When they reached the truck, Eli glanced at the seat, then at each of them, then slid the skeleton onto the seat. "I hate to put this in back where it might get damaged. Leanne, would you mind giving Cole a ride home?"

Cole scowled and tried to resist the temptation to dangle the kid by his throat all the way home. "I'll ride in back."

"No, it's too cold for that. And Leanne's going to the same place, more or less." Eli flashed a grin at her over the bed of the truck. "You don't mind, do you?"

Her smile was tight and unwelcoming. "Of course not."

Cold or not, he could handle the short ride home in the back of the pickup. Come to think of it, it couldn't possibly be any colder back there than the chill he would get sitting next to Leanne.

But no matter how much more appealing freezing was, he didn't climb into the truck bed. No, like an idiot, he passed the truck, circled to the other side of the SUV, and slid into the front seat.

The dirt road curved along the edge of the woods to the far end of the hospital parking lot. If she'd just shifted into four-wheel drive and set off across the grass, she could have cut the trip time in half. But she didn't.

As they bounced over the rutted road at a crawl behind the other cars, he asked the one question that was with him every single day, the one that was hardest to keep in, and the hardest to let out. "How is Ryan?"

She glanced at him. "Do you care?"

"No. I just thought it would be an easy topic of conversation that couldn't possibly piss you off."

She pursed her lips the way her mother did when she was about to get *real* pissy, then quietly replied, "He's . . . okay. We got a dog Saturday—part lab, part who-knows-what-else. His name is Jerome, and he and Ryan have bonded."

"I didn't know he liked dogs."

"All kids like dogs or cats or both." She glanced his way. "Didn't you have a pet growing up?"

"Yeah . . . but they preferred to be called brothers."

Her smile was faint, unwilling, and faded quickly in the dim light. "How many?"

"Five. Too many to keep straight, according to Owen. He just called us all *son*. Said it was easier than remembering our names."

"What are their names?"

"Adam, Bret, David, Eddie, and Frank."

A soft sound came from her side of the vehicle that might have been a laugh if she hadn't stopped it. "They *alphabetized* you, and he still couldn't keep you straight?"

"Owen had a great mind for capers. Not so great for kids."

A minute or two passed in silence before she spoke again. Her voice was quiet and tentative, as if she couldn't believe she was chatting with him, or didn't want to upset the civility they'd managed. "Were you close to him?"

It wasn't as tough a question as she probably thought. He loved his father—loved his whole family with the exception of his mother. He would probably have to spend time on some shrink's couch to figure out exactly what he felt for Eloise. But Owen had been a good parent—nontraditional, but good. He'd done the best he could, had taught them everything he knew, and had never once left them because he didn't want to be bothered. When he had left—for a job or a stint in jail—they had always known he would come back.

"Yeah. I still am. I don't see him or the boys very often, but when we do get together, it's like no time at all has passed."

"But he taught you to steal." The civility teetered.

"Yeah."

"When other parents were teaching their children the difference between right and wrong, he was teaching you to lie, cheat, betray, and manipulate everything and everyone around you."

"Owen taught us the difference between right and wrong," he said defensively. Cole had just learned over the years not to let it matter. Until he'd come to Bethlehem last spring.

"What a wonderful parent he was."

The sarcasm in her voice rubbed him the wrong way. He matched it with his own. "I reckon he was better at being a father, even being crooked and all, than your mother was at being a mother."

"At least I didn't grow up to be just like her."

"Well, I was raised to be just like him. Sorry if that offends you."

She pulled into her usual parking space directly across the street from the Miller mansion, shut off the engine, and faced him. "You could have made a different choice."

Cole stared at the shop window ahead with its Halloween decorations and wished he'd ended this conversation before it had started. All he'd had to do was answer one question—Were you close to your father? A simple yes, no, or sort of would have done the trick.

But no, he'd had to tell her too much, and she'd had to expand on it.

"When was I supposed to make this different choice? When was I supposed to defy my family and my upbringing? How was I supposed to choose a different path when the path I was on was the only one anyone in the family knew? My brothers and I were raised to follow in our parents' footsteps, in our grandparents' footsteps. The possibility of *not* being a crook never even occurred to me until I was grown, and by then it was too late. I didn't know how to do anything else."

"That's a sad way to live."

Not sad. It had served him well for thirty years. But somehow, somewhere, it had lost its appeal. Maybe it was Ryan, or Leanne, or Bethlehem, or a combination of the three. Maybe he'd finally grown up. Maybe he *had* developed a conscience.

"When it's all you've got, you make the best of it," he said flatly.

"But it's not all. You've got a son."

"No." He jerked the seat belt loose, then opened the door. "I don't."

She got out, too, then met him at the back of the truck. "When Danny was born, I would have done *anything* for him. I don't understand how you can't feel the same way about Ryan."

It was easy to say she would do anything for her son when she hadn't been forced to prove it. *He* had. Walking away from Ryan had been the hardest thing he'd ever imagined, but he'd done it because the kid needed other things—stability, a home, a mother's love, a future—more than he'd needed Cole. Leaving Ryan behind had damn near killed him, but he'd done it . . . and she saw it as proof that he didn't care.

He waited until a car passed, then started across the street, grateful that she didn't follow. Once he reached the other side, he turned and found her still there, still watching him. "That's the difference between you and me," he said cockily. "You're one of the *decent folk*. I'm not."

And damned if he could ever forget it.

Chapter Eight

KELSEY GRAYSON'S OFFICE WAS ON THE THIRD floor of the courthouse, a small space that she'd gradually transformed from cramped to cozy. The first time Leanne had been there, between the desk, chairs, and file cabinets, there hadn't been enough air for two people to breathe. The file cabinets had since been moved into the receptionist's office, the institutional green walls painted yellow and the beige metal desk painted white, and the orange vinyl chairs had been replaced with old wooden chairs whose scars gave them character. With family photos on the walls, plus crayon renderings done by the younger members of said family, it was a much more pleasant place.

Not that Leanne's reason for being there was pleasant.

She sat in one of the wooden chairs, legs crossed, nervously bouncing her toes in the air. So far they'd exchanged plenty of small talk, but now it was time to get down to business, and even after thinking about nothing else since Tuesday night, she just wasn't sure she could do it.

After several moments of awkward silence, Kelsey came

around the desk to sit in the other chair. "I take it this visit has to do with Ryan."

Leanne nodded.

"Is everything okay?"

"We're getting along."

"That's an evasive answer."

"Ryan's been having a few problems since"—unable to bring herself to say Cole's name, she frowned—"since his father came back."

"That's understandable." Kelsey's gaze was steady on her. "J.D. told me he's been coming in."

Leanne nodded vaguely. They had another appointment that afternoon. It was a good thing she had Sophy, or the shop would be opening and closing like a revolving door.

"What's on your mind?"

Drawing a deep breath, Leanne plunged ahead. "It occurred to me yesterday that . . . Ryan doesn't seem to feel he belongs with us. He and Danny share a room, but he calls it *Danny's* room. He never says *my* anything. It's as if . . ."

"He's only there for a while?"

She nodded again.

"That's not unusual with foster kids, Leanne. He's very aware that Danny's your child and he isn't. He knows he's there until you get tired of him or we place him somewhere else or his father is able to take care of him. These kids, especially the older ones like Ryan, try not to get attached, to get that feeling of belonging, because they know how easily everything can change."

"I don't want things to change. I want to keep him forever. I want to adopt him," Leanne blurted out.

Kelsey studied her a moment. "Are you sure about that?"

She nodded.

"But—?"

"But I know either his father has to—to give up his rights to him or—or the state has to—to—"

"Terminate them," Kelsey supplied.

Leanne shuddered. She couldn't imagine how awful such a thing would be to most parents. Sure, there were some who obviously wouldn't mind, like Danny's father or Ryan's mother. But Cole, despite all he'd said and done, and all he *hadn't* said and done, would.

Or maybe she was just hoping he would. Maybe she needed to believe that the man she had fallen in love with last spring would be devastated at having his parental rights taken from him.

Yeah, like she apparently still needed to believe that the man she'd fallen in love with actually existed, her inner demon sarcastically pointed out.

"I'm really not comfortable with the idea of asking you to do this," she went on. "I know how I would feel if someone who wasn't even related to me tried to take Danny away from me. But . . . Ryan needs people who love him and can give him a stable home, people who will be there for him today and twenty years from now. He needs a family, and Danny and I want to be that family."

"You're already a single mother, Leanne. Adopting Ryan will more than double your responsibilities because of his experience with his parents. It may take him a long time to trust that you'll never send him away, or it may never happen at all. These problems he's having right now could resolve, or they could get worse as he gets older. You could be letting yourself in for a lot of frustration and heartache."

Leanne smiled dimly. "You know me, Kelsey. I'm an expert at frustration and heartache." Then the smile faded. "I know things could be difficult . . . but that's part of being a parent and a child. The bottom line is Ryan needs us, and we love him, and I really want to give him a real home. A permanent one."

After a moment's silence, Kelsey returned to her desk and jotted something on the pad there. "Mary Therese, my boss over in Howland, and I had discussed a petition to terminate Mr. Jackson's rights when he was arrested in Georgia. Since he didn't go to prison in spite of the guilty plea, we'd decided to hold off. Frankly, I didn't think you'd be interested in adoption and I didn't want to look at placing Ryan elsewhere so soon after he'd moved in with you. I think the child's been bounced around enough in his life."

That was an understatement. Even with J.D., Ryan wouldn't talk much about the years he'd lived with his mother, but in his three years with Cole, they'd lived in two dozen places in a half-dozen states. Ryan had casually explained that was because, in Cole's line of work, the risk of arrest increased proportionally to the time spent in one place.

"I'll have to interview both Ryan and his father. I can't guarantee I'll agree that terminating Mr. Jackson's rights is in the boy's best interests." Kelsey raised her hand to stall Leanne when she would have protested. "I do agree that Ryan needs stability and love and a family . . . but it's possible he needs his father more."

There was no doubt that Ryan loved Cole, Leanne admitted silently. If he didn't, he wouldn't be so angry and hurt. And despite his words to the contrary, if given the chance to take off with Cole tomorrow, to resume their life as it had been before Bethlehem, he would almost certainly go. He might object to the possibility of adoption far more vocally than his father.

But she really, truly wanted what was best for him, and in her heart, she believed that was her and Danny. They could give him everything Cole was unwilling or unable to give—love, acceptance, permanence.

"It's possible," Leanne acknowledged as she stood up. "It's also possible that the moon really is made of green cheese, that the end of the world is nigh, and that Cole's only crime is being misunderstood."

"Such cynicism in one so young." Sliding her arm around Leanne's shoulders, Kelsey walked through the reception area and into the corridor with her. "I'll be in touch about setting up the interview."

"Okay. But I won't hope too much."

"Oh, honey, there's *always* hope."

Not for everyone, Leanne thought as she started down the broad stairs. And certainly not for everything.

IT WAS NEARLY NOON THURSDAY WHEN COLE UN-loaded the last logs of the last delivery of firewood from the City Park trees. He stacked them on the tiny back porch, dusted his hands, then stepped down into the yard and swiped his sleeve across his forehead. It had been cold when they'd left the house that morning, but the sun had finally cleared the clouds and heated the air about ten degrees more than he'd expected. It would be a great day for doing nothing, but was a little warm for physical labor.

"This is so sweet of you," the owner of the porch said as she offered him a glass of milk. She was about five feet tall, well past eighty, and so tiny a stiff breeze could probably knock her off her feet. Her white hair wound around in a bun, and her glasses hovered on the tip of her nose. She offered a plate filled with chocolate chip and oatmeal cookies. "Would you like one?"

"No, thank you." As an afterthought, he added, "Ma'am."

That was another of Owen's rules. *Be respectful to old folks and never mess with people on a fixed income.*

Hmm. Maybe he had a moral or two after all.

"You really should try one. The other boys said they were delicious."

Cole bit back a grin at the thought of anyone calling Murray a *boy.* The guy was old enough to be his father, and couldn't be much younger than the old lady herself. "If you insist," he said, and took a cookie from the plate, though he'd really rather have something more substantial. Breakfast seemed a long time ago.

She waited until he took a bite, then beamed and wandered across the yard to offer thirds to Eli. Cole sat down on the tailgate, a little tired but no longer sore. There was something to be said for real work—at least, when the weather was good and the job wasn't too tough. If Eli put them to work at the sewage treatment plant or mucking out kennels at the animal shelter, he would change his mind.

He was munching the last bite of the cookie when a small child, four or maybe five years old, rolled to a stop in front of him. He—or she; it was difficult to tell with the no-nonsense hair cut, T-shirt, and jeans—settled back on the tricycle, tilted his head back, and fixed a curious gaze on Cole. "Hi."

"Hi," he replied.

"Who are you?"

"Cole. Who are you?"

"Robbie."

That was no help in determining gender. He could ask for a middle name, but it would probably be something like Lou or Jo.

"What are you doing here?" Robbie asked.

"We delivered some firewood."

"Good. Now Gran won't get so cold." Robbie's gaze didn't waver. "I ain't seen you before."

"I ain't seen—I haven't seen you before, either," Cole replied. Then he added, "I'm kind of new to town."

"Huh." Unimpressed, the kid reversed, then pedaled around toward the front of the truck.

Alone once more, Cole glanced at the house. It was tiny, probably not more than six hundred square feet, and shabby. It wasn't the sort of neglect that stemmed from the owner just not caring, but rather from not having the ability to keep up with the regular maintenance. A few screens needed replacing, one of the porch railings was broken, as was a step, and the place hadn't seen fresh paint in at least a decade. Considering the old woman's age, the house really needed a ramp instead of steps, and considering the house's age, no doubt a little weatherstripping would go a long way toward making it more comfortable.

Someone who knew something about houses could probably find plenty of other things to fix, but he wasn't that person. He didn't know anything about anything except ripping people off—and, now, cutting down trees. And hurting people.

"We'd better get going," Eli said, coming toward the truck.

Cole slid to his feet, tossed back the rest of the milk in one gulp, then took the glass to the old lady. "Thank you, ma'am. See you, Robbie."

They returned to the park, where a chipper had been delivered while they were gone. Feeding branches into it would be a fairly mindless job, but once all those branches were mulched, they would head downtown with it.

He would rather cut down the rest of the trees in the park with a butter knife.

"I thought yesterday was your last day here," he remarked to Murray as they began gathering limbs.

"It was."

"So why are you still here?"

The old man smiled and shrugged.

Strange. He had a home—a tiny house similar to the one they'd just left. He'd pointed it out the day before when they were making another delivery of firewood. He didn't seem to have a regular job, though he must have some income to pay for his Jack Black and the car he kept driving while under the influence. He didn't seem to have any family, either, or any responsibilities.

Apparently, he was alone, sad, and lonely. It was a hell of a way to end up in life.

Cole should know, since it appeared he was on the same path.

The park was empty except for the three of them, and quiet except for the sound of the machine grinding up wood. All the school-age kids were in school, and the preschoolers . . . Phyllis Wilson had probably scared every mother in town with her tales about him. The old bat was probably in her house right that moment, watching him through closed blinds with the telephone in her hand, just waiting for him to give her a reason to call 911.

He glanced at the house from time to time. It was kind of stately-looking, built of brick with a big deep porch. It was the sort of house that looked as if it should provide shelter to the perfect family—respectable father, loving mother, typical son, spoiled daughter, obedient dog. It would always be homey and inviting, smelling of lemon oil and roast beef or fresh-baked bread, and everyone would love to visit there.

But the Wilsons hadn't been the perfect family, no more than the Jacksons had. Earl Wilson had run off Chase, and

Phyllis had alienated Leanne. She was a bona-fide witch, Leanne had once told him, and he'd seen the proof for himself.

But they hadn't encouraged her to become a crook, and that counted for a lot in her mind.

Frankly, he'd rather be a crook than have Phyllis Wilson for a mother.

Movement from the parking lot drew his attention that way, and he watched as Kelsey Grayson got out of a van. For a mother of six, she looked pretty damn good. Granted, she'd given birth to only one of them—one was J.D.'s from a previous marriage, and the other four were adopted. Still, he knew better than most what effort went into raising six kids, so he stood by the looking-damn-good observation.

She walked halfway to them, then gestured for him to join her. Cole glanced at Eli, who nodded, then went back to work.

When he reached her, she extended her hand. Looking at his own filthy hands, he shook his head.

"Mr. Jackson."

A knot started forming in his gut, twisting and tightening. It would be too much to hope that this was about the haunted house project, wouldn't it? Besides, Maggie McKinney was in charge of that. Kelsey was just one of the worker bees, like him.

But she *was* in charge of Ryan, more or less, being his caseworker.

He shoved his hands in his hip pockets to keep them steady. "Ms. Grayson."

"Can we talk?"

When he shrugged, she turned toward the nearest picnic table and took a seat on one bench. He straddled the other one. At first touch, the concrete seemed to hold the sun's warmth, but quickly the chill came through.

"You know I'm your son's social worker."

He nodded.

"I'm considering a request to file a petition to terminate your parental rights, which means you would no longer have any legal standing as Ryan's father."

He'd figured this was coming—had been expecting it ever since he'd left town last May, had thought he was prepared for it.

He'd been wrong.

His chest was tight, barely able to accommodate his shallow breaths, and the knots in his stomach turned to a cold, hard weight. He couldn't unclench his fists, hidden beneath the tabletop, or control the thudding of his heart. "I—I—"

He'd known things would never be the same between him and Ryan again. Had known the best thing he could do for the kid was to give him a chance at a better life, then get out of it. Had known Ryan would never understand, never forgive, but would be happier for it in the long run.

He hadn't begun to guess at how badly it would hurt.

"Let me stress that I'm only considering the request right now. Even if my department takes that action, the final decision is the judge's. You'll have a chance to present your side, and at his age, Ryan's wishes will be taken into consideration, too."

He smiled bitterly. "Ryan wishes I'd gone to prison and rotted there."

Kelsey smiled, too, sympathetically. "He's a child."

"A child who's old enough that the judge will consider his wishes."

After a moment's silence, she asked, "Why did you leave him?"

He could tell her the truth, and she might even believe him. Stranger things had happened. But it wouldn't make her decide against the petition. In fact, it would just strengthen her position. When *he* didn't believe he was fit to be a father, how could anyone else fail to agree? It would be a no-brainer for the judge. He could reach the right decision in his sleep.

"Mr. Jackson?"

He lifted his gaze to her face. She really did seem sympathetic. He wondered why. If he dealt with lousy parents all the time, he would despise every last one of them. He would take their kids away, then lock them up forever so they could never cause one more moment's harm to a child.

"You want me to relinquish my rights voluntarily?" he asked bleakly.

"Is that what you want?"

What he wanted had little to do with it. What was best for Ryan was all that mattered.

"I get the impression I'm supposed to believe the answer to my question is yes," she went on when he remained silent. "I also get the impression that's not what you want at all."

"You're wrong," he muttered.

"Which one's wrong?"

"Look, I move around a lot. This"—he spread his hands, indicating the park—"is the only honest work I've done in my life, and believe me, I'm not doing it by choice. I support myself and Ryan with money I've stolen or embezzled or scammed out of some poor sucker. I pay for his clothes and buy his food with that money. When I can't take him with me, I leave him with my father or one of my brothers, all of whom are in the same business. I teach him to look out for himself first, that the law doesn't matter, that no one else in the world matters. If I want something, I take it. If I don't want something, I leave it behind." He fell silent for a long, tense moment. "I left Ryan behind."

"So you're saying you don't want him."

Cole couldn't answer. Tried to, tried like hell to lie, but *couldn't.*

"How long has Ryan lived with you?"

"Three years."

"And what kind of trouble has he been in during those years?"

He scowled at the table. "He got caught shoplifting once."

"Though he'd done it other times, too, hadn't he?"

"Yeah."

"He stole some books, didn't he? And you made him work to pay for them." She smiled. "He told me about it. He said it was the first time he'd realized that most people worked regular jobs to pay for everything. How did his mother support him?"

The sudden tangent caught him off-guard. "I don't know."

"You didn't pay child support."

"I didn't know he existed until he was nine."

"She never told you she was pregnant."

He shrugged.

"He doesn't look anything like you."

He shrugged again. "Your little girl doesn't look like you, either." He'd met the whole Grayson family when he'd met with Kelsey and J.D. at their house one evening, from sixteen-year-old Trey all the way down to the baby, Faith, who was a softer, feminine replica of her father, without so much as a hint of her mother on her round little face.

"Where is Ryan's mother?"

He was positive she'd asked that question of Ryan at some point in the past four months. He gave the same answer he knew the boy would have given. "I don't know."

"So she just showed up on your doorstep one day, said, 'Here's your son,' and disappeared again?"

"Something like that." The evasion made him swallow hard. Truth was, it had been *nothing* like that. But if he told her the truth . . .

He didn't *tell* the truth, though, did he?

"Were you married to his mother?"

"No."

"Did you live with her?"

"No."

"Have a one-night stand?"

He relied on the shrug again.

"Then how did she know where to find you nine years later, to dump your son on you?"

Impatiently, he drummed his fingers on the table. "Look, this is all ancient history. Ryan's mother isn't around to take care of him. Neither . . . neither am I. What does any of it matter?"

"It's not unusual for us to have sketchy background information on children in our care, but Ryan's is even sketchier than most. I'm just trying to get a sense of what his life has been like—how you and his mother have provided for him, and how you've failed him."

"His life has been crappy. He's better off where he is now."

"You mean in foster care."

"I mean with Leanne. Just leave him there. He's got a good home for the first time in his life. Don't screw it up."

"We're not planning to screw it up, Mr. Jackson," she said politely. "In fact, Leanne would like to give your son a permanent home. She's the one who requested the petition severing your rights."

Cole felt a great sense of relief that Ryan wouldn't be uprooted again—almost as great as the shock that it was Leanne who wanted to take the kid away from him, for now and forever, in every way conceivable. It was Leanne who wanted him dragged into court and pronounced unfit to be a father. The woman who'd told him she loved him. The woman who had obviously lied.

God, how she must hate him.

ALEX THOMAS WAS FINISHING UP A PHONE CALL when Melissa arrived for their lunch date. She wiggled her fingers as she moved to a chair, braced both hands on the wooden arms, then cautiously lowered her cumbersome body into it. She was going to the Halloween party dressed as a pumpkin with toothpicks for arms and legs, she had declared the night before. All it would take to pull it off was an orange outfit and a leafy stem curling out of the top of her head. No padding necessary.

He thought she looked beautiful, and had told her so.

On the phone, Melina was winding down. "I haven't heard anything back on Ryan or his mother, and my people are tracking down some stuff on the family. I'll keep you posted, though."

"Thanks, Melina." Hanging up, he smiled at his wife. "Hey, baby."

"Are you talking to me or Junior?"

"Both of you. Where do you want to go for lunch?"

"I would have said Harry's, but I saw Dr. Gregory going in as I was parking, so how about McBride Inn?"

Dr. Gregory was her OB doctor, who had told her last week to watch her calories and continue exercising. The exercise wasn't a problem—they took a long walk every evening—but when she was having cravings at odd hours of the day and night, watching the calories was.

"You afraid of getting caught with a mouthful of Harry's mashed potatoes and gravy?" he teased as he circled the desk and helped her to her feet.

"Sweetheart, when you've stepped on those scales in his office and watched the numbers rise month after month, *then* you can joke about it."

"There are things that happen in that office that scare me a whole lot more than a set of scales—such as anything involving stirrups."

After telling Eleanor where they would be, they started down the stairs at a leisurely pace. "How are things with Melina?" Melissa asked.

"Fine, I guess."

"Is she doing some work for you?"

"Yes."

"On?"

He gave her a dry look. "You don't really want to talk business, do you?"

"I would if you'd ever tell me anything juicy."

He could imagine her reaction if he told her that Cole Jackson had had a lousy childhood. *Now there's a news flash,* she would dryly remark, or *Tell me something the whole world doesn't already know.* Or, more to the point, *Duh.*

"What have you been doing this morning?" he asked as he pushed the heavy door open, then held it for her.

"I lazed around, watching game shows and soap operas, then went by the nursery to see how things are going."

Melissa's Garden was Bethlehem's best nursery—also the only one, though no less the best for that. She'd gotten into the business back when their early efforts to have a baby had failed. If she couldn't nurture a child, she could damn well nurture plants. Last month, though, on her doctor's advice, she'd turned the daily operations over to Julie Bujold. The girl was just out of high school, but she was as responsible as someone twice her age, and she worked miracles with plants.

"And how were things going?"

"Smoothly, as usual. Julie has every—*oh!*" Steadying herself with one hand on the hood of his car, she pressed the other to her stomach and bent forward a bit, breathing shallowly.

"Melissa?"

By the time he reached her, she'd straightened and was smiling wanly. "I'm okay, really. That was one heck of a kick. I felt it all the way down to my toes."

Holding her carefully by the shoulders, he helped her into the car, leaned across to fasten the seat belt, then stared into her face. The color was returning, and her smile was growing broader and brighter. "Really, sweetheart, we're fine. I think that was just Junior's way of telling me he's hungry."

After another moment, he accepted the truth of what she was saying, leaned close, and kissed her, then closed the door and circled behind the car. Though she seemed to, indeed, be fine, he couldn't shake the sudden fear so quickly. After they'd tried so hard, failed so often, then come so far, if anything happened to this baby . . .

He uttered a silent prayer for forgiveness for even thinking such a thing. It was going to happen this time. In another six weeks or so, they would be holding their baby in their arms. They would be parents.

Living proof that miracles did happen.

• • •

Bethlehem High School had an out-of-town football game Friday night. Though she usually attended all the home games—she was a good little civic booster—Leanne decided against driving an hour each way, to freeze in the stands while teenage boys played a game she really didn't care for. Danny and Ryan had gone, though, leaving with Earl and one of his fishing buddies, who happened to be the coach's father, right after school was out. They wouldn't be home until practically midnight, which gave her a long quiet evening to spend alone except for Jerome, snoozing on Danny's bed.

Not that she had to be alone. It was hot-dog night at Chase and Nolie's, and she had a standing invitation to that, with or without the kids. She could go to the Starlite and talk with Rourke for a while or find a handsome man to dance with or hook up with a few girlfriends for a night of giggles and gossip.

Instead, she wandered around the apartment, feeling lost and more than a little blue, and she didn't even know why.

Liar. It seemed she had at least one thing in common with Cole—a propensity to avoid the truth. She felt lousy because of her conversation on Wednesday with Kelsey. Because Leanne had set in motion an attempt to remove Cole permanently from Ryan's life, so *she* could have him. Forget that Ryan was *his son. She* wanted him, so Cole would have to give him up.

She wasn't being that selfish, she insisted as she turned into her bedroom. She truly believed adoption would be best for Ryan. If she didn't, she *never* would have said a word to Kelsey. Besides, it wasn't as if the termination of Cole's rights was up to her. If the judge agreed that Cole was a lousy parent, that Ryan would be better off with Leanne, then *he* would make the decision. The burden would be on *him*, not her.

Liar, liar . . .

She found herself at the side window, where family pictures sat along the sill. She picked up the most recent: a snapshot of Danny, Ryan, and her taken a few months ago. The light in the room was too dim to make out their faces, but rather than turn on the lamp, she reached for the rod that would tilt the slats on the blinds. She twisted it open just enough to get a glimpse of the Miller mansion, then abruptly stopped.

Cole was sitting on the porch steps.

Though he was in shadow, there was no mistaking him. Eli didn't have that thick sun-touched blond hair, and Murray lacked the long, lean lines of that body. It was definitely Cole, and he looked . . .

Lost. Blue.

Probably for the same reason she did.

She dropped the rod, then set the photograph down. It wobbled and fell back against the blinds, but she didn't straighten it. Instead, before she could think about what she was doing—before she could come to her senses—she stopped in the boys' door and snapped her fingers. "Jerome, wanna go for a walk?"

He sprang to the floor as if he hadn't been snoring two seconds earlier, then beat her to the stairs. She paused long enough to grab her jacket and gloves, plus his leash, from the coat tree, then ran down the stairs.

It didn't appear Cole had moved in the time it had taken them to get outside and across the street. She paused in front of the gate, then pushed it open with a creak, and walked to the steps.

"Too bad the barn doors don't creak like that," she remarked as she stood there, one hand clenching the leash, the other knotted in her pocket.

This close, she could see his face more clearly. She

searched for signs of anger, hostility, or bitterness toward her, but didn't find them. She didn't find anything at all besides an unnerving bleakness that made her feel sick inside.

After a moment, he took a deep breath and the bleakness disappeared, as if it had never existed. Leanne found it unsettling, but even his chameleon act was preferable to that unspoken sorrow. "Is this Jerome?"

"Yeah."

At the mention of his name, the puppy left the grass for the steps, climbing up to curiously sniff Cole. He raised one hand to scratch the dog, who immediately flopped over on his back and exposed his belly.

"Do you know how big he's gonna be?"

"Bigger than Danny and smaller than Ryan—I hope."

"You'd better." He scratched Jerome some more, then asked, "If he's the boys' dog, why aren't they walking him?"

"They've gone to a football game with my dad."

"Phyllis the Witch didn't go, too?"

"Heavens, no. The only football games she's ever been to were when Chase was on the team, and even then she complained the whole time. Dad was furious when Chase got himself kicked off, but she was glad, because then she didn't have to go anymore." She moved a cautious step forward, and he automatically shifted to his right, leaving two-thirds of the steps' width for her. Keeping Jerome between them, she sat down on the opposite side.

"Kelsey Grayson came to see me yesterday," he announced.

It was impossible to read anything in his voice or his expression. She swallowed hard and moistened her lips. "I—I'm sorry."

"You say that almost as if you mean it."

"I do mean it."

"Then why are you doing it?"

Another swallow did little to ease the lump in her throat. "Ryan needs a home—a family."

"I've given him a home *and* a family."

"But you can't give him either right now," she said softly. "And you can't give him security. You can't promise you'll always be there for him. What happens the next time you decide to clear out of town in a hurry? Who will you leave him with, and when will you go back for him, or *will* you go back for him? What happens the next time you get arrested and have to go to prison? Who will take care of him then?"

He tilted his head back to stare at the sky with a thoroughly unamused smile. "Thank you for being so certain those things will happen again."

"Have you left him before? Have you been arrested? Have you gone to prison?" Her gesture was impatient. "You know, when you make a habit of doing certain things, before long, people start to expect those things from you."

He didn't respond to that. How could he, without admitting she was right?

She loosely tied Jerome's leash to the railing, then drew her knees up and wrapped her arms around them. "I know it seems cruel, but . . . Ryan needs to believe he belongs somewhere, that he's *wanted* somewhere. On the outside he acts like nothing really matters, but inside there's still a little kid who needs love and security. I can give that to him. I already love him."

Cole tilted his head to skeptically study her. "The way you *loved* me?"

She stiffened. She *had* loved him, and still would—always would—if he hadn't deliberately destroyed it. That was his fault, not hers. "No," she said coolly. "The way I love Danny."

He had no response to that. He just looked at her a moment longer, then turned away, staring off into the distance.

"I just want what's best for Ryan," she said at last.

"You may find this hard to believe, but so do I."

She would give a lot to believe him. Before he'd left, she *had* believed him. He'd been twenty-seven when Ryan's mother had dropped off their nine-year-old son and never come back, and he'd accepted the responsibility with enough maturity that they'd gotten along better than many fathers and sons who grew up together. She had been impressed by their closeness, by their obvious affection for each other. It had been one of several things that helped her fall in love with him.

And yet, when he'd left town, he'd left Ryan, too—hardly the act of a loving father. *Why?*

"If you really mean that . . . will you avoid a court hearing, for Ryan's sake, and sign the papers? Give up your rights?"

That brought his gaze sharply back to her. For a long moment, his expression was harsh, his jaw taut, then everything went blank. "I can't."

Disappointment washed over her. She wanted to swear, to stomp her feet, to find the words to hurt him even half as much as he'd hurt her. But before she could think of anything scathing enough to say, he went on.

"I can't give up something I don't have." He took a breath, and something bleak flickered across his face before he resolutely finished.

"I'm not Ryan's father."

Chapter Nine

THIS TIME LEANNE TRULY WAS SPEECHLESS. SHE stared at Cole, her eyes wide, her mouth rounded in a silent *oh*. She felt so off-balance that if he poked her lightly on the shoulder, she would probably fall over backward, unable to lift so much as a finger to catch herself.

He *wasn't* Ryan's father? How could that be? Maybe he was lying—after all, he'd proven time and again that he was an expert liar. But deep inside she didn't think so. It didn't *feel* like a lie. Besides, paternity was too easy to prove . . . or disprove. And if he *were* Ryan's father and simply didn't want him anymore, he didn't have to lie about it. All he had to do was sign the papers, giving him up.

He *wasn't* Ryan's father. So how did he come to have custody of a child who wasn't his? Because he was related in some other way? Maybe, thanks to one of his many brothers, he was actually Ryan's uncle . . . but why lie about that? People would understand an uncle raising his nephew, especially in Bethlehem, where Nathan Bishop was helping to raise his wife's nephew and two nieces. Of course, Cole hadn't known that when he'd first come to town. Still . . .

She took a breath, the great shuddering kind that trembled through her, then asked in a soft, bewildered tone, "If you're not his father, who is?"

"I don't know."

"What about his mother?"

"I don't know her, either."

"Then how? . . ."

For a long time he didn't respond, but finally he turned so the post was at his back, settling in as if he needed whatever physical comfort he could find, to tell this story. "I was stuck in St. Louis one night, so I passed the time by hustling a few games of pool. When I left the pool hall, I ran into Ryan on the street—literally—and the kid tried to lift my wallet. Of course, I caught him. He wasn't very good at it, while I'd been picking pockets since I was tall enough to reach into them. He was looking for money for food, so I took him to McDonald's and fed him. He didn't have a place to sleep, so I took him back to the motel with me, and . . . we've been together ever since. At least, until . . ."

He'd left the boy with her.

She mimicked his position, then pressed one hand to her stomach, to rub the achy feeling there. "Where was his mother?"

He shrugged. "Three weeks before that, they were taking the bus from Arizona to Chicago and had a layover in St. Louis. He fell asleep on a bench in the bus terminal, and when he woke up, she was gone. Apparently, when they boarded the bus out of St. Louis, she didn't bother to wake him. She got on and rode out of his life. He'd stuck close to the bus station all that time, hoping she would come back, but she never did."

God, no wonder Ryan had nightmares. First his mother left him while he was asleep, then his fath—then Cole did the same. It was a wonder he could sleep at all.

The chill that made her shiver had nothing to do with the cool night. She hugged herself tightly. "You didn't turn him over to the police? You didn't let them try to find his mother so he could join her?"

"Me—call the police?" His expression said all that needed to be said on that matter. "His mother *didn't want* him. She left him without a dime in a bus station in a strange city. If the police had found her and given him back to her, she just would have done it again, only the next time he might not have been so lucky."

Lucky? What had been so lucky for Ryan the first time? That he'd tried to steal from the one person on the streets that night who would reward him for his efforts rather than turn him over to the cops?

Or that he'd tried to steal from the one person who knew what it was like to be abandoned by his mother? The one person who didn't balk at taking in and taking care of someone else's kid. The one person who would care about him.

Still more than a little dazed, she shook her head. "So you just took this child home with you as if he were a stray."

Cole's expression turned stony. "He *was* a stray. He needed a home, and I gave it to him. If I'd called the police, he would have wound up in foster care that much sooner."

Instead, he'd given Ryan a home for three years . . . before putting him through the whole nightmare all over again.

She watched as a car drove past—Georgia Blakely, a friend of her mother's, on her way home from her shift at the grocery store. The morning after Leanne's first night with Cole, the old gossip had seen her leaving his house bright and early, subjecting her to the third-degree from Phyllis. Thank heavens she hadn't been looking tonight, or Leanne would certainly have another visit from Phyllis, and she just wasn't up to it.

When the taillights disappeared down the street, she

looked back at Cole. "I've seen Ryan's birth certificate. It lists you as his father."

He made a dismissive gesture. "He had to have a birth certificate so he could go to school. His mother dragged him all over the country—"

"Like you did."

"—and she changed her name a lot." A grim smile touched his mouth. "Like I did. He didn't know what state he was born in or what name she was using at the time, so . . ."

"Let me guess," she said dryly. "One of your brothers specializes in forging documents."

"Eddie. Actually, it's just a hobby."

Between them, Jerome started to snore. She reached out to rub his belly at the same time Cole did. Even through her gloves, she felt a tingle when their fingers came into contact, and she hastily withdrew, then turned her head, to stare at the stars.

She didn't know whether to be appalled by his story . . . or impressed. On the one hand, a person just couldn't find a kid on the streets and take him home to keep. It was wrong. He should have called the police, no matter how contrary to his nature that was.

But on the other hand, he *had* taken Ryan in. He'd fed him, clothed him, given him a place to sleep, and some measure of security. Ryan's own mother had left him, helpless and defenseless on a bench in a bus station, and if she'd regretted it, it hadn't been enough to make her go back for him. But a complete stranger—a victim of the boy's clumsy attempt at stealing—had been willing to take responsibility for him.

And if Cole hadn't taken Ryan in, he never could have brought him here, and she and Danny would have missed out on a very important part of their lives.

"Okay," she said quietly. "You caught Ryan stealing. You

fed him because he was hungry. You gave him a place to sleep because he didn't have one. Against all logic, you took him home with you. You must have built a pretty good relationship with him, because he obviously loves you. *Why* did you leave him here?"

"Why does everyone keep asking that?"

She didn't know who else was asking. Kelsey, definitely. Maybe Eli. "If you answer, they'll stop."

"Why doesn't matter."

"Yes, it does. If you left him because someone was trying to kill you and would kill him, too, that would be entirely different from leaving him because you were tired of playing daddy and didn't want to bother with him anymore."

"No one's trying to kill me," he said scornfully. "I'm not that kind of crook."

"Were you tired of pretending to be his father?"

His only answer was a scowl.

"Did you want him out of your life?"

Still just the scowl.

"Did you resent having to take care of him, spend money on him, spend time with him?" She paused, but he said nothing. "Did he get in the way of your scams? Or did it worry you that he'd started stealing? Did you think you were a bad influence on him? Did you decide he would be better off without you?"

That last brought a flicker of something to his face. Guilt? Or was it shame?

Too restless to sit any longer, she stood up, walked to the end of the porch and leaned against the railing while she stared at the darkened store across the street. Could that really be it—he'd wanted Ryan to have a better life than he could give him? A more normal life? He'd thought a lying, cheating con artist wasn't the sort of father figure a twelve-year-old boy needed?

Leanne knew about Ryan's stealing. It had happened just a month before they'd come to Bethlehem. He hadn't needed the books, of course, but that hadn't stopped him from taking them. Cole had, in Ryan's words, gone ballistic. It was the only time he'd ever gotten mad at Ryan, the only time he'd yelled at him.

When Ryan had told her the story, she'd thought privately that it had been an overreaction from a man who stole for a living. Now she wondered . . . Was it because he'd seen proof of his influence on the boy? Because he hadn't wanted Ryan to grow up to be like him? Following in the family business was good enough for him, but not his son?

"What are you going to do now?"

Cole's question came from close behind her. How had he gotten to his feet and moved in on her without her hearing? He was there, close enough that she could feel the heat and the tension radiating from his body. "Do?" she asked, and grimaced when her voice managed to tremble even on that tiny word.

"About the petition."

"I'll have to tell Kelsey."

"What if they take Ryan away from you?"

She turned, leaning her hips against the railing. "And do what with him?"

"What if they find his mother and give him back?"

"To a woman who abandoned him?"

The faintest of mocking smiles appeared on his face. "Not ten minutes ago you thought I should have called the police so they could try to do just that."

She didn't try to understand her conflicting feelings. "If she didn't want him then, why would she want him now?"

"I left him in Bethlehem because I knew someone here would take care of him—would give him the kind of life I couldn't. I don't want him sent someplace else, and I don't want him going back to his mother."

"It's not your choice," she softly pointed out. "You have no claim to him."

"I l—" His jaw clenched as he bit off the word, then he muttered a curse and swung away.

I love him. She would bet this month's receipts at the shop that was what he'd been about to say. Had he stopped because the words were hard to say? Because he was unable to admit it even to himself? Or because they weren't true?

Did he even have a clue what it meant to love someone? Or was he so accustomed to deception and pretense that he'd lost touch with such basic, selfless emotions?

Maybe he thought it didn't matter, just as he thought his reasons for leaving didn't matter. But reasons always mattered, though not in the beginning, of course. When he'd first left Ryan, if she could have strung him up from the tallest tree, she would have, no matter what excuse he offered. But now . . . trying to give the kid a better life beat all hell out of trying to give himself a responsibility-free life.

"Will you see him?" she asked.

It was difficult to be sure, standing in the shadows as he was, but she thought she saw him shudder an instant before he said, "That's probably not a good idea."

"For him? Or for you?"

"He's made it clear he doesn't ever want to see me."

"He's twelve years old and hurting. I'm not sure he knows what he wants."

"He's twelve going on thirty. He knows."

She moved a few steps closer, but he didn't turn to look. That was all right. She had no problem with talking to his back. "Then let me ask a different question. Do you *want* to see him? Do you miss him? Do you want to try to explain yourself to him?"

"That's three questions."

Finally she moved around him, stopping a few feet in front of him. Light from inside the house shone through the windows on either side of the door, illuminating the right side of his face, deepening the shadows over the left. "They're simple questions. All they need is a yes or no. In fact, you can answer just one of them."

The sharpening of his gaze indicated he recognized his own words from the other night. But he didn't answer. *She* hadn't answered *his* questions the other night, either. But where he'd let her walk away, she had no intention of allowing him the same opportunity.

"For God's sake, Cole, you're a grown man. You're intelligent and capable. You can charm the rattles off a snake and you can face prison, but you can't say, 'Yes, I miss my son'?"

His mouth barely moved. "He's not—"

"For three years he was, in all the ways that count! What are you so damn afraid of?"

At their feet, Jerome lifted his head, alerted by the frustration in her voice, but Cole didn't react to it at all. Dully he said, "I've got to go in. I'll see you around." Then he disappeared inside, locking the door between them.

WHAT *WAS* HE AFRAID OF?
Cole was up half the night thinking about Leanne's question, and it had occupied his mind all morning Saturday as they worked on the haunted house. She hadn't shown up that morning—he'd heard Maggie tell Kelsey that Leanne was bringing lunch and would stay for the afternoon, while Sophy ran the store. While trying to ignore the tightening in his chest on hearing that, he'd noticed that Eli's attention had perked up at the mention of Sophy. *He sets Sophy's teeth on edge,* Leanne had said one night. *I think she likes him.*

Maybe she'd been right. She was right about a lot of things, it seemed.

He and Eli were working on the system of wires and pulleys that would make the coffin lid open and the skeleton dance, when the gray skies opened up and rain started falling. The fresh scent replaced the mustiness inside the barn, and dropped the temperature a few uncomfortable degrees. A few minutes later Leanne arrived with lunch. She was a bit soggy from the walk from her SUV to the barn, but the food, stored in Danny's old wagon and covered with a plastic tarp, was fine.

"Yea, food's here," Holly Flynn called, and received a tart response from Leanne.

"And hello to you, too."

"Oh, Leanne, I didn't recognize you," Holly teased. "Leanne's here, everyone—and the food!"

Leanne pushed the hood of her navy-blue slicker off her head, then shrugged out of it and hung it on a hook near the door. She snagged a napkin from the wagon to wipe her face and hands, then another to dry as much water as possible from her sneakers. Finally, she looked up and right at him. His stomach knotted, and for the first time since they'd left the house after breakfast, he was warm inside and out.

And *that,* he realized, was what he was afraid of.

Someone who could make life seem better just by being around.

Someone who was that important to him.

Someone who had that kind of power over him.

Hell.

Lunch consisted of sandwiches, chips, cookies, and soft drinks. He took one of each and returned to the back of the barn to sit on a hay bale. The others mostly gathered at the front except Leanne. Her hands empty but for a Pepsi and a cookie, she came to stand in front of him. He slowly chewed the food in his mouth, swallowed, then took a drink of pop before asking, "Are you going to stand there and stare at me or have a seat?"

She moved to sit cross-legged on the next hay bale. If she noticed the frequent glances they were getting from everyone else, she gave no sign. "I talked to Alex this morning about . . ."

"And?"

"He said it will make adoption tougher. The state will try to find his parents. If they can't, the judge can terminate *their* rights the same as he could have terminated yours, if you had any. But it'll take time, and there's always the possibility that his mother's gotten herself straightened out and will want him back, and the judge could decide to give her another chance. Or the father might never have known about him and could be thrilled to have him. Or there could be grandparents or an aunt or uncle . . ."

"So don't tell Kelsey."

She stared at him. "I have to!"

"No, you don't. They think I'm his father. I'll sign the papers and you can have him."

"I can't do that, Cole." Her voice rose, drawing attention from the other women. Face flushing, she lowered it to a whisper. "I can't. It's wrong."

"What's wrong with giving a kid a home where he's wanted?"

"But Alex knows the truth."

"He's your lawyer, isn't he?"

"Yes, but—"

"Then attorney-client privilege would keep him from telling anyone."

"But—"

He watched her as he started on the second half of his sandwich, but he already knew what her final answer would be. She was too honest—maybe too honest for Ryan's own good. She wouldn't go through with an illegal adoption.

Of course, she was right. What if she did, and somewhere down the line the truth came out? What if Ryan's mother came looking for him? The fact that Leanne had known the truth before the adoption would certainly hurt whatever claim she had to the kid, and being taken away from what he thought would be his home and family forever, would seriously hurt Ryan.

While munching her cookie, she stared at the skeleton, sitting up in the coffin where he and Eli had propped him, but he doubted she actually saw it. Her mind was on more serious problems.

"I'm sorry."

She glanced at him. "For what?"

"Everything. I wish . . ."

He'd never believed in wishes—had never wished on a star or birthday candles or a wishbone. Wishes had no place in a con artist's life. Intelligence, planning, execution—that was what made the difference.

"What do you wish?" Leanne asked.

He shrugged. "Nothing."

She shifted on the hay, to look at the skeleton again. "If I were going to wish, I would wish for better instincts about men. This guy here"—she wiggled the skeleton's fingers with her toe—"he looks about my speed . . . unlike every living man I've gotten serious about. Hell, Danny's father left when I told him I was pregnant, because he didn't want to be a father. The next one really seemed to like being part of our little family, but then decided he didn't want to play father to another man's son. The one after him was already married. And then there was you. You not only left me, but you left your son with me." Suddenly, suspicion colored her voice. "You don't have a wife or two out there, do you?"

"No," he said with a scowl, then it faded. "However, I think my brother, Adam, did forget to divorce his first wife before he married the second one."

Her dark eyes widened, then slowly a knowing look came over her face. "You're teasing, aren't you?"

He shrugged. He wasn't, but if it made her feel better to think so, then she was welcome to it.

"Where do your brothers live?"

"When they're not in jail? Your guess is as good as mine." He polished off the chips, then crumpled the trash and stuffed it in the chips bag. "Owen has pretty much settled in Philadelphia, and everyone checks in with him. It's the easiest way to keep in touch."

"Why don't you all just get cell phones and trade numbers?"

"Uh, no. Cell phones mean records, which means a better chance of getting caught for one thing or another."

"It doesn't sound like a very pleasant way to live," she said, sounding a little sad. For him?

"As long as you don't know anything else, it's not bad. The problems start when you do get to know something else." He stood up, held out his hand for her empty can, then took it to the trash with his own. When he returned, he crouched next to the skeleton and began fiddling with the monofilament line attached to its left elbow.

"What problems?"

He barely glanced at her, just enough to see the faded denim of her jeans and the hem of her black sweater. "What do you mean?"

"You said the problems start when you get to know something else. What problems?"

He shortened the line so the arm would lift a few

inches higher, then measured a piece to attach to the left knee. For a moment she let him work in peace while he considered his answer. When her foot started tapping, though, he looked at her again. "Your mother does that."

"Does what?"

"Taps her foot when she's not getting what she wants fast enough."

Immediately her foot stilled, and he grinned. "You don't want to be accused of having anything in common with Phyllis, huh?"

She made a face at him and was about to prompt him for an answer, he was sure, so he saved her the trouble.

"If you've never lived a normal life, you tend to want one of two things—either to have that normal life or to never have it. People who have never had a real home usually either like moving around or they're desperate for a place to call their own. I've never lived in a town like Bethlehem. It's different from the rest of the world out there. It's the kind of place where people can . . . belong. Where everyone pretty much accepts everyone else, and you can fit in, and there's this whole *community* thing going on."

He gestured around them, to emphasize the last words. In Bethlehem, if a person got sick, someone was there to help him out. If there was a crisis, people pitched in to resolve it. People didn't just live there—they were neighbors, friends, and family to everyone else who lived there.

Fifty years ago places like this hadn't been at all uncommon. Even today such towns still existed, or so he'd heard, but Bethlehem was the first he'd experienced for himself. And it had made him want it for Ryan and for himself.

If they were lucky, Ryan could have it.

"So the town tempted you to go straight," Leanne remarked.

"The town." He looked up at her. "You."

Her jaw tightened and skepticism darkened her eyes. She didn't believe him. Now there was a big surprise, he thought as she responded, sarcasm coloring her voice.

"But you managed to resist."

"What could I have done, Leanne? I came here for the sole purpose of stealing from you people. Do you really think I could have said, 'Hey, I've changed my mind. Here's your money back. Can we still be friends?' " He muttered a disgusted curse. "They would have spit in my face while they were cuffing my hands behind my back."

"You don't know that," she challenged, "and now you'll never know, because you didn't have the courage to try."

He knew it was stupid, but when she stood up, so did he. They were so close he could feel her breath, could see the beat of her heart at the base of her throat. He could feel incredible heat—his, theirs—and incredible longing, his and his alone.

"I do know," he whispered, bending even closer. "I changed my mind, sweetheart. I gave the money back. But you still look at me as if . . . as if . . ." He couldn't find words to describe how low she could make him feel with one look. Instead, he trusted her to supply her own.

"As if you stole from me and my friends?" she whispered heatedly. "As if you betrayed us? As if you betrayed your son? You only came back because they *forced* you."

"Damn right they forced me! Do you think I wanted to face these people again after what I'd done? Do you think I wanted to face *you*? I never had much, but at least I had some pride. Until then."

She stared at him a long time before cynically answering. "Gee, sounds like you have a conscience after all, or facing up to what you'd done wouldn't have cost you your pride."

Before he could respond to that, she went on. "Bethlehem is full of generous, kindhearted people. You knew that from the beginning—it's part of what brought you here. You could have stopped at any time, right up to the moment you left Ryan, and they would have forgiven you everything. But you didn't want forgiveness. You wanted money."

Cole didn't bother to argue that point with her as she started to walk away. Instead, he caught her wrist and held her there. "What about you, Leanne? Would you have forgiven me? Will you ever forgive me?"

She looked at his hand, her gaze so sharp he could actually feel it, until he released her, then she took a step back. "I don't know, Cole. I honestly don't know."

He watched her leave, wanting to tell her that she was wrong about the money, wanting to plead with her about the forgiveness, wanting . . . oh, hell, just wanting.

"What was that about?" Murray asked as he came to the opposite side of the skeleton.

Cole wearily shook his head. "Damned if I know."

W ANT TO GO FOR A WALK?"
The look Nolie gave Leanne was chastising. "Gee, let's see. It's about fifty-five degrees, it's raining, it's almost suppertime, and we've been working all day. I don't think so."

Leanne shrugged into her slicker. "You don't have to be sarcastic about it."

"That wasn't sarcasm. That was just me. Want to come to dinner?"

"Not tonight. The boys and I still have costume decisions to make. Maybe we can get that done over dinner."

"It was easier when you were a kid, wasn't it? Chase says you went as a fairy-tale princess every Halloween."

"Until I was thirteen," Leanne admitted with a laugh. "He preferred to be things like blood-sucking ghouls."

"So *that's* why he became a lawyer."

They were standing in the doorway of the barn, watching the rain while they talked. Besides them, the only ones left were Maggie, Eli, Cole, and Murray. Though they hadn't spoken again after their talk about forgiveness, Leanne was way too aware of Cole for her own good.

Apparently, so was Nolie. With a glance over her shoulder, she lowered her voice and asked, "Is everything okay?"

Leanne pretended ignorance. "Sure. Why wouldn't it be?"

"You two seemed pretty cozy."

In spite of the cool temperature, heat seeped into Leanne's face. "You mean Cole and me?"

"No, actually I was talking about you and Mr. Bones."

"We were just talking about Ryan."

"You must have had a lot to say."

A sharp gust of wind blew rain through the open door, dampening their jeans. Nolie pulled her jacket tighter, then stepped back. "You're falling for him again, aren't you?"

If anyone else was asking, Leanne would have no qualms about lying or even telling them to mind their own business. But this was Nolie, family and best friend, who'd helped her pick up the pieces the last time, who offered her the same unconditional love and support she gave her husband and daughter. Leanne wouldn't lie to her, and she couldn't tell her to mind her own business, because family *was* her business.

"Again? I'm not sure I ever got over him the first time. I thought I had. Lord knows, I've had my heart broken enough times to know the drill. But ever since he came back, I've felt *so* . . ." She smiled ruefully. "I know—after everything he did, I'm nuts. Certifiable."

"No more so than any other woman who's involved with a man," Nolie said dryly.

"He's a crook. Trouble with a capital T. He broke my heart and, worse, he broke Ryan's. He can't be trusted. I *know* these things, Nolie. But . . ." Her mouth flattened with dismay as the words trailed off.

"You know them in your head. But your heart knows that you loved him."

"You know, our brains are in our heads for a reason—because our hearts can't be trusted."

Nolie slid her arm around Leanne's shoulders for a comforting hug. "Sometimes our hearts know what's really important . . . and sometimes I swear they're out to get us. Whatever you do, Leanne, be careful. Don't let him hurt you again." Then her voice lightened. "But if it happens anyway, I've got enough recipes for prize-winning cakes to feed your sorrow for a year or so, and two shoulders for crying on."

The smile her words summoned was exactly what Leanne needed. She returned the hug fiercely. "My brother was a smart man to marry you."

"I think so, too." Nolie released her and stepped back before imparting her last words of wisdom. "Think with your head . . . but listen to your heart a little, too."

Leanne tightened her grip on the handle of the wagon as she prepared to dash into the rain. "Give my brother my love, and give Mica a big kiss for me."

"I will."

"And come see us sometime."

"Hey, the road runs both ways."

Leanne stepped into the pouring rain and hustled to her truck. She was trying to manhandle the oversized wagon into the back, when an extra hand easily boosted it inside. She wasn't even surprised that she knew by seeing no

more than the five fingers that it was Cole. Of course it
was. Eli and Murray didn't make her heart catch.

Rain drenched him, flattening his hair against his head
and turning it dark gold. It dripped from his nose and chin
and soaked his clothes, but he didn't seem to notice. In
fact, she thought with a nervous swallow, he didn't seem to
notice anything but her.

She had to clear her throat to speak. "If I had an um-
brella, I'd share it with you."

"And get that close?"

She ignored his jibe. "You're going to freeze out here."

In return, he ignored that. "I *don't* have a conscience."

It took her a moment to think back to her parting words
to him earlier. *Sounds like you have a conscience, after all.* Had
that been on his mind all afternoon? It was a silly thing to
stew over . . . unless the jibe targeted the fundamental
truths his life had been built on. Unless he felt the need to
convince someone he was beyond redeeming. Unless that
someone he needed to convince, was himself. "Is that an insult to someone coming from your background?"

"Damn right. It's a pesky thing that was bred out of the
Jackson family generations ago."

"Right. So . . . wanting a better life for Ryan, leaving
him in a place where he would get it, returning all the
money you stole—none of that had to do with having a
conscience."

He shook his head, sending raindrops flying.

He looked so serious, so intense, that she couldn't resist
leaning closer and clearly, politely, using her father's favorite curse word. It made his eyes widen slightly and left
him staring at her with surprise.

"You didn't take a dime from anyone who couldn't afford it. Nolie told me you wouldn't take her check until
she told you she had other money set aside. You didn't go

near any of the elderly people in town who live on social security."

"I don't target people on fixed incomes."

"Because your conscience tells you it's wrong," she retorted triumphantly.

His grin was faint and sardonic. "No, because Owen says it's wrong—and *he* wouldn't appreciate being accused of having a conscience, either."

Ignoring the cold and the dampness seeping through her jeans and shoes, she folded her arms over her chest. "What else does Owen say you shouldn't do?"

He ticked them off on his fingers. "Never steal from a church. Never admit guilt. Never tell the truth if a lie will suffice. Never bring attention to yourself. Never apologize. Never—"

"Okay. I get the picture." He'd been taught the finer points of living a life of crime, the same way she'd been taught to brush her teeth before going to bed, look both ways when crossing the street, and never play with fire. Obviously, she'd forgotten all about that last one.

"Your father should have been locked up."

The grin flashed again. "He has been. Many times."

"He should have been locked up once and for all, and you and your brothers should have been placed in a home where you could be raised properly."

"We *were* raised properly—for the lives we were going to live."

"The lives *he* decided you should live. He didn't raise sons. He raised six little partners in crime."

How different would Cole's life have been if he'd been removed from his father's influence when he was young enough for it to matter? There would have been no limit to what he could have accomplished. He was smart enough, diligent enough, clever enough, to have done anything, and done it exceedingly well.

But if he'd been a successful businessman, doctor, or lawyer, he never would have been hustling pool in St. Louis. He never would have caught Ryan picking his pocket, or taken him in, or come to Bethlehem. If he'd been raised differently, he would have become a different man, and he wouldn't have had the same empathy for Ryan, and chances were good Leanne never would have fallen in love with him.

And he wouldn't have broken her heart.

"I think it's interesting that you defend your father, yet you did with Ryan exactly what I think Owen should have done with you. You have no problem with being raised by a crook to be a crook yourself, but you don't want Ryan raised by a crook and you don't want him to become one himself."

"He deserves better."

"So the lifestyle is good enough for you, but not him. Why? Why don't *you* deserve better?"

"Because I *am* a crook, plain and simple."

A crook, yes. Plain and simple? No way.

As the rain increased in intensity, she glanced up into the swiftly darkening sky, got a face full of water, then wiped it away. "This is a hell of a place and time for a conversation. Why did you come out here?"

"I was on my way to Eli's pickup, and it looked like you needed a hand."

"I appreciate it, but you should probably—" She glanced to the other side of the road, where the old truck had been parked when she'd arrived. It was gone. So were Maggie's and Nolie's cars. A long look around showed that the barn was locked up, with only the outside light shining, and everyone was gone but them.

How had four people left in three vehicles without her noticing them? Granted, the rush and splash of the rain muted other sounds, but she still should have heard doors slamming and engines starting. For heaven's sake, had her attention been fixed so completely on Cole, that she'd gone deaf and blind to the rest of the world?

He glanced around, too, then finished her statement for her. "I should probably ask my neighbor for a ride home, though I couldn't get any wetter if I had to walk."

"No, you couldn't," she absently agreed, turning away from the rear of the truck.

As she settled in the driver's seat, he did the same in the passenger seat. The moment the engine was running, she flipped the heat to high and shivered uncontrollably for the moment or two it took to warm the air. Naturally, the temperature change caused all the windows to fog, but she absorbed the heat a moment longer, before switching the air to the defrosters.

Gazing idly at the rain-streaked windshield, she wondered what Nolie, Maggie, Eli, and Murray had thought when they'd hurried out into the rain and saw her and Cole standing there, talking as if it were the middle of a warm, dry day. She'd already fielded questions from Nolie and Holly about her conversation with Cole when she'd first arrived. No doubt the speculation about the two of them had already started, and this little incident tonight would just fuel it.

At the moment, she didn't even care. She was getting the feeling back in her toes and fingers and the discomfort of being cold and wet was easing. Besides, she was the only one living her life, so she was the only one who got a say in it.

Finally, when the inside of the truck was as toasty warm as the outside was cold, she switched the wipers on and followed the old road toward the parking lot. "Is Eli irresponsible or overly trusting?" she asked as the SUV bumped over the rough transition to the paved parking lot. "Leaving you behind like that, I mean."

"Probably a little of both. He's convinced he can find me in no time, if I decide to make a break for it."

"And you're convinced he can't?"

He shrugged, making her wonder if his shoulders were so broad or the space between the seats was really so narrow. "I've been running longer than he's been alive."

"So why haven't you taken off?"

"And leave all this behind? Getting dragged into the police station by your mother, for daring to show my face? Not being trusted to carry even a dime in my pocket, or to walk to Harry's for a cup of coffee, or to the grocery store for a newspaper? Getting bossed around by a kid half my age?"

Even though his tone was light and mocking, Leanne knew those things bothered him deeply. According to Ryan, he'd never had to stay around and face his victims before.

She settled for scoffing at the least important of his complaints. "Eli's not that young."

"No, but he looks it."

She pulled into her parking space and shut off the engine. A glance in her side-view mirror showed the green truck in the driveway across the street. "So why haven't you taken off?"

He was quiet a long time, long after the engine noises settled and the windows fogged over again. When he did finally speak, it wasn't to answer her seriously. "Wouldn't you miss me if I was gone?"

"I would survive," she answered tartly. Truthfully, she and Ryan would both be better off if Cole had never come back into their lives. Oh, sure, they would have hurt for a while, but time healed all wounds, her father was fond of saying. Someday in the not-too-distant future, they would have forgotten him and gone on with their own lives.

Unfortunately, foolishly, but also truthfully, yes, in some ways she would miss him. Even though seeing him hurt, even though it was a poor substitute for the future she'd once dreamed of, seeing him was better than not seeing him. Knowing why he'd left Ryan was better than not knowing. Knowing there were reasons—albeit, not always good ones—for the things he'd done, was better than wondering.

Once more she repeated her question. "Why haven't you taken off?"

"Because if I did, I'd miss the chance to do this." Leaning over, he slid his fingers underneath her hair to curve around her neck, and he kissed her. His touch was warm and made her hot. His mouth was gentle and made her hungry. He slid his tongue into her mouth, and she opened for him, no coaxing, no resisting, nothing but a faint whimper of pleasure. It had been so long, and she'd been so lonely, and his kisses were so sweet.

She touched him, just her fingertips to his cheek, and abruptly he pulled back. Before she could grasp that he'd ended the kiss, before she could wonder why, he had opened the door and slid to the ground. Giving her a brash, cocky grin—the phony one—he closed the door once again and dashed across the street.

And he'd never answered her question, she realized. Oh, sure, he'd offered that baloney—*if I did, then I'd miss the chance to do this*—but it hadn't been a real answer.

For the moment, though, it had to be enough.

Chapter Ten

HARRY'S WAS CLOSED FOR THE NIGHT, WITH only a few lights burning here and there. Sophy stood behind the counter, leaning one elbow on it, bracing her chin on her hand. Gloria occupied one of the barstools on the other side, which she occasionally spun in a circle with all the delight of a child. She was easily amused.

Not Sophy.

They'd been in the diner thirteen minutes, and only one car had passed in all that time. Virtually all of their charges were home, tucked in their beds, sleeping soundly and, for a lucky few, dreaming blissfully. Of course, where else would they be at three in the morning?

"Eli's late."

Sophy gave Gloria a dry look. "You do have a talent for stating the obvious."

"You shouldn't be so hard on the boy. I like him."

"Good. Then you work with him, you talk to him, and leave me out of it." Sophy gestured as if she planned to disappear, but Gloria's chastening look stopped her.

"He's just helping—"

Sophy restrained a snort.

"—and it's just temporary. Though I do wonder why."

"Gee, I don't know. Could it have something to do with the fact that you *poisoned* our last charge?"

A delicate pink flooded Gloria's face. "It seemed like a good idea at the time. Besides, Jolie was all right."

"Her name is Nolie—and trust me on this, Gloria. Guardians poisoning the humans they're watching over is *never* a good idea."

"We needed a way to get Chase out of hiding and into town, where he could see his sister. Having Nolie rushed to the hospital accomplished that." Now Gloria's lower lip eased out. "Besides, it was just a little case of food poisoning. Norie didn't suffer too greatly for it."

Sophy rolled her eyes heavenward. No, other than one terribly unpleasant evening, Nolie hadn't suffered greatly. But now Sophy was paying the price, and she hadn't even been involved.

The bell over the door tinkled, even though the door was securely locked, then Eli materialized on the stool in front of her. Caught off-guard, for one instant she was struck anew by how amazingly pretty he was. Not handsome or good-looking, but very definitely, very masculinely, pretty. Perfect blue eyes, perfect nose, perfect jaw, perfect cheekbones, perfect mouth, perfect silky black hair. The most talented sculptor that ever existed, couldn't have created anything to match.

What a shame he was perfectly smug and arrogant to match.

"You're late," she said flatly, straightening so she wasn't so close to him.

"Who made you keeper of the schedule?" he retorted.

"We don't actually have a keeper of the schedule," Gloria said. "In fact, we don't actually even have a schedule. But we could make one up, couldn't we? And then we could have a keeper— Oh. That was a joke, wasn't it?"

"Hardly." Sophy walked around the counter and took a seat at a table nearer Gloria than Eli. Just for fun, since they were meeting at Harry's, she'd dressed in a pink outfit similar to the one Maeve, the waitress, wore. The color went well with her natural blonde hair, but she preferred jeans, overalls, and T-shirts.

Not that it mattered. She wasn't here to think about how she looked. In fact, she couldn't remember a time in . . . well, all of time that she'd given her appearance a second thought. Why now? she wondered while deliberately keeping her gaze and her thoughts from straying as far as the counter.

"So, Soph . . . what's up?" Eli asked, turning to face her, resting his elbows on the counter behind him.

"No one said there was anything up." In spite of her gritted teeth, the words sounded fairly normal.

"Then why the meeting?"

"There doesn't have to be a problem for us to get together. It's something we do—Gloria and I. When we work together. Without interference."

He slid to the floor and came to stand in front of her. She had to tilt her head back, her gaze sliding over jeans and a snug-fitting black T-shirt before reaching his face. "Interference? Is that what you're calling me these days?"

She smiled sweetly. "If the shoe fits . . ."

He swung a chair around, straddled it, and leaned toward her. "You're afraid of being shown up, aren't you? Afraid you can't handle the big jobs."

"Before coming to Bethlehem, I worked in Buffalo," she said with a sniff. "I convinced Tom Flynn to marry Holly McBride. *That* was a big job."

"From what I hear, it was nowhere near as big as convincing Holly to marry Tom." He gave Gloria a wink and a grin in acknowledgment of her role before turning back to Sophy. "Maybe they could put you on nursery duty or something. I could put in a good word for you."

"*Nursery*—You are insufferable."

"Coming from you, I'll take that as a compliment."

"I wouldn't compliment you if you were the last guardian left in all the heavens." She took a few breaths to control her temper, then politely said, "You know, I've finally figured out why *we* got stuck with you."

"And why is that, Miss Know-it-all?"

"Because no one else would have you."

"Oh, right, Soph. Truth is, they sent me here because *you*—"

Before he could say anything more, she faded away, form first, uniform second, clunky thick-soled shoes last.

"Wow, I'm impressed," he said snidely. "Like every guardian can't do that. Is that the best you can manage?" When she didn't answer, he sprawled in the chair and faced Gloria. "She doesn't like me much, does she?"

"No, I'm afraid not," Gloria agreed gently.

"Huh. Wonder why."

Sophy was feeling some small sense of triumph when he shrugged and went on. "That's okay. I don't like her much, either."

Ohhh! She'd been right about him the first hundred times. He was arrogant. Smug. Conceited. Insufferable. Too hateful for words.

In her head, a tiny whisper added one more comment. *Too handsome for words, too.*

ABOUT THE TIME LEANNE WAS EXPECTING RYAN HOME from school on Monday, the phone rang, and it *was* the school—the vice principal to be exact. His name was Pete Harrington, and in her opinion, he was vastly underqualified for the job. Oh, he met the education requirements, but he was every bad teacher she'd ever met, all rolled into one. He took himself too seriously, lived for his rules and regulations, had little compassion, and didn't particularly like kids, so naturally when the position of vice principal had come open a year earlier, the school board had promoted him.

With a sinking feeling in her stomach, after exchanging greetings, she asked, "What can I do for you, Pete?"

"I'm calling about Ryan."

She bit her tongue to keep from tartly informing him she'd figured that out, since Ryan was the only child she had enrolled in the Bethlehem public school system. "What about him?"

"I wondered if you knew he hasn't been turning in his homework."

"In which class?"

"All of them. For a week now."

She sank onto the stool behind the counter. "But he's doing it. I've checked it every night."

"Well, he's not turning it in. He's also been misbehaving in class—talking back to the teachers, refusing to follow instructions—and he got into a shoving match with another student in the hall between classes today. Fortunately, a teacher broke it up." Pete hesitated. "I understand his father is back in town."

If you define "father" loosely. "Yes, he is."

"I presume that's a large part of the problem."

Some foolish place inside her resented a man who'd never even met Cole describing him as a problem, no matter how apt the description. "Yes," she admitted reluctantly.

"I told Ryan to have you call me last Friday. Did he pass on the message?"

She stared at the stack of Christmas sweaters she'd been folding for display, wishing she could cover for Ryan, knowing she couldn't. "No, he didn't. Is it standard procedure to ask a child who's having problems to pass on messages to his parents?"

"We have to show them trust until they prove they don't deserve it."

Or set them up to fail, you pompous jerk. "Well, I'll talk to Ryan the first chance I get."

"Maybe you can get some pointers from your mother. As I recall, your brother was a problem child, too, wasn't he? They used to say that one of the chairs in the principal's office had his name on it."

His remarks made her blood pressure shoot up about ten points, along with her temper. The last thing she needed from her mother was advice, and *no one* called her brother a problem child in that smugly superior voice. For damn sure, no one was going to imply the same about Ryan. She was opening her mouth to say so when the idiot went on.

"When can you come in? This afternoon would be good for me."

"Uh, no. I've got an appointment." This time they would have several new things to discuss with J.D.— Ryan's school problems and her almost uncontrollable need to tell Pete Harrington where he could shove his pomposity and smugness.

"My schedule's pretty full," Pete went on. "How about Friday around four?"

"That's Halloween. It'll be a really busy day for us."

"Perhaps it would be a good idea if Ryan missed Halloween this year."

She made a face at the phone. "I don't think so. Even if I did, I wouldn't extend his punishment to Danny, and I still have obligations for the town celebration that night."

Catching sight of Ryan crossing the street, she abruptly said, "I'll have to call you back about this, Pete. Thanks for letting me know."

She hung up, leaving him sputtering, then hurried to the front window, tapping on it just as Ryan unlocked the apartment door. When he looked up, she waved him inside.

He came two feet inside the door, dropped to his knees to greet Jerome, then finally stood and faced her. "What?"

"We have an appointment with J.D. in a little bit."

He glowered. "I remember."

"Good. I wasn't sure you would, since you didn't remember to tell me that Mr. Harrington wanted to talk to me, and you didn't remember to turn in all that homework you've been doing every night."

Beneath his dark skin, his face flushed a hot red. "So? Homework's stupid. School's stupid."

"And kids who never get an education grow up to be stupid."

"Cole never finished school. Are you saying he's stupid?"

"Not in the least. Cole got an entirely different kind of education." He apparently had an advanced degree from the School of Larceny and Hard Knocks—but what good was it doing him now? "You want to be like Cole when you grow up?"

"Hell, no," he blurted out. Grudgingly, though, he went on. "But there's worse people to be like."

That was certainly true, and she'd dated many of them. She'd kissed more frogs than any female in the gene pool. It was a wonder she didn't have warts.

Sliding her arm around Ryan's shoulders, she drew him to the sitting area at the back of the shop. Jerome followed on their heels and immediately jumped onto the wicker love seat, stretched out, filling it from end to end, and resumed his favorite pastime of snoozing.

"Do you like living with Danny and me?"

He shrugged, pulled away from her, and dropped down hard in the corner of the sofa. "It's okay."

She settled at the opposite end, turning to face him. "We love having you in our family, but, Ryan, they won't let you stay if you don't start behaving and doing better in school. If you fail and talk back and get into fights, they'll think I can't handle you, and they'll place you with someone else. I really don't want that to happen."

He stared at the piece of carpet fringe he was rubbing his shoe across. "It's not like school's a big deal."

"Yes, honey, it is. It's a very big deal. Cole said you're a smart kid. He said you could make A's if you wanted."

"I did it before," he mumbled.

"How about doing it again? Show your teachers and Mr. Harrington and anyone's who giving you a hard time just how smart you are."

"Mr. Harrington's an idiot."

Leanne was pretty sure that agreeing with him was a violation of some parenting rule somewhere, no matter how right he was, so she opted for diplomacy. "He's the vice principal. I think being disliked by the students is part of his job description."

Finally he looked at her, and for the first time—in a while, she realized—he grinned. "He'd be an idiot no matter what he did for a living. It's just the way he is, and you know it. You've got that look in your eyes like you think so, too."

Leaning forward, she grabbed hold of him and dragged him to her end of the sofa, then wrapped her arms around him. Though she was prepared for a struggle, he didn't try to pull away. He didn't lean against her, as Danny always did, or even soften the tiniest bit, but he didn't pull away, and that was something.

"Okay. Swear you'll forget I ever said this, but . . . yeah,

Pete Harrington's an idiot. So's his sister. So are his parents. It runs in their family. *But* . . . Pete isn't the one who matters here. You are. You can't go looking for trouble."

"Why not? That runs in *my* family."

"Is that what the shoving match today was about?"

Immediately he dropped his chin to his chest and stared at his hands. His nails were ragged, as if he'd been biting them, and a callus showed on his middle finger, from clenching a pencil tightly. "Nothing happened."

"So the teacher who separated you and the other boy just imagined the whole thing?"

After a long time, he lifted his feet to the coffee table with a *thud,* then sighed. "No . . . but it wasn't anything. This kid, Kenny, just said somethin' about Cole—they was workin' outside the school—and . . . that's all it was."

This kid, Kenny, in that context, *always* referred to Kenny Howard. He was the only child of the pastor of her church, and was hell-bent on proving that old saying about preachers' kids being the worst *everything.* First and foremost, he was Bethlehem's worst bully. Even J.D., one of the nation's top child psychiatrists before he'd come to Bethlehem, had been known to refer to Kenny as *The Bad Seed* on occasion.

Leanne mimicked his position, placing her feet on the table. "Let me tell you something. When Kenny speaks, *nobody* listens. The kid is a troublemaker with a capital T. I know it's really hard to ignore him when he starts picking on you, but that's what you've got to do with kids like him. If you don't respond, before long, they'll leave you alone."

"Or pick on you even more."

That was true. Years ago, when her brother had become the target of that generation's Kenny, he'd tried the ignoring route, but it hadn't worked. Beating the snot out of the kid, had.

But she couldn't advocate violence. She was *positive* that was against the good-parent rules.

Since she couldn't resolve his problem with Kenny for him, she shifted the subject to another problem she couldn't solve. "What kind of work was Cole doing at the school?"

"They were trimming some bushes and puttin' stuff around them and the trees. Stupid stuff."

"Hey, you helped Miss Agatha and Miss Corinna with their yard work quite a bit this summer. It's honest work." After a moment, she asked, "Did you see him?"

He shook his head.

"Would you like to?"

He opened his mouth to answer, then closed it again and settled for another negative shake.

Leanne pulled his head against her shoulder, then rested her cheek against his hair. "It's okay if you want to, Ryan. He *is* your father"—feeling him stiffen, she corrected herself—"the only father you've ever known, and he's living right across the street. No one would blame you if you wanted to spend a little time with him."

"I don't want to," he said defensively. "Besides, he's not gonna stick around too much longer."

"I don't know about that." She wanted to show a little faith in Cole, but what could she base it on? Gut instinct? Heaven knew, her instincts about the opposite sex were abysmal. Was it her head wanting to believe in Cole, or her traitorous heart?

Ryan showed no such ambivalence. He snorted. "Betcha he's just waitin' for one of his brothers to show up and take him away."

"Why would you think that?"

" 'Cause that's what they do. Whenever one of 'em gets in trouble he can't get out of by himself, he sends a letter to Owen in Pennsylvania, and the first one who checks in with Owen has to go get him."

"But he's been here almost three weeks. Don't you

think someone would have shown up by now if he'd written and asked for help?"

"Nah. Everyone's always busy. It takes a while."

They each checked in with their father, Cole had said. Maybe Ryan was right. Maybe Cole was just waiting for one of them to come around.

Was she a fool for still wanting to believe in him? Probably. But the worst that could happen was he could prove her wrong. And so what if he did?

It wouldn't be the first time, and it surely wouldn't be the last.

With a sigh, she hugged Ryan, then released him. "Why don't you run Jerome outside before we head off to see J.D.?"

He got to his feet, rubbed the dog's shoulder, then said, "Come on, boy, wanna go out?"

Jerome was already dancing in anxious circles at the door when Ryan turned back. He scuffed his foot back and forth before finally looking at her. "Did Cole really say I was smart?"

"Yes, he did."

Though he did his best to hide it, the answer pleased him. With a grunt, he hooked Jerome's leash on his collar and went outside.

A FTER DIMMING THE SPOOK-HOUSE LIGHTS, COLE joined the crowd gathered at the back of the barn Tuesday night to watch the trial run of the dancing skeleton. Dirt was piled around the coffin to make it look half-buried, with the tombstone Leanne had made tilted at a precarious angle at the head.

With a ghostly creak, the coffin lid lifted, then the skeleton rose as if by magic. Hidden between a black sheet and the wall, Murray and Eli worked the monofilament lines like puppeteers, bobbing the creature's head, lifting his arms and legs in a macabre parody of a dance, before slowly lowering him back into the casket, then closing the lid with another creak. It wasn't the least bit scary—though maybe a five-year-old would see it differently—but it was entertaining.

The women applauded before returning to their various jobs. Cole went back to work, too, making the web that would hold the giant lighted spider in the corner of the open doorway. They'd tried using the fake stringy webs that filled every corner of the barn, but the stuff tangled around the spider and even the slightest breeze made it dangle and spin.

Now he was building one out of wire. It would have more substance than a web should, but so what? It was make-believe, like the one-foot-diameter spider that would occupy it.

He was unrolling a length of narrow-gauge wire when the spool slipped from his hand and rolled a few feet away. Before he could secure the end he'd already started and bend over to get it, Leanne picked it up, gave it back, then sat opposite him.

"I told Kelsey the truth."

He carefully bent the wire around one of the spokes that made up the base of the web, then stretched it to the next spoke. "I figured you did, when she walked in here tonight, looking at me like some kind of insect."

"She did not."

"No, she didn't," honesty forced him to admit. Kelsey Grayson had an extraordinary talent for hiding her true feelings toward the scum she worked with. Either that, or she was the most understanding person he'd ever met.

"What did she say?"

"Wouldn't that be easier if the web was standing upright?"

"Yeah, but I only have two hands."

She stood it on end, balancing it in both hands. "They're going to try to find Ryan's parents."

"Don't let them take him away from you."

"How could I stop them? Throw him and Danny in the back of the truck and take off for parts unknown?"

"If that's what it takes, yeah." That was what he would have done if anyone had tried to remove Ryan from his custody. But then, he was used to breaking the law. Besides, in the end, he'd given him up voluntarily.

"She doesn't think they'll have much luck. They don't have much to go on."

"Chances are good his mother, at least, doesn't want to be found."

She nodded at that, then watched as he continued to weave the wire around the web, wrapping it securely around each spoke. When he asked her to steady a particular section, she did. When he asked for pliers or wire cutters, she handed them over. After a while, she finally spoke again. "You know, Ryan's been meeting with J.D. Grayson."

"Yeah. How's that going?"

She shrugged. "Slowly. There's an awful lot he doesn't want to talk about."

Given the kid's background, that was understandable. In his experience, the easiest way to deal with hurt was covering it up and pretending it wasn't there. Smiling when he felt like dying. Hiding behind phony charm. Lying.

But *easy* wasn't good enough for Ryan. He deserved the *best*.

Without giving himself the chance to think better of what he was about to do, he carelessly said, "There's a lot I don't know about Ryan, but if there's anything I can tell him . . ."

She stared at him as if he'd grown a second head. "You would do that?"

He wanted what was best for Ryan, and always had. Clearly she still didn't believe him. The knowledge settled heavily on his shoulders.

He came to the end of the wire, wrapped it off, and clipped it, then measured another length before meeting her gaze. "Yes, I would do that."

"You'll have to actually *answer* questions, you know."

"I answer questions all the time, darlin'."

She made a skeptical noise, then solemnly said, "I'll tell J.D. Thanks." After a moment, she changed the subject again. "Are you dressing up for the party Friday?"

"Oh, yeah, sure. I'll pull out my gray Armani and come as a stockbroker."

The joke didn't amuse her, but that was okay. He wasn't particularly amused by it, either.

"The only thing Halloween's good for is making mischief. I bet when you were a little girl, all you got were the treats."

"And all you did were the tricks."

He grinned. "Bet I had more fun."

"I bet you did. You probably had the biggest collection of masks around. Of course, you used them for professional reasons, too, didn't you?"

"Yes, ma'am. I never had to worry about getting caught with my hand in someone else's pocket when everyone on the street was wearing a mask."

"You still wear more masks than anyone I've known."

He leaned so close the web snagged on his shirt. "No, sweetheart, I don't. You just don't like the me you see."

She shook her head stubbornly. "Sometimes I think, 'Okay, this is the man I knew.' Then you smile, or stop smiling, or blink, or turn around, and you're like an entirely different person. Then I realize I don't know you at all."

Sitting back, he grimly studied her. He wasn't sure

exactly of the reason for it, but he recognized the discomfort in his chest as disappointment. He'd thought . . . he wanted . . .

Hell, hadn't he learned yet that nobody gave a good damn about what he wanted—including himself?

"Does your family know where you are?"

He pricked his thumb on the exposed end of a piece of wire, drawing blood. After watching it well for a moment, he wiped it away on his jeans, checked again, then pressed it hard against the denim to stop the bleeding. While he did that, he watched her.

She was holding the web in one hand, tracing the index finger of her other hand lightly over the wire. Her expression was benign, as if she'd just asked another of her ten million questions. Not as if the question might be significant.

Probably, for her, it wasn't. For him . . . after he'd kissed her Saturday night, he'd gone into the Miller mansion, changed into dry clothes, sat on his bed, and written a letter to his brothers. After bumming an envelope and stamp from Eli, he'd dropped it in the mail on the way to church the next morning. The letter had been short and to the point—*I need a ride. If any of you happen to be in the area, you can find me at the address below.*

They wouldn't bother to write back. That wasn't their way. One day one of them would show up in town, then disappear, and he would disappear with him.

When the bleeding had stopped, he went back to work and answered her question. "I told you, we don't keep in regular touch. Besides, I pleaded guilty, which is a major violation of Owen's rules. If they knew, they would disown me."

"So Owen's laws are more inviolate than the nation's."

He grinned. "In our family, yes, ma'am, they are."

"What about your mother? Does she have any rules regarding her sons?"

"Only one. Once she's birthed 'em, her job is done."

"You're exaggerating."

"Only a little."

"What is she like?"

"Eloise? She has blonde hair and blue eyes. She's a beautiful woman. Put her in a Halston or Chanel suit, with a bauble from Harry Winston around her neck, and you'd never guess she was born dirt-poor." Once more he grinned. "Of course, put me in an Armani suit with a Rolex and diamond cuff links, and you'd never guess I was born poor, either. Granted, I don't *have* the Rolex or the cuff links anymore, since someone saw fit to return them to their rightful owners before he sprang me from jail."

She glanced at Eli, then rotated the web to give him easier access to the section he was working on. "So your mother cleans up good. That doesn't answer my question. What is she *like*?"

It wasn't a subject he'd ever given much thought to. One good thing about the way Owen raised them was that they'd learned not to judge people. To accept most, at least, as they were. They'd always just accepted Eloise without thinking much about her.

"She's . . ." He shrugged. "She's got the face of an angel and lies like the devil. She could sell water to a man stranded in the middle of the ocean or charm a miser out of his last penny. She's the best actress I've ever seen. She can't spend more than a few weeks at a time with Owen, and can't stay away from him for more than a few months . . . barring incarceration. She's great at producing kids and lousy at mothering them. She's . . ." Again he shrugged.

"How long have she and Owen been married?"

"They've been together, more off than on, for about thirty-five years, but they were never married."

That made her look at him, her eyes wide. They were

brown, almost as dark as her hair, and glinted with surprise. Growing up surrounded by blue-eyed blonds, he'd developed a real fondness for brown eyes and brown hair during his short time in Bethlehem last spring.

"They've been together all that time and had six children and never married?"

"They never saw a reason to make it legal. If one of them found someone else, then they would have to go through the hassle of unmaking it." Reaching out, he tapped her chin to close her mouth. "Don't look so appalled. You never married your son's father, either."

"We had *one* son, not *six*. Besides, I would have married him if he'd asked."

That information didn't set well with Cole. She'd told him about Danny's father last spring—they'd dated for months; she'd gotten pregnant; he'd given her the big kiss-off and, for good measure, had moved away. End of story. Somehow she'd omitted the part about wanting to marry him, which suggested she had also loved him. Definitely something he didn't want to know.

So, perversely, he asked her. "Were you in love with him?"

"Yeah. And he broke my heart."

"Want me to beat him up for you?"

She gave him a wry look. "If you go around beating up everyone who's broken my heart, you're gonna be busy. Plus, you're on that list, too. You wanna beat yourself up?"

"I excel at it." He wrapped the last piece of wire around the last spoke, clipped it, then asked, "What do you think?"

His fingers brushed hers as he took it from her. Her gaze flickered and her jaw tightened, then she scooted back on the hay for a better look. "It looks good."

"Now we can stretch the fake stuff across it to give it more substance, then mount the spider right in the middle."

Smiling faintly, she got to her feet. "I'm all in favor of more substance," she murmured before she walked away.

Cole set the web down, then twisted to watch her. She spoke to Nolie, laughed at something Kelsey said, then gathered an armload of ghost-making materials and went to a quiet corner to work. He thought about following her—there was plenty of room for two—and asking what the reason was for her sudden melancholy.

He didn't, though. He still had this project to finish. He'd spent more than enough time alone with her in the past week. He was getting too involved with her—again, and look how badly it had ended last time.

And the most important reason—if he asked her why she'd gotten so blue, she just might tell him.

And he couldn't bear any more guilt.

A PUMPKIN WITH TOOTHPICKS FOR ARMS AND LEGS. That was how Melissa had threatened to dress up for the Halloween celebration. Alex had laughed and told her she was beautiful. As she studied herself in the mirror, rubbing the mild ache in her lower back, she smiled smugly. He would *really* laugh now.

She wore a shapeless orange outfit—she didn't even know what to call it. Sort of a dress with leg holes that hit about midthigh. Underneath it she had on a green turtleneck sweater and green tights, with brown suede Mary Janes on her feet and, on her head, the finishing piece—an orange cap with a brown stalk trailing a piece of leafy green vine in the center.

Alex, of course, wasn't dressing up for Halloween. Few of the men did, although they could always count on Harry, and in the last few years J.D. had gotten in the habit of donning a costume. It was probably easier than saying no to all his kids. In a few years, she fully intended to help Junior badger his father into the same surrender.

"Melissa? Are you read—" From the bedroom door came a great burst of laughter.

She turned to face him, still wearing that smug smile. "How do I look?"

"Wonderful." He gently poked at her stomach, pretended not to hear the rustling of the foam she'd used, and grinned. "And you don't even need padding."

She stuck her tongue out at him. "The prize for the best adult costume this year is a half-dozen of Miss Corinna's triple-dipped chocolate-and-caramel apples rolled in peanuts and pecans. Watch it, 'cause if I win, I might not want to share with anyone who insults me."

He immediately pulled a straight face. "Oh, honey, I'd wondered where every single pillow in the house had gone. Now I know." He nuzzled her neck, then stepped back so she could leave the room ahead of him. "Are you going to be warm enough in that?"

"I'm counting on you and the bonfire to keep me warm." Holding on to the railing, she made her way downstairs and started to turn toward the kitchen, but he stopped her. "I've already loaded the food into the car, along with a folding chair for you and a quilt in case you get cold. I just need to get the apples. Wait here."

As he went down the hall toward the kitchen, she went to the closet, reaching automatically for her very warm, slim-fitting black cashmere coat. With a regretful sigh, she took the very loose-fitting wool swing coat out instead. The cashmere didn't even come near covering her belly, and it wasn't fair to Junior to keep herself warm while letting him freeze, though he did have all that padding of both Mom and foam.

She was struggling into the coat when a sharp pain

sliced through her, making her breath catch. She clutched the closet door with one hand, while pressing the other to the side of her stomach, massaging firmly. Taking slow, measured breaths, she focused her whole being on easing the pain. *It's all right, it's all right.* That had become her mantra to get through these episodes in the past week. They'd been occurring at odd times, but they weren't severe and they never lasted long. When she'd called her doctor, he'd told her not to worry. Backaches and cramps weren't unusual in the last trimester. As long as there was no spotting or discharge, she shouldn't worry.

When she heard Alex's footsteps in the hallway, she gritted her teeth and straightened. She didn't want him to know she'd had another pain. *She* knew how to handle worry—God knew, she'd been through enough of it. *He* didn't handle it so well.

By the time he reached her, she was pretty sure she looked as if nothing more important than getting her other arm into her sleeve was going on. "I could use a little help here," she said, fumbling behind her.

With a chuckle, he held the sleeve, then guided her arm into it. She straightened the coat, then faced him. "Thank you, kind sir. How do I look?"

"With a little whipped cream and a sprinkling of cinnamon, good enough to eat."

"Do my shoes match?"

"Yes, ma'am."

She gazed down with a mock woeful expression. "Do you suppose I'll ever see my feet again?"

"One of these days, honey," he said, sliding his arm around her and ushering her out the door. "One day soon."

Chapter Eleven

PEOPLE WERE STARTING TO ARRIVE FOR THE PARTY when Leanne made her last check of the grounds. All the tables were set up and covered with orange-and-black cloths. The galvanized tubs were filled with water and apples for bobbing, and the few other games were in place. A small stage had been erected for the costume contest that would take place later in the evening, and the wood was laid for the bonfire. Her parents were bringing Danny and Ryan with them, so all that was left for her, was to get dressed.

She got the garment bag from the back of her SUV and ducked inside the haunted house. It wasn't officially open yet, while the final touches were being made, and a corner of it had been turned into a dressing room for the humans who were part of the scenery. She waved at Nolie, dressed all in black, her red hair covered by a stringy black wig, her naturally pale skin turned deathly white, and her smile enhanced with the addition of fangs, before she ducked behind the curtain.

She'd gotten her costume from her cousin, Hailey, whose handmade costumes had become a profitable sideline to her quilting business. Leanne hadn't even had time to peek into the bag since she'd picked it up that afternoon. She'd asked for something beautiful—to be more accurate, for something that would make *her* beautiful. Hailey had assured her the costume was perfect, that the size wasn't a problem, since they wore the same size, and that she needed to wear her hair up and a pair of white tights.

She hung the garment bag on a nail in the wall, then unzipped it. Fabric spilled out, frothy layers of lace and satin and tulle. Her mouth forming an O, she pushed the garment bag behind the dress, then stared.

It was a princess-going-to-the-ball gown, with a pale blue fitted bodice, white sleeves that puffed on the upper arm, then fitted closely all the way to the wrist, and a skirt of sheer white, silver, and ice blue layered one atop the other. It was incredible.

Behind the dress was a cloak in the same colors, trimmed with fur, and in the bottom of the bag Hailey had included a pair of clear vinyl heels and—Leanne didn't know whether to laugh or clap her hands with delight— her very own tiara.

She stripped down to her tights, carefully stepped into the dress, then got the zipper halfway up before peeking through the curtains. "Hey, Vampira," she called. "Can you give me a hand?"

Baring her fangs, Nolie made her way through the maze, stepped behind the curtain, and gave a sharp whistle. "Oh, my gosh, you look beautiful!"

Leanne preened, wishing for a mirror to see for herself. "Can you believe this outfit? I just asked Hailey to pick out something pretty for me. I never dreamed . . ."

"Wait till Prince Charming gets a look at you. He'll be struck dumb." Nolie zipped her up, adjusted the puffy sleeves, then picked up the tiara, to position it on Leanne's hair. When she finished, she stepped back and sighed. "Oh, honey, you're beautiful. But I've got a suggestion. How about next year, *you* be the vampire and let *me* be the fairy-tale princess?"

"My brother already thinks you're the most beautiful princess of them all."

"Yeah, he does, doesn't he?" Nolie's smile was serene in spite of the fangs. "Put the cloak on. You don't want Cole to catch a glimpse of you when you're not ready to dazzle him."

Leanne let her sister-in-law help her with the cloak, grateful for its warmth, then faced her. "Nolie . . . do you think I'm crazy for wanting to dazzle him after everything he's done?"

Of course, she already knew the answer to that. She had passed crazy and was somewhere between reckless and lunacy, and until her sanity chose to return, there wasn't anything she could do about it. At that very moment, there wasn't anything she *wanted* to do about it. Later, though . . . that would be a different story. That would be the time for regrets.

Instead of answering right away, Nolie picked up the jeans Leanne had discarded, folded them, and draped them over the dress's hanger, then slid her sweater over it. "I think there's nothing particularly rational or sane about falling in love, for anyone. Look at Chase and me. What were the odds that a hotshot, big-city lawyer would ever fall for a plump, Arkansas farm girl? But it happened. We fell in love anyway."

"But did he break your heart along the way?" Leanne asked gloomily, thinking back to that awful May day when she'd discovered Cole hadn't just slipped out of bed early to get to work, but had slipped out of town—for good.

"Just once. But the important thing isn't what he did,

but what he does now, what he'll do in the future. The *really* important thing is having faith."

Leanne's voice dropped to a whisper. "I doubt anyone's ever had faith in Cole, not when it mattered." And she didn't know if she had the trust or fortitude to be the first.

Just as she doubted whether she had the sense or fortitude to not get involved with him again.

"Probably not."

She had trusted Cole—the whole town had—before he'd disappeared, but that had been easy. They hadn't known who he was or what he was capable of. The trick was trusting someone when you did know.

"Come on." Nolie swept back the curtain so Leanne could pass through. "They're about to light the bonfire. Let's go find our respective Prince Charmings and let them marvel over us."

Chase was right outside the barn with five-year-old Micahlyn, dressed as a ballerina, on his shoulders. He greeted his wife, kissed Leanne's cheek, and told her she looked beautiful, for a kid sister. She talked with them a few minutes, her gaze constantly scanning the crowd for one face in particular.

She didn't find him.

The fire department oversaw the lighting of the bonfire, officially kicking off the celebration. Holding her cloak together from the inside, Leanne strolled the grounds, greeting friends, searching unsuccessfully for Cole.

She did locate her parents. Her father was dressed in a Star Trek outfit, complete with pointy ears. Her mother, naturally, wore woolen pants, a sweater, a jacket, and gloves, and seemed embarrassed to stand next to Earl.

"Princess!" Her father embraced her, then straightened the tiara he'd knocked askew. "Haven't I always said my girl was a princess?" he asked of no one in particular. "This just proves it. You're by far the prettiest girl here."

"Thanks, Daddy. Where are the boys?"

"Ryan went off with his friends, and Danny's right over there."

She looked to the nearest booth, where her superhero-du-jour son was throwing darts at—and missing—a board full of balloons. Looking up, he grinned and waved, then caught his lower lip between his teeth and took careful aim again. No one looked more surprised than he when the balloon popped—probably because he had aimed for one at the opposite corner.

Finally Leanne couldn't avoid speaking to Phyllis any longer. Facing her, she opened the cloak wide. "Hello, Mother. Do you like my costume?"

Phyllis's gaze was, as usual, as cold as the night. "That's Hailey's work, isn't it? It's lovely. Of course, it's too . . . young for you."

"Too young?" Leanne repeated.

"You're a thirty-three-year-old single mother. Not a princess, no matter what anyone says."

Earl swore, making her mother cringe—the primary reason, Leanne had realized long ago, he did so. "Princesses stay princesses right up until they die—unless they become queens. So, honey, if you want to be a princess forever, you go right ahead and be one."

"Thanks, Daddy. I'll see you guys later." Raising her right hand, she formed a V with the two little fingers pressed together on one side, the other two fingers on the other. "Live long and prosper."

Her father's booming laughter followed her as she walked away. So did Phyllis's sharp, "Honestly, Earl!"

She covered the grounds, finding no sign of Cole, then wandered over to the bonfire. The flames leaped into the air, yellow and red, as the wood popped, crackled, and hissed. The heat it put out was incredible, warming her front to a feverish level, but leaving her backside chilled in spite of the cloak. She was in the process of turning her back to the flames, to even the temperatures, when her gaze fell on a lone figure, leaning against a tree and watching her from the edge of the woods near the back of the barn.

Cole.

Would he come to her if she stayed where she was? Probably not. Was she smart enough to keep her distance? The answer became painfully clear as she strolled across the ground to him, careful in the heels, coming to a stop a few yards in front of him. "You didn't dress up."

He wore snug jeans, faded and soft enough to cling, with a dark T-shirt and a black leather jacket. His boots were black, too, one of them planted in the dirt, the other resting against the tree trunk.

"Sure, I did."

"As what?"

"A thug? A punk?"

"A bad boy?" She smiled. "Women can't resist a bad boy, you know."

"The women around here seem to be doing a fine job of it," he responded dryly.

It seemed safer at the moment to not respond to his comment.

"You look beautiful." He reached out and hooked his finger in the fur at the neck of the cloak. "Are you wearing anything under that?"

As she'd done for her mother, she opened the cloak wide, then slipped it off her shoulders and did a slow twirl for him. When he saw the back of the gown—see-through from her shoulders to her hips—she thought she heard a faint choking sound, and when she faced him again, he looked almost as if he was in pain.

"You like?"

"Oh, yeah. Now put that thing back on before someone else sees you."

"I thought I'd leave it off for a bit—to cool down, you know."

He took the cloak from her arm, swung it around her shoulders, then gathered the edges together in front. "You cool down any more, and I'm gonna go up in flames."

She moved to stand beside him and looked out across the grounds. "Everything seems to be a big success."

"I imagine everything this town does is a big success."

She acknowledged that with a shrug. Folks in Bethlehem loved a party, so of course they were good at throwing one. "Why don't you come on out and join the fun?"

He glanced at all the people, with something in his eyes—wistfulness, perhaps—then shook his head. "I'm fine right where I am. But don't feel you have to keep me company."

Instead of taking him at his word and leaving, she hugged her cloak tighter. "Eli made you come, didn't he?"

"The word 'no' exists in his vocabulary only when *he's* the one saying it."

"Just because you're here against your will doesn't mean you can't have a good time. At least come out to the fire and get warm. You must be freezing." *She* certainly was.

His gaze skimmed over her, from head to toe and back again, and suddenly she wasn't the least bit cold anymore. "I'm wearing more clothes than you are. Though if you're really concerned about me freezing, you could raise my temperature by nothing more than coming a little closer."

Don't do it, don't do it, don't—The voice in her head was silenced by her first step toward him. How close would he let her come? After all, his back was against the tree, so he couldn't easily retreat.

She took another step, and another, and her full skirts brushed his legs. One more, and the fabric was crushed between them.

He swallowed convulsively. "This really isn't a good idea."

"What?"

"This."

"Sharing our warmth on a cold night?"

"Letting me kiss you."

"You haven't kissed me."

"But I'm going to if you don't . . ."

She gazed up at him. There was a look in his eyes she knew well—desire. Hunger. And a look she didn't know at all. Panic? Fear? Was he afraid of kissing her? Afraid of wanting her? Afraid she wouldn't want him? Or afraid she would?

"Leanne," he warned.

"I don't think you'll kiss me. Not here. Not now. Not—"

He proved her wrong. Cupping her face in his palms, he bent his head to hers, claimed her mouth with his. He thrust his tongue inside her mouth, stroking, tasting, then slid his hands lower, down her throat and inside the cloak, across her waist, to her hips, then her bottom. He lifted her to him, rubbing his erection hard against her, all the while stealing the breath and the logic and the reason right out of her.

There was nothing rational or sane about falling in love, Nolie had said, and Leanne was living, breathing, aching proof of it. If she was rational, she would run, screaming, the other way. If she was sane, she would put a stop, once and for all, to the kisses, the conversations, the temptation.

She couldn't say who ended the kiss. Her lungs were aching for breath, her body just aching. His eyes were huge, intense, and dazed. Her heart thudded loudly in her ears, and his breathing was raw and ragged.

Under the cloak, he still held her against him, and was still hard and hot, straining against her. In spite of that, he said, "I don't want this."

"The gospel according to Owen Jackson. *Lie like the devil,*" she murmured recklessly, as she deliberately rocked her hips.

He responded with a nerve-clenching shudder, then tried again. "*You* don't want this."

In the bigger sense—life, the future, the well-being of her heart—he was probably right. But it was hard to consider the bigger sense when he'd lifted his hand to her breast and was gently teasing her nipple through the dress fabric: tiny little pinches, tender caresses that ricocheted all the way through her before settling between her thighs. It was hard to think about life and the future when she'd been alone so long, when she'd missed him so much.

As for the well-being of her heart . . . if four broken hearts hadn't killed her, what were the odds number five would?

She was crazy. Flirting with danger. Her own worst enemy. Good sense had deserted her, and she proved it with her next words. "Come home with me."

"I—I can't."

"Then come behind the barn with me."

He looked scandalized . . . and tempted. "We could get caught."

"We could get caught right here, but that hasn't stopped you from playing with my breast. It won't stop me from . . ." Letting her voice trail off, she slid her hand down his front, over the waistband of his jeans, to the bulge that pulled the denim taut. Choking out a groan, he removed her hand and held it firmly at her side. When she reached out her other hand, he caught it in a similar fashion, then stared down at her.

"You don't know what you're doing."

"Of course I know. I may be dressed as a princess, but I'm the queen of bad choices and lousy decisions. Having sex with you wouldn't be my first mistake. It wouldn't even be my first mistake with you. But at least this time I *know* not to expect anything else."

As he stared at her, bleakness shadowed his eyes. He pushed her a few feet away, then let go and spun off. Startled, she grabbed his arm. "Hey! Where are you going?"

"What? You have more to say? Think of a few other insults? Let me save you the hassle. Liar, thief, cheat, scum, crook, embezzler, lowlife. How about bastard—literally and figuratively? That'll get you two insults in one."

"I wasn't insulting you!" she protested. "I just—"

"Lousy choices? Bad decisions? Having sex? Mistakes? You don't call those insults?"

"I was talking about *me.* I make lousy choices—"

He leaned close to her, barely whispering his reply. "And I *am* the lousy choice. The bad decision. The mistake."

Clutching the cloak tighter, she looked unhappily at him. "I didn't mean—"

"Yes. You did."

He pulled loose and backed away. When he would have turned into the darkness behind the barn, she hastily spoke. "What about my wanting to have sex with you, Cole? Do you consider that an insult, too?"

The cold stares her mother usually treated her to had nothing on the ice in his derisive gaze. "No. I consider that not likely to happen. Not in this lifetime."

With that, he left her.

• • •

HANDS SHOVED INTO HIS POCKETS, COLE CUT BE-
hind the barn to the road, clogged on both sides with
parked cars. He didn't know where he was going—to the
Miller house, probably, though if he didn't make the right
turns, who knew? He could be halfway to Howland before
this angry energy burned off.

Damn it, he didn't care what Leanne thought. He'd
never cared what *any* woman thought. From his mother
on, women had never been more than a temporary part of
his life. His father and his brothers—they stuck around, but
women didn't. They used and forgot the females they came
across, because it was easier than being the one used and
forgotten.

But hearing her say that he was a lousy choice, a bad decision, a mistake . . . if he didn't know better—and, by
God, he *did*—he would think her words had hurt. He
would think she had the sort of power over him no one
else had ever had—not his father, not his mother, not his
brothers.

But he did know better. He wasn't hurt. He was pissed
that she'd seen through the act he'd put on just for her. He
was pissed that she'd seen the real him when no one else
ever had.

Because truth was, he *was* a lousy choice for any woman
to make. Getting involved with him *had* been a bad decision, and having sex with him *had* been a mistake. But only
he was supposed to recognize that so clearly.

He was halfway to the parking lot, the sounds of the
party fading into the distance, when a closer noise slowed
his steps. It came from his left, soft, like a moan or a—

A whimper. Narrowing his gaze, he turned in that direction, looking between the cars parked there. It was

probably a couple of teenagers making out, or younger kids cooking up trouble. But when the sound came again, he recognized the pain in it. It was followed by a gasp, then sharp, heavy breathing and a whispered, "Oh, my God."

Finally he saw the person, standing between two cars, bent nearly double. Even in the dark, there was no mistaking her for a man. The legs extending beneath the costume were too shapely by far.

He took an uneasy step toward her. "Are you okay?"

She raised her head, but seemed unable to straighten. Reaching one pale hand toward him, she whimpered again. "Oh, God, please . . . help me."

It was Melissa Thomas, his lawyer's wife. He recognized her from their one meeting last spring, and from the courtroom when he'd been sentenced. Her face was ghostly pale, dotted with sweat, and even in the shadows, he could see her grass-green tights were stained with—

Jesus, she was pregnant.

And something was wrong.

He bolted to her side and helped her to the ground. Jerking his jacket off, he spread it over her, then said, "I'll get help. I'll be right back."

"Please . . . hurry," she panted.

The last time he'd run all-out, there had been a cop ten yards behind him, gun in hand. Luckily, Cole had been younger, lighter, and faster, and he'd lost the guy on a busy Atlanta street. He covered the distance between the cars and the party at that speed and then some, skidding to a stop in front of the barn and collaring J.D. Grayson. "You gotta come with me! She needs a doctor."

"Who needs—Wait—" Grayson handed his little girl to the teenage boy beside him before Cole dragged him away. "Who needs help?" he asked as they jogged back down the road.

"Melissa Thomas. I think she's having the baby."

"Oh, God, no."

She was easier to find this time. They could hear her weeping a half-dozen cars away. When they reached her, Grayson dug in the pocket of his pants, then tossed a set of keys to Cole. "That truck over there is mine. Back it down here, then lower the tailgate. Melissa, it's J.D. Talk to me, honey. Tell me what's happening."

Cole didn't hear her response as he trotted to the SUV, climbed in, and revved the engine. Having a baby wasn't that big a deal—if it were, Eloise never would have done it twice, much less six times. But Grayson's response—*Oh, God, no*—and the tone of his voice meant this was bad. Maybe the baby was premature, or there was some problem with her pregnancy. He'd heard something about her last spring, about not being able to have kids, but he couldn't remember. He'd never wanted to remember things that might make him sympathetic toward his marks.

He backed up to where Grayson and Melissa waited, then jumped out, opened the back window, lowered the tailgate, and shoved a bunch of gym bags and soccer balls aside. By the time he was finished, Grayson was standing there, Melissa in his arms. "Drive us around to the ER, then come back and find Alex," he directed as he gently lowered her into the cargo area, then climbed in beside her.

According to the truck's clock, it didn't take even two minutes to circle the hospital to the emergency-room entrance, but it seemed a damned long two minutes. Grayson snapped orders to a nurse taking a smoke break outside the door, and a minute later a whole group of staff descended on them with a gurney. After they were inside, Cole pulled away from the entrance, drove to the end of the parking lot, and stopped.

This was his chance. No waiting for his brothers to get his message, then come spring him. He could make a U-turn, head out of the parking lot and out of town. By the time anyone realized he was gone, he would have such a jump on them, that their chances of finding him would be somewhere between slim and none.

He wouldn't even have to worry about Grayson reporting the vehicle stolen for a while, since he had his hands full at the moment. He could drive to Howland, switch tags with a similar SUV, then head for Pennsylvania—or, better, Tennessee. Leanne and Ryan would expect him to go to his father's, but they would never think he would run to Eloise instead.

But when he moved his foot from the brake to the gas, he didn't cut the wheels in a sharp turn. He eased over the bump into the dirt road, drove to the end nearest the barn, and parked there. He found the boy who'd been with Grayson—his third son, Jacob—still in front of the barn, still holding the girl. "Here's your dad's keys. Have you seen Alex Thomas?"

"Yeah, he's right over—"

Seeing the man, Cole headed that way. Thomas was standing with a half-dozen other men, every damn one of them victim of Cole's, and they were talking sports. He didn't wait to be acknowledged, but butted right in. "Grayson just took your wife to the ER. He wants you over there now."

Thomas's eyes widened, and he glanced in the direction where he'd apparently last seen Melissa. A lawn chair sat crookedly, with a quilt draped over it. The cup of hot cider he held, slipped from his hand, splattering to the ground, then, without a word, he raced off toward the hospital.

And without a word, Cole turned and walked away.

This time he made it home, not that he'd ever had a real home. He'd never belonged anywhere.

And Bethlehem wasn't going to change that.

I T WAS TWO HUNDRED EIGHTY-FOUR STEPS FROM THE labor and delivery waiting room to the door of Melissa's room. Alex knew because he'd paced them off about a hundred times while waiting to see her. Many of their friends had come to the waiting room after leaving the party, but he couldn't bear to sit at the moment—couldn't bear the sympathetic looks.

Couldn't bear knowing that after coming so far, he and Melissa might lose this baby, too.

The hospital had paged Dr. Gregory, who'd arrived at the ER, dressed in a clown suit, right behind Alex. Alex had seen him only once since then, when he'd stepped into the hall, to give him an update.

He hadn't seen his wife at all.

J.D. fell into step with him. "She's getting good care."

"I know."

"And everyone's praying for her."

He knew that, too, and he did believe in the power of prayer, in miracles and all those divine mysteries. How else to explain that they were *this* close to holding their baby in their arms? He'd been praying, too—formless, soundless prayers. *Please, God, please, please, please.* It was the best he could manage.

"What are they doing?" he asked as they reached Melissa's door, then turned and started back. Dr. Gregory had told him, but he hadn't heard the words. Alex had been too caught up in the grim expression the doctor wore and his inability to promise that Melissa and the baby would be perfectly fine.

"When she first came in, they started an IV and drew blood for some lab work," J.D. said quietly, his voice soothing as a psychiatrist's voice should be. "They put her on a fetal monitor, to check the baby's heart rate and to measure any contractions, and did a pelvic exam to determine whether the cervix is dilated and, if so, how much. When they took her out a while ago, they went to X ray for a pelvimetry study. That gives them the baby's position and also the size of Melissa's pelvis, to make sure she can deliver the baby."

Alex hadn't seen them taking her out of the room for the trip to X ray, and he'd been at the far end of the hall when they'd wheeled her out of the elevator and back into the room. By the time he'd raced down there, the door was already closed in his face. All he'd seen was hospital staff, and the faintest glimpse of Melissa's dark hair. "What now?"

"They're checking to see if the discharge she's having is amniotic fluid. If it is, they'll have to deliver the baby within twenty-four hours. If the sac is leaking and fluid can get out, then germs can get in, so it's safer for both Melissa and the baby."

"*Safer?* She's only seven and a half months pregnant! Having the baby six weeks early isn't safe for either of them!"

"I know. But it's safer than trying to delay, if the baby has been compromised." J.D. laid his hand on Alex's shoulder. "Is there someone I can call for you? Your Uncle Herb?"

"He's in Hawaii." After retiring and turning his law practice over to Alex, his uncle had thrown himself whole-heartedly into pursuing his other passion in life—flowers in general, orchids in particular. Wherever they grew profusely, he followed.

"What about your parents?"

Alex's smile felt like a fraud. His father was dead, and he got along well enough with his mother, when he saw her, which wasn't often since she'd remarried. Her new husband and his family came first with her now, and he understood that. His kids lived right there in the same town, and his grandkids called her grandma. They needed her more than Alex did, and she really needed to be needed. "I'll call my mother tomorrow, once we know . . ." *Something. Anything* would be better than knowing nothing.

But immediately he discounted that. If the news was bad, he could go on not knowing, indefinitely.

"What about Melissa's family?"

"I called her sister about an hour ago. Their parents will be down in the morning." Alex dragged his hand through his hair. "I *hate* this!"

"I know."

The sympathetic words tore at his raw nerves, making him scowl at J.D. "Stop saying that. You can't know unless you've been through it your—"

Abruptly remembering, he broke off and turned away. Maybe J.D. hadn't ever had to stand by helplessly while doctors fought to save his child's life . . . but he'd had to watch, knowing there was nothing they could do to save his first wife's life. Worse, though the accident that killed her hadn't been his fault, he *had* been driving drunk, and as a consequence, he'd lost custody of their only child. Trey was once more a part of his family, but for a long time they'd had no contact with each other, and Trey hadn't wanted any.

"I'm sorry," Alex murmured.

"Don't be. You're entitled."

As they reached the waiting-room door again, Alex sighed. "I just need to see her. I just need to know—"

"Alex."

He reeled to face Dr. Gregory. If the doctor's expression had been grim before, it was downright morbid now. "We're preparing Melissa for a C-section. The monitor's showing abnormal changes in the infant's heart rate with the uterine contractions. We can't wait to see what happens. I'm on my way to call a neonatologist at the University of Rochester Medical Center, to arrange for a medevac. You can see her for a few minutes before we take her to the OR."

Feeling a rush—of relief or panic?—Alex got halfway down the hall before turning back. "What do you mean—a medevac?"

But Dr. Gregory was already gone.

"J.D.?"

"At seven and a half months, his birth weight's going to be low, probably around three pounds. Plus, the respiratory system isn't as well developed as we'd like. He may be just fine, but if he's not, we don't have the equipment or the skills to take care of him. The Rochester Neonatal ICU can handle anything."

Wonderful. His wife would be in the hospital here in Bethlehem and their child would be hours away in Rochester.

As long as his wife and child *were,* he would be grateful.

He pushed open the door and went into Melissa's room. She looked so small in the bed, with an IV in her arm and wires connecting her to the monitor beside the bed. Her face was pale, her eyes red from crying. When she looked up and saw him, she didn't say a word, but burst into tears again.

Sitting on the edge of the bed, he gathered her close. "It's okay, honey. Everything's going to be okay."

"They're going to do a caesarian!"

"I know."

"I don't want my baby born on Halloween! I want to go home, Alex, please just take me home!"

He brushed her hair back and dredged up a grin from somewhere. "Junior's anxious to get out of there. You think if I take you home, he's just going to settle down and wait patiently until it's time?"

For a moment her lip trembled as if she might smile— or cry—then she clasped his hand. "I'm so sorry," she whispered. "I shouldn't have gone to the party tonight; I shouldn't have gone shopping and to lunch, I should have stayed home with my feet propped up!"

"Honey, going to the party or shopping or to lunch didn't cause this."

"But I bought baby things! I knew better, but I did it anyway, because I thought this time would be different! I thought this time surely—"

The tears started again, so he held her close. The first time she'd gotten pregnant, they'd celebrated by buying everything a baby could possibly need or want. Then, when she miscarried, she hadn't even been able to walk into the spare room they'd designated for a nursery, so it had been left to him to pack up all the baby things and get rid of them.

It was the hardest thing he'd ever done. Please, God, he couldn't do it again.

But this time *had* been different. So the baby was premature. Premature babies were born every day and survived, a lot of them much younger and tinier than Junior. Three pounds wasn't much, but if one-pound infants could make it, then a three-pounder's chances must be that much better.

"Hi, Melissa, Alex," a soft voice greeted. It was Betty Walker, Mitch Walker's sister-in-law and a nurse at the hospital. "Honey, we've got to take you downstairs to the OR now, okay? Alex, there's a waiting room down there on Two where you and the others can wait."

"Okay." He hugged Melissa one last time, then tenderly kissed her. "I love you."

"I love you, too."

Standing back, he watched forlornly as Betty and another nurse wheeled the bed, and his wife, out the door. The door swung shut, leaving him alone in the cold, empty room.

Forget the waiting room. There was a chapel on the second floor, too. That was where he needed to wait. Needed to pray.

Chapter Twelve

POOR MELISSA AND ALEX," SOPHY SAID WITH A heartfelt sigh as Dr. Gregory handed the baby to the waiting nurse.

Gloria turned an astonished look her way. "Why are you feeling sorry for them? They've waited forever for this baby, and now he's here."

"They waited forever for *a* baby. Not this one. They weren't counting on this one." Sophy gestured. "Look at the doctor's face. He knows."

The neonatologist who had come in on the helicopter from Rochester laid the baby tenderly in the transport incubator, and he and his nurse cleaned the infant, suctioned his lungs, and adjusted all the whistles and bells for the journey back to Rochester. There was concern on the doctor's face, and a growing sadness on the nurse's as they took note of what Sophy and Gloria already knew.

"Oh, but isn't he beautiful?" Gloria said with her own heartfelt sigh.

"You think all babies are beautiful."

"They are. Especially this one. Look at that sweet little face and that dusting of hair. It's going to be dark like his father's."

"And his mother's," Sophy felt obliged to point out on Melissa's behalf. The poor woman, fully anesthetized as soon as the baby was delivered, was being stitched back together, but even an excellent doctor like Dr. Gregory wouldn't be able to stitch her heart back together good as new.

Gloria was still marveling over the child. "Look how tiny he is, but so perfectly formed. Oh, babies are such precious gifts."

Usually that was true. Too often those precious gifts were given to someone who couldn't care less, but most babies were welcomed, treasured, and loved. Still, Sophy couldn't help thinking how unfair it was, after all their heartache, that Alex and Melissa were given *this* baby. They deserved perfection.

"He *is* perfect." Eli popped in beside her an instant after murmuring the words in her ear.

She looked sharply at him, then moved to put some distance between them. He didn't seem to notice, but lounged comfortably where she'd been standing.

"No one asked your opinion," she said bluntly.

"It's not my opinion. It's God's truth. What kind of guardian are you that you can look at that helpless, innocent child and find him unworthy of the parents he's been given?"

"I didn't say he was unworthy—"

"You said they deserved better."

"I said they deserved perfection."

"Implying that this child isn't."

Scowling, Sophy watched as the neonatologist and nurse prepared to leave. Within minutes, they would be back on the helicopter and in the air. Soon after, Alex would be off, too, hurrying through the night to his tiny newborn son, never guessing the heartbreak that awaited him.

"You really need to do something about that attitude," Eli said, giving her a sour look that made her face flame with heat.

Feeling a ridiculous urge to cry, she folded her arms over her chest. "I can't believe this—*you* giving me advice about attitude, when you have the worst attitude of any guardian I've ever known. You are so—"

"If you call me arrogant one more time, I'll clip your wings," he taunted, then added, "Metaphorically speaking."

"You—you—oh!" In an instant, she moved from the operating room to her most favorite place in all of Bethlehem, the very top of the First Church. Not on the roof—that wasn't high enough—but on the small steep roof covering the cupola that housed the church bell.

There, with the night all about her, the vast darkness like black velvet, pricked by millions of tiny stars, and the quiet seeping through her, she felt the peace she craved.

Pricked by guilt, shame, and especially disappointment.

Gloria was right—the Thomases' baby was beautiful. And—oh, how she hated admitting this!—but Eli was right, too. He was perfect, and he deserved the best parents any child could ask for. He'd gotten them, too.

She hoped.

But she'd had other hopes that were hard to let go. Hopes that every dream Alex and Melissa had ever dreamed would come true. That after so much trying, they would succeed beyond their wildest imaginings. That this child could be the fulfillment of every hope that lived within them.

That was impossible now.

"God doesn't give anyone more than they can handle."

With an extraordinarily loud groan, she rolled her eyes

heavenward. "Why me, Lord? *I* didn't poison Nolie. Why do *I* have to put up with him?"

"You may as well come down," Eli said from his spot on the roof. He wasn't sitting at the peak, as she and Gloria often did, but had stretched out on the slope, hands under his head, gazing into the heavens. He looked so relaxed.

She felt anything but.

"If you don't come down, I'll have to come up there, and it would be close quarters for the two of us."

She slid off the cupola roof onto the building roof, then grudgingly sat down. "There is no *two of us*," she muttered.

"But you'd like there to be, wouldn't you?"

In an instant, she was ready to explode, but by sheer will she contained herself. He was like a bully, she counseled herself, and, as Leanne had told Ryan, the best way to deal with a bully was to ignore him. If she ignored Eli, soon he would get bored and go off elsewhere to seek attention. The sooner, the better.

He rolled onto his side, then sat up, facing her. He was wearing that insufferable grin again. "I'm not so easy to ignore, Soph."

She ground her teeth. Clenched her fists. Breathed deeply and counted stars.

"Soph?" He moved closer, so his pretty face blocked her field of vision, but she merely gritted her teeth even harder and turned her head the other way. There were millions of stars. Surely by the time she finished counting the first hundred thousand, he would be gone.

"So-oph?" he singsonged.

Still she ignored him.

"You know, I can't resist a challenge," he said as pleasantly as if they were carrying on a friendly conversation. "Let's see . . . what would make you pay attention to me? I could stand on my head. Or dance a little jig. Or . . . hey, how about? . . ."

Moving so swiftly she had no time to guess what he was up to, he leaned forward, brushed his mouth against hers, and murmured, "Try ignoring *this,* Soph."

Then he kissed her. *Kissed* her! Never in all of ever had anyone possessed such audacity. . . .

And never in all of ever had she imagined that it could feel so good.

He drew back, and after a moment, she opened her eyes, half-afraid he would be gone, more afraid he wouldn't. He wasn't. He sat there, still leaning toward her, and all the arrogance was gone from his face. His expression was soft, sort of surprised, and his gaze was intense. He'd kissed *her,* but he'd stunned *himself* into silence.

And she liked that a lot.

Even better, she decided, than the kiss.

OKAY, SO HALLOWEEN HAD BEEN A BUST. OH, THE town party had been great—at least, for most people—and Rourke's party at the Starlite had been fun—for most people—but all in all, to borrow a phrase from the boys, for Leanne the holiday had sucked. She'd been all dressed up like a fairy-tale princess, but there'd been no Prince Charming for her, and certainly no happily-ever-after.

It was for the best, she told herself as she moped around the shop Saturday afternoon. After all, Cole Jackson was no one's idea of a Prince Charming, and he sure wasn't the path to happily-ever-after.

She was in the middle of trading Halloween decorations for Thanksgiving when a customer came in. Grateful for the distraction, she summoned up a semblance of a smile, laid the soft-sculpture witch and the black cat aside, and approached the older woman. "Hi, can I help you?"

"I imagine so. That's what we're both in the business of doing, isn't it?"

"I suppose," Leanne replied, trying to remember where she'd seen the older woman before. The unruly hair was familiar, as well as the ugly but comfortable-looking shoes . . . shoes that she'd last seen peeking out of the hem of a long black robe. "You're the judge who sentenced Cole Jackson. Judge . . ."

"Gloria." The woman gave her a delighted-you-remembered smile. "And how is Jack?"

"Cole."

"Cole what?"

"Cole Jackson. That's his name. Not Jack."

Gloria waved one hand in the air. " 'What's in a name . . .' and all that. How is the boy?"

For starters, he was no boy and, from what Leanne could tell, never had been. Secondly, she was the wrong person to ask. He'd taken off the night before as if he couldn't get away from her fast enough, and when she'd run into him and Eli that morning after getting coffee and pastries at Harry's, he'd looked right through her.

"You'd have to ask Eli that," Leanne said, hoping she sounded warmer than she felt. "Can I help you find something?"

Gloria glanced around. "I'm looking for a gift for Melissa and Alex Thomas's new baby. You've heard the news, haven't you?"

Leanne nodded. Harry's had been all abuzz with it. Melissa was doing fine in Bethlehem Memorial, and the baby was listed in critical condition in the neonatal intensive care unit in Rochester. Melissa's mother and Alex were there, while Melissa's father and sister, Jenny, were keeping vigil in Bethlehem.

"A little boy. Two pounds and thirteen ounces, and born on Halloween night." Gloria's comforting smile came again. "Isn't that special?"

"Poor kid will get Halloween-themed birthday parties and cakes and cards for the rest of his life." *Please, God, let him have a life.* "I just hope he's all right."

"You and everyone else. There have been so many prayers going up for the wee one and his parents that I'm surprised you can't see them clogging the sky." As she talked, Gloria wandered to the side of the shop away from the clothes. She looked at blankets and quilts, gift baskets and toys, mobiles and tiny stuffed animals, then stopped at a display of small ceramic angels.

They'd come in just the day before, and Sophy had unpacked them while Leanne was busy with the party. The tallest was no more than four inches, the shortest only half that, and they came in all shapes, sizes, and colors. They were lovely little whimsical pieces.

"Aren't they sweet? The"—what had Gloria called him?—"the wee one could do with a guardian angel to watch over him, couldn't he?"

"Oh, he has plenty of them, believe me."

Leanne assumed she was referring to the hospital staff that was caring for him. *Angels* was, no doubt, an apt description. She could never work with preemies, could never handle the crises and the fears and the deaths . . . but thank God they could.

Gloria selected the only one of the statues that depicted more than one angel. "I believe I'll take this one."

Taking it from her, Leanne peeled the price sticker from the bottom as she walked to the cash register. It showed three angels, one male and two female, and they looked so . . . protective. She liked to believe that they all had such capable angels looking after them, though if they did, hers, Cole's, and Ryan's must be working overtime.

After she'd rung up the sale and made change, she wrapped the figure carefully in tissue paper, then slid it into a sturdy box. "Would you like this gift-wrapped?"

"No, thank you. I'm in a bit of a hurry. I plan to deliver it to him myself."

"All the way to Rochester?"

"Oh, it's not so far when you travel the way I do." With a cheery smile, Gloria tucked the box in her voluminous shoulder bag, waved, then turned toward the door.

Leanne returned to the side window display and began removing decorations again. After a time, she realized that she'd never heard the doorbell sound when Gloria left. A quick glance around the store showed the woman was, indeed, gone. Styrofoam cauldren clutched in her arms, she went to the door and opened it.

The bell dinged, but she hardly noticed, because a few feet to the right of the door stood Ryan, Jerome's leash grasped tightly in hand. He looked stricken, and a few feet to the left of the door was the reason—Cole. They stared at each other, ignoring the dog, ignoring her, both wearing stunned expressions.

Given a choice, Leanne would have furtively backed into the shop, closed the door, and taken refuge in the storeroom. Unwilling to be such a coward, she took a step forward, extending her hand to Ryan. "Come here, sweetie."

Ryan heard her, but it was Jerome who obeyed, as far as the leash allowed him to. Giving the dog a pat, she crossed to Ryan, slid her arm around his thin shoulders, and walked him to the door, then gave him a push inside. "Go back and sit down."

It was a sign of how dazed he was, that he obeyed without question.

The door slowly swung shut behind him and the dog, and she turned her attention to Cole. "You, too."

"No."

"Yes, damn it!" she gritted out. A passerby gave her a scolding look, and she lowered her voice. "Your son is in there, waiting. Now *go*!"

"He's not my son."

"He is in every way that matters. You took him in, you fed him, clothed him, taught him, raised him—"

"Deserted him."

"—and loved him. Now you're going to walk through that door and talk to him."

"He doesn't want to see me."

"He's twelve years old! He doesn't get to make that choice!" she exclaimed, then took a breath. "Not yet. Not without trying . . ."

He glanced through the glass door, and so did she, but they couldn't see Ryan. There were too many racks of pint-sized clothing in the way. Then he scowled back at her. "Eli told me to go to the hardware store and nowhere else."

"Eli didn't know you would run into Ryan. He won't mind."

For a long time Cole just looked at her, as if he were testing arguments in his mind. His expression was serious and edged with fear. He hadn't denied it when she'd said he loved Ryan, and her statement seemed borne out by the fact that he was afraid to face the kid.

She laid her hand on his forearm. "The worst he can do is reject you."

Abruptly he backed away, letting her hand fall. "Well, hell, I'm getting pretty good at that," he said with a bitter edge. He gazed inside the store again, straightened his shoulders, and pushed the door open. The bell rang just as it was supposed to.

Leanne was tempted to stay out there on the sidewalk, but she was in shirt-sleeves, and there was a cold wind blowing out of the northwest. She would turn blue in minutes, and it wasn't a good color for her.

Reluctantly, she returned inside and set the cauldron on the floor. Ryan and Jerome were sprawled together on the love seat, and Cole stood, hands at his sides, at the edge of the Oriental rug that marked the seating area. He appeared to be staring at nothing.

"Hey, kiddo." Leanne pressed a kiss to Ryan's head as she circled behind the love seat, then sat down on the sofa. "Where were you two off to?"

"We were gonna pick up Danny. I was gonna stop and see if it was okay."

Most Saturdays, Danny went to day care a few blocks away while she worked. Ryan had offered to baby-sit him instead, but she hadn't wanted him to feel as if he had to earn his keep. So she'd partially accepted his offer. Danny still went to day care in the morning, but if Ryan wanted to give up his afternoon to watch him, he could.

"Sure, it's okay." When he moved as if to get up, she added, "In a little bit. First, though . . . I think there are some things you two need to say."

Ryan's gaze never went near Cole, but the sarcastic tone of his voice made it clear who his words were intended for. "You got somethin' to say?" He waited half an instant, then said, "Yeah, I thought so. Me, neither."

"Sit down," she commanded before he got fully to his feet. "You, too," she said to Cole.

After a long stiff moment, he grudgingly obeyed.

"You"—that was directed to Cole—"need to tell him

why you left the way you did, and you"—this to Ryan—
"need to listen."

"It doesn't matter—"

She gave Ryan her sternest mother look. "Listen." Then
she got to her feet, returned to the side window, decided
they needed more privacy, and moved to the front windows. She was peeling fake webs from fake spiders and
tossing them in the cauldron when she finally heard the
low rumble of Cole's voice. She released a tiny sigh of relief, followed by another of regret.

Too bad she couldn't eavesdrop from up front.

S HE REMINDS ME OF ADAM," COLE SAID AT LAST.
"Kind of bossy."

"She's *not* bossy."

"Yeah, right." He rested one ankle over the other knee
and picked at a loose thread in the hem of his jeans. He'd
never been at a loss for words with Ryan, not since the
night they'd met, but at the moment he couldn't think of a
single thing to say.

Come to think of it, though, there *had* been another
time—the first time the kid had scared him out of a sound
sleep, screaming and thrashing in his bed. Cole had rushed
into the room, not knowing what the hell was going on,
and Ryan had thrown himself into his arms, sobbing. He
hadn't known what to do. Any comforting taking place in
the Jackson household usually involved a little friendly
punching, shoving, and teasing until the problem was forgotten. Hugs, patting, soft words—they hadn't been a part
of his life.

So he'd held Ryan. That was all—just held him, and patted his shoulder from time to time—and eventually the kid
had fallen asleep in his arms. Cole had eased him down

onto the bed, tucked him in, and headed straight to the kitchen for a stiff drink to calm *himself.*

Neither of them had ever mentioned that night again.

"You doing okay in school?"

Ryan shrugged.

"Did you have fun last night?" Cole hadn't been able to recognize Ryan at the party, but he'd seen a group of young boys with Earl Wilson, all bloodied and grotesque like something out of a horror movie, and guessed the one Earl hugged was Ryan.

Another damn shrug.

Cole rubbed his jaw, then forced a deep breath. "Look, about when I left—"

"It don't matter."

"I thought you needed a mother, a home—things I couldn't give you. I thought you'd be better off—"

"I am." For the first time since they'd come inside, the kid looked at him, his dark gaze derisive. "Livin' with Leanne is a hell of a lot better than livin' with you ever was."

The dull ache Cole had been vaguely aware of all night and all day sharpened and turned raw. He pressed his hand to his belly as if that would help, then leaned forward, bracing both arms on his knees. "Living the way I do . . . that's no way to raise a kid. You never finished a month at the same school where you started it. You never had a chance to make any real friends. Growing up like that, the only thing you were gonna be able to do as an adult was what I do, and I wanted something better for you."

Ryan's derision didn't ease. "Yeah, right," he scoffed. "That crap might help you with her"—he jerked his head toward Leanne—"but it don't mean nothin' to me. Your whole family's nothin' but a bunch of liars, and you're the worst of 'em all."

Shame heated Cole's face. "You think I'm proud of that? Because I'm not."

"Yeah, sure."

His movements jerky, Cole got to his feet and turned to face the back wall. He couldn't blame Ryan for being skeptical. He'd worked hard to become a master in the art of deception. He'd bragged that his parents were the best con artists Texas had ever produced, and that he was better than both of them. He *had* been proud.

But not anymore.

Finally, he turned back to the kid. "When I took you in, we had an agreement that you would never get involved in the business. Remember? You wouldn't help with any of the scams. You wouldn't lie, cheat, or steal. You would be a normal kid, living a normal life. And then you stole those books."

Ryan propped one large foot on the coffee table. "A normal kid living a normal life? Being raised by a bunch of thieves and cons and lowlifes? That's a joke."

Was that the anger speaking, or how he really thought of Cole and his family? *Thieves and cons and lowlifes.* Maybe they were, but every damn one of them had been good to him. Once Cole had brought him into the family, any one of his brothers would have done anything for him.

Cole leaned one shoulder against the storeroom doorjamb. "You're right. It was a joke." Though it had started out as very good intentions. But just as a mama dog couldn't raise her puppy to be a cat, a con man couldn't raise his kid to follow the straight and narrow. He'd tried, and look what he'd done. "That's why I left you here. Because anyone in Bethlehem could do a better job of raising you than I could. I'm sorry, but—"

His cheeks burning hot, Ryan swore. Cole's warning look only made him repeat the word, louder that time. "If you were so damn concerned about how I was turning out, why didn't you quit dragging me around? Why didn't you quit ripping off everybody you came across? Why didn't you just stop being a crook?"

"I don't know how to change the way I am."

"Don't wanna, you mean. It was just easier gettin' rid of me." Ryan jumped to his feet, and the dog jumped up, too, ready to go. "Well, you know what? I don't wanna see you. I don't wanna talk to you. I don't care what happens to you. So take off when one of your brothers gets here, and don't ever come back!"

Cole wouldn't have thought it possible, but Ryan beat the eager dog to the front door. Leanne stopped him there, talked quietly with him for a minute, then he and Jerome left.

He leaned his head back until it thunked against the wall, closed his eyes, and sighed. "Jesus."

The smell of Leanne's perfume, the awareness of her presence, reached him an instant before she spoke. "That wasn't too bad for the first time, was it? There's no bleeding, no bruises."

"Only on the inside." Opening his eyes, he watched her sit down on the love seat, crossing her legs. She wore a slim green dress that clung to her curves and flirted with her knees. Her hair was loose, the ends curling at her shoulders, and around her neck a gold heart dangled from a chain, just a thin outline with two tiny childlike figures swinging from it.

"The next time he says he's got nothing to say to me, trust him," he said wryly as he moved away from the door and sat at the end of the sofa.

"He had plenty to say, didn't he?"

"Yeah—and nothing I didn't already know."

"But he needed to say it anyway." She paused. "Did you explain to him why you left?"

"I tried."

"Did you apologize?"

"I tried. He wasn't impressed with either one."

"But he listened. He'll think about it. And the next time you talk, he won't be so angry."

"And you know this because? . . ."

"He wouldn't be so bitter unless he was hurting, and he wouldn't be hurting unless he loved you. It's easier to get over being angry than it is to stop loving someone. Trust me. I speak from experience."

He gave her a sidelong glance. "That's right. You're the queen of lousy choices and bad decisions."

"Don't—" Her mouth thinned, and for a moment it appeared that she would rise from the love seat and dismiss him from her presence. But the moment passed. The tension that held her stiff eased, and her mouth shifted into a sigh. "I'm sorry I said that, and sorry you took it so personally. I truly didn't mean it that way."

"I don't see any other way it *could* be taken." And he'd looked for one, too, while he'd spent a good part of the night staring out his bedroom window instead of sleeping.

"Maybe . . ." Her long fingers rubbed across the wicker of the love-seat arm. After a moment, she looked up. "You're right. Maybe Ryan's not the only one who's still got a lot of anger and bitterness toward you."

"You and Ryan don't have a monopoly on it, honey. I've got all sorts of enemies out there."

"We're not your enemies."

Sometimes it feels like it. But wisely he kept that to himself. Instead, he got to his feet. "I'd better get going before Eli figures I made a run for it."

He thought she was going to let him go without another word, but just as he stepped onto the tile that fronted the door, she spoke.

"Why didn't you do it last night? Make a run for it, I mean."

His fingers curled around the metal bar that stretched across the door as he breathed slowly. "When did I have the chance?"

The soft rustle of shoes on carpet alerted him to her approach. Reflected in the glass, he saw her stop at the nearest display and start rearranging little girls' sweaters. "After you took Melissa and J.D. to the emergency room. You were alone, you had his truck and a full tank of gas . . . why not get the hell out of Dodge?"

He was gripping the handle so tightly that his knuckles had turned white. He forced each finger to relax, then to let go, and he turned to face her. "The depth of your faith in me is underwhelming."

Her cheeks pinked a little. "I'm not saying I expected you to. I'm just asking why you let the perfect opportunity pass you by."

Slowly he exhaled. "I thought about it. I sat there in the parking lot and thought about just driving away. Nothing was stopping me. I could change my name, disappear. I've done it before. Someday I'll probably do it again. So your lack of faith in me is justified. Satisfied?"

"There's a big difference between thinking about doing something and actually doing it. I've *thought* about committing a lot of dastardly deeds over the years, but I haven't actually done them." She gave up fiddling with the sweaters and clasped her hands together on top of the pile. "Once again, you haven't answered the question. I didn't ask whether you considered running away. I asked why you didn't do it."

How about another dose of truth? he thought cynically. "It would have been wrong."

She didn't laugh or snort with derision, but simply nodded as if it were a logical answer. As if he could be trusted to care whether something was wrong.

"I—I'd better go."

Once more she nodded. "Thank you for talking with Ryan."

"You're welcome."

She smiled wryly. "And for not pointing out that I didn't leave you much choice."

"I'm used to not having many choices." He hesitated a moment, half-wishing he could stay longer, then forced himself to move. "See you."

So much for his stab at telling the truth, he thought as he walked out the door and turned toward Main Street. Not having many choices . . . that was just so much bull. Life was filled with choices. No one had forced him to break the law—at least, not after he was grown. He'd *chosen* to do it. Taking in Ryan—his choice. Dragging him around the country, with the law always one step behind—his choice. Coming to Bethlehem—no one to blame but him. Scamming these people—him again.

Getting involved with Leanne—done of his own free will.

Disappearing with a quarter million of the townsfolks' dollars—him and only him.

How many chances had he had every single day of his life to change? To make different choices? To make a different life for himself?

Why didn't you just stop being a crook? Ryan had asked.

It was a good question, and Cole had only one answer. Because he'd made the wrong choices.

Chapter Thirteen

J.D. GRAYSON TOOK COLE UP ON HIS OFFER TO DIS-
cuss Ryan with him. At his request, Eli delivered Cole
to the hospital Tuesday afternoon. Before closing the
door to the pickup, Cole bent to see the kid. "What do
you want me to do when I'm done?"

Eli glanced at his watch. "Murray and I will probably
knock off in another hour or so. Give me a call when
you're ready. If I'm not at the house, just keep trying."

With a grim nod, Cole closed the door, then faced the
hospital. He could save them both the hassle and just walk
to the Miller mansion after the meeting with Grayson.

For a moment he stood there on the curb and simply
observed. A young man with his right leg in a cast wheeled
himself out the automatic doors and lit up a cigarette, then
smiled at the young woman with him. A woman on her
way inside patiently matched her pace to that of her elderly companion. A pretty blonde girl pushed a cart filled
with flowers from the delivery van at the curb toward the
doors, and several women—mother and grown daughters,
by the looks of them—hurried past her.

Normal lives.

They were so far outside his experience that he felt as if he'd landed in an alien universe.

Squaring his shoulders, he went inside, got directions to Grayson's office, then located it down the hall. The waiting area was just a wide spot in the corridor, and the desk was empty, the door to Grayson's office ajar. He glanced at the clock—two minutes late. His chest tight, he rapped at the door, and it swung open.

Grayson was sitting at his desk, leaned back, with his little girl asleep on his chest. Cole glanced from the kid to the doctor. "I can come back later."

"No, come on in. My folks are baby-sitting this afternoon, but they left Faith with me while they check in on Melissa. They'll be back for her before long. Have a seat."

Cole chose the nearest chair and glanced around. If he'd ever thought about how a psychiatrist's office should look, he wouldn't have pictured this. There was no dark wood paneling, no comfortable couch, nothing elegant, homey, or austere at all. The furniture was past its prime, and he suspected the walls needed painting, though it was hard to tell with all the photos. The medical degree was all but lost in a jumble of family pictures.

"How is Melis—Mrs. Thomas?" he asked, the first thing he could think of to break the silence.

"She's recovering nicely. She's anxious to get out, so she can go to Rochester and see the baby. She got little more than a glimpse of him Friday night."

"Is he holding his own?"

"Even better. The NICU staff is impressed. He's a fighter."

Cole nodded, shifted in his chair, then gazed at his hands. He, Eli, and Murray had been making repairs on the concessions building at the soccer fields when Eli had gotten Grayson's call. His hands were dirty, and so were his clothes, a detail that bothered him far more in the psychiatrist's presence than it had with Eli and Murray.

He rested his hands on his thighs and fixed his gaze on Grayson. "You wanted to talk about Ryan?"

"Ryan . . . and you. I don't know if Leanne's told you, but Ryan's not thrilled at having to come see me. He spends most of our sessions angry or uncommunicative, or both. I thought maybe you could fill me in on some of the things he doesn't like to talk about."

"Did Leanne tell you that the father-son bit was just another scam?"

"Kelsey did. She's his caseworker," he explained unnecessarily.

"I don't know anything about his first nine years."

"But you raised him for the last three. You must have learned something about him during that time."

"What little I know I learned the hard way. I didn't know he had nightmares until he about gave me a heart attack in the middle of the night. I didn't know how much he liked books until he got caught stealing them." He looked away from Grayson's steady gaze and fixed his attention on the bookcase behind the desk instead. "I do know I was a lousy father."

He'd done his best . . . but when your best was nowhere near good enough, did it matter?

"I understand that you came to Bethlehem first last spring, then Ryan arrived a few days later."

"I left him in Philadelphia with my father, so he could finish the school year. He got Owen to buy him a bus ticket, and he showed up here one day."

"You were here almost two months. Did you routinely leave him with someone else for long periods like that?"

"No. He usually stayed with me. But he always wound up spending a lot of time alone, and he'd gotten to the age where he couldn't get caught up in school as easily as he used to."

"Why didn't you leave him with your father more often, where he could have a more stable home life?"

Cole would have given a lot for some glib answer that would satisfy the shrink without really telling him anything, but that would defeat the purpose of coming, wouldn't it? It was a sorry excuse for a man who couldn't be honest with a psychiatrist.

"I thought . . . *I* was the stability in Ryan's life. What town we were in, where we were sleeping at night, how long we would be there—I thought none of that mattered as long—as long as we were together."

He'd been a fool, living out this responsible-adult fantasy, casting himself as the dutiful father figure, while Ryan thought of him as a thief, a con, and a lowlife.

"What about the nightmares? Has he ever told you what they're about?"

Cole shook his head.

"How long has he had them?"

"As long as I've known him, but he refuses to talk about them. I just figured it has something to do with his mother, but he won't talk about her, either."

Grayson shifted the baby so she lay on her back in his arms. Her face screwed up as if she was going to cry, but she yawned instead and went on sleeping. "What do you know about her?"

He related the story of how she'd left Ryan in St. Louis and how *he'd* taken him in, then fell silent for a time. Ryan had plenty of memories, but few he'd been willing to discuss. Because they were too awful to remember? Or too precious to share?

"She moved around a lot, changed her name the way other people change clothes, and abandoned the kid to fend for himself." His muscles knotted. "She must have been a lot like me."

"Leaving a twelve-year-old boy with a woman who loves him isn't the same as leaving a nine-year-old all alone at a bus station in a strange city."

Maybe not, but it was still unforgivable.

"Did she sing songs to him? Read him fairy tales? Fix a special meal for him? Has he ever shared any memory of that sort?"

Cole shook his head.

"What about family? His father? Grandparents?"

Another shake. "He doesn't know anything about his father, and he's never mentioned anyone else. I got the impression his mother wasn't very maternal. He knew how to cook, to do laundry, and to handle money. He'd been taking care of himself a lot longer than a few weeks."

"Tell me about the nightmares."

"He doesn't like the dark. He wakes up screaming and shaking, then eventually goes back to sleep. He doesn't cry. He never cries, no matter what." It wasn't much to tell. The nightmares were awful for Cole, much more so for Ryan, and Leanne was a hell of a lot better at comforting him afterward. Cole had seen proof of that last spring, when Ryan had awakened them from a sound sleep. She'd taken him into her arms as if it was the most natural thing in the world, had patted and soothed and cradled him, and Cole had known then that Ryan needed a mother.

More than he needed a con-artist father.

"Have you ever asked him about the dreams?" Grayson asked.

"A couple times, but he didn't want to talk and I didn't push him." He should have—should have known how to get the kid to confide in him and then what to do to make everything all right.

Grayson smiled faintly. "We all know how to talk and we do it every day. But when it's really important, it can be the toughest thing to face." After a moment, he changed focus again. "How are things between you and Leanne?"

"Okay." Not that he knew what was between them, besides a lot of anger and bitterness on her part, but there was something. Something vital and intense, something neither one of them seemed able to walk away from. Something like what his parents had with each other.

The thought irritated him. While he was entirely too much like his father, Leanne was *nothing* like his mother. Eloise had never had an unselfish moment in her life. She'd never loved anyone half as much as she'd loved herself, while Leanne was generous and sweet. She loved Danny more than anything in the world, and probably loved Ryan almost as much. Hell, she had even loved *him,* though he hadn't deserved it. He'd been too damn stupid to suspect he might have loved her back.

He might have loved her . . .

Might still love her . . .

No. Loving people who weren't blood-related was just asking for trouble. He already had enough of that, and there was no shortage of it just waiting to find him.

Finally the weight of the silence in the room caught his attention, and he looked up to see Grayson watching him expectantly. Feeling like an idiot, he mumbled, "What?"

"I asked if you'd talked to Ryan yet."

"For a few minutes on Saturday." He related the gist of their conversation, but kept the lowlife comment to himself. Some things weren't meant to be shared.

"If you could have another chance to be Ryan's father again, would you take it?"

The question made Cole stiffen and straighten in his chair, and turned his voice cold. "Nothing's changed. All the reasons I left him in the first place are still there. I can't give him the kind of home he needs. I can't be the kind of parent he needs. If I got another chance, it would take away *his* only chance at ever living a normal life."

"Not necessarily. You could make changes in your own life. You could *become* the kind of parent he needs."

His laugh was short and sharp. "Go straight, you mean? Get an honest job? Stay in the same place? Give up the cons?"

"Does that seem so undesirable? Do you like your lifestyle so much you would choose it over Ryan?"

"It's not undesirable, doc. It's impossible. Being a con artist isn't just what I do—it's what I *am*. It's what I was born and bred for. I don't even have a clue how to settle down and go straight."

"You've been doing honest work in the past few weeks," Grayson pointed out.

"Because they're *making* me. If I hadn't tried to con the wrong woman in Georgia, I would still be doing the same old stuff. I never would have come back here, and I sure wouldn't have taken on an honest job."

"Anyone can change if they want to badly enough."

"Maybe in your world. Not in mine. I come from a long line of disreputable scammers. It's all I know."

"Anyone can change," Grayson stubbornly repeated. "A few years ago I was a drunk. If they'd ever done a blood-alcohol on me, they would have found more alcohol than blood. There were times, when I was quitting, when I would have crawled, groveled, even killed, for a drink . . . but I didn't. Because I wanted to be sober even more. If you find something you want more than you want to be a criminal, you'll find the strength within yourself to change."

Cole studied him. He'd known plenty of drunks—in

his line of work, he'd known all kinds of shady characters. It was hard to imagine Grayson, sitting there with his little girl, looking healthy, at peace, and self-satisfied, as one of them.

Just as it was hard to imagine himself going straight.

Though off and on for months, he'd been tormented by this image of settling down and making a family—him and Ryan, Leanne and Danny.

"You didn't answer my question," Grayson said quietly. "If you could have a chance to be Ryan's father again, would you take it? Even if it meant totally changing who and what you are?"

The three years he'd had with Ryan had been the best of his life. He'd felt like a responsible adult for the first time in his life. There had been times when he'd all but forgotten that Ryan *wasn't* his son . . . and times when he'd thought about retiring from the business for the kid's sake.

Ryan had needed him—to take care of him, to keep him safe, to love him. And *he'd* needed Ryan.

Finally he met Grayson's unwavering gaze. "Yeah, I would . . . but it's not gonna happen. Your wife's looking for his real parents. Even if she doesn't find them, they'll never give him back to me again, and he would never forgive me even if they did. So it doesn't much matter, does it?"

Grayson smiled faintly. "It matters more than you think, Cole."

DO YOU SUPPOSE I'LL EVER SEE MY FEET AGAIN? Less than a week earlier, Melissa had asked that question of Alex. Now she gazed at them without interest. It felt strange to look down without the swell of her belly blocking her view. When she stood up, she was continually caught off-guard by how light she felt—how empty—and when she sat down, she kept forgetting she didn't have to carefully support her own weight on the way down.

It was Wednesday, one of those bright, sunny, warm days that made autumn an even more special season. Dr. Gregory had discharged her from the hospital that morning, and she, her father, and her sister had immediately set out for Rochester. They were almost there, just minutes from her mother, Alex, and their baby.

Their baby. He was doing fine, Alex had assured her in this morning's call, but her fears wouldn't be quieted until she'd seen for herself. She wanted to cradle him to her breast and check his fingers and toes and gaze into his big eyes, and know deep inside herself that he would be all right.

From the front seat, Jenny reached around to pat her knee. "You okay back there?"

"I'm fine." Just chilled inside. Anxious. Afraid.

"You thought about names yet?"

Melissa caught the sharp look her father gave her sister, and so did Jenny, who ignored it. No one had come right out and told her not to choose a name yet—as if she might regret using a good name if the baby didn't . . . didn't . . .

Unable to finish the thought, she drew a breath. Everyone felt she should hold off until his condition was dramatically improved, but she'd named the child months ago in her heart, and that name would always be his, no matter what. "Alexander Maxwell," she announced as the hospital came into sight and her chest tightened. Somewhere inside there, Alexander Maxwell Thomas was waiting for his mother.

"Cool," Jenny said with a grin. "Isn't it, Mr. Maxwell?"

"Cool," their father agreed with a faint smile as he pulled up to the hospital entrance. "You girls go on in.

Mind your sister, Jen. I'll park the car and meet you upstairs."

To the best of Melissa's knowledge, Jenny had never been in this hospital before, but she charged ahead as if she knew exactly where she was going. That was the way she went through life in general—never hesitating, never experiencing a moment's fear or doubt. Melissa didn't know whether to envy her four-years-younger sister or be eternally grateful for her.

She settled for both.

After an eternity and before she was ready, they'd reached the neonatal ICU. Alex and her mother met them, each of them hugging her tightly, then he slid his arm around her waist and walked with her to the nursing station. She was too numb, too nervous, to pay attention to introductions, sympathetic words, reassurances. Practically in a daze, she let him and a nurse lead her away, then help her don a mask, gown, a cap to gather her hair, and paper booties to cover her shoes. She followed Alex, who appeared far more comfortable in the same getup, into the NICU and to their son.

He was so beautiful, and so tiny! He lay on his back, naked except for a pale blue knitted cap covering his head, and it seemed there were tubes and lines everywhere—in his nose, his mouth, his arm, his neck. His color was splotchy, and his little face was screwed up as if he was concentrating intensely on sleeping in spite of all the noise around him.

She bent to gaze at him, tears in her eyes, through the incubator's clear walls. "Hi, Max," she whispered. "You can't imagine how long I've waited to finally see you."

Alex stood beside her, his arm comforting around her waist. "Can she touch him?" he asked, and her pleading gaze shot to the nurse on the opposite side. Oh, yes, she needed to touch him, needed to feel that he was real and warm and alive.

"Sure. But you have to wear gloves."

It was a sorry substitute for skin to warm skin, but she would take anything she could get. She slid her hands into the gloves the nurse handed over, then tentatively reached through the ports in the incubator's side.

He *was* warm and real and very much alive. As she stroked his tiny arm, his fingers stretched, then relaxed. When she gently brushed his cheek, he turned his head her way and his mouth worked a time or two as if he were sucking on a bottle. He was so tiny, so fragile, and if she lost him . . . God help her, she couldn't bear even the thought.

She didn't know how long she stood there, rubbing him, whispering in a voice so low he couldn't possibly hear. Long enough for her back to ache, for the incision in her stomach to throb, for her legs to grow weak. By the time she realized how much she needed to sit, she was leaning heavily on Alex, but he held her without a word of complaint.

"Alex," a male voice greeted him. "How's the little one doing?"

"He's got a name now," the nurse said. "Dr. Bosquez, meet Max."

"Max . . . Maxwell? Your maiden name?" the doctor asked Melissa, then explained, "Your mother's spent almost as much time here in the past few days as your husband. You must be Melissa. How are you? You look like you could use a seat."

"I could," she admitted.

"Come over here and sit down and . . . we'll talk." He led the way to a desk pushed against the wall, held the chair for her, then took a seat on a stool with wheels. Alex leaned against the desk beside her, his hand on her shoulder.

"Max is doing really well," the doctor said. "He's gained three ounces since he got here, which puts him at three pounds even. Even though his respiratory system isn't fully developed, he's doing as well as can be expected there, too. There haven't been any crises, no infections, no problems at all, other than the fact that he got here six weeks early."

But . . . Melissa could feel in her bones that there was a *but* . . . at the end of that speech. Instead of confronting it, though, she asked, "When can he go home?"

"Barring any complications, probably in six to eight weeks. We want him to get up to at least five or six pounds, and we have to give his respiratory system the time it needs to handle breathing on his own."

"Do you expect complications?"

"We pray for the best, but we're always prepared for anything."

She looked up at Alex. He looked tired, as if he'd hardly slept since the last time she'd seen him. Most likely he'd spent every minute possible here at the hospital, doing his own praying.

But in addition to the fatigue and the worry, there was also a joy in his eyes she'd never seen there before. Always, when they'd gotten pregnant, they had celebrated together, and when she'd lost the babies, they had grieved together, but somehow *she* had been allowed to grieve more. She was the one who got the most sympathy from family and friends, while he was the one who'd had to deal with the details of the miscarriages—the one who'd had to pack away the baby things, to break the news to everyone. He had to be the strong one, when his heart had broken every bit as much as hers.

This time their dreams had come true. Max was tiny and fragile and breathing with the help of machines, but he was going to make it. They would never ache with such emptiness again. She wouldn't feel as if she was stealing the pleasure from her girlfriends when they got pregnant. He wouldn't have to watch fathers playing baseball with their kids, or taking them to see Santa Claus, or teaching them to ride bikes, with the bittersweet yearning to have those experiences with his own child.

This time there wasn't going to be any heartbreak.

But she feared she put the thought into words too soon when Dr. Bosquez finally got to that *but . . .*

Obviously uncomfortable with what he was about to say, he reached for her hand, sending chills through her. "There is something you need to know, Melissa, Alex."

Her heart started pounding in her chest, and she couldn't squeeze in enough oxygen to satisfy the ache there. She grasped his hand tighter, to hide the trembling in her fingers, and waited, wide-eyed, for him to go on, all the while wishing he wouldn't say another word.

She didn't get her wish. His eyes dark with sympathy, the doctor took a deep breath, then spoke.

"Max has Down syndrome."

I T SNOWED FRIDAY, THE FIRST SNOW OF THE SEASON. Fat white flakes blanketed the rooftops and covered the yellowed grass in the square with an icy blanket of white. It coated the cars and dusted the firs like Christmas trees.

Christmas, Leanne thought with a jolt. It was less than two months away. Where had the year gone? She'd spent last winter doing her usual nothing, the spring falling in love, the summer mothering the boys and getting over Cole, and the fall . . . she'd spent the fall falling for Cole again.

When would she ever learn?

Maybe after he'd broken her heart again . . . though

probably not. It had happened before, and she'd come back for more. Maybe she was hopeless. Or should that be hopeful?

She'd closed the shop and was working on the bank deposit when the door swung open and a red-haired tornado dashed down the aisle to the register. "Aunt Leanne, it's snowing!" Micahlyn said with delight. "Isn't it wonderful?"

"It's fabulous," Leanne agreed, lifting her niece onto the counter, removing her glasses to wipe away the snow, then replacing them. "If it keeps this up all night, tomorrow we'll be snowed in."

Micahlyn's eyes doubled in size. "I never been snowed in before."

"It's fun. You get to build snowmen and have snowball fights, and your mom can make snow ice cream. You freeze your little toes and your nose—oh, and you've got to make snow angels. You can't have snow without them."

"I never made snow angels before, either. I don't think I ever seen snow before."

"Well, my brother can show you how to do all of that, 'cause he's seen snow hundreds of times. By the way . . . who brought you here?"

Micahlyn looked around to her left, then her right, then giggled when the door opened. "Daddy! He's poky. Is Danny and Ryan upstairs? I wanna see their puppy."

"Yup, they're up there. Better watch out, though, or Jerome will give you a big sloppy kiss and try to stick his tongue in your mouth."

Chase stopped next to the counter as Micahlyn raced back to the door, and peeled off his gloves. "You should be used to males trying to stick their tongues in your mouth."

She stuck her own tongue out, then slid the money and deposit slips into the bank bag. "You guys get lost on your way home?"

"Nope. I'm here to invite you to dinner."

Hot dogs with lots of chili and onions . . . mmm. She'd missed having dinner with the family the Friday before, because of Halloween, and the week before that, because of Cole. Truth was, she didn't much feel like going tonight. It wasn't that she was down or anything. She just wanted . . . well, she didn't know exactly what.

"I . . . jeez, Chase, I don't think I'd be the best company tonight."

"Like you ever are? Someone's got a high opinion of herself," he teased.

"I just think I want to stay home." Maybe. Or maybe not.

He studied her a long time—debating whether to try to change her mind, she would bet. Even though he was no longer practicing law, once a lawyer, always a lawyer. Whatever he saw in her face, though, seemed to convince him that arguing wouldn't work this time. "Can the kids go?"

"Sure. But are you certain you want to take them? With this snow, you might be stuck with them until the spring thaw."

"They're welcome to spend the night. Besides, it's supposed to be in the forties tomorrow. All this is gonna be gone by Sunday."

She dropped the bank deposit into her bag, then shrugged into her jacket. "Come on. We'll go upstairs and you can see Jerome, too. Maybe he's got a brother over at the vet's that you can adopt for Micahlyn."

"Actually, I was thinking about getting her a pony."

She gave him a wry grin as she locked the door. "As I said, maybe he's got a brother over at the vet's. I noticed she called you *Daddy*."

"Yeah." He shrugged as if it was no big deal, but he couldn't hide the pleasure in his eyes. "She had a talk with her grandparents, and they said it was okay."

Micahlyn's paternal grandparents were the only family she had in the world besides her mother, and they hadn't been at all pleased when Nolie packed up their only grandchild and moved her to New York. The grandmother, in particular, had gone ballistic when she'd found out there was a man other than their deceased son in Nolie's life. They'd almost destroyed Nolie and Chase's relationship, but thankfully, everything had worked out for the best . . . more or less. Marlene Harper was still a spiteful witch, in Leanne's none-too-humble opinion, but she'd eventually accepted the changes in her daughter-in-law's and granddaughter's lives.

Not that Nolie, Chase, and Obie Harper had given her much choice.

They climbed the stairs to the apartment, then went into the living room, where Micahlyn and Danny were sprawled on the floor with Jerome. Grinning from ear to ear, she looked up at Chase. "Oh, Daddy, can I have one, too?"

He looked at the dog, then Leanne. "That's not a puppy."

"Sure he is, aren't you, Jerome? You're just a big baby."

At her cooing tone, he rolled onto his back, four long legs stuck up in the air, and waited for someone to scratch his belly.

"Guys, you want to spend the night at Micahlyn's house?"

Danny leaped to his feet, cheering, and so did Micahlyn. On the couch, Ryan shrugged. Spending the night with a four- and a five-year-old wasn't the most exciting thing a twelve-year-old could do, but it was a family thing and for that reason, Leanne suspected, he was willing.

After a whirl of activity, everyone had kissed Leanne good-bye, then trooped down the stairs. She stood in the living room, alone but for Jerome, and wondered again exactly what it was she wanted to do. As her gaze fell on the phone, the answer popped into her head.

Think with your head, Nolie had told her, but listen to your heart, and her heart was telling her she wanted to see Cole. To talk to him. Listen to him. Look at him. Spend time with him. It was foolish and risky, and overwhelming the warning in her head. She wanted to be with Cole.

She changed into gray wool trousers and a burgundy sweater, warm black boots, a coat, scarf, and gloves. After tucking her wallet into one pocket and her keys into the other, she left the apartment and crossed the street.

The Miller mansion looked like something out of a fairy tale, with its layers of snow. It was the sort of house that should be home to a loving, laughing family, with kids overflowing the bedrooms and parents who didn't mind. Instead, it had been home to one lonely old widow for years, to Cole and Ryan for a few weeks, and now to Eli and his charges.

She rang the doorbell, then brushed the snow from her hair and stomped it from her boots. When Eli opened the door, he looked surprised. "Leanne. What brings you out?"

For one moment her common sense whispered that she should rethink her plan. It wasn't smart. It could be disastrous.

Her irresponsible side snickered. As if she hadn't lived through dumb and disastrous before?

She ignored her common sense, told Eli what she wanted, and found herself waiting in the living room doorway while he went upstairs. Murray was sitting on the couch, watching the evening news. He gave her a smile that was part vague, part knowing, and all pleased, but didn't say a word, and before she could think of anything beyond hello, footsteps sounded on the stairs.

It was Cole, not long out of the shower, by the looks of him. Where his hair was still damp, it gleamed dark gold, and his feet were bare, though he carried work boots and socks in one hand. His jeans were clean and pressed, and his sweatshirt had that freshly-laundered smell when he got closer. "Hey," he said in greeting, stopping three steps from the bottom. "What's up?"

"I . . . I asked Eli if I could spring you for the evening. He said sure."

He looked puzzled. "For what?"

She shrugged. "A walk. Dinner. A talk."

The puzzled expression didn't go away as he studied her. She had the distinct feeling he wanted to turn her down, that he felt he *should* turn her down, just as she'd felt she shouldn't even ask. He didn't, though, but sat down on the step and tugged on one sock. "Where are the boys?"

"They went home with Chase."

"And you want to have dinner. With me."

She shrugged again. "If you don't want to—"

"No," he said quickly, then realized how it sounded and flushed. "I mean, I'd like that. I just can't figure why . . ."

"Why? . . ."

Now it was he who shrugged, his broad shoulders stretching the fabric of his shirt. "Why you would want to. Why Eli would agree."

"Judge Gloria said you should learn a few lessons with your punishment and emerge a better man for it. Maybe Eli agrees."

"So dinner with you . . . is that a lesson or punishment, or will it make me a better man?"

The question stung, but she gave no sign of it. Instead she smiled. "Interesting question. I guess you'll have to sit through the dinner to get the answer."

"Are you cooking?" He shoved his foot into his boot and laced it, then pulled on the other sock.

"Hardly. I've had a long week. I thought we could go to McCauley's."

"Go out. To a restaurant. What do you think the good citizens of Bethlehem would think, to see their convicted felon dining at the next table over with you and without his guard dog?"

"Most of them would think you have excellent taste both in food and dinner companions."

"It's not most of them I have to worry about."

She watched him lace the second boot, his fingers working quickly and efficiently. He'd had beautiful hands when he'd come to Bethlehem—long fingers, tanned, strong, and smooth, smooth skin. They were still long, tanned, and strong, but a month of hard work had taken care of the smooth part. There were nicks and scars and calluses now, but they could still take her breath away.

Finally he looked up and caught her staring. The hint of a smile quirked one corner of his mouth. "How about Harry's?"

"How about McBride Inn?"

"How about I cook?"

"In my apartment?" Heat began building inside her, so sudden and so hot that she half-expected to hear the snowmelt begin. She wanted to see him, wanted to sit down to a meal with him like any other man and woman who each found the other attractive. But him, her, her apartment . . . did she want to be that alone with him? With the boys gone for the night? With her bedroom just down the hall?

Yes.

She did.

"Okay," she replied, and her voice sounded breathy and hopeful.

"I'll be right back." He pulled himself to his feet and went down the hall to the kitchen. She could hear his voice and Eli's, but couldn't make out the words. When he returned a moment later, he got his jacket from the coat closet, zipped it up, then pulled on a pair of black gloves before opening the door.

The snow was coming down harder. When they reached the sidewalk, she gazed up at it, catching flakes in her hair, on her lashes and her cheeks. "I'll have to go to the grocery store. I don't keep much besides snacks and sandwich stuff in the house. You can come with me or wait at the apartment."

He gestured toward the store down the street, and she started in that direction. He walked beside her, hands in his pockets.

Because the silence was too comfortable, she wanted to break it, and latched onto the first thing to come to mind. "I thought Murray's sentence was only for a week or so."

"It was."

"Then why is he still there?"

"Damned if I know. When I asked him, he just shrugged. I asked Eli, and he said Murray would leave when the time was right."

"Which means?"

He shook his head, sending snowflakes scattering.

"Maybe he just likes living there—being a part of something. I know he's been alone a long time."

"No wife or kids?"

"His wife is dead, and his kids . . . I don't think they have much to do with him. I think . . ." She tried to recall the gossip she'd heard not long after Murray moved to town, but it had been years ago; she'd been younger and more self-centered, and the problems of a fifty-some-year-old stranger hadn't particularly interested her. "It seems they blamed him for his wife's death, but I'm not sure."

"Maybe he was responsible, and that's why he drinks."

"He certainly looks healthier than he did before this last arrest. Still, it's hard to imagine anyone staying in a program like this once his time is served, or a program that would let him stay."

"Eli is nothing if not unconventional," Cole responded in a dry tone. "Like your town."

She smiled brightly as they crossed the grocery store parking lot. "Thank you."

"I'm not sure that was a compliment."

"I'll take it as one anyway."

A blast of welcome heat greeted them as they walked into the store. Leanne pulled a cart from the corral, stuffed her coat, scarf, and gloves into the basket, then headed for the produce. There she indicated the fruits and vegetables with an open hand. "Your choice. What do you want to cook?"

He got mushrooms, onions, peppers, baking potatoes, bananas, brown sugar, butter, steaks, whipping cream, and a packaged pound cake. If he noticed the curious looks they got from other shoppers, he gave no hint of it, but concentrated on his choices instead.

When they reached the checkout and she dug her wallet out of her coat pocket, he shook his head. "I'll get it."

"But—"

He gave her a stern look. "I said I'll get it."

She'd thought he had gone looking for Eli to verify that it was okay for him to go out, and maybe he had. Apparently, though, he'd also talked the kid into giving him some of his own money, since not being trusted with so much as a dime had been one of his earlier complaints.

"I would have been more than happy to have you just do the cooking, but if you want to pay, too, go ahead," she said. "And if you want to play dish fairy afterward . . ."

"To quote Ryan, 'Dish fairy, my—' "

She smiled at the memory from last spring. She had invited him and Ryan, Nolie, Micahlyn, and Chase for dinner and, after the meal, had innocently wondered aloud if the dish fairies might visit. Danny and Micahlyn had been awed by the prospect of fairies, but Ryan hadn't been so easily fooled.

That was okay. Fairies or no, the kids had done the dishes anyway.

He paid for the food, then they split the bags between them and strolled back to her apartment. They left their shoes at the top of the stairs, then she drew a barstool to the dining room side of the counter and watched as he started dinner. He placed the steaks in a garlic, Worcestershire, and soy sauce marinade, cleaned and sliced the mushrooms, and scrubbed the potatoes.

"I can help," she offered as he rummaged through the island drawers before coming up with a grater.

"I don't think there's room for two in here."

She knew. That was why she'd offered.

"I can grate cheese, sitting here, out of the way."

In response, he set the cheese, grater, and a plate in front of her. She circled the counter to wash her hands, bumping against him as he put the potatoes in the oven, then she sat down again.

"I like the tile work," he remarked as he chopped onions.

"Thank you. I did it myself." Slowly she dragged the chunk of cheddar across the tiny holes in the grater while gazing at the backsplash. The tiles ranged in size from one inch square to twelve, in blues, whites, and yellows, and it had taken her more hours than any sane person would give up, to get them laid perfectly. And the first person who'd seen it besides Danny—her mother—had wrinkled her nose and moved on without a single comment.

How foolish she had been, expecting Phyllis's approval for anything she did.

How insulting and angry her mother would be if she knew Cole was in her daughter's kitchen at that very moment. And how sad that her mother's opinions meant nothing to her.

"You could open a restaurant." Her sudden pronouncement surprised Leanne as much as it did Cole. She'd been thinking about her mother and watching him place a mixing bowl and the beaters in the freezer, and without any thought on her part, the comment just popped out.

He smiled sarcastically. "Sure, and our slogan could be, 'Welcome to Cole's, where we fill your stomachs and empty your pockets.' "

"Actually, I think 'wallets' would sound better," she remarked. "But seriously, you like to cook and you're very good at it."

He was unwilling to even consider the idea. "The last thing Bethlehem needs is another restaurant."

Her breath caught, and a butterfly somersaulted in her stomach. Gripping the cheese tightly enough to crumble it, she tentatively asked, "You . . . you're thinking . . . about staying? In Bethlehem?"

He looked at her, realized what he'd said, then scowled. "I've still got about forty-eight hundred hours left on my sentence. There's no point in thinking about doing anything at the moment."

"There's always a point to thinking about the future," she disagreed.

"Why? So you can arrange it to death? Then there are no surprises, no point in living it."

"Life is full of surprises," she said reprovingly, "no matter how carefully you arrange it. When you went to work this morning and the sun was shining and you didn't need more than a light jacket, did you think we would have six inches of snow on the ground by dusk? Did you imagine for a minute that you would be cooking dinner for me tonight? When you walked away from me at the party last week, were you surprised to find Melissa Thomas alone and in labor? When you sneaked out of my bed five months ago, did you ever dream someday you'd be back?"

He gave her a long steady look, the knife still in his hands, the onions forgotten on the chopping board. "Is that what you *sprung* me for? So you could make another mistake?"

Heat flooded her face. "I didn't say that right. When you sneaked out of my bed and *out of town* five months ago, did you ever dream someday you would be back *in town*?"

Slowly he positioned the onion half-cut-side down, then sliced through it three times before chopping it. "You didn't answer my question. Is that how I'm supposed to thank you for the unexpected night out?"

Because sex hadn't been on her mind when she'd given the invitation—at least, not consciously—she didn't hesitate to pretend it wasn't on her mind at all. "I don't expect anything, Cole, except a good dinner."

He scraped the onions into a skillet on the stove, set the knife down, and came to lean on the counter in front of her. "Too bad," he murmured, his voice husky. "Because tonight . . . I wouldn't mind being your latest mistake at all."

Chapter Fourteen

ANY FOOL COULD SEE SHE DIDN'T KNOW WHAT to say to that. Cole remained there, too close but not close enough, for a minute, or three or five, just to see what she would come up with. When she remained silent, he returned to the island and the green and red bell peppers waiting to be chopped. "How's Melissa Thomas and her baby?" he asked, sounding as normal as if he hadn't just raised the temperature between them by twenty degrees or so. As if he weren't disappointed that she'd had no response to his come-on.

As if he hadn't harbored some stupid hope that she would forget all about dinner and invite him into her bedroom.

"M-Melissa?" she echoed, her voice hoarse. "She's—she's fine . . . out of the hospital and . . . gone to Rochester. The baby . . . he's okay, too, as far as I know. I—I haven't heard anything in the last few days." Still speaking in that unfocused tone, she asked, "Is this enough cheese?"

"More than enough." He hadn't told her half the block would be plenty for the baked potatoes, so she'd grated all but a small piece.

Calling the dog over, she fed that chunk to him, then

covered the plate with plastic wrap and set it in the refrigerator. "What else can I do?"

Oh, he could think of a few dozen answers to that, and not one of them had to do with cooking . . . though he'd seen a few items in her refrigerator that could come into play if she was adventurous enough.

But he knew too well that wasn't what she meant, and there was no sense in pretending otherwise. Just being alone with her was torment enough. He didn't need to shovel it on.

"You can wash the mushrooms if you want. Other than that, everything's pretty much done."

She did as he suggested, then covered them with a damp paper towel. While he finished chopping the peppers, she took a bottle of wine from the refrigerator and filled two glasses. He wasn't much of a drinker, but he would take anything that might cool the heat in his blood a few degrees.

She leaned against the counter, ankles crossed, and sipped her wine. "When you came here, you said you were moving from California. Was that true?"

"Nope. I've lived just about everywhere *but* California."

"Why did you lie?"

"Because I've lived just about everywhere *but* California."

"Meaning you're probably wanted just about everywhere."

He shrugged and copied her position on the opposite side of the island. "Everywhere and nowhere."

"Ryan says you never finished school."

"I dropped out in tenth grade. I had more important things to do with my time."

"Like what?"

He shrugged again, and she frowned. "Stop doing that. Ryan does it all the time, and it drives me crazy. Say 'None of your business' or 'I don't want to talk about it,' but don't shrug again."

"Okay," he agreed slowly. "When I was sixteen, Owen went to prison for a while. Someone had to look out for the younger kids, so——" He started to shrug, then caught himself. "I did."

"What about social services? Why didn't they place all of you in a home?"

"They didn't know about us. Owen wasn't using his real name, and he didn't volunteer the information."

"Wasn't he worried about you?"

"He knew we would take care of one another."

"Taking Ryan when no one else wanted him . . . that was just natural for you, wasn't it? After spending all those years taking care of your brothers."

"I guess." He stood her steady, thoughtful gaze for as long as he could, then pushed away from the counter and took his wine into the living room, where Jerome lay on the sofa. He took a seat near the mutt's head, and she sat by his feet.

"Of all the places you've lived, which one did you like best?" she asked in a conversational, getting-to-know-you tone that they should have been hell and gone past, but weren't.

This one. "There are different reasons for liking a place," he hedged. "Winters are great in Palm Beach. Atlanta was great for things to do. If you like skiing, Denver's convenient. For a party town, you can't beat New Orleans. People are more trusting in small towns. My kind of scams rank lower on the cops' priorities in big cities. People tend to take paybacks more seriously, in my experience, out west."

"So you've never thought you might like to stay in any particular place."

Just this one. "I don't know *how* to stay in any one place. Even when I was a kid, growing up around Dallas, we never had the same address longer than a couple months."

She drew her feet onto the sofa and balanced her wineglass on one knee. "You've never stayed anywhere, and I've never left. Never wanted to. I've always loved Bethlehem—have always been happy right here. It's home."

Absently he scratched behind Jerome's ears. "I've never had a home. Just a long line of places I've settled for a few weeks or a few months. I've never had neighbors or roots or ties to the community." Or friends or connections or that warm sense of familiarity people like Leanne had for their hometowns.

"Have you ever wanted any of that?"

He glanced at her, but she was gazing off into the distance. Because the question was casual, unimportant? Or because it wasn't?

The smart answer would be the lie. *Never. Why settle in one place when you can wake up someplace new every day? Why be bored when there's a whole world of excitement out there?* "Sometimes," he replied quietly. "When I'd wake up and couldn't remember where I was. When it was time to move on and I didn't have the energy for it. When Ryan's new school would comment on all the schools he'd gone to in the past year. When I'd have to tell him it was time to quit and find another new school."

She gazed into her glass as she swirled the wine in lazy circles. "Did you ever want to stay in Bethlehem?"

A lot more often than was safe. She'd been a large part of it, Ryan another part. But it had been the town, too. The feeling that he'd found a place to belong, when he hadn't even known he was looking for one. The sense that he and Ryan could both have everything they needed right there.

He opened his mouth to lie, but sudden impatience

with the old habit made him change his answer. "For a while, I did . . . but I screwed that up."

Finally she looked at him with a hint of a shrug. "But you're here."

Yeah. He was there. Granted, coming back hadn't been his choice, but . . . staying had been. But staying because the judge had ordered him to and staying once he was free to leave were two different things. People had to put up with him now, because the court said so. Once his sentence had been served, they would be justified in running him out of town.

Before she could say anything else, the timer in the kitchen buzzed. He left his wine on the coffee table and went to shut it off. While butter melted in a saucepan, he sliced the mushrooms, then added them and brown sugar to the butter. He set the onions and peppers to cooking in olive oil over the back burner, put the steaks under the broiler, then cut the potatoes in half.

"I had a meeting with the vice principal at Ryan's school this week."

Leanne's voice came from behind him, much closer than she'd been two minutes ago. He didn't startle, though, because some internal radar had alerted him to her nearness an instant before. "Is he in trouble?"

"He thinks school is a waste of time. But what twelve-year-old boy doesn't?" Crossing to the refrigerator, she opened the door. "What would you like to drink with dinner? We have more wine, Kool-Aid, orange juice, Pepsi, and milk."

"Eli gives us milk with every meal. I realize he's still a growing boy, but I gave that stuff up when I was eight. How about more wine?" It had a nice bite to it, and if he drank enough of it, he might get the courage to go for what he wanted. Hell, he could even drink enough that

not getting it wouldn't hurt . . . at least, not enough to notice, with all the other hurts inside.

Taking the wine bottle with her, she set the table while
he finished up the dinner. As soon as she was seated at the
small wicker table, he served it.

"Steaks broiled to perfection, caramelized mushrooms,
sauteed onions and peppers, and cheese-stuffed baked potatoes," he announced. "And you can sit barefooted and cross-
legged to eat. Isn't that better than a noisy restaurant?"

"And a handsome waiter as well." She saluted him with
her wineglass. "Hope I have enough on me for a good tip."

It was a surprisingly comfortable meal. Anyone watching would never guess that he'd betrayed, hurt, and disappointed her, that she'd sworn to hate him forever. They
were like any man and woman, talking about nothing in
particular, even laughing a time or two.

Of course, if they were *any* man and woman, they
would be in a restaurant, one too elegant and expensive to
be noisy, instead of hiding out from disapproving eyes at
home. After dinner they would stroll through the snow to
the car, and he would take her home and walk her to the
door, where she would slide her arms around his neck,
brush her mouth against his, and ask in a sultry voice,
Would you like to come in?

And he *would* like. Very much. And would say so. And—

Leanne's long slender fingers waved in front of his face.
When he blinked and focused on her, she smiled. "Where
were you? On some warm Florida beach?"

"Uh . . . no." He shook his head to clear away the fantasy. "What did you say?"

"I asked if you wanted to go with us." She gestured to
Jerome, who was watching him intently from the other
side of the table. "The baby needs to go out."

"He looks like he'd prefer that *we* go out and let him clear away the food." The mutt was practically grinning, and he started drooling once he caught the whiff of the leftover steak on Leanne's plate.

"That would be his first choice, I'm sure, but it's not going to happen." Rising, she picked up both their plates and took them to the kitchen. Jerome was right on her heels.

There weren't many leftovers—the piece of steak, a few mushrooms, and a helping of onions and peppers. She filled a plate, covered it with foil, and put it in the refrigerator, then left the dishes in the sink. "Let me get my shoes, sweetie, and we'll go."

As she disappeared into the hall, Cole took the rest of the dishes in and found the dog, his front feet on the counter, his big tongue swiping the dinner plate on top in the sink. "Get down," he murmured, giving him a push. "Don't make me rat you out."

He got his boots, earning a glance but nothing more from Leanne, sitting on the steps, and took them back to the dining table to put on. He had never intended to stay in Bethlehem past June—or any other place that knew the meaning of winter. He was going to have to squeeze some more of his money out of Eli and buy a heavier coat if he wanted to survive.

A month ago survival had meant nothing if it had to be done in Bethlehem.

He wasn't sure, but he thought it came damn close to meaning everything now.

When he returned to the top of the stairs for his jacket, Leanne had put on the long wool coat that flapped around her legs, and wound a woolen scarf around her neck. She took another scarf, this one black and softer than anything he'd ever felt, and wrapped it around *his* neck. "Are you sure you won't freeze?" she asked as she clicked the snap on the leash and Jerome came flying.

"You have this real concern with me freezing. Do I look that delicate to you?"

She studied him as if seriously considering her answer. "You look like a surfer boy who rarely leaves the beaches."

He grinned. "Another reason I said I was from California. But I'm tougher than any sissy surfer boy."

Her only response was a soft grunt as she released the leash and let Jerome dash to the bottom of the stairs. There she looped it around her wrist, opened the door, and stepped outside into the cold.

The dog loved the snow, dashing here and there, diving headfirst into every drift they came to, then emerging all coated in white, to shake himself dry and shower them. They crossed the slush that covered the street and went into the square, where Jerome slowed his frenzied explorations long enough to do what he had to do, then immediately dove into another drift.

"I think that dog wakes up in a brand-new world every day," he commented.

"Are you implying unkind things about my baby's intelligence?"

"Not at all," he lied dryly. "Just making a statement."

"It might not be a bad way to live," she remarked as they followed the dog's lead toward Main Street. "He was dumped and left to die or survive on his own by people who didn't want him, but in spite of that, every day's a wonderful new day. I admire his resiliency."

Still following the dog, they turned onto Main Street and walked a block in silence before he stiffly said, "I didn't dump Ryan to survive on his own."

The look Leanne gave him was surprised. "I was talking about Jerome and his worthless owners, not you and

Ryan . . . though I admit to noticing a few similarities between Ryan's situation and Jerome's." Then she nudged him with her elbow. "Feeling the sting of that conscience you claim you don't have?"

Instead of admitting or denying it, he turned his gaze to the storefronts. Harry's, back in the other direction, was the only business still open. The others were locked up tight and dimly lit, most with Thanksgiving messages or scenes on their windows. "Eli told us today that we'll be handling the Christmas decorations for the town."

"That'll keep you busy for a good long while. Christmas is our favorite holiday, and we do it up right. How could we not, with a name like Bethlehem?"

"He's got us scheduled to work on floats for the Christmas parade, string lights, and put out tacky decorations." He scowled. "I'd rather chop wood and pick cotton."

This time the elbow in his ribs was substantially more than a nudge. "Our decorations aren't tacky! They're beautiful. And the lights look incredible on the trees and buildings when it snows, and the bandstand is always gorgeous—like a scene from a Rockwell painting. And the Christmas parade is the best time to be had in this part of the state in cold weather."

"Funny. I thought that was you. In any kind of weather."

She stopped abruptly and lifted her gaze to him. Her dark eyes were wide and alive with emotions, most of which he couldn't name. Wouldn't name. Slipping her hand from her glove, she laid it, warm and soft, against his cheek. "I'll take that as a compliment," she whispered as she leaned closer. Before he could tell her he'd meant it as one, she was kissing him.

It was a great kiss—sweet and warm, tasting of wine and dark sugar, promising everything and doing a pretty good job of delivering. It made him forget the snow, and the cold, and the discomfort in his toes, and stirred a hunger in his belly that all the steak dinners in the world couldn't touch. It made him want more than was wise, need more than was possible. It made him greedy, and grateful, and . . . sweet damnation.

It ended too soon—about the time he slid his hand into her hair and used the other to pull her against him. She drew back, gave him a few chaste little kisses, then pulled away, took his hand, and started walking again.

"Does the Jackson family have any Christmas traditions?" Her voice sounded almost normal, as if she hadn't just turned him on beyond bearing, as if the kiss had left her unaffected. But her voice was a shade breathier than usual, her tone a shade more satisfied than usual.

It took him half a block to get his brain functioning again. "You mean, like bail money in our stockings, stealing from the rich to give to ourselves, or ripping off the Salvation Army Santas?"

"I mean, like putting up a tree after Thanksgiving or making gifts for each other. Hanging mistletoe and drinking eggnog, getting together on Christmas Eve to go to church and having a big traditional dinner on Christmas Day."

"We didn't go to church the rest of the year. Why would Christmas Eve be different?"

She gave him a chiding look. "I'll let you in on a little secret. A great many of the people in church on Christmas Eve don't go the rest of the year."

He shoved his free hand in his pocket, then flexed his fingers around hers. It was a little thing, holding hands and walking the dog in the snow, but it didn't feel little. It felt like one of the best gifts he'd ever been given.

And because that sounded way too dopey even for him, he turned his attention to answering her question. "Yeah, we had a tree." Most years, at least. And most years it had even had presents under it. "We never bothered with mistletoe—the Jackson boys never needed an excuse to kiss their girls—and we didn't much care for eggnog, so we doctored it with rum. We still didn't care for it, so we quit adding the eggnog and just drank the rum. Usually Eloise would come back from wherever she was, and we would have the big traditional Christmas dinner in whatever restaurant Owen could afford that year. Sometimes it was the ritziest place in town. Usually it was more along the line of Harry's."

At the next intersection, they turned right onto a street just as deserted as and even more snow-covered than Main. The sidewalk stretched ahead of them, unmarked by footprints, smooth, clean, damn near pristine.

"Now that they're grown up, how do the Jackson boys celebrate?"

"Anyone who can make it to Owen's does. He still has a tree, still no mistletoe, and plenty of rum, and Christmas dinner is still eaten in a restaurant somewhere."

"You should invite them here."

This time he was the one who stopped and stared. She and Jerome walked ahead a few steps before his grip on her hand stopped her, then she came back and gently closed his mouth. Immediately he opened it again. "Invite my family *here*?"

Her head bobbed. "I'm telling you, Bethlehem does Christmas right. They would love it."

"*I'm* telling *you,* the last thing this town needs is the whole Jackson family here at the same time. They would carry off anything that wasn't nailed down and half the stuff that was."

She smiled blithely. "At Christmas? When they're being welcomed like long-lost members of the family?"

"That's what I did," he said bitterly. "You people welcomed me, and look how I repaid you."

She nodded as if his words didn't mean much, then tugged his hand, silently coaxing him into walking again. At the end of the block, they turned right again. A few blocks ahead, the Miller mansion was brightly lit against the night. Out of sight from their vantage point was Leanne's apartment: smaller, cozier, more dimly lit. After their stroll through the snow, he would walk her to her door. Would she slide her arms around his neck? Kiss him again? Invite him inside?

He hoped so. If the snow hadn't obliterated all sign of the stars, he would even wish for it.

Even at their lazy pace, they were at the door in just minutes. She unlocked it, climbed the first few steps, then looked back. "Aren't you coming in?"

"I wasn't sure . . ."

"Hey, we still have bananas, cake, and whipping cream, remember?"

Dessert. Of course. So much for hoping and even wishing.

Then, when they were about halfway up the stairs, she gave him a look too innocent by far for the gleam in her eyes. "Besides, I haven't yet tipped you for the excellent dinner."

HE SLICED THE BANANAS, CARAMELIZED THEM, THEN served them over slices of pound cake, with sweetened cream whipped to soft peaks. It was simple and incredible, and made Leanne want to purr with satisfaction. After indulging, they shared the dish-fairy chores, then stood on opposite sides of the island, each drying their hands while sizing up the other.

"About that tip," he said, his gaze dark and heated.

She hung the towel over the rack, then turned her pants pockets inside out. "We may have to negotiate that. My pockets have already been emptied."

"What would you be willing to offer?"

With an innocent shrug, she raised her brows. "Maybe a kiss?"

"Just one kiss?"

"Sweetheart, I could give you one kiss that would curl your toes and make your eyes pop."

"One kiss?" he asked skeptically.

"It's not the number of kisses that count. It's how—and where—they're done."

For a long moment the only sound in the apartment, besides her own nervous breathing, was Jerome snoring in his kennel. Then Cole broke her gaze, hung up the towel, then glanced at the clock. "When will the boys be back?"

"Sometime tomorrow, weather permitting."

"When is Eli expecting me back?"

"He didn't say." She smiled. "It's not as if he doesn't know where you are and who you're with and what you're doing."

"He's such a kid, I'm not sure he has the faintest idea what I'm doing." Slowly he circled the island, caught Leanne's hand in his, and started toward the bedroom.

The first time they'd had sex, it had been easy. She hadn't been in love with him yet. She had suspected he could break her heart, but hadn't expected it. She'd thought she could handle the attraction to him, spending all that time with him, and having sex with him without getting in over her head because, hey, she was the queen of bad relationships. She'd gone into that one with her eyes wide-open.

And she was going into this with her eyes open even

wider. Now she knew what it was like to love him. Knew how easily he could hurt her. Knew this was more than attraction, more than sex, and wanted it—wanted him—anyway.

A single lamp burned as a night-light in her bedroom, a silly little frilly thing with tinted glass and fringe sitting on the dresser. Along with the light filtering in around the edges of the blinds, it was all the illumination they needed.

He stopped next to the bed and drew her into his arms. It was the one place she'd longed to be. It was like coming home—warm, familiar, comforting.

For a time he just held her and kissed her and proved her right—that it wasn't the number of kisses that counted, but how and where they were done. Sweet kisses, lazy kisses, all-the-time-in-the-world kisses, accompanied by gentle, tormenting touches. Kisses that made her skin hot, her muscles quiver, her knees weak. Even one kiss that curled her toes. He removed her clothing as easily, as familiarly, as his own, then lowered her onto the bed, and he remembered the condoms in the nightstand drawer as if he'd put them there himself.

The room was warm, the night still, its usual sounds muffled by the heavy snow Every place they touched, her skin rippled, and every breath she took grew sharper, thinner, more ragged. When he suckled her nipple, she would have gasped if she'd been able. When he slid his strong, calloused hands beneath her and lifted her hips to meet his, the best she could manage was a groan.

The pleasure was intense, the need inside her growing more urgent with each thrust of his hips. It had been so long . . . felt so good . . . so necessary . . . so . . .

A cry wrenched from her as the long, shuddering waves of completion washed over her. With her vision reduced to starbursts of blinding brilliance, with her lungs struggling for the faintest breath, she clung to Cole as if she was never going to let go. As if she needed him to survive. As if she loved him, plain and simple.

And she did. No matter how crazy it was, how irrational and illogical and downright stupid. Knowing he could, and likely would, break her heart again. Knowing he couldn't stay, while she wouldn't leave. Knowing he couldn't fit into her life, while she wouldn't fit into his.

She loved him.

And she didn't know whether to laugh about it . . . or cry.

I SHOULD GO."

Leanne took a deep breath, and the sensitive tips of her breasts brushed his arm. "What time is it?"

"Ten-thirty."

"Does Eli do a bed check?"

"So far it hasn't been necessary, since we weren't allowed to go anywhere without him." Instead of getting up, though, he turned onto his side and drew her nearer. For a long time he looked at her, his expression grave in the dim light.

What did he see? An enormously satisfied woman? A grateful lover? Or a woman who loved him in spite of everything?

She truly hoped not on that last. She'd said the words to him once last spring, early one morning when she'd awakened in his bed across the street. She had thought he was asleep, looking so sweet and . . . special, and she'd blurted the words out on a rush of emotion.

Only he hadn't been asleep. His eyes had popped open, and he'd look stricken. Appalled. Terrified.

Definitely *not* the response she was looking for.

Once he'd regained his equilibrium, he'd hustled her and Danny, then himself and Ryan, out the door. He'd canceled his lunch with her, and missed their dinner with Nolie and Chase. She'd thought she had seen the last of him, but he had come back that night, and every other night . . . for the next week.

Then he'd disappeared.

Most of that Saturday she'd thought he was working. She'd worried a little all day, but it wasn't until evening rolled around that she got really concerned. She'd gone to the Miller mansion, but no one was home—had called his office and gotten only the answering machine. Her next call had been to Fred Miller. Yes, he had an extra key to his mother's house, but no, he didn't feel right just letting himself in when Cole was in the process of buying the place.

She'd talked him into it, though, and around seven-thirty, he'd met her and the boys there and unlocked the door. The house had been too still, too empty. Immediately she had known in her gut that Cole was gone, and a check of his bedroom confirmed it. Ryan's belongings were all where he'd left them. Cole's . . . all gone.

All she had to do was close her eyes and she could feel that stillness, that emptiness, again. Back in the summer it hadn't taken long for her to realize that the feelings hadn't come from the house, but from herself. Some secret place inside her—the place that expected all men to leave her—had known he was gone. The stillness and emptiness had been her life without him.

And the hurt. The anger. The bitterness. The disappointment. The hostility.

And here she was, back again in the same place. Facing it all over again. And there was nothing she could do to stop it.

Nothing she *would* do.

It was better to have loved and lost than never to have loved at all, or something like that. Nonsense, she'd believed after her first broken heart. Pure and utter nonsense, spoken by one who had never loved and lost.

But every bad relationship had given her something. Sometimes it was just experience. With Greg and again with Cole, it had been a child. Whatever the gift, all those things had gone together to make her the woman she was today, and she loved that woman a lot.

Even if no man had ever loved her back.

She stroked her finger lightly across his mouth. "You look so serious."

"You look so beautiful."

"Oh, yes, my beauty is so great that it always makes men look as if they're in pain."

He bit the tip of her finger gently, then wrapped his hand around hers. "Actually, I was thinking about the fact that I'm thirty years old and I have to go home when the evening's hardly started, so some kid half my age won't get annoyed and come looking for me or, worse, call the cops. That's no way for a man to live."

His last words, quieter, grimmer, than the rest, stirred a faint hope to life inside her. He didn't know how to stay, he claimed. He was a crook, plain and simple. He looked out for himself first, and screw everyone else. But the first step to changing was to *want* to change, and before he could want it, he had to find dissatisfaction with the way things were. *That's no way for a man to live . . .* sure sounded like dissatisfaction to her.

But was it enough to overcome a lifetime of honing the finer skills of con artistry?

"It's not ideal," she agreed. "But life isn't, is it? We all make mistakes, and either we learn from them and become better people or we're doomed to repeat them."

"And you and I are repeat offenders," he said with a wry smile. "For most men my age, prison isn't an acceptable alternative, which makes breaking the law an unacceptable occupation, but here I am. . . . And you . . . hell, here you are naked. With me. Again."

"Being intimate with someone you"—she lowered her lashes so he couldn't possibly read anything in her gaze—"you connect with isn't automatically a mistake."

"Being intimate with an idiot who's already broken your heart once *is*." Releasing her, he sat up on the edge of the bed, then reached for his clothes.

Leanne missed his warmth immediately. After settling both pillows behind her, she tucked the covers tightly around her. "Careful. You almost sound as if you regret it."

He stood up to pull his jeans to his waist, buttoned and zipped them, then sat down again, putting on his socks and boots as he faced her. "Don't you?"

"Do I regret getting my heart broken? Sure. I'm all in favor of suffering as little as possible. Do I regret having the affair? No. I would have wished for a different outcome, but I wouldn't undo it if I could."

He pulled his sweatshirt on and tugged it into place, leaving his hair standing on end, then leaned forward, placing one hand on each side of her. His blue gaze hard and intense, his jaw clenched, he asked, "Do you regret loving me?"

His voice was silky, soft and smooth slicked over steel. He wanted to be sarcastic, she suspected, but couldn't quite pull it off. Wanted to show how little he cared, or what a bastard he really was, but couldn't quite manage that, either.

She cupped her hand to his cheek, and he automatically turned, pressing a kiss to her palm. "No," she replied as she lifted her gaze to his. "I don't regret that at all."

Suddenly, frantically, he kissed her, a hard quick assault that left her short of breath and long on heat. Then he left her and the bed, left the room and, a moment later, the apartment.

She slid out of bed and into her robe, then went to the side window and raised the blinds. The snow had stopped and a few stars had finally broken through the cloud cover to gleam on all the white below. She watched as Cole crossed the street, then reached the Miller house with long, purposeful strides. He cleaned his boots on the porch, went inside, and closed the door, but still she watched. A moment later she was rewarded when a light came on in his bedroom and, seconds after that, he appeared at his own window.

For endless moments they just gazed at each other. Finally, with the cold creeping into her feet and along her legs, she waved her fingers lazily. He raised his own hand, though not in a wave. He just held it, fingers apart, palm pressed to the windowpane, in a gesture so forlorn it made her chest tighten around her heart.

Swallowing hard, she turned away, shut off the lamp, then snuggled back into the bed that retained the heat, the scent, and the memory of him.

As she did.

BE CAREFUL WHAT YOU WISH FOR. YOU JUST MIGHT get it.

As soon as they'd arrived at the hospital Saturday morning, Alex and Melissa had gone straight to the NICU to check on Max. She was still there, all gowned and gloved, touching the baby's tiny body through the incubator ports, talking and singing softly as if he were . . . as if nothing was wrong. As soon as he could leave, Alex had excused himself and come here to the chapel, to . . . what? Be alone? Feel bad? Stop pretending? Pray?

That last didn't much appeal to him at the moment. He'd prayed a lot of times for a baby, but they'd had to go through hell to get one and once they finally had, he'd come early. He'd prayed for Max to live, to be healthy, and then he'd prayed for the doctor's diagnosis to be wrong. Well, Max was still alive and his condition had been upgraded from critical to serious, but as for being healthy and the diagnosis . . . God apparently wasn't listening.

After dropping his bombshell on Wednesday, Dr. Bosquez had shown them the signs—Max's smaller-than-normal size, even for a preemie; the shape of his head; his ears and mouth, disproportionately small, and his nose, disproportionately wide; the epicanthic folds on his eyelids and the size and shape of his hands and fingers. Melissa had listened, all the while looking at the baby as if he were the most perfect baby in all the world, and Alex . . . all he could think of was that old cautionary saying and how true it had proven.

Be careful what you wish for. You just might get it.

He'd wanted a child—had prayed, begged, pleaded for one. He'd watched other men with their children and felt such a longing inside. He'd dreamed of coaching a five-year-old's soccer team, of being a scoutmaster, of being the proud-to-bursting father of a football player or honor student, a drama star or even a class clown. He'd dreamed of someday changing the name of his law practice to Thomas and Thomas.

So much for dreams.

"God must hate me."

A gasp sounded a few feet away. "Don't say such a thing! God doesn't hate!"

Startled, he glanced at the woman sitting farther down

on the pew. He would have sworn the chapel was empty when he'd come in, and he hadn't heard anyone else enter, but there she sat, a pretty blonde with curls, wearing the standard uniform of cotton top and pants. She didn't look old enough to be a nurse, though he knew well looks could be deceiving. After all, to the uninformed, Max looked like a very small but perfect baby, when he was anything but.

"You're Max Thomas's father. I've seen you around the NICU. I'm Sophy."

When she offered her hand, he grudgingly shook it, then swung his gaze back to the front of the chapel. On Sunday night he was returning home to Bethlehem for a few days, to get caught up on his work, while Jenny and her parents stayed with Melissa. Everyone would want to see pictures and hear updates and would be so excited for him and Melissa, and he would have to tell them . . .

He *always* had to be the one to break the bad news.

"You're disappointed, aren't you?" Sophy asked sympathetically. "I understand. So was I at first. You've waited so long to become a father, and you thought this time everything was going to be perfect, and then . . . *boom!*"

He didn't say anything—didn't even look at her. No one knew he was disappointed, not even Melissa, and he intended to keep it that way. It wasn't a reaction he was proud of—truth was, it shamed him all the way through his soul—but there wasn't much he could do about it. He felt the way he felt.

"He has tremendous potential."

This time he couldn't stop himself from looking at her. "To do what? To *be* what?"

"To be a healthy, happy, loving son. To make your life, and Melissa's, and the lives of everyone around him, better. To make a difference."

"He'll never be a lawyer, a doctor, a teacher, or a father."

"Neither will an awful lot of other people."

"He'll never make the high-school football team or play in the band or go to college. He'll never drive a car or go out on dates or live on his own. He'll never have the chance to travel without someone to take care of him. He'll never hold a job or be a productive member of society. He'll never be anything more than a child, no matter what his age."

The look she gave him was chastising. "You don't know many people with Down syndrome, do you?"

He'd known a few over the years, but not well. They were . . . different.

He wanted his son to be different in only one way— better. Smarter. More talented. More outgoing. More accomplished.

"*Every* child is different, Alex. Max's differences will just be more readily apparent. As for what he'll do or never do, no one will have a clue for several years, at least. He could be very high-functioning. He could go through school, hold a job, and live in a group home, if not on his own. He could even marry and have children of his own." She laid her hand on his arm. "Yes, there will be things he can't do, but there are things that every infant in this hospital, 'normal' or not, won't be able to do. Not every child can throw a football, learn the piano, or become fluent in multiple languages. Not every child can do math or pick up chemistry or interpret the finer points of the law. And not every child can be sweet and loving and generous and kind . . . but Max will be."

Maybe . . . but he wouldn't play soccer or baseball. He wouldn't memorize lines to act in a play, as his mother had been doing when Alex met her. He wouldn't fit in in a regular classroom, wouldn't advance with other kids his age, wouldn't have the wide-open future other kids faced.

"But he'll think you hung the moon and the stars," Sophy murmured, "and he'll love you without reservation for the rest of his long, happy life."

Alex looked at her, at the utter serenity of her expression, and the tightness in his gut eased a little. Loving and being loved—something else that not all kids could do. Something important. Something that mattered, that made a difference. And, after all, the world already had enough lawyers and doctors, didn't it?

Even so, he couldn't stop being disappointed. Couldn't stop thinking.

Couldn't stop wishing . . .

Chapter Fifteen

WHILE ELI AND MURRAY WATCHED A football game on TV Saturday afternoon, Cole stood at his bedroom window, staring out at the town and thinking—about Leanne, last night, Ryan, Owen and Eloise and his brothers, about mistakes and complications and screwed-up values.

He hadn't been kidding when he'd told Leanne that this was no way for a man to live. It was the only life he'd prepared for, the only one he'd ever known. For the first time in thirty years, he wanted to break with tradition.

He didn't have a clue what he would do, or how he would do it, or if he stood even the smallest chance of succeeding. He didn't even know if he would like whatever respectable life he might make for himself any more than, or even as much as, the disreputable life he lived now. He just knew he wanted something different.

Stability. A chance to fix things with Ryan. A chance to pursue things with Leanne. He wanted to know how it felt to face himself in the mirror each day and know he hadn't done anything to be ashamed of. He wanted an occupation and a lifestyle where prison wasn't one of the costs of doing business.

He wanted to reinvent himself.

And he wanted to believe he could do it.

The sun hadn't come out all day, but the temperature had warmed into the high thirties. Snow melted in a steady drip from the rooftops and trees—so steady that a few of the older women out running their Saturday errands carried umbrellas to keep them dry. A snowman built in the square that morning by Sebastian Knight and his little girl had shrunk into a featureless lump of snow, and the streets were filled with dirty slush that splashed onto the sidewalks when cars drove past.

By Monday there wouldn't be any sign of the snow left—a good thing, since they were scheduled to start work on the town's Christmas decorations that morning. There were miles of lights to check for burned-out bulbs and bad wiring, as well as painted decorations that would require touch-ups, and others needing a good cleaning.

Though he could think of a lot better ways to spend his time than decorating for a holiday he didn't care much about, Cole wished it was already Monday. The weekend was dragging out one endless moment after another, leaving too much time to think.

He was about to turn away from the window when movement across the street caught his attention. It was Ryan and Danny, both bundled against the cold, and heading toward Small Wonders from Danny's day care center a block or so away. Ryan was holding Danny's hand and listening as the kid chattered.

When they drew even with the Miller mansion, Ryan's gaze shifted across the street, and Cole automatically took a step back and to the right. He watched through the lace curtains as Ryan stared at the house.

Sometimes Cole was surprised at how much he missed the kid. There was an empty space inside him that had appeared last spring and wasn't going away. He missed the friendship, the teasing, the arguing, the affection, the responsibility. He missed the needing, and being needed.

If you could have a chance to be Ryan's father again, would you take it? J.D. Grayson had asked during their appointment.

He missed being Ryan's father.

When the boys turned the corner and moved out of his sight, Cole turned away from the window, his gaze falling on the nightstand. Next to the lamp was Kelsey Grayson's business card, complete with the state seal and her home phone number as well as the office number. Jacksons had always made a point of being unreachable except through Owen, but here in Bethlehem, *unreachable* was a foreign concept. Unlisted phone numbers were rare, and if you couldn't get a person on the phone, half the town would be happy to give you directions to his house.

He picked up the business card and tapped it against one palm. He didn't want to talk to Kelsey—didn't want to hear that she'd had any luck in locating Ryan's birth parents. He didn't want to even think about the fact that she was looking, that if she found them, they could take the kid away from the family who loved him.

But Kelsey's home phone number was also J.D.'s, and he had a question or two to ask the good doctor.

Folding his fingers over the card, he went downstairs to the kitchen phone and dialed the number. One of the Grayson brood answered the phone, then a moment later, J.D. came on. "What can I do for you, Cole?"

"Sorry to bother you at home, Doc, but . . . I want to see Ryan."

"Okay." Grayson sounded a little confused. "Shouldn't you be discussing that with Leanne instead of me?"

"I just . . . I want to be sure . . ." Cole clamped his jaw

shut. It was easy enough to put into words—*I want to know that my being around won't do him any harm*—but giving voice to those words was another matter. It was a shameful thing to admit that just spending time with him could hurt Ryan.

"You want to know that seeing you won't cause Ryan any further problems." Grayson paused. "What made you want to see him?"

I miss him didn't seem a good enough response. Neither did *I feel guilty* or *I need to feel needed*. He didn't know that any answer he might give could be good enough, but he tried. "He deserves to know that it wasn't his fault—that he didn't do anything wrong. I didn't get tired of him. I didn't think life would be easier without him. I *knew* it would be damned hard . . . but I left him anyway."

That was the bottom line, the one that was so hard for him to explain, and so hard for Ryan to understand. *I left him anyway.*

"One of the toughest concepts for kids to understand is doing something for their own good. You left him here so he could have a better life than you could give him, but all he sees is that you chose a life that didn't include him. You were right the other day, Cole—you *were* the stability in his life. Your leaving turned his whole world upside down, and it hasn't been right since. When he's older, your reasons for it will matter, but right now they don't. All that matters now is that he loved you and you left him. Now you're back, and he's got all this anger and hurt inside that he doesn't know what to do with."

"So he's acting up at school. But if I'm around, he can take it out on me."

"It would certainly be easier on him to vent all that emotion on the person responsible for it, though it might get kind of rough for you."

"You think it's not kind of rough anyway?" Seeing him, knowing how deeply he'd hurt him, unable to talk to him, to make him understand . . .

"He'll want to hurt you the way you hurt him, and to some extent you'll have to let him. You can't blow up at him or try a time or two, then write him off. That would just validate his belief that you didn't want to bother with him anymore."

"I understand."

"And this can't be a short-term thing, Cole. If you're not intending to be a part of his life for the rest of his life, don't even start. He doesn't need your pity or your guilt. He needs a father who will always be there for him. If you can't commit to that, then leave him alone. Let him work through things with Leanne and me."

Commit. Cole smiled thinly. He'd committed a life's worth of crimes, but he'd never truly committed himself to any sort of relationship.

Until now.

"I'm not going to hurt him again. I just want to make things right." He paused, closed his eyes, then quietly added, "Please."

Grayson was silent for a moment before exhaling. "Let me talk to Leanne, then I'll get back to you, okay?"

"Thanks." Cole hung up, his fingers wrapped tightly around the receiver for a long time before he finally let go. He'd asked. Pleaded. Now all he could do was wait.

The answer came nearly two hours later. He was back in his bedroom, studying the patterns in the pressed-tin ceiling, when Eli knocked at the door, then came inside. "Leanne Wilson called. She and Dr. Grayson agree that it would be a good idea for you to spend some time with Ryan."

Cole sat up, swung his feet to the floor, and took a deep

breath, but didn't get much air. His chest was too tight to let his lungs expand, leaving him feeling starved for oxygen and vaguely panicked. He had asked for a chance, and they were giving it to him. Now if he just knew what to do, what to say, how to make Ryan believe in him again. . . .

"She said to tell you that they'll be having dinner at Harry's at six-thirty. She thought meeting in public might keep things a little restrained this time."

Jacksons had never been particularly restrained about their emotions, no matter where they were. He'd seen some wild celebrations in public places, as well as knock-down-drag-out fights. Hell, he'd taken part in both.

But Ryan wasn't a Jackson.

Funny how easy it was to forget that.

Eli started to leave, then turned back. "I understand this was your idea."

Cole nodded.

"Good." With that, he left.

G OD, HE HOPED IT WAS A GOOD IDEA, COLE THOUGHT as he stood in the darkness across the street from Harry's and gazed inside. The café was brightly lit, and a couple dozen diners were spread around the room. Harry, as usual, was in the kitchen, visible only occasionally when he delivered food to the pass-through, and Maeve, as usual, was waiting tables.

Leanne, Ryan, and Danny sat in the corner booth, a round one big enough for twice their number. She was on one end, and Danny on the other, which left Ryan in the middle with no escape. Probably a smart move on her part. Danny was on his knees, chattering a mile a minute, using his facial expressions, his hands, and his entire body to tell his story. He looked so young and innocent, exactly the way a four-year-old should look.

Had Ryan ever been that young or that innocent? Probably not. He'd never had the security Danny took for granted—a permanent home, family who loved him, a parent who would die for him. Cole had given him what he could, but it hadn't been enough. The story of his life.

Maeve delivered drinks to the booth, then laughed at something Danny said. Her pen was poised over the order pad, but she was in no hurry to move on to the next customer.

Suddenly cold, Cole forced himself to step out of the square, to cross the sidewalk, then the street, and walk into the diner. The bell announced him, bringing everyone's attention his way. Some looked at him, then away, without interest. Some glances were speculative, some censuring. Still frozen on the inside, but now flushed hot on the outside, he pretended to ignore them all and went to the booth.

Maeve gave him a cool excuse for a smile, Leanne gave him the real thing, and Danny leaped into his arms. "Hey! Where've you been? I been wishin' you'd come and see us, but you never do. We've missed you, ain't we, Ryan?"

Ryan shot a pissed look at Leanne, then started to slide around the bench. She stopped him with her hand on his arm. "You're not going anywhere, sweetheart."

"I'm not eatin' with *him*!"

"Yes, you are." She tugged his arm until he had no real choice but to slide back toward her a few inches. Okay, so he could have twisted his arm, twisting hers, too, in the process, and jerked away, but he didn't. Cole knew he would never risk physically hurting her. He'd been taught better than that.

"Danny, sit down. Cole, you, too. Maeve, could we have one more menu?"

Looking as if she would much rather show him the door, Maeve left, then returned to slap a menu down in front of him. "I'll come back for your order," she said stiffly before walking away.

"This isn't fair," Ryan said hostilely. "You could have told me this was a setup."

"Then you wouldn't have come willingly, and you would have been embarrassed when I carried you in over my shoulder."

"I wouldn't have come *at all*." He slumped down in the seat, chin on his chest, arms folded.

Leanne brushed a strand of hair from his eyes and gently teased, "Sweetheart, don't make me remind you that I'm your boss. Until you're old enough to live on your own, you have to do what I say."

He snorted.

Resting his arms on the table, Danny leaned close to Ryan. "And even after you're all growed up, you still have to do what she wants, 'cause she's the mama, and you're the kid, and that's the way it is. Ain't it, Mama?"

Leanne rewarded him with a serene and loving smile. "It certainly is, sweet pea."

Ryan slumped lower and scowled harder. "I'm not your kid."

"Says who?" she challenged. "I say you're mine, and so does Danny, and there's no one around brave enough to argue with us."

That stumped him. He looked at her for a moment, and Cole could actually see him softening a bit. Then, as if he caught himself, he frowned again, clamped his jaw shut, and said nothing.

"You ready to order?" Maeve asked as she returned,

giving smiles all around except to Cole. He wondered if she would pour salt in his tea and sugar in his gravy. He wondered if he could possibly stick around long enough to earn a genuine smile from her, or to make people stop looking at him as if he were alien to their experience—long enough for Ryan to forgive him, or to die trying. That could be his epitaph, he thought grimly. *He died trying.*

Maybe just this once it could be enough.

I T WAS A SHAME THE PURPOSE OF THE EVENING'S dinner hadn't been to get Danny together with Cole, because Danny was having a ball. Ryan, on the other hand, was dealing with Cole by not dealing with him—not speaking to him, not acknowledging him at all.

But Leanne had to give him credit—at least he hadn't left. He could have, even though they'd blocked him in. He was an agile kid. He could have gone under or over the table if he'd been really determined to get away. Instead, he'd sat there, scowling, barely picking at his food, ignoring everyone.

It was a start. A pitiful one, but a start.

When they were finished, she slid to her feet, put her jacket on, then looped her arm firmly through Ryan's when he would have bolted. Keeping him at her side, she leisurely strolled to the cash register near the door, paid the tab, called goodnight to Harry and everyone else, then joined Cole and Danny outside on the sidewalk. "What now, guys?" she asked as cheerfully as if the meal hadn't been excruciatingly tense.

"Ice cream!" Danny shouted, jumping up and down.

"Ice cream? With all that food in your tummy, you couldn't possibly have room for ice cream," she teased.

"Uh-huh. See?" He pulled up his shirt, exposing his little round belly, then smiled sweetly. "Please?"

"What do you say, Ryan?" she asked. "You want some ice cream?"

The child might be able to turn up his nose at a hamburger and fries, but he liked ice cream every bit as much as Danny did. He obviously considered that before shrugging as if he didn't care either way.

"What about you, Cole? You like ice cream?"

"Sure." He sounded about as enthusiastic as Ryan had looked. She had to give him credit, too. He'd tried to talk to Ryan, to draw *some* response from him, and had kept trying—though without success—long after she would have given up.

They crossed the street and walked the short distance to the ice cream shop. With its wooden floors, little round tables, and curlicued chairs, it was one of Leanne's favorite places in town. It had been in the same spot for more than sixty years, with the same furnishings and the same employee. Mr. McCormack had been dishing up cones and banana splits ever since he was fifteen years old. Back then, his grandfather had owned the place, then his parents had taken it over, and now it was his. His children had no interest in following tradition, but his granddaughter had been helping out ever since *she* was fifteen.

Tradition could be such a wonderful thing, she thought as they waited in line. Alex Thomas came from a family of lawyers and little Max would probably become one, too. The McCormacks had brought smiles and wrecked diets with their ice cream shop through five generations.

And then there was Cole's family tradition.

Each armed with their own cones, they found a table near the door and squeezed in. She took a bite from her cappuccino-almond ice cream, then sighed. "The woman who invented ice cream should have been granted saint-hood."

"I think it was a man," Cole said. "Men made all the great discoveries."

"Did not—and the ones they did make were probably because of women."

"What? They nagged, so they get to share the credit?"

"Big talk coming from a man with so little imagination he orders plain vanilla." She sniffed superiorly. "That's only good for holding fudge sauce or fresh strawberries, or for serving with birthday cake."

Danny grinned. "Ryan and me like—what *is* this again?"

"Cherry pecan," Ryan mumbled.

"Yeah. It's our favorite."

"Remember the first time you had that?" Cole asked. "We were in Memphis—"

Ryan interrupted, his tone cold and snotty. "And you were stealing from that woman you were seeing."

Cole's features tightened and his mouth thinned.

"You left me then, too, remember? And Eloise had to come pick me up so we could meet you in Alabama." He made a derisive sound. "I should've known you'd do it again someday."

His fingers gripping the cone almost hard enough to break it, Cole leaned toward him. "I left you that time because damn near every cop in the city was looking for me. It was too risky to go back for you. They would have taken us both into custody, and who knows if I ever would have gotten you back?"

Ryan leaned forward, too, until they were practically nose to nose. There was no physical resemblance between them at all—Cole was too blond, Ryan too dark—but their scowls were identically fierce. "Like that mattered? It would've just saved you the trouble of dumping me here."

"I didn't *dump* you."

"Oh, that's right. You thought I'd be *better off.* You thought if you left me here, I wouldn't turn out to be as big a loser as you are." The contempt in Ryan's voice made the words sound even uglier than they were, but only the twitch of a muscle in Cole's jaw showed that they'd hit their target.

"I always wanted you to be a better person than me. What's wrong with that?"

Ryan swore, making Danny's eyes open wide. "All you ever wanted was whatever was best for you. When it was okay for me to be around, you kept me. When it wasn't, you dumped me on someone else."

Leanne hated to interrupt when Ryan had finally started talking, even if he was just venting his anger, but they'd drawn attention from practically everyone in the shop. She laid one hand on Cole's arm and gripped Ryan's hand with the other. "Why don't we continue this conversation at home?"

"Why doesn't he just go to hell?" Ryan pulled free, tossed his ice cream in the trash, then stalked outside and across the street.

Leanne started to rise, but Cole grimly pushed her back. "Let me."

Danny watched him go, then looked fearfully at her. "Why's ever'one mad?"

She opened her arms, and he slid into her lap, resting his head on her shoulder while continuing to lick his ice cream. "Don't worry, babe. Everything's going to be all right." And that wasn't just words. She believed it with all her heart.

But it wasn't going to happen tonight.

• • •

By the time Cole caught up, Ryan had made it to the bandstand, where he leaned against the railing and hung his head. Cole climbed to the top of the steps, but didn't go any farther. He wanted to—wanted to wrap his arms around the kid and hold him until everything was all right.

But it might not ever be all right.

Instead he shoved his hands in his pockets. "I know how bad it hurt when your mom left, Ryan. Eloise was always leaving us. If she hadn't been so hung up on Owen, I doubt any of us kids ever would have seen her again after we were born. It hurt, knowing she didn't love or want us the way a mother was supposed to. I can only imagine how bad you were hurt, to have your mom take off the way she did."

"You don't know anything about my mom," Ryan muttered. "Besides, it don't matter. People don't matter."

"You're wrong. People are the only thing in life that *does* matter." He wasn't sure, but he thought he heard another of those obnoxious snorts in disagreement. "Maybe I didn't do a good job of teaching you that. I put too much emphasis on the cons and not enough on the important stuff, like family."

Ryan stared out at the street, his back to Cole. "I don't have any family."

"Maybe not the regular kind. God knows, the Jacksons don't qualify. But you've got some kind—Owen and the boys and me, Leanne and Danny and Micahlyn and her folks."

"Phyllis doesn't like me."

For the first time all evening, Cole felt a bit of relief. "Son, Phyllis doesn't like anyone."

"Don't call me that."

"Okay. Sorry." He'd hated being called *son* himself, but unlike his father, he hadn't used the word because he couldn't be bothered remembering the kid's name. That made a difference—to him, at least.

He watched Leanne and Danny come out of the ice cream shop, then start on the long way home, bypassing the square. She wiggled her fingers in a wave, then tucked Danny's hand securely in hers. A car drove past, then the porch lights came on at Jillian Freeman's house. It was prime-time Saturday night, and the town already seemed to be half-asleep.

Five years ago the payoff on a score would have to have been significant to make him settle even temporarily in such a quiet little place. Even then, he would have taken off every chance he got to find some excitement elsewhere, and he would have celebrated getting *out* of town as much as the payoff.

Tonight it seemed peaceful. Full of promise. A place where a man could atone for his past, live with himself, and make a future worth living.

With the cold seeping into his joints, he went to lean against the railing across from Ryan, crossing one ankle over the other. "I'm sorry for leaving you the way I did. I can't tell you how many times I wanted to turn around, come back, and get you."

"But you didn't," Ryan said belligerently.

"No, I didn't. And if the cops hadn't picked me up, I probably never would have set foot in Bethlehem again." He watched the kid's thin shoulders stiffen before adding, "But I would have regretted it as long as I lived."

"Easy to say now."

"No, Ryan, it's not easy to say, and it damn sure wasn't easy to do. But I *know* what I am. I *know* what I have to offer, and it's not enough. You're a smart kid, and you have so many chances ahead of you. You can be anything you want. You can make a difference in people's lives. If you settle for being no better than me because that's the only choice I've given you . . . I couldn't live with that. My own life has been screwed up from the beginning. I can't screw up yours, too."

Finally the kid faced him. "I could be anything I wanted *with* you! I stayed out of the cons. I didn't lift wallets or pick pockets for fun. All I did was get caught stealing once—one freakin' time! And it was just the excuse you were lookin' for to get rid of me."

"Nobody made me take you in. Nobody made me drag you around for three years or tell people you were my son. Nobody made me love you—" Realizing what he'd said, Cole stopped abruptly, the words echoing through him.

Ryan didn't notice, though. "And nobody made you dump me, either! You did it because you wanted to—because you didn't want me anymore!"

"That's not true—" Weariness settled over Cole, cutting off his denial, weighting his shoulders, and stirring an ache behind his eyes. It's not gonna be easy, Eli had said. The damn kid had to be right, didn't he?

"What's it matter anyway?" Ryan asked. "You tryin' to impress Leanne? Tryin' to make her think you can be a good father? Why, when you're just gonna dump her again, too?"

"I'm not dumping anyone."

"Yeah, sure. One of these days Adam or Bret's gonna show up in town and you'll be outta here like that." He snapped his fingers. "By the time she even realizes you're gone, you'll already be in another state, running another scam."

His life in a nutshell—change his name, change his hair

color, add a pair of glasses, or grow a beard. Play up the inbred Texas twang, affect a Southern drawl, or maybe mimic a clipped Boston accent. Be somebody else, conning someone else, until either he took all he could get or the law got too close. He'd lived his entire life like that.

"I'm not going anywhere," he said flatly, but to his own ears, the words lacked conviction.

Ryan stared at him, long and hard, before shaking his head. "Yeah, sure. Guess we'll see about that." Turning, he walked away.

After a moment, Cole headed after him, catching up as he reached the apartment door. Ryan took the stairs two at a time and disappeared down the hall. The bedroom door slammed about the time Cole got to the top.

Leanne came out of the kitchen and slid her arms around him. After a moment, she sighed softly. "I appreciate your doing this. I know it's tough."

"For God's sake, Leanne, I'm not doing anyone a favor. I *owe* the kid."

Her body stiffened against his, making him regret the words and the tone. When she would have pulled back, he wrapped his arms around her. "Don't . . . I didn't mean . . ."

After a moment, she softened against him once more. She smelled of things too exotic to name, sweet and sexy and desirable, and he knew she would taste just as sweet, just as sexy. Before he could prove it, though, small footsteps interrupted.

"Hey, Cole, wanna see me and Ryan's room?" Danny asked. "It used to be just my room, but then Ryan came, so now it's his, too. Wanna see?"

The kid was like a monkey, climbing halfway up Cole's leg. He gave him a boost and settled him on his hip. "I think Ryan wants to be alone."

"That's okay. He don't mind if I come in," Danny said matter-of-factly. It had never occurred to him even once in his life that his presence could ever be unwanted. Lucky kid.

"Why don't we give Ryan a little time alone?" Leanne suggested, then scooped him away from Cole and to the floor. "You go take your bath, then Cole can see your room when you go to bed, okay?"

"Okay. He can read me a story, too." Danny clumped off, his boots echoing on the hardwood floor.

When he was gone, Leanne turned back to Cole. "Why don't you get comfortable and warm—"

Her face cupped in his palms, he kissed her, sliding his tongue inside her mouth to taste her. Yep, sweet as spun sugar, sexy and sinful as hell. Just that one kiss was enough to make him hard, to turn the chill inside him to feverish heat.

When he ended the kiss, she looked a little dazed. He felt it.

He brushed his thumb across her still-parted lips, then said softly, "All warm now." But uncomfortable as hell, in a pleasurable way. "Go take care of Danny. I'll wait."

LEANNE GOT DANNY'S BATH STARTED, CHECKED IN ON Ryan, then went into the living room. She knew better than to think she and Cole might have five minutes uninterrupted, and naturally she was right. On weeknights, Danny usually dawdled through his bath, but this time he was serious about it, in and out—and even clean—in no time. She knew why, too—he wanted Cole's attention again.

As soon as he was dressed in his pajamas, he showed Cole all around the bedroom, as if it had truly changed since the spring. The walls were still tomato-red, the shelves were still filled with toys and books, and the video games still spilled out onto the floor. The only real differences were that his twin bed had been traded for bunk beds and some of the books on the shelves were Ryan's.

He insisted that Cole lie down in bed with him and read his favorite book about dinosaurs. Though she could practically recite it from memory, Leanne remained in the doorway and listened, enjoying the sight of her sweet little boy curled up in Cole's arms. Though she'd never regretted Greg's disappearing act, she had always wished Danny could have a real father. It helped, having her dad around and now Chase, but the real deal would mean so much to him—and to her.

Ryan could practically recite the story from memory, too, but he lay motionless in the top bunk, listening to the words. Had anyone ever read bedtime stories to him, then tucked him in and kissed him and said *I love you?* It didn't seem likely that the mother who'd abandoned him had made a routine out of anything that didn't benefit her.

Not that Leanne really knew what kind of mother the woman had been. Yes, she'd abandoned him, but the reason for it could make all the difference. Maybe she'd been a good mother, but had suffered a breakdown and become unable to care for him any longer. Maybe she'd never meant to leave him in that bus terminal but something had happened to her.

Or maybe she'd just realized one day that she no longer wanted to be a mother.

That possibility boggled Leanne's mind.

As soon as Cole finished the book, Danny dragged another one from under his pillow and shoved it at him. "Now this one."

Looking at her, Cole raised one eyebrow, and she nodded that it was all right, then left the room. She was in the kitchen, making brown-sugar-and-cinnamon-flavored coffee when he eventually followed her. He came to stand behind her at the stove, where she stirred the coffee in a saucepan, sliding his arms around her and nuzzling her neck.

"Hmm, that smells good. And the coffee's not half-bad, either."

She smiled. "So Danny couldn't talk you into a third story."

"Just a very short one. You read to him every night?"

"Ever since he was a few months old. Now Ryan does it sometimes." She watched the muddy-looking brew boil, the coffee grounds bubbling up, then subsiding, only to do it again. The last thing she needed tonight was caffeine, but she figured the sugar and spices, along with the whipped cream that would go on top, would counteract it. If not, maybe Cole would.

When the timer went off, she reluctantly pulled out of his embrace and took a mesh strainer from a drawer. If she were a more proficient cook, she would have cheesecloth to go inside it. Instead, she lined it with a paper towel, then strained the coffee into a heat-proof carafe. She was spooning whipped cream into mugs when Cole chuckled.

"You planning to have a little coffee with your whipped cream?"

Making a face, she scooped one heaping spoonful from each mug back into the carton. For good measure, he took the spoon and removed that much more from his. Once she'd filled the mugs, they each took one, then went into the living room. She sat on the sofa, kicked her shoes off, and drew her feet onto the cushions. He walked to the nearest window.

"Eli says I should go to church with you guys tomorrow," he said after a while.

"It couldn't hurt."

"Are you sure? Ryan's friends will be there."

"They know who you are, and they know what you've done. Besides, most kids their age aren't too happy about the parents they've been stuck with."

He gave her a dry look. "Danny will adore you as much when he's sixteen as he does right now."

"Because I've trained him well," she replied with a smug smile.

"Why isn't his father around?"

She tried to remember if he'd ever asked about Greg before. It was something everyone eventually got to, but she couldn't recall him ever bringing it up. Because he hadn't cared?

"He wasted no time getting out once I told him I was pregnant. He'd thought we were having fun—dating, sleeping together. He hadn't signed on for anything as serious or long-term as fatherhood."

"Has Danny ever met him?"

"No. Greg not only got out of the relationship, he got out of *town*. He was afraid I would hit him up for child support or something. I never knew where he went and never cared."

"But you were in love with him."

"I was," she agreed slowly. "It's funny, though, how quickly you can fall *out* of love with a man when he tells you he wants nothing to do with his own child." She didn't realize the double meaning of her words until Cole's jaw clenched and he stared outside again.

"Like me, you mean."

Rising from the sofa, she set her coffee on the table, then went to wrap her arms around him. "No, that's not what I mean. You and Greg are nothing alike. His reasons for taking off were purely selfish. You wanted Ryan to have a better life. Greg wanted his own life to be better. He didn't want to give up his fun, marry me, run into me around town, or tell his new girlfriends that he had a son. He certainly didn't want to take on eighteen years of financial responsibility for a child he hadn't chosen to have. I doubt he even remembers Danny exists."

"What is it with parents?"

"It's not parents. It's just people. Some people are generous and loving, and some aren't. They're that way in all parts of their lives, not just with their kids."

"Some should never be parents."

Leanne rested her head on his shoulder while she considered that. "I don't know. I know more than my share of parents who have done an abominable job of parenting. My own mother wouldn't win any awards, and no matter how good my father was to me, he was lousy with Chase. But if they'd never become parents, Chase and I wouldn't be here. If bad parents were prohibited from procreating, none of us in this apartment would be here, and that would be a terrible shame. The four of us have a lot to offer."

"At least three of you do."

She elbowed him gently. "Ryan and Danny love you. That says a hell of a lot about you."

He gazed down at her, his blue eyes shadowed, his expression intent, and his mouth opened, then closed again. Ask, she silently urged. *Ask me if I love you.*

But the moment passed and the words didn't come. Instead, he set his coffee on the windowsill, pulled her hard against him, and grinned that phony grin. "Wanna make out while the kids are quiet?"

Deep inside she was disappointed. She didn't like the fake front he presented—didn't like that he felt it necessary, after all they'd been through, to present it to her. But there was nothing fake about his arousal, or about the heat building inside her. There was nothing fake at all about his need for her, or her love for him.

She managed a seductive smile and rose onto her toes to brush her mouth across his. "Oh, darlin', I wanna do a whole lot more than make out."

She gave him a hungry, greedy kiss, then grabbed a handful of his shirt and headed for her bedroom, dragging him behind.

I T WAS NEARLY ELEVEN O'CLOCK WHEN COLE WENT home. Leanne belted her robe around her waist and walked with him through the quiet, cool apartment to the top of the stairs. "See you tomorrow?"

"For church?" His look was wry. "After what we just did?"

"Some would say we need it more than ever after what we just did."

"Some would . . . but damned if I'm going to repent for it."

"See if Eli will let you skip just once. We could take the boys to the lake—go hiking, have a picnic or something."

"I'll ask." He kissed her, a sweet goodnight kiss that wasn't intended to stir her blood but did. "Either way, I'll see you in the morning."

Hugging herself, she watched as he took the steps two at a time, then let himself out. With a sigh, she turned off the lights they'd left burning, then quietly opened the door to the boys' room. The lamp on the nighttable showed Danny sprawled across the bed, his pillow on one side, his covers on the other, and snoring softly. Jerome lay on the fallen covers, also snoring softly, and Ryan was curled on his side, reading by flashlight.

She nudged the dog off the blankets, retucked her son, then leaned her arms on the edge of Ryan's bunk. "Let's go to the hardware store Monday and get one of those lamps that clamps onto the bed. You'll ruin your eyes using that flashlight."

With a faint smile, he nodded.

"Not sleepy yet?"

"Not really." He paused. "Is he gone?"

This time the faint smile and nod were hers.

"He says he's not goin' anywhere."

For a moment his words puzzled her. Of course Cole had to go home; it wasn't as if it was his choice. Then she realized he meant in the larger scheme of things. "Do you believe him?"

"He's a liar and a con artist. You can't trust him."

"Did he ever lie to you, Ryan? Did he ever con you?"

Because his answer was no, she suspected, he didn't say anything, but merely glowered.

"Come on, sweetie. You opened the subject—now you've got to answer. Did he ever lie to you?"

Grudgingly he muttered, "No."

"Did he ever con you?"

"He made me think I could stay with him, that he wanted me, and then he dumped me. That was a con."

"No, it wasn't. He thought he was doing what was best for you. That's what parents do, no matter how much it hurts them. If he was conning you, what did he get in return? What was the payoff?"

Again, Ryan chose not to answer.

"Why would he bother with you at all if he didn't want to? He wasn't the first person whose pocket you picked, was he? But no one else took you in. No one else offered you a home and food and clothes and security. Just Cole."

"Because he felt sorry for me."

"Probably, in the beginning. But if that was all he felt, don't you think it would have been easier for him to turn you over to the authorities? If he didn't care about you, he could have gotten rid of you so easily, without even a guilty conscience to bother him."

"Cole don't have a conscience," he mumbled.

"He has one. It's what made him take you in and look out for you and be a father to you, and it's what made him leave you here with us. He wanted what was best for you, just like I want what's best for Danny."

Ryan let his book fall shut, then clicked off the flashlight. "Yeah, but you didn't give him away."

"No. But if I *truly* believed he would be better off living with someone else, that living with me was hurting him in some way, I would find someone to take him. It would break my heart, but I would do it."

"But that'll never happen, 'cause you're a good mother. He's a lousy father."

"He's a pretty good father for someone who's never been one before, who was raised the way he was. You liked having him pretend to be your dad. You liked living with him, or you wouldn't be so unhappy without him."

"I'm not unhappy."

"So failing school and getting into fights is just a hobby with you."

He gave an elaborate shrug, then repeated, "I'm not unhappy. He did me a favor. I like it here with you and Danny. We don't need him."

I do. Wisely, she didn't say so out loud. Taking the book from the bed, she laid it on the nightstand, then brushed her fingers through his hair. "There's nothing wrong with needing someone," she said, then sang deliberately off-tune. " 'People . . . people who need people . . .' "

With a great groan, Ryan clutched his pillow to his ears. "No singing, please!"

Lifting her nose into the air, she sniffed. "Obviously, you have no appreciation for musical genius." Then she spoiled the effect by laughing. "You'd better get to sleep, kiddo. Me, too. I'm not as young as I used to be."

Stretching onto her toes, she tucked him in, pressed a kiss to his forehead, then said *I love you* and *Goodnight*. She was at the door when he spoke again.

"Hey, Leanne?"

She paused.

"He—he said that, too."

"He told you goodnight?"

"No. That—that he . . . loved me."

A lump formed in her throat and made her voice husky. "Well, of course he does, sweetheart. Didn't you know that?"

He shook his head.

She wondered whether to make a big deal over it—to explain how some people had trouble expressing their emotions verbally, but showed it through their actions, just as Cole had. Deciding that would be too much, she settled for a quiet reassurance. "Well, now you do. Goodnight, babe."

Chapter Sixteen

B y Monday morning, the only sign of the weekend's snowfall was the wet ground and layers of dirt deposited on all the cars around town. Though Cole had made a point of spending all his winters in warmer climes, he hadn't minded the snow as much as he'd expected. In fact, there was something to be said for a walk in the snow with a pretty woman . . . especially when it was followed by a roll in the sack with her.

Of course, the real test of his winter adaptability would come when Bethlehem got its first serious snowstorm, the kind that shut down the highways out of the valley and kept everyone close to home. Then he might be a good candidate for going stir-crazy.

He, Eli, and Murray had spent the morning at the city garage, where most of the town's Christmas decorations were stored. *Bethlehem did Christmas right,* Leanne had said, and their morning's work had proved her point. They'd unpacked literally miles of lights, giant velvet bows, jingle bells, acres of ribbon, and enough wreaths and garlands to create a forest of fake spruce. In a room off to the side were the nutcracker soldiers—five dozen of them, six feet tall, painted blue, red, or green, and wearing black hats with tall feathers curling overhead. When they went cross-eyed from checking wiring and bulbs on the strings of lights, Eli had said they could take a break by starting the touch-up painting on the soldiers or hauling in the bigger displays from the summer camp outside of town where they were stored.

Cole's eyes were *already* starting to cross from the work, and the mindlessness of it was making him antsy. Too bad they'd finished cutting all the trees. Getting outside and burning off a little energy was starting to sound really good.

Eli came to stand in front of him, stepping over boxes of bulbs. "You ready for lunch? I figured we could walk down to Harry's."

"Sure. Where's Murray?"

"Washing up."

"How long is he gonna stay here?"

Eli shrugged. "As long as he needs. He'll know when the time is right to leave."

"And you're just gonna let him hang around?"

"It's not like he's taking a bed that I need for someone else. We've got plenty of room, and as long as he's finding something he needs here, who am I to turn him away?"

What was Murray finding that he needed? It wasn't as if he was outgoing or even particularly friendly with either Cole or Eli. He did his share of the work, but pretty much kept his thoughts to himself. What was his life like, that he preferred living with them to being back on his own again?

The answer popped into Cole's head too quickly for comfort.

Lonely.

He wasn't thinking of himself a little there, was he?

"Why don't you wash up, too, then meet me outside," Eli suggested.

The bathroom was in the main part of the garage next door, the sturdy built-of-brick-to-stay-around-forever part. Their workspace was corrugated metal, a tacked-on afterthought devoted exclusively to housing the Christmas stuff. He ran into Murray on his way out. The old man smiled as he passed, and Cole realized that the gesture wasn't as vague as it had once been. His eyes were clearer, too, and his color better. Cole understood that staying sober could do that for a man.

Thank God he'd hadn't had to find that out for himself. Booze was one vice he hadn't embraced wholeheartedly. Other than the occasional eggnog-free rum at Christmas, he could go years without so much as a beer and never miss it.

He'd gone nearly six weeks without committing a crime, and he didn't miss that, either.

As soon as he'd washed away the grime, he grabbed his jacket and caught up with the others outside. It was only a few blocks to Main Street, then a few blocks more to Harry's. Eli and Murray walked ahead, with Cole bringing up the rear, hands in his pockets, gazing in the store windows they passed. He was thinking idly about showing up in church with Leanne and the boys the morning before— Eli had insisted they could go to the lake *after* the services—and the hike they'd taken around the lake's rocky shore. Danny and Leanne had both moved like mountain goats, and had laughed and called him "city boy" when he complained. Even Ryan had said it once, his tone not exactly friendly, but not dripping with disgust, either.

Later, when Cole had cooked dinner for them, Ryan had even grudgingly helped out in the kitchen. He wasn't giving in easily or gracefully, but he *was* giving in. A little. Very little.

Abruptly he came to a stop. He was in front of the bookstore, where a display of old books had caught his eye. The once-bright covers were faded, the pages were yellowed, and they showed signs of heavy wear, but that didn't matter. He'd read that series—a lot of them, at least—when he was a kid. Owen had teased that his interest had been professional—the series was about crime-solving kids, while he'd been a crime-*committing* kid, just looking for tips.

Truth was, he'd read them for the reason a lot of people read—to escape from his life through the pages of a book. Anything could happen in a book, while in real life, the possibilities were far more limited, though it didn't always feel that way in Bethlehem.

He didn't have a clue what had happened to his old books. They'd probably been left behind in one of their many midnight moves. When you had to take off at a moment's notice, you tended not to accumulate much in the way of possessions. The kind of things normal people kept—letters, photographs, baby clothes—had never been a part of his life.

"What are you doing?"

He glanced at Eli, then Murray, waiting ahead at the corner. "Ryan's birthday is Thursday."

"The kid likes to read, huh? You thinking about getting him those old books that you used to read?"

Cole gave him a curious look. "How do you know—"

"All boys used to read those books. Why don't you tell Betty to hold them for you, and you can come back tomorrow to pay for them. We're going on to Harry's. Want me to order for you?"

"Yeah, just a burger."

As Eli walked on, Cole went inside, his gut knotted. Betty was the full-time help at the store, working for Elena, the owner, and they'd both invested in his scam last spring. He wouldn't be surprised if they refused to do business with him now. Tired and discouraged, but not surprised.

Both women were working. After exchanging wary glances, Elena left the box she was unpacking and approached him. "Can I help you?" Her tone was neutral, polite enough under the circumstances, but nowhere near as polite as it had once been.

He asked about the books, and for a moment she looked as if she wanted to say they weren't for sale, at least, not to the likes of him. But she pasted on a grim smile, told him the books had just come in as part of a library she'd purchased at an estate sale, and gave him the price for the set.

"Can you hold them for me until tomorrow? I don't have any cash on me right now, but I can bring it by first thing in the morning."

Her gaze turned speculative as she considered it. Was she wondering who he would steal the money from, or whether, if she refused, he would come back after closing time and take them anyway? Whatever her thoughts, after a moment she shrugged. "Would you like them gift-wrapped?"

"Yeah, please."

"A special occasion?"

"A birthday. My son—" He caught himself, grimaced, then went on. "Ryan's birthday is Thursday."

"We'll have them ready."

He nodded, then headed for the door, eager to escape. Something stopped him there, though, and made him turn back, glancing from one woman to the other. "About what happened—what I did . . . I'm really sorry."

Elena offered that grim smile again. "So were we."

He nodded once more, walked through the door, and collided with someone on the sidewalk. "Sorry," he said again, catching his balance and extending a hand to steady the man. His gaze got only as high as the priest's collar. There was only one priest in town, and Cole had ripped him off, too. Facing three of his victims in less than a minute was more than he was prepared for, so he ducked his head and set off toward Harry's. He hadn't gone more than five feet before a familiar voice in an unfamiliar brogue stopped him.

" 'Tis too lovely a day to be rushin' about, laddie. You should slow down, take a look around you."

Cole spun around and stared, his eyes opened wide, his breath caught in his chest. *"Frank?"* he whispered, the best he could manage.

"That's Father Francis to you, son." Frank slid his finger between his neck and the collar, then reverted to his normal voice. "I guess it's true what they say—the clothes make the man."

"What the hell are you doing?"

"Answering your call. Well, your letter, to be more precise. You remember—*I need a ride. If any of you happen to be around Bethlehem . . .* I was closest, so here I am."

Cole rubbed the tension in the back of his neck, then looked around anxiously. The last thing he needed was for someone he knew to see him and Frank together. The resemblance between them wasn't so strong that seeing Frank alone would automatically make a person think of Cole, but standing side by side was too risky. They had the same blond hair, though Frank's was a few shades lighter, and the same blue eyes, though Frank's appeared guileless. He was masquerading as a priest, for God's sake, and managed to look innocent doing it.

"What did they get you for, bubba?"

"An investment scam."

"What was the haul?"

"Quarter mil."

Frank gave a low whistle. "Damn. So the town's as prosperous as it looks. Or, at least, it was. Is the money safe?"

Across the street, Leanne's father came out of the building that housed his insurance office and walked to the curb. Cole grabbed Frank's arm and hustled him back the way he'd come. As soon as they turned the corner, he released his brother. "Don't you know you'll burn in hell for pretending to be a priest?"

Frank laughed, his dimples showing. "Don't you know we're all gonna burn in hell anyway? Our fates were sealed by the time we turned ten. So . . . where's the take?"

Shoving his hands in his pockets, Cole leaned against the brick building and scowled at his brother. There was something wrong when a man felt a twinge of shame, not for stealing $250,000, but for giving it back. He *wouldn't* be ashamed if he was admitting it to anyone but family, and there was something damned wrong about that, too. "I returned it."

"You . . ." Frank made a big show of rubbing his knuckle into one ear, then cupping his hand behind it. "I didn't hear you right. Can you say that again?"

Cole started to cuff him on the shoulder, then wondered what any passerby would think about him punching a priest, and drew back. "I gave the money back."

Frank couldn't have looked more surprised if the Father, the Son, and the Holy Ghost had taken on physical form right in front of him. *"Why?"*

"Because it was the right thing to do."

"Right for *who*?" Dolefully Frank shook his head. "Jeez, Cole, remember the rules? *Admit to nothing, deny everything, lie like the devil, and always look out for number one. Never tell the truth if a lie will suffice. Never apolo—*"

"I remember," he said dryly. "I've heard them five years longer than you have."

"Damn! A man makes a score like that, he doesn't give it back. He goes to Tahiti or Australia or, hell, he blows it right here in the good ol' U.S.A. He lives it up until it's gone, and then he goes out and starts it all over again. Are you out of your freakin' mind?"

Maybe. But Cole didn't offer the answer out loud.

Frank leaned against the building, too, his gaze on the street, his brow drawn together. "Let me get this straight. You conned a quarter of a million dollars out of these people, they caught you, you gave it back, and they're letting you walk around free?"

Cole didn't bother to correct him on the order—that he'd given the money back long before he'd been caught—but focused on the last part. "I'm not walking around free. I'm part of an experimental work-release type program. My watchdog is waiting for me at Harry's." If he wasn't already on his way back, to find out what was holding Cole up.

"Okay, so what's the plan?"

"The plan?" Cole repeated stupidly.

"We gonna take off now? Do you need to get your stuff first? Is there a better time for getting out, when no one will be around to notice you're gone? *The plan,* bubba. A man needs a plan." Frank's tone turned impatient. "Jeez, you still want to split, don't you?"

Cole stared into the distance. He'd *wanted* to—when he'd written the letter, and for a time afterward. But now . . . well, hell, if he skipped out now, Eli would be short a man in getting the decorations up, and the cops and the judge would surely be pissed that he'd managed to lose his only real criminal. They would probably shut down his program, which wouldn't be a problem for him—he was young and energetic, and Bethlehem took care of its own—but Murray was neither young nor energetic nor, technically, one of Bethlehem's own.

If he skipped out now, he could kiss Leanne good-bye forever. She'd forgiven him once. She wasn't likely to do it a second time. That would be a greater loss than he was prepared to deal with.

And if he skipped out now, three days before Ryan's birthday, when he'd just told him Saturday night that he wasn't going anywhere . . . *Yeah. Sure. Guess we'll see about that,* Ryan had said. He hadn't managed to forgive Cole even once. He would damn sure never do it if Cole proved he didn't deserve it.

"Well, bubba?"

His gaze jerked back to Frank. "I can't just— There are things I have to—" He swore. "Your timing sucks."

"Oh, well, hell, pardon me for dropping everything to help you out, but doing it with lousy timing. I'll tell you what—I'll go back to Connecticut, where I've got a flock to fleece, and when you find time in your schedule to skip town, you can give me a call. Or better yet, you can get yourself the hell out of town."

Cole rubbed his forehead, then let his hand drop to his side. "Look, Frankie—" He broke off as a car pulled into the parking space in front of them and an elderly woman got out. He aimed for polite with his smile, but wasn't sure he managed anything more than a grimace as she stepped onto the sidewalk. "Miss Corinna."

"Cole." She smiled, gave Frank a curious look and a nod, then turned the corner onto Main.

Cole watched until she was out of sight, then became aware of Frank's gaze on him. Without looking, he could feel the censure, and confirmed it when he faced his brother again.

"They're doing it, aren't they? Setting you on the straight and narrow. Jeez, I don't believe this . . . unless . . . You have another con in mind, don't you? You ripped them off once, they forgave you, and now you're gonna do it again. What'll it be this time?"

"Nothing. There's no con."

"Yeah, right. I *know* you, bubba. No way you're gonna stick around a hick town like this, doing scut work for free, unless it's gonna pay off somehow."

Cole couldn't deny there could be a payoff if he was lucky, though not the kind Frank was envisioning. Like the rest of the Jacksons, Frank thought in terms of cold hard cash. But Cole wanted the big prize—Leanne, Ryan, Danny. A family, a home, a place to belong.

But hadn't he learned from the cradle that wishing was a waste of breath? He'd been born and bred for one kind of life, and what Bethlehem offered, wasn't it.

But people could change. Leanne believed it. So did Ryan and Eli and everybody else. If Leanne and Ryan could believe in him, wasn't believing in himself the least he could do?

"It ain't gonna happen, Cole," Frank said quietly. "Being a thief, a liar, and a cheat isn't what you do—it's who you *are*. It's in your blood. Like I said, our fates were sealed by the time we turned ten."

Cole walked to the corner, saw Eli going into the bookstore, then ducked back. "Look, I've got to go. There's a motel just outside town called Angels Lodge. Get a room there, and I'll be in touch."

"Don't take too long. You'd be surprised what a crimp this outfit puts in my social life." He fell into the phony brogue again. "When you call, laddie, ask for Father Murphy." When he reached his car, he turned back. "Hey, where's Ryan?"

"He's here. In a foster home."

"Good. We'll pick him up before we leave."

"No." Vehemence made Cole's voice sharp and heated his face. "He's staying here. He's not going to grow up like us."

"And that would be so bad?"

Rather than argue the point with him, Cole shrugged, then walked away. As soon as he turned the corner, he spotted Eli, heading his way. The kid's expression went blank before he mildly asked, "Take a wrong turn on your way to Harry's?"

"I was giving directions to this guy looking for the motel," he lied, gesturing as Frank, with a friendly wave, turned left onto Main.

Eli raised his brows. "New priest in town?"

"I think he's just passing through."

"Maybe he'll enjoy his visit so much he'll stay."

That was doubtful. Frank enjoyed a lot of things, but small-town honest living wasn't one of them. And since the Jackson boys were all alike, didn't that mean small-town, honest living wasn't for *him,* either?

WHEN ALEX LEFT HIS OFFICE MONDAY EVENING, HE was torn between going to church, where the doors were always open for those in need of spiritual solace, and the Five Pines Lounge, where the doors were almost always open for those in need of spirits of another sort. The desire for peace of some kind was strong, and he was leaning toward the oblivion offered by the Five Pines when he backed out of his parking space.

Instead, he found himself heading home. For a time he

sat in the driveway, looking at the dark house. In all the years of their marriage, he'd spent so very few nights in that house without Melissa that it seemed wrong somehow to walk through the door when she was hours away. He could delay it by going back downtown to Harry's or McCauley's for dinner, but that would mean facing people who now knew the truth.

All it had taken was one phone call Sunday morning to Miss Corinna. He'd asked her to tell their friends about Max, so he and Melissa wouldn't have to. He had thought that would be easier for him, but as he'd discovered when he'd gone to the office that morning, there was nothing easy about any of it. The expressions of sympathy he'd gotten, the sorrowful looks, the hugs and pats on the arm . . . it was almost as if someone had died.

In reality, part of him had.

When the cold shivered through him, he got his briefcase from the seat beside him and went inside the house. He didn't bother turning on lights, but climbed the stairs in the darkness and made his way, as he had hundreds of times before, to the nursery. There, finally, he flipped on the lights.

Once he and Melissa had allowed themselves to hope that this time there would be no miscarriage, he'd painted the room at her direction. There'd been no blue-for-boys or pink-for-girls discussion, no gender-nonspecific pastels. She had chosen a rich, dark green for the walls, with a wallpaper border of carousel horses about halfway up. The crib was made up with flannel sheets, a quilt, and a receiving blanket, and hanging above it was a colorful mobile.

There were shelves built into one wall, with figurines and baby books, stuffed animals, empty picture frames, and Alex's old baseball glove. Melissa had been optimistic when she'd put that there.

He picked up the glove, smelled the aged leather, and rubbed the signs of hard use. His father had given it to him when he was five or so, and on every warm day for months they'd played catch in the backyard. All that effort hadn't made him more than a passable catcher and a so-so pitcher, he recalled with a faint smile.

If Max wasn't much of a baseball player, he would just be following in his father's footsteps. If he didn't excel at riding a bike, he could thank his mother's bike-challenged genes for it. If he couldn't carry a tune . . . well, his grandfather *was* tone-deaf, and if he lacked the coordination to march in the high school band, he could blame his Aunt Jenny, who could trip in the middle of a perfectly clean floor, pick herself up, and do it again.

Every child was different, Sophy had pointed out in the hospital chapel. He knew that, of course. He'd gone to school with kids who couldn't behave to save their lives, as well as ones who couldn't misbehave to save *their* lives. There'd been the kids who had sailed through every class with effortless A's and the ones who'd struggled for C's. They'd had the actors who could become someone else in the blink of an eye and the kids who couldn't even be themselves without time to prepare. The graceful and the uncoordinated. The outgoing and the reserved. The kind, the cruel, and the indifferent.

Everyone *was* different. How boring life would be if that weren't true.

He and Melissa were different now. They weren't just husband and wife, lawyer and nursery owner, members of the community. They were parents. Mother and father to a beautiful little boy who would be sweet, loving, generous, and kind—who would think they'd hung the moon and the stars, and would love them dearly all his life.

Who deserved to be loved like that himself.

Alex had wanted a child, had pleaded and prayed for one. He hadn't specified a child who would become a lawyer or a teacher or an athlete—just a child who would be happy and healthy and loved.

He was a lucky man.

His prayers had been answered.

You've been a million miles away all evening," Leanne remarked as she shifted on the sofa to face Cole. "Where are you, and what are you doing?"

He glanced at her, his gaze shadowed before he hid his moodiness behind a smile. "I'm right here, darlin'."

"In body only. Your mind is far, far away." It had taken about two seconds to realize that when he'd arrived for dinner. His kiss, quickly given and accepted in the hallway, had been about as sizzling as her brother's kiss might be, and she and the boys had found themselves repeating things to him all through the meal. For the past half hour he'd sat at the other end of the sofa, a cup of coffee growing cold in his hand, an air of melancholy surrounding him.

If he were anyone else, she might wonder if he was homesick, missing his family, or regretting the life he would be living if he wasn't in Bethlehem. But he'd never had a home to miss, and his contact with his family was sporadic. As for missing his guilt-free life of crime . . . she wanted to believe he didn't. Wanted to believe he never looked at an object he coveted and thought how easily he could acquire it. Wanted to believe he'd changed.

She just wasn't a hundred percent positive about it.

The television was tuned to her favorite Monday-night drama, and they were alone in the living room. Danny had been bathed, tucked in, and read to, and was now snoozing in his bed. Jerome was snoozing there, too, warming

Danny's feet, while Ryan read in the top bunk. The apartment was quiet except for the television, and she and Cole had been quiet, too—for too long.

Using the remote, she muted the TV. "Seriously, what's on your mind?"

"Nothing. I'm just tired."

That was a lie. He was distracted, distant, troubled. About what? The aspects of this life that agreed with him and the ones that didn't? The parts he wanted to change and the ones he couldn't change?

Which category did she fall into? The good? The bad? Or the convenient?

"Is work going okay?"

"Yeah."

"No more run-ins with my mother?"

"If there had been, you would have heard."

That was true, she acknowledged. The whole town would have heard, but as it was, Phyllis had been quiet lately.

Wishing for something to occupy her hands, she settled for hugging her knees to her chest. She couldn't force confidences that he didn't want to give, so she settled for the next best thing. "If you need to talk, you know I'm here."

His smile was faint and slid away as soon as it formed. "I know. But right now . . . I think I need to go."

"Okay." Her smile was no more successful than his. When he took his coffee cup into the kitchen, she followed as far as the bar that separated the kitchen and dining room and stood there awkwardly, arms hugging her chest, one foot balanced on top of the other.

After rinsing the cup, he faced her. "Before I go, can I use the phone?"

"Sure." She freed one hand to gesture to the phone a few feet away, but he gave it a wary look.

"In your bedroom?"

"Sure." Retucking her hand, she watched him leave the room, then listened to her bedroom door close. A private call. To whom? He didn't have any real friends in town. There was no reason to call Eli when he would be home sixty seconds after leaving the apartment, and no reason, as far as she knew, to call his lawyer.

So maybe it wasn't a local call. Maybe he was calling his father or one of his brothers. Granted, he and Ryan had both said they kept in touch through their father's post office box, but maybe he'd heard from one of them and gotten a temporary number to reach him.

Maybe one of them had shown up, as Ryan had predicted, to take him away. That's what they do, he'd said. *Whenever one of 'em gets in trouble, he sends a letter to Owen, and the first one who checks in has to go and get him.*

That was an awfully big assumption to make from one phone call, she chastised herself as she loaded the last few dishes into the dishwasher. Cole wasn't leaving. He'd told Ryan, and her, too. He intended to serve his time, and then . . . *then* he would be free to go wherever he wanted.

Please, God, let him want to stay right here.

She wasn't sure what alerted her to his presence—a quiet footstep registered subconsciously or the soft, steady sound of his breathing. More likely pure feminine instinct that tightened her nerves. Whatever it was, when she turned, he was standing in the doorway, his jacket in hand.

"I'm leaving now."

Not trusting herself to speak without pleading, she nodded.

"I told Ryan goodnight."

She nodded again.

"I'll see you tomorrow."

She went to him, slid her arms around his neck, and

kissed him, long and deep and hungrily, and was rewarded with the first stirring of desire swelling against her belly. Breaking the kiss, she breathed softly of his scents. "Yeah. Tomorrow."

Now that he was leaving, he looked as if he would rather stay, but he walked out anyway. She stood where she was, a chill that came from the inside making her tremble. She could be so terribly insecure when it came to the men in her life. Maybe that was because they kept leaving her—first Greg, then Steve and Richard. Cole had been number four on the heartbreak list. Surely she could be forgiven for wondering if he might also be number five.

She picked up in the living room, started a load of laundry, and paid a few bills. Shortly after ten o'clock, Ryan came out to say goodnight. She hugged him and told him she loved him, and he mumbled, "Me, too," for the first time ever. For ten minutes the wonder of that kept her smiling and warm on the sofa.

Finally she got ready for bed, following through her nightly routine, changing into a T-shirt, folding back the covers, sitting on the bed to rub lotion into her hands. She was lying down and leaning on one elbow, about to turn out the lamp, when her gaze fell on the telephone next to it—or, to be more accurate, on the REDIAL button on the phone.

Who Cole had called was none of her business. She knew that, just as surely as she knew what she was about to do was wrong. That didn't stop her, though. She braced the receiver between her ear and shoulder, took a deep breath, and pushed REDIAL.

The call was answered on the second ring. "Angels Lodge. Can I help you?"

Cold emptiness spread through Leanne as she quietly hung up.

• • •

JEEZ, COULDN'T WE HAVE MET AT A BAR?" FRANK grumbled. "This place must have a couple, and I could use something strong to drink."

"No, we couldn't," Cole replied shortly.

They were sitting in Frank's car in the darkest corner of the hospital parking lot. It was the only place Cole had been able to think of, where people sitting in a parked car this late in the evening could go unnoticed. He'd considered the town square, but decided it was too public, and its proximity to both the police and the sheriff's departments hadn't helped. He'd thought about City Park, too, but the proximity to Phyllis Wilson had persuaded him against that. He wouldn't put it past her to lurk at an upstairs window with binoculars, just waiting for the chance to get someone in trouble.

Leaning across the console, Frank rummaged in the glove compartment before coming up with a flask of booze. He offered it to Cole, who shook his head, then took a swig. "I take it we're not leaving tonight."

Cole stared across the lot to the emergency entrance. Less than two weeks ago, he'd driven Melissa Thomas right up to the door in Grayson's truck, then debated whether to keep on driving. His decision to stay that night hadn't been too difficult. Now the decision to go shouldn't be difficult, either.

"How is Owen?" he asked in a deliberate attempt to distract himself from the fact that it was.

"Same as ever. He's moved again, but he's still around Philadelphia."

"What name is he using now?"

Frank shrugged. "The only one I bother to remember is Delbert Collins."

That was the important one—the one to whom the post office box belonged. It was the only alias Owen had ever used that had never been tied to his real name or his criminal record. It was a safe name, one made up out of thin air and kept scrupulously clean.

"What about the others?"

Frank took another swallow of liquor. "Adam's doing six months down in Georgia. Bret's out in California, doing what, I don't know. David's gone to Jamaica with some lonely widow, and Eddie's got a sweet deal running down in Louisiana with a little rich girl whose family is big-time into all the Mardi Gras crap."

"And Eloise?"

"She's the reason Owen moved again. She came for a surprise visit and caught him entertaining the woman next door. She wasn't exactly pleased."

It was a hell of a way for two people to live—they couldn't stay together and couldn't stand to be apart. Watching them as he'd grown up, Cole had always sworn he would never get caught in a situation like that. So what had he done instead? Fallen in love with a woman he didn't deserve, in a town where he wasn't fit to live, where she was raising his son—because, damn it, legalities aside, Ryan *was* his—who wished he would rot in jail.

He shifted in the seat, listening to the vinyl creaking beneath him. "You ever think about going straight?"

"I considered it once," Frank replied, then slid into a fair impression of their father. " 'But I laid down and soon the temptation went away.' "

"Seriously."

Frank pretended to think about it before brashly answering, "Nope. Not for a minute. Hell, what would I do? Sell used cars? Unclog toilets? Mow yards? 'I can't do much—' "

Cole finished another of Owen's sayings with him. " 'But what I do, I'm damn good at.' Jeez, can't you carry on a conversation without quoting the old man every five minutes?"

"I don't know that I've ever tried. Besides, the old man gives good advice—the best for people like us." Frank gave him a sidelong look. "And you *are* like us, Cole. You always have been. You always will be. There's no changing that."

"People can change," Cole said quietly.

"Oh, sure. That's why you never see any repeat offenders in the joint," Frank retorted. "Maybe people like us *can* change, but they *don't,* not for long. Not for good. Remember when Adam married his first wife, and she made him promise to straighten up and fly right? He tried, he really did, but he just couldn't do it. He didn't even last four months before he was back to his old ways."

But he didn't try for the right reasons, Cole wanted to protest. He hadn't had any real desire to live an honest life. He'd been making the effort just for Beverly.

Cole didn't want to do it just for Leanne or just for Ryan, though they were both damned good incentives. He wanted it for himself, for his own pride and dignity, for his self-respect. *Those* were the right reasons.

But no matter what the reasons, Adam really *had* tried. And he'd failed. Why should Cole's luck be any different?

"You need to get out of this town, bubba. They're putting bad ideas in your head. You can't stay here. You stole a quarter of a mil from 'em. You think they're ever gonna forgive or forget that? Besides, what would you do? How would you support yourself and Ryan? You never even finished high school. You don't have a mechanical bone in your body. No one's gonna buy a used car from you after you already ripped 'em off, you don't know how to unclog toilets, and the yards up here won't need cutting for the next five months. What can you do, besides lie, cheat, and steal?"

He could cook, he could follow directions, and he could learn. He could get his GED and even go to college. People seemed to think that cheating and stealing came easily, but the sort of scams he'd run had required a solid grounding in a wide array of subjects. A man couldn't pretend to be an investment broker without having a firm understanding of investments and how they worked. Ditto for a pseudo-art appraiser, a phony lawyer, or a fake home security expert.

"I'm sure there's a woman involved," Frank went on, "you being a Jackson and all. But get real, bubba. There hasn't been a Jackson in four generations that ever held a legit job. What are you gonna do when you get bored with it? Start driving by convenience stores on your way home? Casing her friends' houses? Lifting the family valuables just to stay in shape?"

Cole couldn't even deny he'd wondered about that. This time in Bethlehem was the longest he'd ever gone without committing *some* crime—excluding the months he'd been incarcerated, of course. He wasn't at all tempted now, but who was to say that wouldn't change in six, twelve, or eighteen months? How could he *know* he could go straight when he'd never even considered it before?

But how could he know he couldn't, if he didn't try?

"Man, it's freakin' cold." Frank started the engine and turned the heater to high, then tossed the flask into the console. "These people around here . . . they're just messin' with your head, Cole. Making you think you can fit in, when you can't. Making you think you can be just like them, when you've *never* been like them. You weren't raised for this kind of life and you know it. The sooner you accept that, the sooner we can get out of here and life will get back to normal."

He didn't want to accept anything. He just wanted to go back to Leanne's apartment and spend the rest of the night making love with her.

He wanted to spend the rest of his life with her.

Frank didn't bother to cover his yawn. "I've gotta get some sleep. Why don't we plan on taking off tomorrow night, after your do-gooders think you're in for the night? We can be hell and gone before they even realize you've slipped out."

"I can't," Cole said to himself, then realized Frank was frowning at him. "Thursday is Ryan's birthday. I can't take off this close."

"Jeez. You're gonna make me masquerade as a priest three more freakin' days?"

"You could have taken the collar off when you left Connecticut."

Frank's smile showed the dimple that made him look oddly angelic. "I kind of like it. I feel a kinship with men of the cloth, what with so many of them being in the same business we are. Can I give you a ride home?"

"Nah. I'll walk. It's not far." Cole opened the door and was halfway out when Frank spoke again.

"Don't disappoint your family, bubba. We're the only ones who have accepted you the way you are, and we're the only ones who will."

With a grim nod, he slammed the door, shoved his hands in his pockets, and set off across the parking lot. It was true that they'd always known him for what he was and loved him anyway. That probably wouldn't change if he cleaned up his act . . . but things with Leanne and Ryan *would* change if he didn't. They deserved better than what he was.

They made him *want* to be better.

Chapter Seventeen

—

THE WEATHER TOOK A TURN FOR THE WORSE ON Tuesday, matching Leanne's mood. She sent the boys off to day care and to school under a sky the color of pewter, and the wind blew down the street with such force it actually whistled. The temperature, starting in the high thirties and dropping fast, left no doubt that for all practical purposes, winter had arrived. Oh, there would be a few more lovely days, some even warm, but the next several months promised to be downright chilly.

When the doorbell dinged shortly after noon, Jerome looked up from his snoozing spot on the floor, his ears pricked with interest. A person could be forgiven for thinking it was the noise that had disturbed him, or the blast of frigid air, but she knew it was the fragrant aromas of the food her visitor was carrying. He sprang to his feet and greeted Nolie with a nuzzle and some eager sniffs. Farm girl that she once was, she unconcernedly nudged him aside and approached Leanne at the counter.

"It's *cold* out there," Nolie said, and her cheeks were red to prove it. "I hope this is the worst it gets here."

"Oh, darlin', it'll get much, much colder," Leanne teased. She accepted one of the bags Nolie offered and headed toward the sitting area. "Doesn't it get cold in your part of Arkansas?"

"Not like this. At least, not very often."

Jerome beat them to the back and leaped onto the sofa. Nolie set her load down, removed her coat, scarf, hat, and gloves, then pointed to the floor. "Down," she said sternly, and Jerome hastily obeyed.

"How'd you do that?" Leanne asked. "I tell him to get down and he grins and wags his tail and gets more comfortable."

"You don't tell. You politely suggest, and when he refuses, you let him. You're lucky Danny's not a manipulative child, or he would obey like the mutt does."

As Leanne sat down on the love seat, she blew a kiss to Jerome, then began unpacking the bag. When Nolie had called to say she was bringing lunch, Leanne had been grateful—a visit with her sister-in-law was exactly the distraction she needed. The foil-covered plate giving off incredible aromas was a bonus, when she'd expected takeout from Harry's or the deli. "You cooked," she said, inhaling deeply.

"Jambalaya, left over from last night's dinner. But it's better the second day anyway." Nolie unpacked silverware, unwrapped a large foil packet of steaming cornbread, and tossed a plastic bag on the coffee table. "And for dessert, pralines. My dad had some Louisiana relatives somewhere way back who generously donated these recipes to the family cookbook."

Leanne peeled the foil from her plate, sat back, and took a heaping bite of sausage, shrimp, chicken, rice, and vegetables, then gave a great *mmm*. "Oh, Nolie, this is wonderful."

"Food like this is where I got these hips," her sister-in-law said matter-of-factly.

Though it was difficult with her mouth full, Leanne snickered. "My brother adores those hips."

"Yes." Nolie smiled as if pleasantly surprised. "He does." Without hesitation, she changed the subject. "How is Tall, Blond, and Handsome?"

Leanne used the food as an excuse to delay answering. Tall, Blond, and Handsome had been her nickname for Cole when he'd first come to town last spring. Then she'd looked at him the way all single women viewed single men—as a prospective date, a fling. How quickly she'd moved past that, to naming him Mr. Right, and how quickly she'd gone beyond that to heartbreak. Was she on her way there again?

Finally, her mouth empty and her nerves starting to prickle under Nolie's gaze, she shrugged. "Exactly as the name implies."

Nolie didn't verbally chide her for the evasive answer. The steady look in her blue eyes did it for her.

"He's, uh . . ." At a loss for words, Leanne shook her head. He'd stopped by earlier that morning. He, Eli, and Murray had been stringing lights over on Main Street, and he'd dropped in for a moment. His skin had been cold when he leaned close to kiss her, and even through his gloves, she had felt the chill in his hands. He would cook dinner for them, he'd said as soon as the kiss ended, and then he'd headed back out to work.

He'd been in and out so quickly that she hadn't had a chance—he hadn't *given* her a chance—to ask about his phone call to Angels Lodge. She'd spent every quiet moment since wondering what answers he might have given. Calling a friend? He had no friends. Making a date with another woman? She didn't want to believe it. Setting a new scam in motion? She really didn't want to believe that.

Making contact with one of his brothers, newly arrived in Bethlehem?

The possibility made her stomach hurt and tightened her chest so breathing became difficult. Even just wondering made her feel disloyal, but under the circumstances, how could she *not* wonder?

"You guys having problems?"

Blinking, Leanne focused her gaze on Nolie. "No," she murmured, and hoped it was true. "Nothing that you wouldn't expect."

"You're still in love with him, aren't you?"

Leanne scooped up a shrimp on her spoon and chewed it slowly before responding. "When Danny's father broke up with me, it was so easy to stop loving him. I was angry and hurt, and I was disappointed in myself for misjudging him, but the day he told me he wanted nothing to do with our baby, I stopped loving him. It was that simple. But with Cole . . . he lied to me. He betrayed my trust. He abandoned his own child. He broke my heart. But still . . . "

Before he'd come back, she'd been convinced she was over him. She'd been angry and hurt and she'd hated him, but that was it. She'd had no gentler feelings for him at all. No sweet memories. No forgiveness. Certainly no love.

And then he'd come back and . . . Had she been kidding herself all along? Had she ever really fallen out of love with him, or had it just been so easy to fall back into it?

Either way, what did it matter? She did love him. It was that simple. And that hard.

"I would guess that the way you loved Greg is different from the way you love Cole," Nolie said. "I loved Micahlyn's father with all my heart, and when he died, I thought I would never care for anyone that way again. Now I love Chase with all my heart, but it's not the same as it was with Jeff. They're very different men, and I'm different, too."

That made sense, Leanne thought as she polished off the last of her food. She'd matured a lot since she'd found herself pregnant and alone. Danny had taught her the meaning of unconditional love. Life had taught her a few lessons, too—hard lessons on what was important and what wasn't.

Greg, ultimately, hadn't been important, but Cole was.

"How does he feel?"

Leanne scowled at her. "Oh, gee, there's the million-dollar question. If I knew the answer to that, I'd be planning a wedding or crying my eyes out."

"You haven't discussed the future?"

" 'There's no point in thinking about the future,' " she parroted. "Not when he's got some forty-eight-hundred hours left on his sentence."

"That's forty-eight-hundred work hours. If you figure he's putting in eight hours a day, then you've got about double that to persuade him otherwise. For a woman of your charms, that's not even a challenge."

"A woman of my charms," Leanne repeated dryly. "If I were so charming, he wouldn't have left me in the first place."

"His leaving had nothing to do with you and everything to do with our $250,000. Though I think his returning the money had plenty to do with you."

Leanne took a break to wait on a customer, then sign for a shipment of winter clothing. When she returned to the sitting area, she caught Nolie slipping Jerome a chunk of cornbread. "Ha! You talk so tough, but you're a sucker for big brown eyes, too." Settling in, she took a praline from the zippered bag. "You guys are coming Thursday night, right?"

"We'll be here with bells on—and my blue-ribbon banana-split cake. Want me to provide candles?"

"I have some." She'd been tempted to get a regular birthday cake for Ryan—white with buttercream frosting—but Danny had insisted Ryan loved banana-split cake better than any other kind. Traditional or not, there would be candles and presents and birthday wishes. She intended it to be a birthday Ryan would never forget.

"How is the birthday boy getting along with Cole?"

"They talk. Some. Cautiously. It'll take time, but I'm hopeful."

Nolie studied her a long time, then nodded in agreement. "Yes, you are. Stay that way. It'll pay off in the long run."

After a few more minutes of conversation, Nolie gathered her dishes, bundled up again, and headed out into the cold. Leanne unpacked the new shipment of clothes, cleared space for them on various racks, and tagged them, then alternated the rest of the afternoon by waiting on customers and thinking about Nolie's advice. *Stay that way. It'll pay off in the long run.*

That was all she wanted—the grand prize. Love, marriage, happily-ever-after.

Sophy breezed in a few minutes late, wearing an overcoat that brushed her ankles and swallowed her hands. Her hair curled around the edges of her knitted black cap, and the scarf around her neck practically matched the color in her cheeks. She greeted Leanne cheerfully, then gave Jerome a vigorous belly rub before stripping down to her overalls and T-shirt.

"You're certainly in a cheery mood," Leanne observed.

"I usually am. Hey, did you hear that Melissa and Alex's baby's condition has been upgraded? He's gained nearly a pound, and he loves cuddling with his parents."

"That's wonderful." She'd heard the news that Max had Down syndrome from Emilie Bishop, and had felt so sorry for the Thomases. She couldn't imagine how it must feel, to want a baby so badly for so long, and to have to face a lifetime of difficulty once they got him. But if anyone could give him the love and care he needed, it was Melissa and Alex. "Any word yet on when he'll be able to come home?"

"Probably another four or five weeks, maybe a little longer."

At the front of the store, Jerome pressed his nose to the glass, then whined. Leanne checked the time. Ryan was due home from school within the next few minutes, and the first thing he usually did was take the dog to the square. But judging from the animal's next whine, louder and longer, he wasn't going to wait one second longer. "Watch things, will you?" she asked as she pulled on her coat and gloves, then grabbed the leash.

Jerome circled impatiently as she hooked the leash to his collar. As soon as she opened the door, he dived outside, dragging her with him, and made a beeline for his favorite bush in the square. Of course, it couldn't be a simple matter of taking care of business. No, he had to sniff first, to determine if anyone had strayed into his territory, then he had to mark it all over again just in case. She stood there, shivering and softly urging the dog to hurry. Her ears were going numb and her nose was slowly freezing solid, and—

Abruptly, Jerome lunged, pulling her off-balance before jerking his leash free. Catching herself on the wet, frozen ground was easier said than done. If not for a strong arm wrapping around her waist, she could have added *dirty* and *damp* to *frozen*. "Jerome!" she shouted, then looked up at her rescuer. "Thank you so—"

She wasn't sure which registered first—the priest's

collar or the familiar features. She'd never met the man before—who would forget a sinfully sexy priest?—but she knew those eyes, that jaw, that nose . . .

Clutching Jerome's leash in one fist, Ryan stalked up to them and gave the man a vicious shove that sent him stumbling back a few feet. "What the hell are you doing here?"

"Ryan!" she exclaimed, stunned by his display of violence. "Stop that! You can't treat him like that!"

He spun to face her, tears in his eyes. "Do you know who that is? It's Frankie, Cole's brother! He's come to get him!" Unexpectedly, he punched the man, earning a grunt of pain for his effort. "I *knew* he wouldn't stay! I *knew* he would skip town the first chance he got! He's a liar, and I hate him! I *hate* him!"

Still holding tightly to Jerome, he ran toward the street. Leanne looked from him to the priest, trying to decide which one needed her attention more at the moment. When Ryan darted into the street in front of a car, causing the driver to brake with a loud squeal, the decision was easy. Giving the guilty-looking man a glare, she spun around and ran after Ryan.

He was younger, faster, and had a good head start. By the time she jerked open the apartment door, *bangs* and *thuds* were coming from the living room. She took the stairs two at a time, then caught her breath at the top and tried to slow her racing heart. She'd been right—there was no friend, no other woman, no new scam. No, this was the worst possible truth. Frank Jackson had come to town.

Cole intended to leave.

She hung up her coat, then went through the kitchen, forcing shallow breaths into her lungs. Ryan's coat was on the floor, one glove on the dining table, the other dangling precariously from the television. His backpack rested on the coffee table, and its contents were scattered around the room, flung in anger and disillusionment. She sidestepped an airborne algebra book, hardly flinching as it crashed onto the hardwood floor, walked right up to him, and forcibly pulled him into her embrace. His thin body shook, and his breaths came in ragged gasps that punctuated his words.

"He said he would stay . . . he promised . . . he said he loved . . ."

"It's all right, babe," she murmured, stroking his hair with one hand, rubbing his back in soothing circles with the other. "It's okay."

His tears seeped through the fabric of her shirt, dampening her shoulder. "I hate him! I knew better than to believe him! I knew how good a liar he is! But he said . . . he promised . . . "

In the corner where his kennel resided, Jerome peered out, head resting on his front paws, his eyes huge and doleful. He stood and stretched, then wandered over and leaned against Ryan's leg. Finding the boy's hand hanging limply, he positioned his head underneath it, then rubbed it back and forth in a parody of a scratch.

Ryan's sob turned into a choked laugh. Shrugging away from Leanne, he knelt next to the dog and hugged and scratched him at the same time. "You always want attention, don't you?" He sounded stuffy and embarrassed. "You'd probably let me scratch you twenty-four hours a day if I could, wouldn't you?"

"He thinks it's no more than he deserves." Leanne sat down on the coffee table next to the backpack. "Hey . . . has it occurred to you that you might be jumping to conclusions?"

Ryan scowled. *"No."*

"Just because Frankie is here doesn't—doesn't mean that Cole's planning to run off."

Sitting back on his heels, Ryan gave her a look that made her feel naive in the face of his great understanding. "You think he just dropped by to say hello? They don't do that. They only show up when they've been asked for help. *He* asked them for help. He had to, or Frankie never would have come here."

"Maybe he was just in the area. Maybe he just wanted to see the brother he hasn't seen in months."

Now his look made her feel stupid as well as naive. "They *don't* do that," he repeated. "Ever. Frankie's here because Cole sent for him. Trust me."

She didn't want to. Didn't want to believe Cole had lied to them about leaving. Didn't want to think for a moment that he would work his way back into their lives and their hearts when he was planning all along to disappear again. Didn't want to know he could be so self-centered and uncaring.

She didn't want to know she could have been so terribly wrong about him.

She combed her fingers through Ryan's hair. "Honey, we can't just assume the worst. He deserves the benefit of the doubt."

He shook his head in the same disdainful way Cole did. "Cole says people like you are what makes life easy for people like him. He's already proven he can't be trusted, but you just keep on doing it over and over. Frank wouldn't be here if Cole hadn't written, asking for help gettin' out. He's gonna leave. I know he is."

What were the odds that Frankie Jackson's sudden appearance was as innocent as she hoped? Ryan was convinced otherwise, and he *knew* the family. All she knew was what Cole had told her—that he didn't see his brothers often. That he didn't even know what state they were in most of the time. That the only way he knew to get hold of them was through a letter sent to their father. *Gee, I'm in the area, so why not drop in and spend a few days with Cole* didn't seem to be their style.

Besides, if Frankie's visit *was* innocent, why was he pretending to be someone else? And a *priest*, for God's sake. She'd once thought Cole should worry about retribution for simply walking through the church doors.

"You gonna call the cops?"

Startled by Ryan's hesitant question, she focused her gaze on him. His eyes were red and filled with more emotions than she could name. A few were easy, though. Anger. Betrayal. Bitterness. Hurt.

And fear. He was so sure he was right . . . and so afraid.

Was she going to call Mitch Walker? But what if she was wrong? What if, by some quirk of fate, Frankie's visit *was* innocent? Cole would be devastated by the proof of her distrust.

And what if she wasn't wrong and she did nothing and Cole did take off with his brother? She would bear some of the responsibility for his escape. She'd never helped anyone break the law before, and she didn't want to start now.

But she also didn't want to cause trouble for him and Eli's program, or to be the reason he wound up serving the rest of his sentence in prison.

"Well?"

"I think we should talk to Cole, babe, and listen to what he has to say."

He snorted. "He'll say what he wants you to believe, just like he did before."

She couldn't deny that he'd played her for a fool before, but she also couldn't deny him the chance to prove he deserved their trust.

"We have to talk to him," she repeated. "We have to believe in him until he gives us a reason not to."

Ryan gave a derisive shake of his head. "Cole says there's a fool born every minute."

"He stole that line from someone else."

He shrugged as if it didn't matter. "He steals everything."

A glance at her watch showed at least two hours, maybe three, before she could expect to see Cole walking through the door. She couldn't wait that long to talk to him. "Want to go with me to find him?"

"To *try* and find him, you mean. He's probably already gone."

"Do you want to go or not?"

He shook his head. "He's just gonna lie to you."

"You stay here in the apartment and do your homework, okay? Don't go out—and pick up your stuff, please." Leaning forward, she kissed him on the forehead, then stood up. "I'll be back."

He let her get to the kitchen doorway before grimly responding. "*You're* not the one who runs off."

THERE MUST HAVE BEEN WORSE JOBS THAN STRING-ing Christmas lights all day when the wind chill was hovering in the single digits, but at the moment Cole couldn't think of any. He'd lost contact with his extremities hours ago. His eyes were watering and his nose was runny, and he was pretty sure he wouldn't thaw out until spring. But Eli and Murray didn't complain, and if they could stand it, so could he.

They were on the roof of the building that had once housed the office of Jackson Investments, stringing icicle lights along the top. Every single building in the business district would be outlined with the clear lights and, when the switch was flipped sometime around Thanksgiving, would put out enough wattage to persuade any nocturnal creature around that night had become day. Mere stars wouldn't be able to compete with the display, and airliners thirty thousand feet up would be able to see the town a thousand miles away.

It sounded like quite a sight.

The door that provided rooftop access creaked loudly enough to be heard over the traffic below and the sniffling closer at hand. He glanced over his shoulder, saw Leanne, and stopped breathing.

Would he ever reach the point where he could look at her without noticing how amazingly beautiful she was? He couldn't imagine it.

She stopped a few feet from the door, the wind whipping her black coat around her ankles. A red hooded scarf covered her hair and wrapped around her neck, and matching gloves provided a splash of color at her waist, where her hands were loosely clasped. Her face was pale except for the bright spots on her cheeks, and her breath formed white puffs before disappearing with the wind.

"Can I take a break?" he asked Eli. When the kid nodded, he moved away from the roof ledge and walked to her. "Hey."

She didn't smile, and there was something in her eyes that made his own smile fade. Wariness? Uncertainty? "Can we go inside?"

In response, he opened the door, then followed her into the stairwell. He expected her to head downstairs, but instead she gathered her coat close and sat on the top step. He joined her.

For a time she stared toward the landing below, as if she was putting her thoughts in order. The impatient part of him wanted to tell her to just spit it out. The fearful part wanted her to say nothing, not until that look was gone from her eyes, not until she could smile at him and mean it.

Finally she drew a breath. It sounded loud in the stair-well and made his gut clench almost as hard as her words did.

"Are you planning to leave town?"

It was his turn to draw a breath, but he couldn't. His chest was too tight, his throat closed off.

"I only ask because I met your brother this afternoon—well, sort of. Ryan punched him, then took off, and I went after him, and Frankie went . . ." She shrugged as if it wasn't important where Frank had gone. "Ryan's convinced that Frankie's here for only one reason. He insists you wrote to your father, asking for one of them to help you get out of town. He believes you lied to us when you said you weren't leaving. Did you?"

Aw, jeez, this was *not* a conversation he wanted to have, especially with her looking so pale and wary. He surged to his feet and took the stairs to the landing, his boots echoing loudly. There he stared at the wall, wishing he had never written the damn letter, or had sent Frankie away the day before, or had skipped the conversation with his brother on the sidewalk and jumped in his car with the order to—

No. He didn't wish he'd left. It may have been what he'd wanted in the beginning, and from time to time since then, when everything seemed impossible, but not anymore.

Not anymore.

Slowly he turned and climbed the stairs to crouch a few steps below her. "No. I didn't lie."

She studied him, the expression in her dark eyes intense, searching for a reason to believe him. He didn't flinch, but let her look all she wanted, let her see what she wanted, and hoped—prayed—it was enough. He barely breathed while he waited, just short little puffs that did nothing to ease the tightness in his chest or the knots in his gut. He needed her to believe him. It wasn't logical or reasonable, not when he'd given her two-hundred-fifty-thousand reasons not to, but he needed it more than he could say.

After what seemed like forever, she took a ragged breath, then nodded. "I didn't think so."

Relief washed through him, loosening his muscles in an instant. Too unsteady to stay as he was, he sank down on a step, the wall at his back, and exhaled loudly. She knew what he was and trusted him anyway. No one but Ryan had ever done that before. No one but Leanne might ever do it again.

"But you did write to your father, didn't you?" She leaned forward, arms resting on her knees, hands fisted against the chill, her chin dipped into the folds of the red scarf. "You did ask for your brothers' help."

He didn't want to admit it, didn't want her to reconsider her faith in him, but couldn't lie to her now. "Leaving Bethlehem last spring was the second hardest thing I've ever done. Coming back was the hardest. I *couldn't* come back—couldn't face you and Ryan after what I'd done. When the cops picked me up in Savannah and turned me over to Nathan Bishop, I figured getting shot would be better than that, but I never got the chance. I tried to escape on the way here, but Bishop was ready for it."

He gazed off at nothing, remembering the despair and dread that had eaten at him on the long drive from Georgia to New York. He would have gladly bypassed a trial and gone straight to prison if it had meant avoiding the people he'd betrayed.

"I didn't want to be here. Waking up every day in that

house, seeing your shop every time I looked out the window, seeing you and Ryan, and knowing you both hated me . . ." He grimly shook his head. "Yeah. I wrote Owen and asked for someone to come and get me."

But things had changed since then. *He'd* changed. Not as much as he could, nowhere near as much as he should, but he'd made a good start. It was the town, the people, and especially Leanne. She'd made him want to stay, to clean up his act, to be a part of her family. She'd made him want a normal life—going to bed and waking up in the same place, not just week after week, but year after year. Being a father to Ryan and Danny. Knowing what was really important. Living an honorable life.

For a time, silence settled around them. Not complete silence—the wind rattled around the building and carried faint snatches of Eli and Murray's conversation, a door opened and closed two flights down, a car horn sounded. But between him and Leanne, there was nothing but the ragged tempo of his breathing. She seemed lost somewhere inside herself, and he wondered bleakly if he could find his way to her.

After too long, she spoke, her voice low, her tone empty of emotion. "And now Frankie's come."

"Yeah. But I'm not going anywhere."

"Does Frankie know that?"

"He suspects it." For the first time since seeing her outside the rooftop door, he managed a faint grin. "The idea of me going straight scares him. He's afraid he might catch whatever I've got and have to settle down himself."

Her smile was pale but genuine. "He might even develop a conscience. That would surely throw the rest of the family into a panic."

"No kidding."

She unknotted her fingers, then slid her hand into his. It

was a simple gesture, but it formed a lump in his throat and made him forget the cold. When he tugged, she came to him willingly, letting him lift her onto his lap and hold her close. She smelled of cold and sweet, spicy flowers, and she felt . . . right. As if she belonged in his arms.

As if he belonged in hers.

"I'll tell Frank tonight. He's got a scam running back in Connecticut. He won't stick around."

She rested her head on his shoulder and slid one gloved hand inside his coat to press against his chest. "Why don't you invite him to dinner?"

"Are you sure you want him in your apartment and around the kids?"

Her soft laughter warmed him. "He's not going to corrupt them in one evening."

"Don't count on it. I've seen him corrupt plenty of young women in an evening or less. He might even corrupt you."

"I've already got the best Jackson of the bunch."

The best of the bunch. Considering who *the bunch* was, it wasn't saying a lot, but he'd take it.

Though his hands were still frozen, he pulled off one glove and raised his fingers to her cheek. She was so beautiful, her dark eyes so trusting. He wanted to kiss her, but there was something he needed to say first. With an odd, funny feeling in his chest and his throat dry as the desert, he said, "You know, darlin', I lo—"

The door above slammed open with the wind, hitting the wall and bouncing on its hinges. Frigid air blasted over them as Eli and Murray hustled in, then forced the door shut again. "It's colder than the North Pole out there," Eli said, stomping his feet to get the blood circulating again.

Leanne didn't startle or jerk away from Cole, but gracefully eased to her feet. "And you know that because? . . ."

"I've been there, of course. Just about everyone in my field goes there at least once, even if it's just on the way to somewhere else."

Why would a do-gooder social worker go to the North Pole, especially when it wasn't on the way to *anywhere* else? But Cole didn't waste much time pondering it. Instead, he was regretting the declaration he hadn't gotten to finish, and feeling a little relieved by the interruption, too. He'd never said *I love you* to any woman before, and it was damn near as scary as the prospect of becoming an upstanding, law-abiding citizen with roots. There would be another, better time, and when it came around, he would have built up enough courage to overcome the fear.

"We're knocking off for the day, Cole," Eli went on. "Let's get the stuff back to the garage, then head home to thaw out."

With a nod, he stood up, let the other two men pass, then followed them downstairs, Leanne's hand in his. When the others left the stairwell, he paused, pulled her closer, and kissed her. It wasn't the kind of kiss he wanted, certainly not the kind she deserved, but it would hold him for an hour or two.

"Want me to invite Frankie to dinner?" she asked as they entered the first-floor corridor, where the temperature was a good thirty degrees warmer.

He would really prefer that she tell Frank to get out of town and save him the arguments his brother was sure to offer, but that would be the coward's way out. Not that he was truly adverse to being a coward . . . "If you're sure you want him there. He's staying at the motel."

She paused at the main doors. Outside, Eli and Murray loaded two large boxes of lights into the back of the truck, then climbed in to wait for him.

"Who should I ask for?"

Cole's face flushed with regret that she knew enough about him and his family to ask the question. "Frank Murphy. Father Murphy."

With a rueful grin and a roll of her eyes, she nodded, pressed a kiss to his cheek, then pushed through the door. On the sidewalk, she glanced back to wiggle her fingers in a little wave, then set off toward the shop.

He was a lucky man.

God, please don't let me screw it up.

Chapter Eighteen

FRANK JACKSON WAS A CHARMER.

Handsome, funny, and entertaining, he had a natural talent for storytelling, as well as a way with words that could turn any woman's head, to say nothing of a killer grin and dimples. Before they even sat down to dinner, Ryan had come around and was trading jokes with Frank as if he hadn't punched him just a few hours earlier, and even Leanne found herself enjoying his company.

Almost as much as she wished he would disappear and resurface a thousand miles away.

Cole didn't see his brothers often, he'd once told her, but when they did get together, it was as if no time at all had passed, and that certainly seemed to be the case. When she'd reunited with Chase last spring, it had taken a while for them to find the closeness they had once shared. Not so for Cole and Frank. There were times through the evening when they seemed to pick up conversations that had been dropped months before, no prompting, no reminding needed, and it took no more than a word or two to send them off on reminiscences about times past.

There was a lot of affection between them, she thought

as she watched them good-naturedly argue over something that had happened ten years earlier. Maybe Owen
Jackson hadn't been the best father around, and no doubt
about it, teaching his sons to follow in his footsteps had
been wrong. But two of those sons, at least, obviously loved
each other and weren't afraid to show it, which was more
than she could say for a lot of people raised in more con-
ventional ways.

So Owen wasn't the worst father around, either.

She was sitting in the armchair, her feet drawn into the
seat, a glass of wine from the bottle Frank had brought
clasped in both hands. Dinner was long over, dessert a
sweet memory. Ryan and Danny had done the dish-fairy
chores, then gone off to get Danny ready for bed. It was
late, fiercely cold outside, and as fiercely comfortable inside. If not for the faint churning in her gut, she would be
well and truly contented this evening.

But there was that churning.

"So . . . Leanne."

Frank's voice startled her out of her thoughts. She
looked up to find him and Cole, sitting at opposite ends of
the couch with Jerome between them, watching her.

"You gonna make an honest man out of my brother?"

The question was asked as if in jest, merely a play on
words, but there was a sharp challenge underlying it that
set off her internal warning bells. He believed that when
he left town, Cole would be going with him—thought
this evening was just another part of just another scam.
Cole had said he would tell Frank he'd changed his mind
and was staying in Bethlehem, at least for the duration of
his sentence. Now seemed as good a time as any for that to
happen.

"The only person who can make an honest man of
Cole is Cole," she replied, her gaze on him. He was idly

scratching Jerome and looking back at her with the faintest of smiles. He looked very much at home—on her couch, in her apartment, in her life—but she still had that queasy feeling. It wasn't going to go away until Frank did.

"Leanne knows why you're here," Cole said.

The look on Frank's face was comical—his jaw dropped, his eyes widened, his brows reaching for his hairline. "You trust her not to go to the cops?"

"About you?"

He snorted. "About *you*. How far do you think we'll get if she rats you out?"

"You'll get wherever you want to go. Me—I'm already there." He fell silent for a moment—not a hesitation that implied uncertainty, but more a pause to give weight to his next words. "I'm not leaving."

Leanne's gaze shifted from Cole to Frank, then back again. Sitting a few feet apart as they were, the family resemblance was unmistakable. So was the difference in demeanor. The younger brother didn't know whether to be dismayed or disbelieving, appalled or wheedling. The older was calm, relaxed, even relieved. The butterflies in her stomach started to settle one by one, and that contentment she'd been thinking about earlier began growing.

"You're kidding, right?" Frank said at last. "Come on, bubba, I *know* you. There's no way you're gonna make it in a nowhere little town like this. I admit, Leanne's pretty, but you don't go straight for a pretty woman."

Cole was still looking at her, still wearing that hint of a smile. "I'm not doing it for her. It's for me."

Frank muttered an obscenity. "You don't even know how to go straight."

"I've got a couple years left on my sentence, to figure it out."

Springing from the couch, Frank paced to the nearest window, then back again. "Why? Why are you doing this?"

Finally Cole looked away, focusing on his brother instead. "Because I'm tired, Frankie—of ripping people off. Of lying. Of pretending to be someone I'm not. I'm tired of dragging Ryan all over the place, of not having a place to call my own. Most of all, I'm tired of not—not liking who I am or what I do."

Frank dragged his fingers through his hair before planting both hands on his hips. "You think it's that easy to change who you are? You think you can just say, 'Okay, I'm one of the good guys now,' and that makes it true? 'Cause it's not gonna happen, bubba. What're you gonna do? You don't know how to do anything that doesn't involve breaking the law. You've never made a dime in your life that wasn't dirty. You've never stayed in one place more than a few months, or with one woman. You don't know how to live any life besides the one you were raised for."

Cole's reply was simple, his tone stubborn. "I can learn."

Frank's was even simpler, a snort of disgust.

For a long time silence hung in the air. Frank stared at Cole with something akin to horror, and Cole stared back, his expression resolute. He looked like a man who'd made up his mind and wasn't about to change it, Leanne thought. She hoped her own expression was as steady, but inside the butterflies had started turning cartwheels.

Abruptly, Frank shrugged, as if literally casting off his concerns. "You wanna stick around here? Fine. Give it your best shot. See how well you can fit in with these small-town, small-minded yokels. When you find out you can't . . . you know how to reach me."

"That won't be necessary."

Frank looked from him to her, then smiled an ugly smile. "Sure, it will. Maybe not tomorrow or next week or even next month, but you'll call. You're a Jackson, and no matter how hard you try, no matter how hard she wants you to try, you'll never change that."

Leanne spoke up at last. "I don't want to change who he is." She loved who he was. She just hated what he did.

The look he gave was pure cynicism. "Yeah. Right. Well . . . guess I'd better get back to the motel. If you're not going with me, bubba, I want to get an early start in the morning."

Cole didn't argue with him, a fact for which she was dearly grateful, but got to his feet. "Let me tell Ryan you're leaving."

Once he was out of earshot, Frank turned his attention to her. "You're dying to get up and do a little victory dance, aren't you?"

"Just a small one."

"You know you're both kidding yourselves."

"I don't know that at all."

"Cole's a con artist—the best I've ever seen. And right now he's running the best con I've ever seen—on you and himself."

"Why does it bother you so much that he wants a better life?"

He looked insulted. "Better? Stuck in one place? Working nine-to-five? Struggling to make ends meet? Doing the same drudge job day after day, living the same dreary life? How does that qualify as *better*?"

"Someday maybe you'll grow up and find out the answer to that for yourself."

"Not if I have anything to say about it." He let his scowl fade, then said, "I'll be back."

"Maybe." For a wedding or Christmas with the family. For a family reunion or to get acquainted with the newest member of the Jackson family. But *not* to take Cole away, her inner voice whispered delightedly. He wasn't going. Not tonight, not next week or next month, not *ever.*

Digging into his hip pocket, Frank removed his wallet, then withdrew a fifty-dollar bill. "Cole said Ryan's birthday is Thursday. Do me a favor and give this to him, will you?"

She looked at the money, then at him. Good sense told her to snatch the fifty, then hustle him to the coat tree in the hall. He could say good-bye to Cole and Ryan while putting on his coat, then she could push him down the stairs and out the door.

But her thoughts from a moment ago kept repeating in her head. *Christmas with the family, a family reunion, meeting the newest member of the family . . . see a pattern?* Frank was a part of Cole and Ryan's family and deserved to be treated as such, especially now that Cole had told him unequivocally that he wasn't leaving town or her. Instead of reaching for the money, she stood up, then folded his fingers over the bill. "Why don't you give it to him yourself, at his party? Whoever's waiting for Father Murphy to return can wait a few extra days, can't they?"

He grinned, showing the dimples. "You want me to stick around? Aren't you afraid I'll try to change Cole's mind?"

"To the contrary, I'm sure you will. *Try,* that is." But trying was a long way from succeeding. She didn't believe for an instant he would succeed. "Let's make a deal. You stay for Ryan's party, and I won't sic the police on you when you leave."

The grin broadened. "Blackmail, huh? Maybe I shouldn't worry about you corrupting Cole. Maybe next time I see you, you'll be working right alongside him in his newest scam." He returned the money to his wallet. "Okay.

It's a deal. I'll stay for Ryan's birthday, and then I'm outta here."

As Ryan's voice drifted in from the hallway, Frank headed that way, but turned back before he reached the kitchen. "But I'm not making any promises that I'll be leaving alone."

Leanne summoned her most serene smile. She didn't need promises from him. She had them from Cole, and that was all that mattered.

A SENSE OF ANTICIPATION SWEPT THROUGH LEANNE as she surveyed the living and dining room, though she couldn't honestly say whether it was because it was Ryan's birthday, she would be seeing Cole again very soon, or Frank would be leaving town in the morning. It wasn't that she was afraid Cole would change his mind and leave with him. He'd made up his mind. He'd chosen Bethlehem, Ryan, an honest life, and her over his lawless days.

It was just that resisting temptation was always easier when it wasn't staying a few miles away, sitting down to meals with you, and frequently reminding you of old times, good times, cons that had gone hilariously wrong and ones that had been textbook perfect. To hear Frank tell it, the Jacksons were damn near legendary in the right circles, Cole more so than the others. Leaving that life behind, in his opinion, was *not* the act of a sane man.

But hadn't Nolie said there was nothing sane about falling in love?

It was almost party time, and she was as ready as could be. Sophy was downstairs minding the shop, Danny was still at day care, and Ryan was over there with him, helping the teachers and staying out of the apartment until Leanne was ready for them at six.

As was their custom, he'd picked the menu—salad, spaghetti, and garlic bread. The salad was chilling in the refrigerator, the sauce simmering on the stove, and a huge pot of water simmered, too, ready to bring to a boil as soon as everyone arrived. The bread was sliced, buttered, and sprinkled with garlic and waiting in a cold oven, out of Jerome's reach.

The dining table and a card table were set with festive tablecloths and balloons tied to the kids' chairs, and a stack of presents waited on a table in the corner. She might have gone a little overboard—okay, so a present from Jerome was a bit much—but she wanted to overwhelm Ryan with the fact that he was absolutely part of the family.

The doorbell rang, bringing a lazy *woof* from Jerome. Figuring it was Cole, she ran down the stairs and opened it . . . to Eli. The young man looked uncharacteristically serious. "Hi. Is Cole here?"

"Of course not. I mean, he's supposed to be, later, but . . . he's been with you all day."

"No, actually, he hasn't. Not for the last couple hours. I thought maybe he came straight here when he got back, because of Ryan's birthday."

The chill that made her shiver came from the cold, nothing else. That was why her voice was the slightest bit unsteady when she asked, "Got back from where?"

"The town keeps some of their Christmas displays at the camp out on the lake. I sent him out with the truck, to pick up some of them around three this afternoon, and . . . we haven't seen him since."

The cold was making it difficult to breathe, too. Her lungs must have been rejecting the chilly air, because she couldn't fill them adequately. "Have you gone out there? Maybe he had a flat tire or—or ran out of gas or something."

"He took the truck. I don't have a way to go check."

The sound of a cheery, "Happy birthday, sweetie," drew her attention to the corner. Chase, Nolie, and Micahlyn had just gotten out of his truck, and Ryan and Danny had just come around the corner from the day care center. It was Nolie who had spoken and was giving a hug and a kiss to a bashful Ryan.

"Hi, Mama," Danny greeted, stretching onto his toes to give her a big hug. "Ryan comed to day care and stayed and teached us. It was *cool*."

"I bet it was." Absently she bent to kiss his forehead, then hugged Ryan. Micahlyn, cradling a prettily wrapped gift, lifted her cheek for a kiss but declined a hug on account of the present. Chase, carrying Nolie's famous banana-split cake, accepted a kiss on the cheek, too.

"You guys go on upstairs," she murmured. "I'll be up in a minute."

"Everything okay?" Chase asked, glancing curiously at Eli.

Acutely aware of the kids listening, she smiled. "Yeah. I'll be right up."

Once they were inside, she stepped out and let the door close behind her, hugging herself against the cold. She should have grabbed her coat when she passed the coat tree in the hall, but she'd been expecting one of Cole's hello kisses that curled her toes and heated her internal temperature to scorching.

"I'd better notify Chief Walker," Eli said before she could get her thoughts straightened.

"Do you have to? If Cole's run out of gas or gotten lost, it'll make him feel really lousy that you sent the cops after him."

"The truck had half a tank of gas, and I don't think it's humanly possible to get lost going to the camp and back."

She knew that. She'd spent weeks every summer at the camp when she was growing up. You took the street that ran past the hospital, followed it to its end after the pavement gave way to dirt, and you were there. There were no confusing directions, no intersecting roads for wrong turns, and only one house along the whole stretch. You just couldn't screw it up.

"Maybe . . ." The buzz of the street lamps distracted her. It was dark, cold, and sure to get colder. What if something had happened to Cole?

Like Frank, her been-fooled-before voice suggested. What if he'd sought out Cole today and resumed his efforts to persuade him to leave with him—and succeeded?

"I'd better talk to Chief Walker," Eli said again.

"He *didn't* leave. It's Ryan's birthday. He's expecting Cole at his party tonight. There's no way Cole would disappoint him."

"He disappointed him before," Eli quietly pointed out.

"But he wouldn't do it again." She was sure of it. Absolutely positive. Ninety-nine percent convinced.

Oh, God.

"Let me get my keys and we'll drive out to the camp—" Breaking off, she watched as Mitch Walker crossed the street from the Miller mansion. His expression was grim, and made her breath catch in her chest.

"Murray said I could find you over here," he said to Eli when he joined them. He gave her a curt nod. "We just got a call from Isaac Lester. He reported a pickup parked on the road up near his place—*your* pickup. Were you driving it?"

Eli shook his head.

"Was Jackson?"

He nodded.

"Where is he now?"

"Your guess is as good as mine."

"He *didn't* leave," Leanne insisted. "He promised me . . . he promised Ryan . . ."

Neither man looked convinced, and why should they? That lone house on the way to the summer camp was Isaac Lester's. Cole had last been seen in the truck, which had been abandoned on a rarely traveled country road. All they needed to convict him was to find out that Frank had unexpectedly checked out of the motel. . . .

Her stomach clenching, she abruptly spun around and raced up the stairs. She hardly noticed the heat or the fragrant aroma of the spaghetti sauce as she grabbed the phone book from its place in the junk drawer and thumbed through to the listing for Angels Lodge. Her hand trembled when she punched in the number. As it rang, she turned her back so she couldn't see Ryan, Nolie, and Chase watching her from the living room, or Eli and Mitch standing just inside the hall doorway.

Bree Aiken, the manager, answered with a friendly, "Can I help you?"

"F-Frank Jackson's room, p-please."

"I'm sorry. We don't have anyone registered under that name."

Of course not. *Never use your real name* was probably number sixteen on Owen's endless list of rules. "Murphy," she said breathlessly. "Frank Murphy."

"Oh, Father Murphy. Let's see . . . he checked out this afternoon."

Leanne's stomach dropped to her toes and her vision went blurry. "Can you tell me what time?"

"I'm sorry, ma'am—"

Pressing one hand to her eyes, Leanne interrupted. "Bree, it's me, Leanne Wilson. Please—it's very important. When did Frank leave?"

"Oh, hi, Leanne. I guess it's okay to tell you. He'd said earlier he was leaving tomorrow, but then he checked out about three-fifteen today."

Too shaken to even think, Leanne slowly hung up without another word. She felt as if everything had been drained from inside her—warmth, life, faith, hope. If she tried to speak, she would sob. If she tried to move, she would collapse in a heap.

A hot, sweaty hand covered hers where it rested on the counter. "He's gone, isn't he?" Ryan whispered. "Frankie's gone. Cole's gone."

She managed to turn on her unsteady legs and wrap her arms around him. "Frank's gone . . . but not Cole. He said he would stay. He said . . ."

"He lied."

"No." She couldn't offer any reasons for believing that, but she did believe. She knew in her heart he never would have voluntarily abandoned them again—*knew* it. She couldn't possibly love a man like that, the way she loved Cole.

But she'd loved him before . . . and he'd voluntarily abandoned them that time.

"Who is Frank Murphy?" Mitch asked.

Reluctantly she lifted her gaze to him, standing next to the refrigerator with his hands on his hips. "His real name is Frank Jackson. He . . . he's Cole's younger brother."

"And he's been here in town?"

She nodded.

"For how long?"

Feeling the censure in his gaze and his tone, Leanne straightened her shoulders, ignored her blush, and lifted her brows. "A few days. I'm not sure."

"And you've known that and didn't bother to tell anyone."

"We found out Tuesday," Ryan volunteered, hostility creeping into his voice. "But Cole promised he wasn't going anywhere. He *promised*."

He hadn't promised, she thought dully—just spoken with great conviction. Lied with great conviction? her hated inner voice whispered.

"I'm sorry, Mitch," she said coolly. "I didn't know I was supposed to report back to you about anyone Cole spoke to."

"His brother is hardly *anyone*. He's also his frequent partner in crime, and if you didn't know that, Ryan certainly did."

The peal of the doorbell saved her from having to respond to that. Hope surged, but just as quickly faded. It wasn't Cole. Somehow she knew it all the way down to her toes.

"Want me to get that?" Eli offered, and she nodded.

"Where would they go, Ryan?" Mitch asked, coming to the island as Eli started for the door.

Ryan stared at him, his mouth clamped shut and his expression blank.

"I understand your grand—Cole's father lives in Philadelphia. Do you think they would go there?"

He got an answer this time, but not from Ryan. Chase came to stand next to him and rested one hand on the counter, the other on Ryan's shoulder. "Questioning a minor without permission from his guardian or his attorney?" he asked mildly. "I'm sure they taught you better than that in police chiefs' school."

Mitch scowled at him. "We all want the same thing—to find Jackson."

"Yeah, but they want to find him because they're worried about him. You want to lock him up."

"Look, guys, I'm not the enemy here. He's innocent

until proven guilty, right? But until we find him, it looks real likely that he's fled the jurisdiction, and if he has, he'll have to suffer the punishment. If he hasn't, he'll be real pleased to know you folks had faith in him."

"Have you sent—" Leanne broke off as Eli returned, carrying a large box. It was beautifully wrapped in red embossed paper with gold wired ribbon—the signature wrapping shared by several shops downtown.

"Elena, from the bookstore, brought this by. She said Cole was supposed to pick it up before closing time today. When he didn't show, she decided to deliver it. She didn't want to miss Ryan's birthday." Eli grinned. "Happy birthday, son."

Ryan stared at the package, an anguished look in his eyes. "Maybe he did leave," he whispered. "Maybe he thought sending a present would make up for it. Maybe—"

"Maybe nothing." Leanne gave him a shake. "He intended to pick it up and deliver it himself—that's all. He wasn't trying to make up for anything."

More determined than ever, she returned to the question Eli had interrupted. "Have you sent someone out to the camp to look around?"

Mitch nodded. "When Isaac called in about the truck, Sheriff Ingles sent a deputy to check it out. He drove all the way to the camp and saw no sign that anyone had gone beyond Isaac's place in weeks." As he finished speaking, his cell phone rang. He stepped into the hall to answer it.

"Something's happened," Leanne murmured.

"Yeah," Chase agreed just as softly. "Like maybe brother Frank met him on that dirt road because they knew it would take several hours for anyone to find the truck and realize Cole was gone."

She glared at him over Ryan's head. "No, not like that! I know you don't like Cole—"

"I don't like or dislike him. But I knew a hell of a lot of guys just like him in Massachusetts. I defended them, and I served time with them. I never trusted those guys, and I don't trust Cole." Chase's gaze shifted to Ryan. "I'm sorry."

"It's okay," he mumbled, still staring at the red gift Eli had placed on the island. "Only a fool trusts a Jackson. Cole says so himself."

And was she a fool? Leanne wondered, tears clogging her throat. When she'd asked him about Frank on Tuesday, had he told her the truth . . . or what she wanted to hear, as Ryan had predicted? And that whole scene with Frank Tuesday night . . . had that been an act for her benefit, to throw her off-guard? Was he well on his way to parts unknown to start his next scam? Had he betrayed them again?

Abruptly she released Ryan and pushed away from the counter. "Nolie, can you cook the spaghetti for me? The water's already heating. There's salad in the refrigerator and garlic bread in the oven. It just needs to be browned."

"Sure," her sister-in-law answered from the couch, where she'd been reading to Danny and Micahlyn, to keep them distracted from the adults' conversation.

"Where you going?" Chase asked.

"To look for Cole."

"Where?"

"In town. Outside town. Anywhere. Everywhere." She wouldn't accept that he'd left, until she'd proven to herself that he was nowhere around.

"Let the cops do that, Leanne. It's their job."

"Maybe. But it's my responsibility. I can't stay here knowing that he—" Could be hurt, lost, dead, or dying. "If

I'm not back when you leave, please take Danny and Ryan with you. Thanks a lot."

She didn't wait for further argument, but went into the hall, sidestepped Mitch, grabbed her coat, scarf, gloves, and purse, and headed down the stairs as she donned them. She was climbing into the SUV when the sound of running footsteps made her look up. Ryan and Jerome came flying toward her, the boy struggling into his jacket as he ran.

"Chase said we should come with you." He opened the rear door so Jerome could hop in, then jumped into the passenger seat.

She wanted to send them back, but he was worried, too—a good sign. As long as he believed looking for Cole was worthwhile, then he must believe they hadn't been abandoned again.

"Where are we gonna look?"

She shrugged as she started the engine. "Your guess is as good as mine, sweetie. The logical place, I guess, is the summer camp."

They'd driven a mile, maybe two, when Ryan turned his head her way. The dashboard lights made him look young and achingly vulnerable. "Do you think we'll find him?"

She had to try twice, but managed a smile. "I do."

She just wished she knew if she really did think so, or if she was lying to herself as well as to him.

O H, Gloria . . . you really should be more careful."

The voice seemed to come from inside Cole's head, though it was hard to tell with the deafening rhythm already beating there. It was a soft voice, warm and sweet, and reminded him of Leanne, who was also soft, warm, and sweet, and waiting for him to show up for dinner. Too bad he lacked the energy to even open his eyes.

"*Me* be careful?" a second voice asked indignantly. "*I'm* not the one who stepped off into thin air!"

That was followed by a third voice—male, vaguely familiar. "No, you're the one who *appeared* out of thin air and startled him into falling."

Thin air . . . falling . . . was that what had happened to him? Why he was lying on the cold, damp ground? Why every shallow breath he took hurt like a son of a bitch?

"Do you think he's alive?" A female voice, not like Leanne's. Gloria again.

The man responded. "You don't see any death angels around, do you?"

Death angels? An involuntary snort of laughter slipped out, double-timing the pounding in his head and tripling his aches and pains. Was he laughing at the idea he could be dead, or the existence of angels? Oh, they probably did exist, but only for people who deserved them. Not for lowlifes like him.

It was a struggle, but he opened one eye, then the other. At some time while he was unconscious, darkness had fallen and the temperature had dropped. Stars twinkled overhead in the clear night, and a quarter moon shone brightly. He was in the forest and, judging by the silence, too far lost for anyone to find him. But how had he gotten there? The closest he'd ever gotten to the country was when he and Leanne had taken Danny and Ryan to the lake—

Ryan. Today was his birthday, and Cole was late for his party. He hadn't picked up the kid's present from the bookstore yet, and he needed a hot shower and a strong drink and— He tried to sit up, but the agonizing fire that shot through him made his vision go dark and his stomach heave. Sweet damnation, mainline painkillers, and a cast or two might be nice.

Lying still, he took inventory. He was freezing, of course. Knocking himself out in the forest on a frosty night could do that to a man. His head throbbed, his neck was bent at an awkward angle, and his left leg was bent at an impossible angle. His ribs hurt, and his chest, and he wasn't sure, but he thought his ankle was sending out occasional twinges to remind him it was still there. Gritting his teeth, he raised one hand to the knot on his forehead. His fingers came away sticky with congealed blood.

He was in trouble.

Bad.

"Look!" Gloria exclaimed. "He's awake! He's not dead!"

"Hey . . ." His voice was little more than a croak. "I could use a little help here."

When no answer came, he lifted his head, groaning, sweating, swearing, and took a look around. There was no one there. Nothing but trees, rocks, darkness, and cold. "Hello? Gloria? Somebody?"

No answer.

Weakly he laid his head down again, closed his eyes again. It had seemed such a simple job—take Eli's old truck to the end of the dirt road, load some super-sized plastic decorations in the back, and drive back to the city garage. Any moron could have done it without a problem.

But not Cole. First, he'd passed his brother on his way across town, and Frank had turned and followed him. When Frank passed him, then stopped, blocking the road, Cole had stopped, too, shut off the engine, and listened to his brother's arguments for leaving all over again. This time, though, he'd persuaded the kid he wasn't going, had said

good-bye and watched him drive away . . . only to find
out the truck wouldn't start.

He should have left it running. Shouldn't have gotten
out to talk to Frank. Should have made it clear beyond a
doubt that he wasn't leaving Leanne and Ryan, though in
his own defense, he'd thought he'd done that Tuesday
night.

Failing all that, when he realized he had to walk back
into town, he should have stuck to the winding road. So
what if it was three times farther than cutting through the
woods? At least on the road he wouldn't have . . . what did
Gloria say he'd done? Stepped off into thin air.

He remembered it vaguely. He'd been going down a
steep hill, slipping and sliding but making better time than
he would have on the road, and time had been important.
He couldn't be late for Ryan's birthday dinner. Then she'd
appeared. One second he'd been alone in the woods, and
the next she'd been there ahead, hovering in midair, it had
seemed, and shaking her head regretfully. "Should have
stayed on the road, Jack," she'd said, and that was all he recalled.

Apparently he'd fallen, cracked his head and maybe
some ribs, and broken his leg. The injuries weren't life-
threatening, but the dropping temperatures were. Barring a
miracle, he wasn't going to survive the night, and he wasn't
exactly deserving of a miracle.

It was a hell of a way for a city boy to die. But at least it
was peaceful. If Leanne was with him—and he wasn't
banged up—it could be damn near perfect.

But Leanne wasn't with him . . . and he'd never told her
he loved her . . . and things were still wrong between him
and Ryan. So many regrets, and no time to fix them. He
was worthless, Leanne had told him the day she'd come to
see him in jail. Since then, he'd come to believe he could

prove her wrong—sometimes believed he *had* proved her wrong—but in the end, he was the one who was wrong. He wished . . .

He wished . . .

I WISH WE COULD JUST TELL EVERYONE WHERE TO find him," Gloria said worriedly. "He doesn't look good."

"He could hear us talking when he wasn't supposed to," Eli responded. "Of course he doesn't look good."

Ignoring them both, Sophy gazed at Cole. He appeared unconscious, but she could hear his shallow, steady breaths, could feel his life force, however weak. Like Gloria, she wished they could take a proactive approach to getting him found, but that wasn't a guardian's job. All they could do was watch over him until he *was* found.

Sheriff Ingles's deputies and Chief Walker's officers were looking for him, but not actively. They considered him a fugitive and would be happy to take him into custody if they saw him, but they weren't out beating the bushes for him. No, Cole's best hope lay with Leanne and Ryan, who were just arriving at the summer camp. Did he know they believed in him when no one else did? Could he imagine the depth of their faith in him?

He would find out soon enough.

Sophy just wished they would hurry.

She knelt beside him. His eyes were closed again and he was shivering uncontrollably. His mouth moved, whispering pleas, prayers, mindless words that had no voice. She laid her hand against his forehead and found his skin cold on the outside, burning from inside. For a time she simply touched him like that, and gradually the shivers subsided, his lips stilled, and his breathing deepened as much as his injured ribs would allow. He looked as if he was merely taking a nap—comfortable, peaceful. Thankfully, it was a nap from which he would awaken.

Feeling a steady gaze on her, she looked up and into Eli's eyes. A blast of heat flamed through her. "Go away," she said quietly, as she hastily lowered her gaze to Cole again.

"No can do. He's my responsibility, too. Besides, if I leave you and Gloria alone with him, God only knows what will happen."

"Yes, He does, doesn't He? So beat it."

"What's the matter, Soph? Afraid to be this close to me? Afraid you can't keep your hands off me?"

She gave him her most disdainful look, when what she really wanted was to slap that smug arrogance from his— Good heavens, what was she thinking? She was a guardian, a protector. She'd never resorted to violence, not in all of forever. She'd never even *thought* about it.

But now that she had . . . "The only place I'd be likely to put my hands is around your throat," she said with a sugary smile.

"Yeah, right. When we finish up here, why don't we see about that?"

Her gaze caught on his mouth, as smug and arrogant as the rest of him, but also finely shaped and eminently kissable. "When we finish here, I've got better things to do," she replied. "Like watching the leaves rot or counting the dust particles in the atmosphere."

He leaned closer and grinned. "What is it you're afraid of, Soph? That I'll kiss you again? Or that I won't?"

Oh, yes, she thought as she gritted her teeth in a vain effort to ignore him. Physical violence was looking more appealing by the minute.

• • •

T HE SUMMER CAMP WAS A COLLECTION OF RUSTIC buildings—a large kitchen and dining hall, a covered pavilion for rainy-day activities, and six cabins that slept fourteen each. Several docks extended into the lake for boating and swimming, blackened fire rings dotted the shore, and with a change of nets, a concrete slab converted from a basketball court to tennis.

A half-dozen flood lamps shone on the camp, and that many more were burned or broken out. Leanne kept her headlight beams on high as she followed the dirt lane that wove between the buildings. There was no sign of life, nothing to suggest that Cole had ever made it there. Which meant he was somewhere between the truck, three miles back down the road, and town.

Or a state or two away with Father Frankie.

The road looped around to go out the way it came in. Ryan sat in silence beside her, staring out the side window so she couldn't see his face. In the backseat, Jerome took in the view from one window, then the other. She tried to think of something reassuring to say, but her mind was too blank, numbed by fear and worry and more fear.

They passed Isaac Lester's house, a bright spot in the night, then soon left the glow behind for the quiet dark of the forest. If Cole had left them again, she would never forgive him. She'd let him go last time, but not again. She would track him down and make him damn sorry he'd ever heard of Bethlehem or her.

But if he'd left them again, he might already be sorry he'd ever heard of her. If he could walk away from her a second time, he certainly couldn't love her, not the way she loved him, or need her the way she needed—

A sob caught her off-guard, sounding choked and stran-
gled and jerking Ryan around to look at her. Realizing it
had come from her, she smiled unsteadily and gripped the
steering wheel more tightly as they rounded the curve that
would reveal Eli's old truck. She wondered why the sheriff
hadn't had it towed yet, but was grateful he hadn't. It made
the next step of her so-called plan easier.

When she parked nose to nose with the pickup, Ryan
gave her another curious look. "What're we doin'?"

"Looking." She turned the key and climbed out,
quickly zipping her coat to her throat, then pulling the
collar around her ears. The pickup looked forlorn and
abandoned in the moonlight, exactly the way she felt. She
walked around to the driver's side, looked through the
window, and saw nothing out of the ordinary. There were
plenty of tire tracks in the soft ground—the deputy's, hers,
some no doubt belonging to Mr. Lester. Maybe some to
Frank?

There were footprints, too—the deputy's, hers, now
Ryan's, and surely Cole's. He hadn't just been beamed out
of the truck. He had climbed out and gone somewhere . . .
but where?

Whining, Jerome strained at the leash. Leanne smiled
faintly. "Why don't you take him into the grass? All the
new smells are probably overloading his senses."

Ryan obeyed, letting the dog pull him around the truck
and to the edge of the trees. Ryan stopped there, but
Jerome didn't. Mulishly, he ducked his head and moved as
far into the woods as he could, stretching the leash taut.

"Stop it, Jerome," Ryan admonished, pulling on the
leash. It was a losing battle, though. Jerome tugged back
and dragged his master a good three feet before Ryan
caught himself. With a whine, the dog jerked again.

Curious, Leanne moved beside Ryan and called Jerome.

He glanced at her, whined, and pulled in the opposite direction.

Was it possible? . . .

He was a big overgrown baby, she reminded herself—not a tracker. Granted, labs were supposed to be very good trackers, but that required training or, at the very least, a strong bond between the dog and the person he was tracking. As far as Jerome was concerned, Ryan and Danny were the important people in his world. She and Cole were just the caretakers on the sidelines—the ones who took him out, scratched him when the kids weren't around, fed him . . . and Jerome did love his food and everyone who provided it. Maybe . . . *maybe* . . .

She looked at Ryan. Judging by his expression, he was wondering the same thing she was. She nodded into the trees. "Let's see where he wants to go."

"J EROME!" SOPHY CALLED SOFTLY, ONLY TO BE SHUSHED by Eli.

"That's cheating," he said in his most annoyingly superior manner, then he gave a sharp whistle, the kind dogs everywhere responded to. Jerome's bark was muffled by the distance.

"Oh, and that's not?"

"What? All I did was whistle," he said innocently.

"You two stop fussing," Gloria said testily. "Why, you're worse than any children I've ever dealt with. This is serious business here. We've put considerable effort into reaching this point with Jack and Louanne, so hush."

Chagrined, Sophy gazed into the woods. They were a fair distance from the dirt road up above. Even so, she could hear the crash of Jerome's oversized feet crunching over fallen leaves and rocks, nearly drowning out the softer footfalls of his master and mistress. It would take them a while, but they would reach Cole in time.

She lifted his hand into hers and briskly rubbed her heat into him. "You're going to be all right, Cole," she said so softly only he could hear. "Help is on the way."

He tried to move, groaned, and became still except for his fingers clenching hers. "Leanne?"

"She'll be here in just a minute. Just hold on, Cole. She's coming."

WHEN SHE STOPPED TO CATCH HER BREATH, LEANNE had no clue how far they'd come from the road. Her lungs insisted a mile or more, but common sense suggested less than half that. It was rough going, making their way through the trees with only occasional flashes of moonlight to guide them. They'd slipped along the downward slope toward the valley, grabbing handholds where they could, sliding where they couldn't. She'd tripped over a fallen log and bruised her shin, and had lost her knitted cap on a leafless branch some distance back.

Jerome didn't seem to face any of the hazards she and Ryan did. Of course, his night vision was vastly better than theirs, and his four monster paws gave him a better grounding. Plus, he was on a mission. The excitement that made his whole body tremble made that clear.

Up ahead, Jerome barked. It wasn't his usual *feed me, walk me, I've gotta go* sort of bark, but an excited, urgent alert. As she headed in that direction, Ryan frantically called her name.

The boy was standing on an outcropping of rock at the edge of a bluff, staring wide-eyed and pale. Jerome's next bark came from down there, still urgent. She skidded to a stop next to Ryan and saw the dog fifteen feet below, crouched low to the ground and warily confronting the form lying motionless a few feet away.

Cole!

"Wait here." Spotting a break in the outcropping, Leanne headed down, sending showers of dirt and rocks to the forest floor below. Halfway down, her feet slid out from under her, making her land hard on her butt. She skittered the rest of the way down, then scrambled across the ground to Cole.

Except for the knot and the blood on his face, he looked as if he was merely sleeping. His eyes were closed, the corners of his mouth turned up in the beginnings of a smile. Heart pounding, she jerked off her glove and touched her shaking hand to his cheek. He was cold, dangerously so, but she felt the faintest movement, the slightest puff of breath against her skin.

Leaves and rocks rattled behind her, then Ryan appeared at her side. "Is he—is he dead?" he whispered, his voice choked and trembling.

In the moonlight, he appeared as pale as Cole, bringing the fear etched on his features into stark relief. She gave him a reassuring smile as she stripped off her coat to cover Cole. "No, babe, he's not. He's going to be all right."

Ryan scrambled to the other side, tugged off his own coat, and carefully laid it over hers. Almost immediately it seemed that Cole rested easier.

"Cole?" Ignoring her own chill, she bent over him. "Can you hear me?"

His lashes fluttered before he managed to open his eyes to slits. He smiled crookedly. "Didn't . . . leave . . ."

Tears stung her eyes. "Of course you didn't. We knew that, didn't we, Ryan?"

"You—you said you wouldn't," Ryan whispered.

With some effort, Cole shifted his gaze enough to see

the boy, and the faint smile came again. He lifted his hand a few inches, as if to touch one of them, then winced and let it fall again. "You . . . believed . . ."

That earned her warmest, brightest, most confident smile. "Of course we believed. Listen, I'm going to call for help, okay? We've got to get you to the hospital." She pulled her cell phone from her pocket, saw the signal strength was weak, and started to push to her feet.

"Wait." This time he touched her in spite of the pain, wrapping his fingers loosely around her wrist. "Have to . . . tell you . . ."

"Tell me at the hospital."

He shook his head. "Can't wait . . . I . . . love . . . you . . ."

Suddenly the night wasn't so cold or so dark, and the fear that had kept her going ever since Eli had appeared at her door disappeared. She looked at Ryan, whose lower lip was trembling as he swiped at his eyes, then she leaned close to Cole again and gazed into his glazed eyes. "I love you, too, Cole, forever and ever."

"Marry . . . me."

She'd always wanted to get married someday, but had never found the man worth it. What a hoot that the man seemingly the most unworthy of them all turned out to be the one and only man for her.

"Ask me again tomorrow when your brain's not addled from pain and the cold, because, sugar, once I say yes, you're stuck with a life sentence." She kissed him as gently as she could, then unwound his fingers from her wrist and lowered his hand into Ryan's. "Let me make that call, city boy."

She had to climb back up the hill to pick up a signal. After placing the call to 911, she stood on the outcropping of rock and watched the scene below. Ryan still held Cole's hand in his, and Jerome, not wanting to feel left out, had curled up against them both, sharing his warmth.

"I'm . . . sorry." Cole's voice drifted up on the chilly air, lacking substance but not conviction.

"For what?"

"Screwing up . . . your birthday . . . your life. Being a . . . lousy father."

Ryan shrugged. "Nothin's screwed up."

"I never meant to . . . to hurt you. Just wanted . . . you to have . . . good life."

"Yeah." It was Ryan's usual response, but this time it lacked the usual cynicism. "Well . . . don't let it happen again."

A chuckle escaped Cole before it faded into a grunt of pain. "I . . . love . . . you."

Leanne held her breath, and it seemed as if everything around her had gone utterly still as well. As the seconds dragged out, an ache started deep inside her, growing, knotting, and then—

"I love you, too," Ryan whispered.

Their little spot in the forest brightened and warmed a few degrees, or so it seemed to her. Truthfully, it was probably just the pure joy rushing through her. She returned the cell phone to her pocket, then started the journey back down the hill. As dirt and rocks slid beneath her feet, a slight breeze blew through the valley, and for an instant she would have sworn it formed words in an enormously satisfied voice.

And they'll live happily ever after.

I T HAD TAKEN A YEAR OR TWO FOR COLE TO GET warm again—quite a feat, considering that less than eighteen hours had passed since he'd foolishly decided cutting through the woods was a good idea. Some lessons took a while to sink in, but staying out of the woods without Leanne at his side was one he wouldn't forget. He was more grateful than he could say that he'd had a chance to live and learn it.

It had taken around thirty minutes for a deputy to reach them the night before, plus another ten minutes for him and the dispatcher to pinpoint their location and find a quicker, easier route for the paramedics. Cole hadn't minded the wait, though, not with Leanne on one side and Ryan on the other. They had both cried over *him*. The knowledge humbled him.

So did the understanding that when anyone else would have expected the worst, they had trusted him. Not one person had ever shown that kind of faith in him. On the contrary, people were usually quick to judge him, even his own family.

Rather, the Jackson family. Leanne, Ryan, and Danny—*they* were his own family now. They were where he belonged.

When the door to his hospital room swung open, he lowered his eyelids and looked through the lashes. If it was the nurse with another of her needles, he intended to fake sleep. Surely if the pain was manageable enough that he could sleep, she wouldn't wake him up to give him medication for it so he could sleep.

But it wasn't the nurse. Mitch Walker came into the room, hat in his hands. Stopping at the foot of the bed, he took off his uniform jacket, then fixed his gaze on Cole.

He knew he wasn't a pretty picture today. He'd been shaved where the laceration on his forehead extended beyond the hairline, and a row of black stitches stood out starkly against his skin. He was slumped against a stack of pillows, his broken ribs too sore to allow him to either sit up or lie down. His left leg was in a cast from hip to toe, and his right ankle was wrapped with an elastic bandage. He had bruises and scrapes elsewhere, but they couldn't begin to compete in the pain department with the other injuries, so he discounted them entirely.

"How are you feeling?" Walker asked.

"A hell of a lot better than I did last night."

Walker nodded, then glanced around the room. There weren't any flowers or cards—just sterile walls and furnishings designed for function rather than comfort. A TV bolted to the ceiling, a chair with little padding, another with none, a table to slide over the bed, a telephone on a night table he couldn't reach.

Finally the chief looked at him again. "I came by to apologize."

Cole blinked. "For what?"

"When the deputy found the truck and Eli said you'd been driving it and no one had seen you . . . I assumed you'd seen the chance to take off and grabbed it. I instructed my officers to keep an eye out for you, but . . . if you'd had to rely on our help last night, you wouldn't be here today. I'm sorry."

Cole started to shrug, but caught himself with the first sharp stab. "Under the circumstances, you made a logical assumption—you being a cop and me being a . . ." What was he exactly? Not a crook, not anymore. Not a thief, a liar, or a lowlife.

"You being a reformed con artist," Walker finished for him.

Reformed. Remade. Reborn. Cole smiled. He liked that.

"It was a logical assumption," he said again. "There were times when even I wasn't sure I was going to stick around. It's no big deal."

Walker looked as if he'd been let off too easily. He was

opening his mouth to say something when the door swung open again. This time it was Leanne, still wearing the same clothes as last night, looking tired and in need of a dozen hours' sleep, but beautiful just the same. She was carrying a cup of coffee in one hand, a sweet roll from the hospital cafeteria in the other, and she was . . . radiant. It was an extravagant word, but the only one that fit. There was an easiness about her, a peacefulness so pure that she practically glowed.

"Morning, Mitch." Balancing her breakfast, she raised onto her toes and kissed his cheek. "You haven't come to move the patient to the prison ward, have you?"

Walker scowled at her. "The hospital doesn't *have* a prison ward, and he's not in custody."

"Ha. He's in *my* custody." She set her breakfast on the bedside table, then grinned. "I found him. Now I get to keep him."

"The state might have something to say about that," Walker said dryly, then pulled on his coat. "You two take care."

"You, too." Leanne pulled the padded chair close to the bed, broke off a piece of the roll, and popped it into her mouth. Just watching her made Cole's mouth water, though it was debatable whether he was hungry for the roll or her. "How do you feel?"

He offered a shortened version of his answer to Chief Walker. "Better. Did you spend the night here?" He had vague memories, blunted by pain and dulled by medication, of gentle hands, a soft voice, her sweet fragrance. The attention from her had done him more good than the drugs the hospital staff had pumped into him, and he'd tried his best to stay awake and savor it, but he'd failed.

"Of course I was here. Do you think I could have gone home?"

She *could* have. She could do anything that was necessary—raise her son alone. Start and run a successful business. Take in Ryan and love him as if he were her own. Find *him*. Help him find himself.

Breaking off another piece of roll, she offered it to him. "Have you had breakfast?"

"If you can call it that," he said with an absent shake of his head. "Scrambled eggs, oatmeal, and applesauce, all with no salt, pepper, sugar, ketchup, hot sauce, raisins . . ."

"Already complaining about the food. You must be feeling better."

Gritting his teeth, he shifted on the bed so he could see her better, then for a long time just looked at her. She continued to eat her breakfast and let him look, a faint smile playing over her lips. It faded when he finally spoke. "You saved my life."

Her cheeks turned a pale pink and her gaze shifted away, then back. "We just did the logical thing—start where you had last been and go from there."

"I don't mean last night. From the beginning. When I first came here, when I was gone, when I came back . . . being friends with me and loving me and hating me and forgiving me and trusting me and loving me again. You saved my life."

She neatly wiped her hands on a napkin, stood up, and leaned over him, careful not to bump him. "Does that mean you belong to me from now on?"

"Whether you want me or not. Guess this means I do have a conscience," he said with a grin. He couldn't lift his arm to pull her closer or even raise his hand high enough to touch her face, so he settled for lacing his fingers through hers. "You never answered me last night."

"You never asked me anything."

"I tried." He stroked the palm of her hand, then slowly

lifted it to his mouth for a kiss. "I told you I love you, didn't I? I know, because you said it back. I didn't imagine it." Not something that important, that far outside his experience.

"No, you didn't imagine it."

"And I asked you . . . pleaded with you . . . to marry me. And you said—"

"Yes."

"No. You said, 'Ask me again tomorrow.' "

She smiled gently. "Guess your brain wasn't as addled as I thought. And now it's tomorrow."

"So? . . ."

"You still haven't asked."

He tried on words in his mind, wanting exactly the right ones, but the whole idea was so new to him, and she was so important, and if he screwed this up—

You can't screw up, Jack, a voice whispered in the distance. *She loves you, and you love her. It's meant to be.*

Meant to be. That was a hell of a notion. That his coming to Bethlehem, ripping off everyone, abandoning Ryan, leaving, returning the money, getting caught, and coming back again . . . all of that was *meant* to happen, just to get him and Leanne to where they were right now. All of it somehow fated, because *they* were fated.

Maybe it *was* fate, or luck, God, divine intervention. Whatever it was, it was also definitely one other thing.

It was right.

"I don't imagine this is the proposal you've always dreamed of," he said wryly. "I look like hell, I can't hold you, I can't even kiss you properly. But . . . I love you, Leanne, and I want to stay with you forever. Will you marry me?"

Her eyes were teary again even as she smiled at him. "The doctor tells me you have a mild concussion, and it really isn't fair to hold a man to anything he says in that condition, but I warned you last night, didn't I? Once I say yes, you're stuck with a life sentence. No appeals, no pardon or parole."

"So go ahead and say it."

She leaned closer, her lips brushing his. "Yes. Yes, I love you, I want you to stay forever, and I'll marry you."

Her kiss was cautious, her mouth barely touching his, her tongue sliding inside only tentatively, as if she was afraid of hurting him. It was sweet and full of promise, stirring aches that had nothing to do with last night's fall, and damned if he could do anything about them at the moment.

But that was all right. They had the rest of their lives to stir aches and satisfy them, then do it all over again.

A life sentence had never sounded so appealing.

Life had never sounded so appealing.

He was vaguely aware of the door opening, of footsteps coming into the room and a snicker or two, before Leanne finally ended the kiss with a soft sigh. When she stepped back, Ryan, Danny, and Eli came into view, standing just inside the door. Danny, at an age where his mother kissing a man was enough to send him into a fit of giggles, was grinning from ear to ear. Eli looked as if he hadn't expected anything else, and Ryan . . .

Ryan had told him he loved him last night. That alone had been worth breaking half a dozen bones and freezing half to death.

"You look better than the last time I saw you," Eli said.

"Thanks," Cole said dryly even as he frowned. As far as he could recall, the last time Eli had seen him, he'd been all in one piece, getting into the truck for the drive out to the camp. This morning was definitely not an improvement over that.

But lost somewhere among the pain and cold that had almost killed him last night was a faint memory—something about angels and thin air, a vaguely familiar voice. Eli's voice?

Impossible. Eli hadn't been in the forest when he'd fallen. If he had been, he would have called for help. The memory was so elusive because it wasn't a memory, just a trauma-induced hallucination.

Danny came to the bedside, wrapping his fingers around the side rail. "You got a lot of owies."

"Yeah, but I'm okay."

"That's what Ryan said." He bobbed his head with complete faith. "Everything's gonna be okay."

Cole shifted his gaze to Ryan, who'd made it as far as the foot of the bed and now stood, staring down at the covers. Was he embarrassed by his display of emotion the night before? Showing affection to anyone but a woman was something none of the Jacksons excelled at. His brothers did it with punches and insults. *Bubba* was the closest they ever got to an endearment. But crying, hugging, and saying *I love you* just didn't happen in their family.

That was one more way he intended to depart from family tradition, and there was no better time to start than the present.

He lifted his hand a few inches from the bed. "Come here, Ryan."

Dragging his feet, the kid circled around, hesitated, then offered his own hand.

Cole wrapped his fingers loosely around it. "I meant what I said last night."

Ryan's dark eyes widened.

"You thought maybe I forgot?"

He shrugged.

"I didn't. I love you, Ryan, and I'm sorry for everything

I did wrong. If you'll give me the chance, I'll do everything I can to make up for it."

Ryan's mouth worked a time or two before he finally muttered, "Yeah, well, don't let it happen again."

He'd said that the night before, Cole remembered, parroting the final warning Cole had given him months ago after the book-stealing incident. Smiling faintly, he offered the same words the kid had. "I won't." Ryan had made good on his promise. Cole fully intended to make good on his.

For a long time Ryan just looked at him, then he swallowed hard. "I know." Bending, he gave Cole an awkward hug, mumbled, "I love you," then abruptly turned away.

It was a better start than he had any right to hope for.

"Well," Eli said cheerfully. "I just wanted to check in on you. I've got to get back downtown. Those lights aren't going to finish hanging themselves."

As the door swung shut behind him, Danny scooted a chair close to the bed, then climbed up to stand on it. "Hey, Cole, when're you gonna get out of here? 'Cause Ryan won't open his birthday presents 'til you can be there, and I really wanna know what he got." Without waiting for an answer, he plunged ahead. "Hey, Ryan says my mom's gonna be his mom for real and you're gonna be my dad, and him and me's gonna be real brothers, so can I call you that? I never had . . ."

Tuning out Danny's words, Cole looked at Ryan, who was watching him with a hopeful sort of expression he'd never seen before, then at Leanne, who wore the same look. He figured he had it, too, for the first time in thirty years.

The promise of love.

The gift of a family.

And hope for the future.

About the Author

Known for her intensely emotional stories, Marilyn Pappano is the author of nearly fifty books with more than six million copies in print. She has made regular appearances on bestseller lists and has received recognition with numerous awards for her work. Though her husband's Navy career took them across the United States, they now live in Oklahoma, high on a hill that overlooks her home town. They have one son.